Brian Dennis Hartford

WITHOUT

To Karen,
What is forever anyways....
between souls.

To a new evolution,
Love and adoration!

Namri'd Publishing, LLC
2 Marietta Court Ste A #117
Edgewood, NM 87015

www.namridpublishing.com

Cover Art: Brian Dennis Hartford

Warning: This book contains adult content, violent images, and sexually graphic material.

ISBN-13: 978-0-9985432-4-6
ISBN-10: 0-9985432-4-1

First Printing: December, 2017

10 9 8 7 6 5 4 3 2 1

Printed in the United States of America

A Very Special Thank You;

To my wife, twin flame, best friend, and forever love as the centuries pass from us. To Dawn Marie Imel, (12/29/55-09/07/2017) for raising my wife to be the woman she is today. To friends and family who helped to see this through. To the Vampires. To Andreas Bathory for his spiritual guidance and friendship, too another century my friend! To Anne Rice, Bram Stoker, and all the rest. To H.P. Lovecraft, keeper of things best left unknown. To God, for all these wonderful things and most ugly truths. And lastly, to Stoya Tepes Dracŭ and Ianthe Gold, the whisperers in the dark.

"What is forever anyways..."

Stoya Tepes Dracй

CHAPTER 1

Charlotte sat across from me as we prepared to dine at one of West Hollywood's most beautiful restaurants, Café La Bohème on Santa Monica Boulevard. I had reserved a table upstairs in the crystal booth seating area for us, center table. I wanted to ensure we had privacy, yet have a clear view of the entire restaurant and its patrons below. I was starving.

La Bohème was a favorite of mine; a small slice of modern 1930s-era France; with its neo-boudoir like soft Gothic, candle-lit, red velvet feel. It brought back memories of more simple and glamorous times. It was eloquent, sensual; a perfect place for a first date.

I was nervous. She looked so beautiful. Her powder blue eyes, the way her mouth seemed to always be about to whisper something; a great secret, maybe? A want, a message, a longing of some kind that she was unable to articulate, lacked the power to actuate, I believed.

Her long, pure blonde hair flowed lightly around her soft, rounded face. Its natural golden hue glowed angel-like in the low lighting. I couldn't help but to melt at the sight of her. And I couldn't help but know that we had met before.

I had come across her quite accidentally while shopping at the Santa Monica Place Mall. I noticed her instantly through the Coach Store window. Her soul beckoned me and I knew that I had to meet her. She was cute, beautiful, a bubbly mid-western blonde full of ambition and love for life.

I watched her as she compared attaché cases for her job. She worked as a finance and securities lawyer for the firm Sandalwood and Associates. I could not resist her radiating charisma the minute I walked in to meet her.

I stood frozen; enamored by the way she so delicately fretted over her dilemma. The black conservative one, or, the classic brown and Coach emblemed canvassed one? The latter was a little flashier and defiantly more stylish.

I watched as she bit at her lower lip, standing with her right ankle slightly bent, her full weight on her left leg. I could tell money, too, was a bit of an issue. I stood spellbound, watching while she ached over her decision. Then I finally spoke.

"Black…with the gold buckles," I said smiling at her finally working up the courage.

"It's classic, classy, will go with everything, and makes the statement that you are a professional," I told her as I watched her blush, looking back at me in surprise.

I remained entranced as we stared at each other in a knowing, eager silence.

"Well…OK...," she managed to finally speak softly.

"Black, then?" she asked again, a confirmation really.

Her voice was articulated, clear, calming, thoughtful, and seemed to soothe me; to draw me in.

"Yeah, the black one!" I confirmed to her once again.

I fidgeted internally over the vision of her, wanting this moment to last.

"Well, you two, would you like me to ring that up?" Ihsan the store manager interrupted, bringing me out of the trance I was in.

"Gift wrapped, or…?" Ihsan smiled and winked at me as she gently took Charlotte's choice for purchase from her hands.

Charlotte smiled, then blushed, realizing what had been occurring, our interlocking stare; the instant infatuation.

"Oh…yes…sure, yes…," she said shyly, slowly, then promptly spoke up.

"Oh, yes, I'm sorry! Yes, please, I like this one, if I may…but no gift wrapping, I'll be using it today for work. This afternoon, I have court."

Charlotte looked back at me again, waiting for me to approve.

"Yes, this one!"

I nodded assuring both Charlotte and Ihsan.

I felt flush, realizing what I had said was in reference to Charlotte; "This one."

Ihsan was flittering about, laughing and kissed me on the cheek.

"So, this one…then…Ianthe?" she quietly exclaimed as she glided playfully behind Charlotte pointing at her and laughing again.

I rolled my eyes at Ihsan and pursed my lips to her.

"Yes! This one!"

I stood tall, condemning her obvious irritation at my intrusion into all this, hands on my hips; scowling at her in playful defiance.

"Ring it up!"

I ordered playfully twirling my finger at her. "And my usual discount, please, thank you!" I sternly confirmed, feigning annoyance.

I turned back to Charlotte smiling, closing the distance to talk more intimately.

Ihsan always liked to fuck with me when I flirted with anyone but her. But that's the kind of relationship we had; fun, flirty, friends with benefits. However, I had detected a bit of jealousy in her in that moment, maybe a little bit of resentment even, over my "moving in" on Charlotte.

Ihsan was forty-five, Iranian born, had money, was very intelligent, and very sexual. Ihsan had been a possibility for a deeper relationship, until I met Charlotte that day.

I had swung a fifty percent discount on the attaché case and a handful of freebees and samples which seemed to thrill Charlotte more than the discount, or her new bag. I would owe Ihsan a nice dinner, possibly more.

In return for hooking her up at Coach, Charlotte insisted on buying me a coffee and we hit it off right away. She was smart, adorable and very funny in both mannerisms and thought. She had me laughing almost the whole time, not so much for her sense of humor, as funny as she was, but in the way that she did things, approached life, the innocence of her being.

I found her alluring in the way she placed our order, and then clumsily poured me sugar and cream, making sure that my coffee was perfect, just as I had wanted.

She was just so damn funny as she gingerly, hurriedly wiped down our little table and my chair with a handful of napkins. She was delighted over how I pulled out her chair and seated her. Like a perfect lady.

I laughed even more as she fretted over the fact that she had wanted me to have the Christmas themed cup like hers. It was April and the coffee shop was attempting to phase out its special run holiday season cups like they always did. She kept offering to switch cups.

I just laughed, cupped her face in my hands and whispered. "No, but thank you sweetie for being so thoughtful."

She fawned at that, that I appreciated her.

We soon found ourselves sitting in silence staring into each other's eyes in nervous anticipation, seeming not to need words. Each longing, remembering something to say, but neither knew what.

It was clear to the both of us this was going to go somewhere and so agreed to a first date for that Friday night; tonight. It was a struggle for me to wait this long.

I knew Charlotte was deeply attracted to me from our first meeting and had a hard time not demonstrating it now as she leaned forward in her chair, posturing with a straightened back while slightly condensing her shoulders inward which assured me a view of her near perfect C-sized, soft white breasts. Her skin glowed as her breasts bubble up over the top of her slinky black Ann Taylor dress.

I could tell that she long to touch me. I felt the tip of her high-heeled shoe gently, but deliberately touch my calf from time-to-time testing the waters for full contact. I smiled back at her, she was so silly.

"This place is so beautiful!" Charlotte exclaimed looking around excitedly.

"I have always wanted to come here but…," she trailed off in thought looking down at all the stylish, well-dressed people below.

We listened for a moment to the murmur of their conversations, the clinking of dinnerware, and the occasional intimate toasts between friends and lovers.

I thought it funny that she seemed to think herself unworthy of this, this treatment, this place. But it's what I had noticed about her right away. She was humble, thankful, unassuming despite the way in which she carried herself. It was evident she had breeding, a good upbringing, a first-rate education, and wanted for nothing.

She was happy, glowing, excited. I was glad to be able to give her this experience. She had mentioned during our coffee date that she always wanted to dine here, but she was practical, conservative with her money; just staring out really, in life and wealth.

"You look so beautiful…," I managed to finally tell her. Afraid I might sound stupid at stating the obvious. I sipped at my drink, a smoked Manhattan in its crystal-clear glass with a large, square ice cube. It calmed my nerves, the first date butterflies.

"Well, thank you!" Charlotte replied, sounding a little nervous also.

"But I'm…not, I, well…you are so…"

I could detect a rise in her heart rate. She had become flush, her face and neck turning slightly red.

It was funny actually; two drop dead gorgeous women both thinking that they are not good enough for the other.

"So…what...?" I asked of her.

Charlotte blushed and seemed afraid for a moment, then relaxed, sitting back; her hands clasped in her lap.

"You're, well…," she squirmed, looking at me rolling her eyes playfully. "Really fucking hot!" she blurted out enthusiastically, approvingly as she blushed again.

I busted out laughing, smiling, allowing myself to straighten up and show case my goods playfully like a model on the runway; then sat back again, smiling back at her. She was adorable in every way.

"Well..., I paused looking her over. "I'm not so sure about that anymore."

She giggled as we both relaxed further, our first date tensions slipping away; an old, familiar comfort slowly creeping in.

We looked into each other's eyes again for a while in silence. It was clear to both of us already how this night was going to end.

"So, what is it that you do, Ianthe?" Charlotte finally asked, anxiously taking another large sip from her wine while slowly looking me over with her big, bright eyes.

I saw that they were a little grayer now in the low light, like the gray of the frozen, North Sea ice.

We had not gotten that far in our first conversation over coffee, discussing my profession, my life. I was content to just let her ramble on about herself; to take her in and experience her personality, her thoughts, and actions.

I leaned slightly forward, closing the intimacy gap between us. Both elbows on the table; my left arm down upon the crisp, white table cloth, reaching in her direction; open to a touch, to interlock our fingers if she so desired, the other gently swirling my drink.

"I'm retired mostly but still dabble in the stock market and model once in a great while," I mused.

"Wow, a model?" Charlotte exclaimed, flushing a bit over the fantasy that all have of dating a model at least once.

"For whom?"

I choked for a moment. I had revealed something about myself. Would she find me, recognize me, the photos through the years, the fact that I had never aged?

"Elle Magazine and Sports Illustrated, mostly; 2012 and 2014 were my last shoots," I paused. "But like I said, it's been a while."

"Oh! I love Elle magazine! I've been a subscriber since I was sixteen." Charlotte countered. "What issues?" she asked inquisitively.

I sank back in my chair; shit! I thought, of course she had.

"Fall 2012, Chanel evening-wear," I added. "Slinky black leather dress and boots…," I trailed off.

"And the Sports Illustrated?" she inquired.

"Yeah, cover shot actually; girl in the gold bikini, Hawaii, June 2014." I squirmed hoping she would draw a blank.

"Not ringing a bell, but…but I don't ever look at Sports Illustrated." she said rolling her eyes at the idea of sports articles and such silly manly things.

I sighed out in relief.

"Well, cool, Ianthe, I'll look you up later. Check ya' out, if that's OK?" she blushed.

I sighed, chuckling to myself and hoping she would forget to do so.

"Sure, sweetie-pie, I don't mind." I winked back at her.

I sat quietly, thinking for a moment, wondering what an internet search would reveal of me, photos from many, many years ago; decades to be more precise.

I chuckled again, would she make the connection? I thought of my early 1900s Chanel and Lanvin photo spreads. I really need to do an internet search, see what is out there. I thought to myself in that moment. Then catching myself, the look I might have been reflecting, I chuckled to myself, lost in personal thoughts.

"Immortality…," I thought aloud and smiled, "Immortality…" as I took another long sip of my drink.

Thankfully, Charlotte seemed to ignore my personal private joke. The word "immortality".

"So…retired then?" she asked more curious, probably over my reaction.

"Yes, retired, I've made my money in stocks actually."

"Stocks?" she queried.

"Yes, stocks! Gold mostly...," I replied, knowing she'd want to know what kind.

"Do you make a lot of money, in gold?" she asked innocently, putting her empty wine glass down.

"Yeah, a lot!" I smiled back at her, smirking a little.

In truth, I owned more than just stocks in gold. I had my hand in everything. My wealth was beyond compare. It had no equal, at least on this world anyway. A vague estimation would be in the billions, a trillion or two actually, of non-earth precious metals held in private vaults.

"Wow, my portfolio really sucks, I should have you look at it sometime...maybe I should get into some gold!" she gleamed.

It was an invite to a follow-on date already. And yes, I thought, get into some Gold! I couldn't help but to smile devilishly at the thought of her in my bed.

"Sure anytime," I said enthusiastically, leaning forward again finishing my drink.

"So, do you like being a lawyer?" I asked Charlotte seizing the chance to make this about her and to hide my truths.

"Yes, it's interesting work. I'm challenged daily. Besides daddy said that I had better put that Stanford degree to work after spending all that money," she giggled again biting at her lower lip.

We laughed together. She was so damn cute.

I was feeling more and more aroused in her presence. She glowed in a way I had not experienced in a great while. Her body and soul drew me in, made me long for her. Images flashed in my mind of a frozen sea, I wondered over them, a memory of which I could not fully recall.

"Awesome!" I replied. "It's good that you're doing what you want to do. So many aren't these days...That you are helping others..." assuring her I thought her work was important. That she was important.

We sat for a moment in silence looking into each other's eyes; contemplating us. This thing, our coming story.

CHAPTER 2

"Are you and Ms. Aberdeen ready to order, Ms. Gold?" Tim our waiter, yet another personal acquaintance of mine, asked.

He was smooth and gentle at the interruption, reverent to the amorous situation, an expert waiter in every way.

He knew I was the primary; I ate there frequently. Service here, for me anyway, was never second best.

"Yes," I stirred. "You first, Charlotte?"

"I will have the salmon, well done, please," Charlotte said rocking back and forth slightly in her chair, excited. "And another glass of Pinot Grigio, please!" she squeaked polite and sweet.

I silently chuckled at the thought of "well done" salmon. She was so funny.

Tim turned toward me with his big brown eyes and inviting smile. "And the usual for you, Ms. Gold?"

"Yes," I replied. "The usual, and bring me a nice Burgundy, a red to go with it, the best you have; the bottle," I smiled.

"Yes, ma'am, right away!" he turned to leave.

"And Tim, remember, no garlic, you know it doesn't settle well with me."

"Yes, ma'am. No garlic!"

There never was but I always made sure anyway.

Charlotte leaned in toward me again once Tim left, incredulous at the fantastic service we had been receiving. But of course, the service was always spectacular.

When dining there, I always handed the manager $1,000.00 in cash, letting the staff keep the remainder as a tip to show my gratitude. It was the least I could do. I believed that one must be generous in this life, because not all lives are gracious ones. Some are downright painful; I should know, I have lived them.

We talked some more about Charlotte's dreams and aspirations; her family.

"Ultimately, I want to open my own law firm and advocate for women and children suffering from domestic abuse; hopefully, a not-for-profit firm." Charlotte smiled broadly as she spoke.

She was passionate about it, helping those in need, but frustrated at the lack of power and finances to do it. But I doubted that she had the emotional capacity for such things, she seemed a bit fragile in that way.

Such things are ugly, hard to deal with. Often one must force themselves to be cold and analytical. Compassion, unfortunately, can crush your heart.

She had a good meaningful soul, a soft heart, she cared; it's what I was looking for. If only this world had more like her.

When our meals came, Charlotte sat back looking slightly repulsed at the sight of my 12-ounce porterhouse seared only, extra, extra rare; swimming in its own blood and juices. No sides, just meat, and a light au poivre sauce.

I did my best to hide my repulsion at the grilled fish carefully lain over its bed of rice pilaf and asparagus. Though I love the ocean, I wasn't a fan of the things swimming in it; a memory of a less than pleasant time in my life when everything was wet and slimy. I shuddered slightly at the thought of that world again.

I like land, terra firma, dry earth; the desert suited me well. I like four-legged and two-legged animals, red meat, warm blood. Cow, actually, was my favorite animal here on this world, next to man.

"Sorry," I lamented. "Is this…OK? Charlotte?" I motioned that I could have it taken away is she had so desired.

"S, s, sure, I'm sorry, I'm just not that much into cows and such, I feel sorry for them, the way they're often treated."

I couldn't help but to chuckle to myself again.

She became more comfortable as I ate my steak. I wasn't a pig about it. I was gentle, caring, well versed in table manners. I slowly cut off small petit bites like a lady of the court, of which I had been, many, many times. I made sure the seared, cooked end remained orientated in her direction, shielding the dark red, nearly raw flesh from her sight, as we talked about all manner of things.

It was a delightful dinner; her presence especially.

When the last of a shared fresh fruit topped crème brûlée with extra whipped cream for Charlotte and my Burgundy were finished, Charlotte insisted that she pay for her part of the bill. We argued playfully over it.

"No, sweetie, your money isn't good here; the bill has already been paid!" I protested leaning back to enjoy the elegant Parisian-like atmosphere, and the vision of her.

I smiled, soothed, thinking of old memories, of Charlotte sitting before me, as I swirled an 83' Kopke Colheita Port. She had begun to remind me of someone more and more with every minute, an old memory, a time and world that I just couldn't place. A frozen sea I did not know of where. I sat quietly pondering her, the memory, as the image of a sea of ice played within my mind. There were strong winds and the ice chimed like tiny bells.

"So, Paris, it's like this…the restaurants?" Charlotte innocently asked as she scraped at the large Ramekin with her spoon for the last of the brûlée.

"Yes, even better!" I stirred; then sighed happily at that thought. "You have never been?"

"No, daddy was going to take us, but well, he's a workaholic, and, well…the next thing you know, I've graduated college and work like 50 hours a week now."

She smiled dreaming again, looking about at the sensual atmosphere. "One day. I guess…," she trailed off.

"I'll take you there, one day," I paused, hoping she would say "yes, now, tonight!"

"Oh, I'd love that! One day, soon!" she cooed, looking back at me as she soaked in the ambiance and let out a long, gentle sigh, then leaned forward to me again, day dreaming of a Paris she longed to experience. Of me, I think, taking her there; the perfect romance story.

I felt her foot that by now had hooked itself just below my calf clinging there; wanting. I smiled at her playfulness, then reached down and took up both of her feet, removed her shoes, and placed them squarely into my lap to massage them. I let her left foot slip down under the hem of my dress, and encouraged her to leave it there, to press into me where my smooth, excited pussy awaited.

I wore no underwear.

She quivered at the touch of it, my sex, the warmth of it, the smoothness of it; the slight wetness of it. She pulled her foot back for a moment, ashamed, blushing as I let out a rather loud devilish laugh and pulled it back against me there again while massaging her toes and the sole of her right foot.

I drew her blood to me; then pushed it back into her, warmed and electrified, a thing that I can do.

She let out another low, soft sigh at this; the most unusual touch I had. Her facial expressions looked as if she was being sneaky, naughty, her hand in the proverbial cookie jar as it were. As if she was ready for me to take her home. My cue.

"What would you like to do next tonight?" I asked her as she melted back into her seat to fully relax; keeping her feet in my lap.

I watched her become flush again, seeming to try to find the right words. She looked at her watch as she fidgeted, then leaned forward to me again. She looked into my eyes, then cocked her head a bit biting at her lower lip again as if in some great dilemma, like at the Coach store.

"Home...," she whispered. "I, I'd like for you to take me home."

"Home?" I pouted, teasing her as if I was being rejected.

She smiled and pressed her foot deeper into me, against my sex, as she smiled seductively.

I almost came, mentally, at the suggestive look within her eyes, the almost whisper upon her lips now wanting, the way in which the inflection her voice seduced me.

"Yeah...home. I'd like you to tuck me in tonight, if...?"

I smiled, leaning forward as my body anticipated that thought, the coming sex. I was entranced by the look in her eyes, the tone of her voice, and the meaning of the word home.

"Yes..., I would," I spoke quietly back confirming to her our mutual desire.

I smiled warmly as I sat back again and let out a long, contented sigh. I looked back into her eyes, her soul, her being. That's what she had reminded me of, home, life and a long-lost love.

CHAPTER 3

Outside, the evening had begun to cool off, the city re-born into romantic dark rosé and red hued colors as the sun began to sink into the horizon of the great Pacific Ocean only a few miles West of us.

I stood behind Charlotte as we waited for the valet to get my car, warming her shoulders with my hands. She had forgotten to bring a light sweater; she seemed to get cold easily.

We had met at the restaurant. Her roommate had borrowed her car to go out dancing and had dropped her off.

Charlotte snuggled back into me, a physical suggestion that "I" should be doing the warming.

Charlotte was a little light headed from the wine. She didn't drink much. She told me that three glasses were more than she was used to, most times.

I embraced her at the hips and let her rest against me as I tenderly nuzzled her neck with my lips. Her natural human scent was intoxicating, the smell of cinnamon, just barely masked by a light application of Soma's "Enticing" perfume. I took in the sensual notes of it, the light currant, gardenia, freesia, and warm, white musk. I marveled over her smooth, buttery, milk-soft skin and the way she gently breathed in as I caressed her. She was all together completely irresistible; completely intoxicating.

"Holy shit, is that your car?" Charlotte squealed, rapidly clapping her hands, moving to it, as my Bugatti Chiron came into view at the front steps of the restaurant.

"Yeah," I replied playfully, moving to open the door for her.

Charlotte, unhesitant, slipped into the deep burgundy colored leather interior, reinvigorated, excited.

I closed the passenger door making sure it was secure. Once I was in the driver's seat, we sat for a moment looking into each other's eyes.

She was glowing, enamored with this luxury as all women, and men for that matter, are with things so fine and grand.

I smiled again, pleased at yet another experience I could give her. I adjusted the heater so that she would be warm.

"Speed" she blurted out nervously. "Don't go too fast, I was in a wreck once!" she said sadly.

"Your safe with me sweetie, I won't let anything happen. Ever!" I assured her.

I leaned forward, placing a hand on her cheek and kissed her gently on her lips. She was so gorgeous, so gentle. I took her left hand and placed it upon the primary shifter knob and then set mine upon hers. I wanted her to be in control of this moment, of me, and her fears.

We eased my Bugatti into gear; the engine was not used to taking it so easy. It began to strain against the idea of not going fast.

But fast is easy. Fast is sloppy. I preferred finesse, the smooth motion of moving through traffic like a great, silent beast, never meeting a red light, never encountering a pedestrian, perfect timing always. Never speeding up nor slowing down too much, just smooth steady moving through traffic as if it wasn't there. It was hard here in LA, but it could be done. I had mastered it.

As we glided effortlessly to Charlotte's home, Charlotte leaned over the center console and let her left hand slowly move onto my upper thigh, touching the refined satiny material of my Chanel dress. She then let her hand slip beneath the hemline as she timidly caressed my inner thigh. Her little pinky coyly, innocently, and ever so lightly, touched my clitoris from time to time. Her hand trembled with that excitement.

I smiled, looking back at her seductively. She was wanting, she needed this night; to escape, to love, to be ravished.

"Here?" I asked Charlotte.

"Right up there," she pointed to her condo and its carport below.

I shifted quickly into high gear, letting the Bugatti have its release, as we quickly accelerated from 45 to 65 in a mere fraction of second. The car lunged forward as Charlotte's hand clenched my thigh in terror.

As I came upon her condo and its carport, I turned sharply letting the Bugatti's rear end swing out and around, positioning me for a perfectly straight shot into the awaiting parking space.

Charlotte let out a loud "ooo, oh!" as we came to a sudden perfectly aligned stop inside of her carport.

I had mastered this machine. I was a part of it on a much deeper level than any human could ever be with the devices they made. It was as my body was, how our kind interacted within your world and its machines; intuitive, synchronous, harmonious.

Charlotte sat back, overcoming her panic.

I laughed slightly, biting at my lower lip. "I'm sorry...," I offered up leaning in toward her, feeling a little devilish again for making that move.

She leaned into me, her pulse racing. She was excited; flushed.

"N…no, that was awesome!" she gasped out, catching her breath.

"We'll take a drive, up Highway 1, sometime soon; I'll show you what he can do," I spoke quietly referring to my Bugatti.

She smiled back at me playfully, at me referring to my car as a "him".

Silence came over us, an eager silence; then an electrical charge which descended upon us. That feeling of the coming first kiss, that first real physical connection which told us both that there was going to be something more in this than just a date.

We moved to each other in slow motion and completed our first full kiss of this most romantic night. It was a kiss that told me that she was the one.

My thoughts tumbled, that kiss, her mouth, her tongue, her taste; the intense tenderness of it. I teared just a bit at the corner of my eyes. I had found it hard to catch myself, to breathe in that moment.

"Yeah, I think I'd like that soon," she replied quietly pulling back slightly, whispering just barely upon my lips at the idea, the possibility of escape, a little danger, fun, the way that I am with her; an escape to anywhere.

"Yes, real soon, Highway 1, then Paris…," I said kissing her again, drowning in her absolute being.

CHAPTER 4

In her bedroom, we lay naked upon her silk-sheeted bed embraced in a lock of passion. The soft yellow light of vanilla and spice-scented candles softly illuminated her bedroom.

She had good decorating taste; a fondness for "Shabby Chic". A little out of style, but still relevant. She was nostalgic, a romantic, her style, her mementoes and photos of family life told me so. I had to laugh at her large collection of Vampire love novels piled up on her dresser. But I felt at home now, filled with fond memories of things that had been gone a long while for me.

We touched each other in near silence; save for our breathing, the occasional sudden in or out of it, which identified the places that felt the most stimulating.

We wondered over each other, the other's thoughts, the other's bodies.

She was exquisite. Soft, supple, delicate skinned; her body was rounded and soft, healthy. Charlotte was a little thick, chunky most would say. But I loved that about her, too. She didn't work out much. Time and stress of her job often left her tired. She was perfect to me, her body, her breasts with soft, tan-colored nipples, her soft stomach. I had found that she was definitely a natural blonde.

We looked into each other's eyes as I traced the outline of her face, her perfect little nose, and soft, pale pink lips. She was angelic, innocent looking. Her light brown eyebrows were expressive with every word and touch. I loved the way in which she bit at her lower lip expectantly and the almost secret whisper that seemed to escape with each breath.

She shuddered as she caressed me; admitting to me that she was excited by me, by my touch.

I was completely different to her. My Egyptian-Bedouin heritage was as exotic to her as her romance novels. Yet another experience I was pleased to give her.

The way I made love was also different; the peculiar calming, the tracing of my fingers upon her, the way in which I made her blood feel; the way I could make it tingle. How I could make it seem to wash through her like gentle waves upon the sand. I could make it swirl and ebb throughout her entire body and slowly fade back into her heart.

I know she wondered about me, the way in which she looked at me so inquisitively. I was different, but in what way she was unable to fully conclude.

I smiled as we kissed again, teasing her with the exotically alien way in which I touch and feel.

She breathed in a low, slightly rapid fashion, quietly moaning, cooing. Her tongue, her taste teased at me.

The warmth of her blood just below the skin enticed me; the feeling growing with intensity with every touch and kiss of her. Her blood moved to me, seethed to be released by me. I could taste it through her skin. Feel her soul within it long for me.

She was flush, longing; ready though perhaps in her mind she had wanted to take it slower. But it was not possible now, I could feel her surrender to me, begin to absolutely desire me.

After a while, I began working my way down her soft supple stomach, pausing to kiss her breasts, her nipples, teasing them with my tongue. Then, I moved lower to nibble at her belly button, to kiss the area just below it slowly, which made her giggle and squirm with expectancy.

Her back arched a little as she rolled gently from side-to-side in pleasure as my tongue glided over her most sensitive areas and the curves of her stomach.

She ran her fingers firmly, wantonly through my long, dark brown, violet undertone hair and across my tanned, well defined shoulders. Her hands ran across my body and down my stomach. She marveled over me and my unusual warmth.

I teased her, working my way closer to her sex. Taking up her legs and kissing the full length of them. I kissed her feet and the arches; she moaned at this in pleasure.

As I readied to go down on her, she caught and held my face, searching it, looking into my eyes, to make sure for a moment and to search within her own mind that she was ready for this so intimate completion. I smiled up at her waiting, then without hesitation, slowly began to kiss her there as she parted her legs wider in acceptance.

I could smell her sex; soft sensual, a sweet salted cinnamon. I breathed gently back onto her, her clitoris, her labia, then slowly moved to caress her with my lips and then my tongue. I started slowly, gently, licking her up and down and in a light circular motion, building up into a rhythm until I found what elicited her body's approval. My tongue, my lips, drew the blood there also. She tingled like with no other lover; the ocean like tidal rush of the orgasm building up within her.

It took only a couple of minutes until she began to move forcibly, her back arcing as she moaned, building into orgasm. She clutched at my shoulders, encouraged me with firm squeezes to continue. I was skilled in this, I had great experiences with women due to my centuries on this world.

As Charlotte was coming close I pulled away seductively, tauntingly, teasing her with my eyes.

I slid back up and onto her, projecting my full sexual power over her, kissing her mouth and mounting her like a man does a woman.

She seemed to hesitate at my boldness for a moment; then gave in to me, excited over the sensation.

I gently pulled her legs up and around my waist, then gently stretched her hands up above her head pinning her to the bed. Her head tilted back, her eyes half closed and mouth partially open. She began to moan and breathe heavier as her legs tightened around me.

I slowly began to lower myself, my pussy, my clitoris onto hers, slowly pushing down onto her as if thrusting a penis inside of her. It took years to perfect, to get it just right. I laughed gently, lovingly, as I let myself sink down onto her fully and slowly began to pump into her, gently thrusting, grinding; the action rocking our clitorises together arousing us both even more.

Her juices began to flow, wetting me as I slowly moved upon her, kissing her mouth then biting gently, lovingly, at her neck; small innocent bites. Playful bites so that I could taste her skin and the blood waiting just below it.

It pleased her. It was a totally different experience for her I think, the biting; the way in which it feels. She began to grip me tighter with her legs, her back stiffening; her arms still trapped but squirming as she began to cum.

I ground and pump into her harder adding often erratic, counter intuitive circular motions for extra effect. Her eyes closed as her mouth opened to responded audibly, groaning more and more as she began rocking hard against me. I shuttered in that moment; full of love and adoration.

She was beautiful, sweet, and kind. And I thought about taking her away and sheltering her somewhere safe and serene. To live with her forever. I thought of forever in that moment and then had another image in my mind. It was Charlotte, or, I think it was her. There in the blowing snow upon a frozen sea, I saw her dancing. Tall and graceful, alien, she had the same powder blue, ice-gray eyes. The same almost whisper upon her lips as now. I watched in my vision as she danced gracefully to the tinkling sounds the ice made in the wind so long ago.

I found myself cuming at this image and the love felt in that memory, at the thought of Charlotte as her human self. I let her arms and hands free, so she could take hold of my shoulders.

As she clutched me, we came together, our bodies tensing, straining, wet with the smell of cinnamon-sex, "Enticing" perfume, and the vanilla spice-scented candles permeating the air.

As she released, she began to relax, softening her grip on me, a small tear dripped down from the corner of her right eye as she breathed out fully exhausted from the intensity.

I gently kissed her face and her single tear. My lips caressing her eyebrows, her lips as she breathed in deeply contented. I took her in as I smiled down upon her, her angelic face, the soul within.

"I do!" I confirmed to myself in my mind, at the memory of the girl upon the ice.

I knew inexplicably in that moment that she was the one for me on this world; "this one", Charlotte Bell Aberdeen.

CHAPTER 5

When Charlotte had fallen asleep in my arms, I gently removed myself from her bed and tucked her in, gently kissing her goodnight.

I watched her sleep, warm and content, for a moment then went to let myself out securing the front door behind me. Outside, I leaned against the door for a moment to catch myself, my breath, to hold onto myself, to feel my own embrace. I was warm, and felt my own heart beating and my blood move through me contented and energized. I hesitated to leave in that moment, I was already missing her.

It was late, maybe 3AM. I ascended the steps to the front door of my condo across from the white sandy beaches of Santa Monica. The air was cool. I heard the ocean drone upon the sand. Oh, how I loved that sound.

A young, desperate-looking man in a dark blue hoodie charged out from the darkness rushing toward me as he pointed a gun in my direction.

"I'm going to rape and kill you bitch!"

I thought of others like him from across the centuries, always taking; always wanting; always seeking out the innocent, the weak. I turned and looked at him. I could smell his sweat and the blood within his body; his fear.

I thought of Charlotte in that moment; that this event could have happen to her tonight. I thought about how I had promised her I would never let anything happen to her. I looked to the stars and thought of the circle of life; of this universe, of why God had made me, our kind.

Cracking a smile and wetting my lips, I would comply with his desires.

"Sure, let's go!" I chimed seductively. I was starving again.

CHAPTER
6

My name is Ianthe Gold and I am the vampire. But, that is such a simple word; vampire. To explain who I am is so much more complex. I am the drinker of blood and the consumer of flesh, yes, but that too, is a narrow view of it. For I am, we are, far greater than that.

To be clear, I am human, at least my host body on this world. But I, the creature within; is not. I am a visitor; an alien life form from another world. I am the inhabitor of the flesh and soul.

My species, a complex, sentient, symbiotic being, has existed since the dawn of life. I am proof of God and that life exists beyond your world, beyond your solar system, and the microscopic section of the universe of which you know so little.

I am ancient. Much of my kind is. My body, the human body of which I inhabit, is only 3,000 years old. But the creature that exists within it, what I truly am, is much, much older.

We are true immortals, birthed as first souls, first bodies of flesh, a corporeal being that is eternal and continual in its existence. Beings that do not suffer breaks in its life-journey as your kind does. Beings uninterrupted by death and the resulting transfer of the soul as most life forms are meant to be; mortal but transitory.

We move through the ages, to live a thousand different lives, in a thousand different bodies, across millions of years or more in time. Always knowing, always remembering, always with the same thought and persona but ever growing. We are eternal in all ways, but to the will of God, and its one inevitable fate; the end of time.

We are the Nosferatu, the name of our kind; a word adopted by your world. A title that has over the centuries, become imbued with mystery, violence, and death. But, also of glamour, seduction, and sex. An idealized fantasy for many, an uncomfortable self-reflection for most.

We are real in body and being, an existence that lives and breathes behind the myth. Behind the glitz and glam of what your imagination has made of us. We walk plainly in the open among you, for in fact we are as you. And, I am not alone.

On this world, there are three of us besides myself.

Stoya, who is the last of us to arrive to this planet, fell from the stars in a small spacecraft which crashed into the Boreal forest of greater Russia a little over 1,200 years ago. She has ruled entire galaxies, is powerful, mysterious, and dangerous.

E'ban, with whom I fell from the same shattered world upon our individual meteorites, is near me in age. We are life-long friends and lovers; always seeming to find each other somewhere on some world, in some galaxy, as we travel through time and space. I could not have a better companion as we face forever together, assured that the other, somehow, is always near.

And lastly, there is Tyr; who arrived upon this world before the primordial seas had yet spawned life. It is said that he is the first of our kind to learn how to inhabit bodies not of our own. He had become a mighty ruler on our world, and a great destroyer of life. He lay now in the "great sleep"; weak, trapped, and unable to fully awaken in the moment. The human body no longer sufficient for him; he would need a more advanced life form to truly thrive again.

I had fallen to this planet encased within a large meteorite in a spectacular once in a century meteor shower sometime in the year 1,000 B.C. A celestial event common and quite frequent to this part of the universe. The meteorite was a remnant of a long dead world from a dark and dangerous solar system over 16 light years away, just beyond the star you call Gliese 832. A world that was my home until its core superheated and de-magnetized, causing a loss of stabilized orbit.

The body of which I had previously inhabited survived, laid dormant inside a piece of that world. There I rested; asleep as I hurled through space and time until its eventual, but random collision with this earth. I had lain suspended in a kind of hibernation, something my kind can do. Something I can make my host body do to survive.

My meteor, my tomb, shattered upon impact with your earth's surface releasing me after an 8,000-year journey through space. My physical body was broken and dying, no longer of any use to me. I, the creature within, was in need of a new body to inhabit; a new host in which to survive. It would not be long.

CHAPTER 7

I knew the adventurous young Bedouin girl who found me upon the desert sands would suffice. Instinct and collective knowledge had identified her as the apex species here. She would become mine.

She was young, healthy, strong, and beautiful. Her body would serve me well.

She tried to run from the horror she found there in the torchlight illuminated sands. My host body, an enormous six-armed anthropoid-like reptilian creature laid dying in the cool desert night among the space rock debris.

It, I, lay sputtering, gasping, crumpled, and dying. Its antenna-like tendrils waved and flopped around trying to make sense of this new environment, trying to find a way to survive. It was strong in that way. An apex predator, a first-class survivor. It squirmed, crawling in agony, torn open; bleeding. Parts of its exoskeleton were crushed, and I, the creature within it, was severely injured.

I would have to abandon that body to survive; an act which revealed yet another incomprehensible horror, my true physical being.

She shrieked at the sight of me, my true form, the violet-purple-colored, amoebic, mucus-like blood oozing out onto the earth, crawling out from within the beast, collecting, forming, searching, needing.

She was looking for something magical, I am sure, as she followed the red and white-orange streaking object falling from the sky. A gift from the heavens, a gift from her God, she had thought. In so many ways she found that gift; me, her time immortal.

Turning to run from this unearthly collective horror, she tripped, falling into the soft sand.

Seizing that moment; I lunged forth upon her as she froze in absolute terror. Enveloping her, I tore into her flesh trying to find a way inside her as she desperately cried out for her parents in the quiet night air. I used the first major orifice I could find, not understanding fully the indecency of what that place meant to your kind. That place which births life.

Pain erupted within her as I poured myself up into her. She screamed out in agony as I filled her, crawling deep into her like some horrible reverse birth. But I did have sympathy for her, I wanted her to have no pain, but there was little I could do in that moment, the process of initial inhabitation can be painful for many species.

She screamed and wailed as her insides ruptured and I tore through her body weaving and streaming, radiating throughout her as I began to flood her like water, searching, exploring every organ, vein, and vessel, nerve, flesh, and skin, trying to connect, to understand. Her blood boiled like an acid as the chemical composition of our two separate chemistries collided. Another unfortunate side effect of our immediate inhabitation.

Hot with pain, she collapsed; writhing, crying.

I found my way to her nervous system and shut it down. She would, as her individual self, her sentient human being, know no more but the soft velvety blackness and the calming surrender of time falling into stasis, what it feels like when you become as us.

When the inhabitation process was done, she, we, I, would be reborn and would soon set out upon this world to experience it in ways that she, the little girl, would have never been able to ever conceive of.

This is what it is to be inhabited by us. To be a life reborn; a union of two so completely different species that become as absolute one; a new creature, a new form of being; an evolution.

We, the creature within, offer up immortality, the stoppage of the natural aging processes of the body and the mind. Time. Life, its often hurried journey, ceases to matter. We give the gift of perfect health, strength, and other physical attributes not normal for your bodies. We also gift our host with great physical beauty and knowledge that goes beyond man's understanding. And, you will remember your past lives, lives you thought were but dreams and distant memories.

The human body offers up to me greater mobility, sensory perception, and the ability to interact with earth's physical environment and enjoy emotional, individual life experiences, the things I value most. Your bodies also allow us to breed more efficiently in order to create a new child of our kind. In this case, on your world, your human bodies are a perfect union for us.

The one condition; your soul, your inner being, your very essence, becomes absorbed by us forever. We are the absolute loss of that one identity, all that is you, that which stares back at you when you look in the mirror, you, the sentient-individual, the greatest gift to you from God.

The young girl was buried by sundown the following day as was her people's custom. Not understanding the truth, they claimed that a devil had taken her. A demon, it looked like to them, the shattered broken body of the beast from another world. It had no name, that species of which I had inhabited. It was primitive, powerful, and dangerous and lived a secluded life.

She, we, I, lay in the earth wrapped in a burial shroud, listening to the grieving wails of her people. I wept for her. She would lose everything she had ever known; her family and friends. She would be deprived of her life, of what was in her future as she was meant to live it. Though it could be argued that I was her destiny as God had ultimately intended for her.

What was clear on that night upon the desert dunes, was that Ianthe Aida Thahab, human being, would be no more to the world.

CHAPTER 8

It would take nearly a year for me to fully incorporate into her human system. My being was damaged; I needed to rest. I had to repair my own physical body, as well as hers at most every level, to fully incorporate myself into her biological system. I had to re-structure, re-align, and re-model it so that we would be perfectly synchronized with each other. Become as one at all levels. One mind, one breath, one movement, one thought, one being.

My successful inhabitation of her would make us stronger, faster, more powerful, and godlike beautiful. Her limited knowledge and her life-soul's experiences were assessed and filed along with my own collective knowledge and memories. It is how I learned of you, became as you, as with all beings that I inhabit.

Ianthe Aida Thahab would forever be me from then on, that day we arose from the desert sands. The human body with a creature within, the alien collaboration that is our unique life-journey. Forever to become the eternal human being that I am now on this world, Ianthe Gold.

CHAPTER 9

Awaking from the dry, parched Saharan sands, I was eager to see this new world, to participate in it, to experience it, to live in it as you do. It is what I have done over the millennia as I traveled time and space, adopted bodies and lived as one of them. I feed off them and, sometimes, fall utterly in love with them.

For this is what and who we are, assimilators of life and death. Of what God has made us to be. I travel and inhabit and enjoy and learn, and most importantly, I love. Always looking for that one being, that one special soul, if it's at all possible. It is a journey as you could never conceive of. But not all lives are great. Some lives are, well, down-right simplistic, literally, to put it mildly; uneventful at best even. Like my last one. I was glad to have moved on from it.

Earth is a world as I had not experienced before; a perpetually, fast-paced evolutionary, ecological model. Your kind is primitive in thought and body, but with advanced technologies and grand imaginations. You strive to change, endeavor to evolve, to move ever forward; to explore while at the same time work so very hard to destroy it. Your planet, your existence is a part of a very complex social eco-system that utterly intrigues me. Your human being fascinates me. Your evolution, your past, present, and excitingly unpredictable future and the fact that your time in this universe will be so very short.

On this world, I found that I had few physical issues. It was easy to adapt. Your bodies are quite a remarkable feat of engineering. They are graceful, sexual, well proportioned, flexible, and adaptable in many ways. But as with all bodies that I have inhabited there were always little kinks, minor compared to some other bodies, but easily overcome after minor adjustments.

The visual receptors I use through your eyes are sensitive to the strength of the earth's sun. I am from a much darker world. One illuminated almost exclusively by our great moon, Namri'd. In fact, many worlds are darker than yours. Earth's solar system is special in that way, night is as if day for me here on earth.

Direct sun light brings a slight blurriness and an inability for fine details without the protection of sunglasses. When I first arrived on this planet, I used thin veils and scarves to protect my eyes. Then I switched to colored-glass spectacles as the craft of glass-smithing became more refined. Now I use mirrored Prada sunglasses custom focused for my unique needs.

I can eat most any food found here on earth. But blood and flesh are essential to my existence. I love beef, porterhouse specifically, but any fresh, rare red meat will do. I partake of human flesh only as my system demands. I am conservative in that manner, unlike the others of my kind here and elsewhere.

Garlic, the plant species Allium sativum, I did find; however, was dangerous to my system, not for some mystical repellant reason, but because of its unusual chemical reaction that it has within our species digestive process. I have never really figure out why exactly, but it is not unusual. There are many things I have come across that are unpalatable or downright dangerous for our kind to eat on other worlds. But, it won't repel me or burn my skin or anything dramatic like that. Instead, it offers up stomach cramps, indigestion, belching, farting, and at times diarrhea, woefully uncomfortable, not at all becoming.

Aesthetically, physically, we are near perfect. Our second greatest gift after our unique biologic-immortality, is the power of beauty. I, my host, had died at the age of sixteen, but with a little chemical and genetic manipulation, emerged to look as if I was thirty. A good age, I felt, to project my power and social status as I walk through the ages.

My human body is of Middle Eastern decent, Egyptian-Bedouin to be exact. I, she, was the daughter of the ruler, a Sheikh, of a once powerful nomadic clan so she had been well cared for. I, the creature within is also of royal lineage. Funny this coincidental pairing of her body and mine, a fate of which I still ponder over.

My skin is a light olive color of classic Middle Eastern tone. My face clearly reflects my Egyptian-Bedouin heritage. I have large, almond-shaped eyes framed with elegant thick eyebrows and long, black eyelashes set into an angular, thin, moderate, cheek-boned face and a nose somewhat sharp but well formed. My lips are full but sharply cut. My hair is long and thick, a shiny black-brown, which possesses a violet-purplish hue undertone in the full sun light, an after effect, like my eyes, of our kind's habitation of a body.

I am of average height for women of your world, standing at five feet, six inches. I am lean, tight, muscular. I move gracefully and exude a confident sexual prowess. My skin is smooth, hairless, unusually warm and exotic to the touch. I had chosen to eliminate the gene designator which affected hair growth anywhere else on my body, save for my head and eyebrows. I found the other places of where it grew distasteful. I have no tattoos, an anomaly in this day and age of often excessive body ornamentation. The ink fades quickly in us, making it all but pointless to endure the process.

My scent is fresh, clean, human; a womanly musk, but with the slightest scent of the rose an hour before it dies; the universal tell-tale scent of our species.

I prefer the clean, simple look in all things fashion. An elegant Versace or Chanel sheath dress and a pair of Louis Vuitton high heels suits me well most times, even when at home.

I avoid too much ornamental flash, believing that the expense of the brand and materials say it all. I wear little in the way of jewelry save for some small antique gold hammered hooped earrings, the earrings that my host body had come with, and a half carat diamond belly ring which makes me feel sexy and aroused when tugged on. I have a great fondness for all things Chantecler, their bells specifically, and wear an anklet of them often. The tinkling of them, when I walk soothes me and reminds me of a long-lost love.

There are other clues that might betray me as not entirely human. It is my eyes and my voice, if you really pay attention, which could also give me away.

My eyes are abnormally clear, crystal-like. They reflect a dark, deep violet or purple color depending on the light, and in some ways, can seem almost luminescent. My irises and pupils are slightly larger than that of human's as well, allowing me to see more clearly at great distances in the darkness. But the difference is slight and goes unnoticed by most. My gaze is captivating, irresistible, powerful, all knowing. Some find it quite disturbing if not completely spellbinding. There is an "infinity" within them, a sense that they are endless, like staring up into the stars out into the cosmic abyss, the sometimes, unnerving sense that there is something not entirely human staring back at you.

My voice is clear, soft, eloquent, with an ever-mild sultry husk to it; hypnotic and sexy. I speak eloquently, concisely, confidently. But to those who really pay attention, you might detect at times that it is as if two people are speaking in unison; another anomaly of our inhabitation, another clue that we are not entirely as we portray. But it is barely audible to most human ears and those that do pick up on it think it nothing more than some form of speech impediment on my part, or auditory malfunction on there's.

I possess no long sharp nails to tear at you, preferring instead a short conservative cut, smooth rounded and painted with light, neutral colors. I have no evil, growing fangs either. When it is time to feed, I simply tear out the neck-arteries of my victims with strong, sharp, perfectly human teeth. But, I prefer subtler means. I make it sensual, pleasurable, and take only what I need to satisfy my hunger, little nips and cuts that go unnoticed, love bites in the throes of passion.

My brand of death comes to those who truly deserved it, the evil, the wicked, or the sick and dying that are deserving of mercy. I can; however, eat a human in its entirety, including the bones, and do so from time-to-time, I suppose that is monstrous enough.

CHAPTER 10

My wealth is infinite. When humans were still discovering the beauty of gold and pondered over its uses, I showed you its true future value not only as a thing for ornamentation, but it's coming market value as a resource material. I have capitalized upon that precious metal for centuries now, creating a quiet empire that spans the globe. There isn't an ounce of it sold that I do not receive my portion in monetary compensation.

But it remains a fairly silent business, a proprietary holding with false names, embedded within layer upon layer of corporate entities both big and small, exact profits obscured under a myriad of names and titles all of which lead to a Swiss bank account that receives payment in the thousands at the end of each and every day.

I am the owner of gold and its namesake. And it will serve me until the earth's very existence ends. As I have said, I am worth billions; a trillion or two actually.

To me; however, gold and the associated investments are only a means to an end. I care little about such things. For in truth, the only real worth here on your world, is the life you live, alone, together, collectively in this infinite cosmos; you are unique and so very special in that way.

I live, and have lived, all over the world. I own many homes and consider myself a global citizen. But I am an American first. And it has been my primary country of residence, my pledged citizenry for almost 280 years. I have been here since its inception. Here, there is still hope, a promise, and a dream. I love the vibrancy here, the multi-ethnicity, the diversity, the creativity, and the dream of being more than what someone tells you that you can be.

The possibilities are endless in this nation, for anyone wishing to try. It's why I was drawn here, the great possibility. I worked behind the scenes to make it all happen, the concept of America, the War for Independence, the Constitution, and the birth of a new age. This nation and its people's full potential are still just being born.

CHAPTER 11

Humans have developed funny ideas about us. I blame Stoya for much of that, the vampire mythoi that your books and movies portray of us. We are for the most part as human as you in appearance and body with a few genetically evolved exceptions.

Aside from our beauty, we are physically and mentally powerful. We possess strength five times or more of that of the average human male. We can run faster and farther. We can suffer horrific wounds and still be able to function. We heal completely in a short amount of time. We can see far with great clarity and detail, hear the slightest noises, and smell things from many meters away. Blood in particular and fear.

We can draw your blood to us from within your body when we are near you. We draw it to the surface of the skin and out of the tiniest wounds for easy feeding. We move and manipulate it electrically, magnetically, utilizing a kind of current that we can generate, pulling the iron mineral content of it to us. For you it feels sensual, seductive; orgasmic. Most of my victims die quickly, peacefully, erotically, when I chose to kill.

Environmentally, we can tolerate temperature extremes of both heat and cold, dry and wet, both in our natural form, and of the host body through chemical manipulation and alteration. We are immune to the vacuum of space and can endure long periods without food or water, months, sometimes years when necessary.

We possess an intelligence level way beyond your human understanding. We have seen, lived, and absorbed life-knowledges from other beings that you could not even conceive of. We understand the true laws of the universe and the chemical and mathematical narrative of how things happen and why. We understand God and the grand design and that this is just one of many universes both physical and dimensional.

There are other human beliefs which amuse us. We cannot climb walls, walk across ceilings, or even fly. Our movements are nothing special, just graceful, eloquent, and purposeful. Though you might detect the fact that we never stumble or fumble at any time. We never drop a thing, nor demonstrate any form of inability even under physical exertion or stress, a thing uncommon in even the fittest of people.

We are immune to the effects of the sun and in many ways, it strengthens us, makes us healthier, and more alive. Though in truth we flourish at night. Darkness is what we were designed for, what most predators in this universe are designed to hunt in.

We cannot vanish into thin air or turn into a cloud of bats or a pack of rats. We cannot summon wolves and other dangerous things, nor manipulate the night in any way. And, we cannot turn other humans into the mindless bloodsucking undead. Or, for that matter, into another like us with a simple bite or a blood transference of some kind. There is no venom or some other form of biological infection either. These are the works of fictitious minds. We are a species, not a disease.

We cannot be killed by conventional or unconventional means; easily anyways. Attacks with wooden stakes, axes, swords, and silver bullets mean little save to our host body. These things will destroy it, but not what is within. Inhabitation is quick, and it could be that you find that I have become you.

Attempting to kill us would prove most difficult. Our physical bodies, the creature within, are not as yours. We are too fast and too powerful. I will know of your intentions before you can act. Though I cannot read minds per se, instinct and experience will tell me of your true intentions beforehand. I have millions of years of experience in the struggle of life and death. I am quite adept, I assure you, of defending myself.

As for holy water, well, all water is holy, for water, the chemical compound H_20 is the blood of God. So how could something which already exists within all species, be any risk? But, please, I implore you, never use holy water, it will stain my $6,000.00 Versace dress.

We do not hate religion as most would believe. I personally have no real feelings toward Christianity, the holy cross, or any other religious ideologies or instruments. Human notions of God and faith mean little to us save for some amusing conversations. I know for a fact that God exists, it is in my blood to know I am of It, of God, as you are of God, when God paid attention to such things.

God, Its purpose, Its reasoning, is beyond your understanding. God is indignant of us, of you, and of Its other creations. It serves a higher purpose of which none will ever know, save perhaps some other elder god from before our time. It is the creator-being and nothing more. But I say this; It should not be blasphemed, nor does It need your praise and devotion. It simply is, and does. And It will do so until It is done.

CHAPTER 12

My life has never been about the feast of flesh or of death. It is about living and learning all that I can of it. It's about meeting and talking to strangers, about meeting new entities. I like making friends and learning all about them, their unique lives and their journey upon their world, within time and their purpose within the context of the grand design, the journey of their individual souls. I accept all walks of life. I am indifferent to color, economic status, or sexual preferences, all are equal in my eyes. It is the way it should be.

Sex, love, and intimacy are of great interest to me on this world as it was on others. My chief life study actually. As you can already tell, I have a preference for women; female beings. I am, the creature within, the feminine, a female. But I am not exclusively lesbian, nor am I purely heterosexual. I enjoy both sexes, even transgender from time-to-time. It is how most of us are, our culture; bi-sexual, multi-sexual; separate from the God-made male-to-female sexual constraints assigned to much of this universe's creatures. Our kind takes and loves whom we choose. But we each have our preferences, what we relish most. For me on this world it is women.

Smooth, intoxicating, and complicated, your planet's females are strong, liberated, and sexual. I like breasts, the roundness of your bodies, and especially your sex organ; pussy. Women's bodies, are intoxicating to me, the way they look and feel, their scent. It's what I desire most, to press against you, the feel of you, taking you in, the way you kiss me, hold me, the way you feel under me. The taste of your blood. Old or young, all races, it makes no difference. Short, tall, thin or chubby, small breast or large, I care not. Only that you are fun, intelligent, and have a love for life.

No. I am not the monster of fictitious myth, save for the blood and flesh that I must have. I am just a passenger of time, the watcher from within. Here on this world I am as human as you are, maybe even more so. It is how our species has evolved. We are passengers on an endless journey through time, space, and eternity, waiting for it all to end, if it ever ends.

But I will not lie and tell you how grand we are, nor exalt our existence above any other. For we started as any other, nameless crawling things, searching, evolving, longing to be something we were not in that moment. We were fashioned into predators, a kind of mucus membrane that absorbed other organic materials. But, in time, we evolved in body, learned in mind. Through the process of evolution, we soon learned that we could inhabit others, to become as them, live as them, and feed from them.

We are immortal because God had seen fit to gift to us no life-limits, both of the body and spirit, it's what sets us apart from all others.

Our DNA and stem cell construct are perpetually self-replicating at all levels. Like the Hydra, the Turritopsis Dohrnii Jellyfish, the Planarian flatworm or earth's humble Bdelloid or Tardigrade, we grow and learn from absorption of other DNA, that of other beings, your human being.

We had become a plague at first, feeding too rapidly upon the alchemy of molds and fungus, the other prenatal amoebas, almost causing an extinction of all life, and ourselves, before it could fully begin. Had we not forced ourselves into conservation, you quite possibly would not have had the chance to exist.

It is that conservation; however, where we first developed our reverence for life; most of us anyway. We found that we could get by through nursing on our prey, drinking its fluids one drop at a time. And as we grew stronger with the ages, and as creatures of all kinds grew larger and more advanced, we found we could enter them, coexist within them, become as them.

In time, we thrived, but only for a short moment. Our lust to devour and grow in capability threatened us to near extinction as before. Harnessing the bodies of new beings that called themselves Angels, near perfect translucent humanoid life forms that had emerged from our evolving world, we turned upon ourselves again for nourishment and the power that comes with that consumption. Wars raged as we fell into near extinction.

But, many of us found ways to flee our world seeking escape, refuge from our self-made god-kings, to see new places, to live and feed. Just or not, it is the cycle of life. It is God's design; the eaters and the eaten. In time we thrived again, evolved into nomadic flesh hunters amidst the stars.

We are no more of a monster than anyone or anything else on this world or in this universe. We are, quite simply, a part of the cycle of life, the apex predator existing to keep the cosmic balance in check. We are here to cull the herd. Not out of malfeasance or any other motivation. We are what we are meant to be; the balancer, the scale. But I am also love and hope, and proof that God, the creator-being, does exists. That life beyond your world exists.

So, do you see me now; understand of whom it is that I am? I am the vampire, but so much more than that. I am as you are. I am that woman or man you saw at the coffee shop, the clothing store, on the street corner crossing, so remarkable, so beautiful you fell in lust right then; a fantasy come true perhaps. I, in turn, smiled back at you, letting you know that I saw you also; that I am approachable. Do not be afraid of me. I am just as you in many ways. I breath, and laugh, and live. I bleed, and hurt, and cry, and suffer all the earthy pains that you do both physically and emotionally. I experience life as you do, suffer love and loss as you do. My only real advantage is that I am forever.

CHAPTER 13

“Hey?” Charlotte spoke investigative like on the phone.

“Hi!” I replied, excited at the sound of her voice.

“You, you left…last night, didn’t you?” she queried afraid of the answer.

“Don’t be silly, sweetie,” I replied quickly. “I just wanted to make sure you had your space, that’s all,” I said hoping to remove any negative ideas from her head.

“I’m definitely wanting more of you…,” I trailed off, blushing at that thought, the way I messed up my words, *“wanting more of you.”*

“Can we do lunch?” she asked, brightening after confirming that I was still interested.

“Hmm…,” I thought. “How about dinner again, at Mélisse, and then dancing? It’s Saturday night, I know a place. We should party!” I paused. “It will be an adventure!” I spoke, portraying a bit of mystery to what I had in mind.

She was thrilled at that prospect, adventure. “Ooo…awesome!” she exclaimed, excited.

“OK then, how about eight? For dinner that is...?” I asked.

She mused. “Yes, eight is perfect! And…Oh! Can we take the Bugatti again?” she pleaded.

"Sure, just for you, cutie-pie," I laughed at her. "Pick you up at seven, let's just see where the night takes us after that."

She giggled excited at that prospect; *"where the night takes us."*

I hung up and made some calls; priority access and first-class service. I have friends and associates everywhere.

CHAPTER 14

My last real love was in the year 1946, shortly after the Second World War. A young American Officer in the OSS. He was heroic, stoic, an officer's officer, but most of all he was kind like Charlotte. An old soul.

I was in France to ensure that my funding for European reconstruction efforts were being used to its full advantage. I was also involved in helping local area churches find funding and means of support from back in the United States for the orphans of war, which were numerous. I hadn't been back to France since before the German invasion at the start of the war.

He was there to aid in the investigation of, and, if possible, recover British and French gold stolen from European banks during the occupation. But there was something else he was there to do, lay the groundwork of resistance for the coming Cold War with the emerging Stalinist Soviet Union.

I still think of him often, his picture hangs on a wall in my lair. His smile, the confidence he exuded, was indicative of the passion he had for helping and for understanding others' pain. He spent a considerable amount of his own money and time towards reuniting those war orphans with extended family across Europe. He was killed not two years after we met, shot dead on the politically contested East-West German border in Berlin while helping a young family escape, in exchange for vital information, from the clutches of Stalin's grasp. I was devastated for months, and withdrew from the world for many years.

The music pulsed and vibrated in the low, pale red and blue-violet lights of the Vampyr Club in LA. Charlotte and I danced together as small strobe lights blinked and flashed in unison to the beat. She was afraid of that place at first; the dark vibe. But soon found it intriguing, even a little exciting.

It was a bar for human vampires so by its very nature was kept dark, low key, Gothic. Dark secrets were expressed there; quiet whispers of inner desires and fetishes. Its blacked-out, red velvet booths assured this privacy and provided space to play out such things.

The bone bar was reminiscent of the infamous Paris catacombs, the house of millions of dead since the 17th century, and assured a common place for the lonely to meet, to talk over a few drinks before retiring to a secret alcove to discover hidden pleasures. But there was life here and a deep reverence for things long past.

I was a regular, Stoya and I were silent business partners actually. Making money was not the goal, but the celebration of things most mysterious, sex, and memories were. For Stoya, a place to feed.

Charlotte was getting drunk and having the time of her life. She was carefree to the worries of the world and her job in that moment, in this place. She had begun to embrace the fact that the majority of the club's patrons were composed primarily of steam punk romantics, Goths of every make, and vampires. The very sorts she read about in her vampire love books. She was even beginning to make new friends.

I wanted her to see things outside of her box and knew that Stoya was in town and would be there.

"Charlotte, so nice to meet you." Stoya glared at me as she took Charlotte's hand into hers, feigning sweetness and caring.

Stoya stood tall and powerful, disapproving, jealous. Her thin, porcelain white skin seductively revealed the delicate violet veins just below like a great spider web tattoo or that of a fine clear marble. Her hair was jet black, waist length and full with the violet-purple hue indicative of our kind. Her violet eyes blazed in the dark; a piercing glow, penetrating our souls. I watched them, they were as if a fire, a thing unique only to her and no other of our kind.

I was Stoya's lover. More hers than she would ever be mine. An obsession to her, my nobility status amongst our kind, my beauty, our history. But it was one of those loves; conflicting souls, desperate, broken, and never to be.

At times, she could be quite ugly. Emotionally racked with hate and sentimental remorse that was deep and painful, but she was still unbelievably beautiful; awe-inspiring to behold in person.

It was Stoya who was the real vampire on this world; the drinker of blood and eater of flesh without discrepancy or remorse. The devil if you ever wanted to know a real one. Domineering, obsessive, abusive, and mysterious; she played the part well. She relished it in fact, that word, the sentiment; monster, vampire. It was she that perpetuated the myths of us. Exaggerated our powers. Demonstrated our ability for explicit sex and great cruelty.

"It's nice to meet you, too!" Charlotte squeaked as she wobbled, a little drunk, waving at people.

"Stoya, is that Russian?"

"No!" Stoya commanded, scolding her. "Bulgarian! But I am Russian," she condemned Charlotte's ignorance, sneering.

Charlotte recoiled from her but tried her best for me.

"Wow, that's awesome! So, you're into vampire stuff too?"

Poor Charlotte asked, simply not knowing, not understanding. But it was an obvious observation.

Stoya stood before us as the quintessential vampire mistress of the dark. She was dressed in a very old vintage black velvet dress, its short train flowing behind her. It was slit at the front exposing her long exquisite legs and her elegant front laced, knee high, high heeled riding boots; also vintage. Her garb literally came from another time, Italy, the 1600s, maybe a little older. She was oh so sentimental. The dress, a gift probably from some hideous aristocrat lover.

Her makeup was dark. The eyeliner, the shadow, the deep, wet, blood-red lipstick were contrasted by a face so perfect it was like white marble or a glass, a mirror in which you saw your inner most perverse desires; your death when it suited her.

She had a fondness for Bvlgari jewelry. Her necklace flowed upon her neck, sparkling radiantly with a million dollars' worth of diamonds and several hundred thousand in platinum; her favorite metal. She spared no expense in that regard.

We had become surrounded by many patrons clamoring for Stoya's attention. They wanted to be seduced by her, loved by her. She was the ideal; the aspiration, the deepest desire. She ignored them, which made them love her even more.

Stoya glared, looking down at Charlotte. "Sure, and I sleep in a coffin, too!"

I laughed, because Stoya wasn't joking. She did at times, Vlad Tepes III's coffin, her most important earthly love.

"Awesome!" Charlotte replied sipping on her drink beginning to feel more and more uncomfortable with Stoya's blunt approach and leering personality.

"Let's dance later?" she asked of Stoya trying to be nice.

"Sure, but be careful, I bite!" Stoya said laughing again at Charlotte with her shrill condescending tone. She wasn't joking about that either.

Charlotte had found an out, taking off to dance with some other girls, beautiful vampire Goths who had beckoned her to join them, enticed by the fact that she could command such a presence as Stoya, and my obvious affection.

Stoya and I stood together in silence for a moment looking at Charlotte dancing in the red-blue violet lighting with the girls who had invited her. I knew Stoya was desirous of her, of me, of what I had. She grinned, licking at her lips, red, wet, and wanting.

"Careful sister, you are not the only predator in this house," Stoya turned laughing at me, taunting me, watching intently as Charlotte wiggled her perfectly plump little ass.

Stoya favored men; however, cruel, horrible men. Women, for her were sexual play things to be used and discarded wantonly. I was her only exception, so that I knew.

"So, what brings you to LA, Stoya?" I asked already knowing she was here to see this Charlotte of mine, of which I had so bragged about.

"Entertainment," Stoya flippantly replied, eyeing a young man, in his white, frilly, Gothic, French-style shirt and tight fitting black leather pants and European riding boots, as he was dancing and moving his hands as if he were conducting the music as it boomed and echoed.

I chuckled slightly at her absolute disregard to answer anything in full.

"Well, then…," I said as I yanked her out onto the dance floor by her thin, elegant hand.

The music pumped and vibrated in surreal techno dark trance Gothic tones as we began to dance, Stoya and I, writhing in our unique and alien way.

It is the dance of vampires, the Nosferatu, of our kind. A slow rhythmic dance that, if anything, was more similar to some ancient forgotten belly dance, a ritual-dance possibly, performed for some ancient evil god. We were slow, controlled, and other worldly in our movement. Stoya and I danced as two beings joined together physically and mentally, a soul-to-soul connection, knowing and sharing thoughts and emotions, knowledge, and physical feelings together. It is how our kind are, connected beyond the mind and flesh.

On the dance floor we had become desire, sex, death, and life as we moved to a beat made for us. Unable to deny the desires that lay within themselves, other patrons began to join us, one-by-one, timidly at first, lured by our unique alien vibe and Stoya's dark, drawing magnetism. They began to open themselves up for whatever we may please. Enticed, seduced, by the way in which their blood move oddly within them, orgasmic, as we pulled it to where we pleased. We would drink of them unabashed, reveling in their undying devotion to the fantasy of blood. It was what they were there for, the fetish of the flesh.

When Charlotte joined us, Stoya and I encompassed her, absorbed her into our being. She clung to us as we loved her, pleasuring her, draining her of inhibition as we kissed, the three of us, touched provocatively, explicitly. Charlotte became lost to us, our sex and Stoya's all engulfing aura. Powerless to the way we made her feel. Charlotte, was hers too by default. It's how our beings are; the sex, the relation. We claim all the lovers each other has. It is just how it is done with our kind. And what Stoya would demand. Charlotte found herself powerless to it; to her.

The three of us moved in elegant unison to the sounds of brooding darkness, the cataclysmic-like end of low drum and base pulses of some deeply mourned Gothic dystopic scene, a death, a funeral. "Bella Lugosi's Dead", the music, the voice told us, the remixed sounds of Bauhaus solemnly informed all as we came in unison to the beauty of such a dark prospect.

We moved in rhythm as the unearthly lyrics spoke of a dark and lonely death. An unfinished life. A languishing, the searching for what lay beyond the veil of the mortal soul.

And as I fell into the trance of our sex, I had become aware of the warning within the song, the story of an unfinished life. The fact that we are all held captive in some way to a thing which we cannot seem to ever truly find, immortality, completion, love.

Stoya reveled and fevered with the scents of human flesh and blood, to the music and lyrics of songs which reflected her inner most thoughts. We allowed others to pass between us, writhing, pulsating, and orgasmic. We would pleasure them as no other on this earth can.

Charlotte had become lost in a sensuality she had never experienced before; that of mass sex, the orgy. Stoya would have her fill, the warmth, the blood. She was there to feed, to feel the world again for a moment before returning to her own personal torment.

We were sisters despite the love-hatred she had for me. I had broken her heart. We were lovers, she and I. But never to be together in the way that she had wanted. She owned me in her mind. And now there was Charlotte; betrayal. She seethed over that, unable to find a resolution in us, her place in the order of things. It was all or nothing with Stoya. I was able to love both.

At 4AM, exhausted and sated, I drove Charlotte home as she cuddled against me sound asleep. The neon flashes of a modern world swept dreamlike over us hiding the optimism of a decaying city. Inside I felt that warm, electrifying contentment that one only gets once they realize they have fallen completely in love.

Carrying her up to her home and into her bedroom, we slid naked under the cool, soft, silken sheets. I held her tightly and fell fast asleep.

This is why I fell here, to this world, I thought in that moment, to find her, this one beautiful soul.

CHAPTER
15

I helped Charlotte with the last box as she struggled to get it up the stairs to my condo. She was tired from a full day of moving. I had paid out the rent for the year on Charlotte's place so her roommate had time to find another tenant. Charlotte insisted we move her stuff ourselves, a kind of bonding; a symbol of a new life and promising future.

It was November. We had been officially dating for six months and our relationship had already become more akin to a marriage than anything else. And like any married couple, we quibbled occasionally over stupid things, like not completely screwing the cap on a salad dressing bottle, leaving hair in the sink, or drinking milk straight from the carton. All of which Charlotte was guilty; especially hogging the sheets. But I adored it. She made me feel alive again; so very human.

My place was a far better place for her, allowing Charlotte easy access to work, a twenty-minute drive, the beach which she loved, and designer shopping when she had time.

My condo had a giant balcony overlooking the sea and its beach going worshipers. Its sliding glass doors could fully retract into the walls to allow unrestricted access to the large wrap around patio providing us with ample living space.

She loved the gourmet kitchen and quickly set about brushing up on her cooking skills when she found the time. She struggled with red meat, especially when cooking my beloved porterhouses; however, it was so adorable watching her do so.

Charlotte, in turn, would get over my seemingly lackadaisical attitude toward being on time, my obsession with economics and politics and my limited diet which consisted of red meat, wine, certain fruits, and desserts. I had a close doctor friend of mine write me up a diagnosis which outlined my special medical issues and discussed the restrictions to my diet. She wasn't buying it.

"Sometimes, I think you think you're a vampire. Like the people at the club, like Stoya does," she would accuse me.

I couldn't help but smile devilishly every time she slung that accusation.

We soon settled into a routine. Charlotte would leave for work as I set about checking on my accounts and other business, then go for my morning run, some yoga, or a round or two of volley ball on the beach. At noon, I had lunch dates with various friends or with Charlotte when she could get away. At six, I would have dinner ready. Take out mostly, I never did care for cooking all that much.

My most favorite time of the day with her was morning. I purred with contentment as I watched her rush to get ready for work. Flustered, often trying to carry her case load files, coffee, pop tarts, and other stuff, wobbling, limping on one high heel as she tippy toed around trying to put her other shoe on with her one free hand as she would rush out the door to start her day.

I had bought her a Mercedes S-Class sedan fully loaded for our six-month anniversary. It was already a wreck inside, filled with an ever-growing pile of clothes needing to go to the drycleaners and case files that were long over and settled. It was cute; annoying, but cute.

My second most favorite part of the day was Charlotte coming home. Flustered and tired her hair was ruffled and partly undone, a strand or two wafting down onto her face as she tried to blow it off her since her hands were too full with office work, it was impossible to smooth it back.

She would stagger in, her arms filled with her suit coat, files, and both shoes; her feet hurt. She'd have her blouse undone three or four buttons at times to get in some air.

Shortly after she'd return home, I'd watch as she gritted her teeth while plunking down in her favorite chair with yet another case to review; exacerbated by yet more deadlines. I hated the suffering part of it all, the work, her deadlines, but I was in love with that facet of her life, proud to be a part of it. It made me melt, her work ethic, the way in which she was so determined to make her way in it. It made me feel whole.

I did my best to serve her every need. I had wanted her to quit her job and offered to help her start her own not-for-profit firm which was her dream. But she refused, insisting that she had to get there on her own. It was just one of the many things I so deeply love about her; her independence and iron will which lay hidden deep within in her under the mushy, sentimentally kind persona.

So, I did all that I could to make her life as easy as possible. I worked on my cooking and kept the house clean and neat, ran errands for her, and massaged her feet and back nightly. I bought a state of the art hydro therapy hot tub that seemed to help also.

We were very happy and soon became content to stay home on most Friday and Saturday nights. We would play checkers, her favorite game, and eat Chinese take-out with hot chocolate if it was cold and rainy outside. With the lights turned low, we'd listen to the rain and the sea beyond the patio, while Sade played in the background.

Other times we would cuddle up and watch a movie and eat popcorn. She loved classic "B" horror movies, black and whites and Vincent Price. Elvira was a particular favorite. She had the complete series on DVD. And of course, all the romantic classics as well. It was just the two of us against the world. The way most couples are and should be.

I was complete again, like when I was with my officer lover in France just after the war. It was at times, hard not to tear, both at her in my arms and the thoughts of him.

The sex only got better too, slow passionate, kind, and loving. At times, she would release her kinky side, although it was pretty tame to me.

Eventually, I met her parents and attended a family wedding in Upstate Pennsylvania, where much of their family resides. I was a smash hit despite the general reservations toward our lesbian relationship.

Charlotte came from a well-bred, self-made family. Her father was very conservative, overly capitalistic, ambitious, and driven to achieve perfection and to make money at nearly any cost.

I eased her father's fears over the financial well-being of his daughter by presenting him with my financial portfolio and telling him my intention for her to have a pre-nuptial agreement if she so desired.

He stammered over my documented "Net-worth". He had no idea about what my "actual" worth was, let alone what I had hidden away long ago. If I had told him, he might have had a heart attack and died.

I told him that it was real, my love for Charlotte; our love. And that I was going to marry her when she, we, were ready to do so. I would wait. I had forever.

I laid out a basic plan for our lives together and how my wealth could take care of the entire family, his family and how, together, her father and I, could invest in new business ideas. I was going to share everything. I would make him richer than he ever thought possible. His greed and desire for money made it easy for him to compromise in his personal and religious beliefs.

So, in the end, it was settled, we were a couple, blessed by her family, more or less.

I intended to ask her to marry me when the time was right. She would have everything she could ever want or need or dream. I would sit up in bed at night looking out at the stars over the great Pacific holding her, her head on my chest, as she quietly slept, thinking of how blessed I was. Dreaming of that day when we would say "I Do!" But God, time as always, had other plans.

With increasing frequency, as I would drift off to sleep, a dream would descend upon me. A vision of a girl dancing in the far distance upon an endless sea of ice would enter my mind. She would dance and dance and beckon me farther and farther out into the endless frozen-black horizon. Whispering things I could not hear. A great secret, maybe? She seemed ever to fall farther and farther away from me as I ran and ran after her. And then, suddenly, a great storm would come and there in the snow where she once had been, lay my anklet of Chantecler bells, tinkling like ice, chiming in the driving wind, fading under the driving snows.

For all my alien-born advantage, my senses had still been blind to the thing now growing within Charlotte, the one true, great devourer of your kind, of the universe. Of perhaps, even, time itself. A thing more monstrous than my kind could ever be, God's most horrible unstoppable creation; cancer.

CHAPTER 16

Charlotte had made it clear that she wanted us to stay home on the eve of our first anniversary. It was April again. I wanted to take her to my home in Capri, Italy, or Zakynthos, Greece, or anywhere in the Med. And honestly, she needed a vacation.

She had become over worked and seemed to be suffering from frequent exhaustion. But she had nested, insisting we needed to stay right there and celebrate in what had become "our" home. We both agreed that we'd do a little partying the following night, Saturday, at the Vampyr Club if she felt up to it.

She was beginning to feel at home there. She felt safe and could be uninhibited. She was adored by everyone, having made many, many friends. She had her own little following actually. It was so cute to see her there, little Miss Perfect surrounded by punk rockers, steam punks, Goths, death rockers, and vampires. They were enthralled by her. She was so far outside their lives, this Gothic lifestyle. But they could not resist her, she seemed to heal them and their personal pains. But that was Charlotte's real power, to understand, to heal, to love.

I had arraigned for us a special five course meal prepared at our home by Chef Curtis Stone of the restaurant Maude. I had allowed him a large budget and requested only that he be as eclectic as possible while maintaining an underlying theme; a congruency of taste.

He chose to emulate man's culinary history. An idea of his he had been toying with for some time. It started, of course, with Africa, The Mediterranean, and Asia, the primary cradles of man. Then crossing into Europe; France, Spain, Great Britain and finally, America; the New World and its greatest melting pots, New York and LA; the now cataclysmic palette of the most modern dining experiences. It was quite simply, fantastic!

We dined on the balcony overlooking the sea, taking in the salt scented air under the stars and lights of Santa Monica. We enjoyed a tasting menu that was elegant and rich with experiences for the palate, and as always Chef Curtis made the perfect Porterhouse; lightly seared with a sauce which eloquently reflected Egyptian, Asian, and European flavors. It brought back many memories.

Even Charlotte had to agree that porterhouse was very tasty. Dinner was bold, challenging to both chef and palate, and worth every penny.

Stoya would have been impressed. She was also, in her own right, a master chef.

When Chef Curtis and his assistants had cleared our kitchen and quietly left, we opened another bottle of Château Lafite Rothschild 2000. Rich, full bodied, lengthy in flavor and linger, it had paired well with our dinner.

I couldn't help but to fire up a Cuban cigar after dessert.

The wine had been a gift from Stoya. It was rare, both the wine and her generosity. But Stoya was very sentimental about love. It told me we still had a chance, her and me; and Charlotte.

We sat and savored the wine and each other's company on an outdoor couch while the gentle blue flame flickered in my artistically rusted steel, glass shard filled open fire pit. Charlotte was happy. I gave her anything and everything. She was living the high life, the LA life.

I had given Charlotte a green emerald necklace with a matching bracelet and earrings. The necklace contained three enormous emeralds which were set amongst a diamond pavé and hung radiating out from her neckline upon an intricately woven gold chain-like mesh. The matching bracelet sported three smaller emeralds surrounded by more pavé. They were antique Tiffany, and I was particularly drawn to that set because of the intricate gold Art Nouveau-like Arabic letter styled filigreed design which spelled out "I Love You" and "Only time stands before us."

Filigree, or Nam'hul-urithlé in our language, the more modern, Arabian calligraphic designs of it, is similar to the written language of my kind. Some of which, its elder stylings', I had personally created for early Egyptian artists, which still can be found now and then, though filigree is not as fashionable of a design as it once was.

The necklace with its matching bracelet and earrings hearkened back to the mid-1800s, reminiscent of Egyptian-stylized jewelry and writings just being newly discovered amidst the Anglo-Egyptian political conflict of that time. It was intricate, three dimensional free-form filigree of the highest order; expertly crafted, work that seldom exists in this day.

Our language is beautiful in written and spoken form. Written, it takes a three-dimensional form in nature, often utilizing multiple colors intertwined to convey thought. Though on this world it is difficult to achieve on paper and is most often executed in simple black and colored ink brush work. But it translates well sculpturally, in jewelry specifically.

I have given you the best words from our language through art; "Cherish", "Admire", "Respect", "Understand", "Care for", "Grow", "Strong", "Love", and other power words and phrases of goodness and prosperity. I always smile at that art-craft, filigree; our secret language worn boldly upon your world. I wondered if the artists or wordsmiths through the ages could ever guess it; the mass-on-mass of random swirling lines. Could they ever have known of what they created? The fact that not only are they words, but mathematical equations and a form of music for us as well.

"Oh…oh, Ianthe it's beautiful!" Charlotte had gleamed excitedly jumping up and down like a little girl capturing her first firefly by a secret magic pond under a full moon.

"Oh…you shouldn't have!" she squeaked. "But I love it, oh thank you, thank you, oh…"

She proceeded to hug and kiss me saying "smoochies, smoochies!" before each kiss as she peppered me in them.

It was hard to keep from telling her about the filigree, what the words meant in my language, my message to her.

It sucks sometimes, being me, us, our little otherworldly secrets.

Charlotte was the first to suggest that we move inside. She seemed anxious for something, giggling and laughing, moving to the bedroom like a young girl in love. I had wanted to stay outside and be intimate there under the moon and stars.

Once inside sitting on our bed, we kissed for a while; touching, feeling, understanding, when she handed me a gift-wrapped box. Yet another gift in a myriad of little gifts that I had received all week.

It was beautifully wrapped; she had talent for such things. The box was covered in a deep pink wrapping paper and a sexy red colored bow.

The card simply read "XOXO" which beckoned to me to open it.

Charlotte leaned back into me with growing excitement, and I thought a little bit of hesitation, as I opened her gift.

She rushed me, squeaking. “Hurry, hurry, o, o, o.” Her hands waving rapidly in excitement.

I was taken back a bit when I saw what was inside. It lay there embraced within the thin, delicate, light pink and red tissue paper, shiny and pink, a simulated silicon phallic; a dildo. A strap-on with its black, but tastefully executed leather straps and gold buckled harness. I was shocked, it was unexpected.

Charlotte recoiled embarrassed at my reaction.

“Oh, no… no sweetie, I, I just didn’t…expect…well, you little devil you!” I exclaimed pulling her back to me and kissing her.

“I just, well, you know, wanted, needed…,” she stammered out, rolling her eyes to the side her head sinking back looking at me embarrassed, possibly ashamed.

“What sweetie?” I pawed at her, working to regain her enthusiasm; her trust.

I kissed her again. “For me or…?” I inquired, curious. I was the dominate.

“Oh...,” she spoke enthusiastically, seeming re-enticed now as to her original intention. “That’s for you to give to me!”

“If… that’s… OK?”

“Well, yes, anything for you!” I paused smiling and aroused. “I love you, you know…,” I assured her. “Anything!”

I could tell this was a big thing for her; the next level in our deepening relationship.

I smiled and kissed her again, standing.

She lay back open to me. She eagerly watched as I put on our new toy. It was elegant, the highest priced device one could buy. It was eight inches in length with a varying girth not exceeding two inches toward the front. It had slight undulations for its texturing, random, smooth. Its silicone rubber, hard enough but supple enough to flex and move around like the real thing.

I blushed standing there looking down at her, my little devil.

For me, at my end of things, a gently formed cup of sorts to collect me, my clitoris and labia. On its surface, a sort of sticky ribbed silicone which massaged and coaxed. It felt good down there. I had not done this sort of thing for long time, a few years at least.

I thought of the Bordellos of France, late 1800s, my first experiences with this sort of new pleasure. I fawned over the memories of my lovers, both men and women, but especially the men who enjoyed such things. Devices then weren't so elegant. Glass or porcelain rounded shafts tied on with a simple silk bow.

She breathed in, in anticipation as I moved closer to her beginning a slow descent onto the bed, onto her. Charlotte's eyes widened as she strained her hips back toward me, wanting its tip to tickle her. She bit at her lower lip, her eyes euphoric, half closed. She moaned out long and sensually. With great expectation of what was to come.

She produced some lubricant, sweet smelling, like flowers, Hibiscus possibly. She gently coated the shaft, massaging it sensually as if it were me.

I was prompted then, to move into her, and as I did so she seemed to become anxious again.

I was no more than three inches inside of her when I stopped, concerned for her well-being.

She seemed hesitant suddenly as I began to withdraw she stopped me, holding by the base of it.

"N…no, I, it..., I," her eyes rolled around, her mind trying to find the right words, fearful of my reaction to what she wanted to tell me, to instruct me to actually do.

I was puzzled, we used vibrators regularly.

She seemed embarrassed suddenly. "Well, yes…but…tonight I…I…"

I kissed her again gently. "It's OK sweetie, anything, just tell me!" I encouraged, waiting suspended there in time, I had time, we had time for this most intimate of things.

She bit at her lower lip looking deep into my eyes, my soul; this was a big thing for her, to demonstrate this fragility, this level of trust.

"Oh, well…fucking shit!" she finally burst out blushing smacking her hands on the bed.

I tried not to laugh at her; she was so damn funny.

"Here!" she finally let out.

Charlotte reached down for me, my elegant artificial phallic, as she bucked her hips up slightly, quickly guiding it, the tip of it into her anus.

I felt flush suddenly. I began to sweat, to wet immediately at the intention of the act. Anal sex was an exotic prospect, meant only for the closest of lovers. It meant everything to me, this newly revealed secret desire.

She pulled me into her gently, steadily, letting out a long seemingly painful moan as I tried to be as delicate as possible.

"Oh…oh, yeah, yes… fucking shit, oh, oh God, that…uh…oh, ahhh, fuuuck…yes…," she let out softly, gritting her teeth slightly, trying, I think, to keep in check her real feelings.

She had wanted to let loose but was trying to be sensitive to me as well, not knowing how I might react. Trying not to scare me over the fact that her precious adorable little angel had within her, a deep and longing desire, a taste for something of which many might find rather scandalous, and sometimes disgusting.

She pulled me all the way in now in one long, slow move save but an inch or so, the space biomechanically inhibitive when two bodies come together in such a way.

It was shocking by normal standards, the rapidness and the deepness of which she took it in. I had experience with this form of sex, and have engaged in it often, but it wasn't my personal favorite; receiving or giving.

Her eyes rolled back, closing as she slipped away into another part of herself, a dark desire, slowly coaxing me with her legs, to pump into her, gently at first to work the muscles there to get them to relax, then steadily faster, and deeper. It was completely unexpected to me, she like to be fingered there; one usually, two at times. She liked me to lick there too. I didn't mind. I liked such things. I wanted always to please her.

I knew she was a little more open there, larger than normal, but it wasn't unusual, people's parts are different. But it had become obvious now she had experienced this before, relished it in fact, as she began to buck at me losing control like I hadn't seen her do before in sex. I thought of the other vibrators in the nightstand; visions of her pleasuring herself in this way when I was not around.

Oh, my naughty, naughty little Charlotte, I thought to myself as I slowly began to pump in and out of her.

I smiled at the vision of her, joyful that she had shared this most intimate of secrets with me, joyful I could provide this, her ultimate pleasure.

I, too, let myself go. I let my body attach itself emotionally to my artificial phallic, my nerves connecting to it, the vibrations, the way it felt as it made its way in and out of her. It became like me, an extension, as the way our kind can do.

I could feel her insides, the gentle bump like ridges; her anus clutching at me as I slid in and out. I could smell the bitter sweet that is anal sex fill the air. I was becoming intoxicated by it, by her, by this act, because it was with her.

Charlotte began to undulate and roll side-to-side, then reaching down she began to vigorously stimulate herself, fingering her clitoris, her other hand grabbing at me, tussling my hair, grabbing at the back of my neck, my throat lightly. Another unexpected thing. She began to moan out loudly and without shame. I thought of the open glass doors and the beach front below, the people on a midnight stroll, I laughed at that thought.

I began to thrust harder into her, trying my best to please her. She guided me, ravenous of it, wanting long steady thrusts deep into her. I felt her begin to tremble; her body begin to climax in response to me as I moved into her. My eternally hard plastic phallic making gentle sexy sloshing and sucking sounds as it moved in and out, wet from both of us, our cum, our sweat, and the sweet Hibiscus lubricant.

I myself began to buckle uncontrollably; less aroused by the kneading of the rib filled cup upon me, than from the emotion of it all which was more erotic than the physical act.

It pleased me greatly pleasuring her in this way; her new-found openness to me meant everything. It was a next level in our being.

I came, mentally really, as I drove into her trying to balance between the violence and the sensual aspects of this sex, shuddering, trying to maintain the placement of the harness and the cup upon my pussy as I sweated and dripped. I let out a long and soulful groan, not usual for me, I was kind of quiet in that regard, as we both came together.

As the last trembles rippled through my body I pushed into her as deeply as I could, as if "releasing" myself into her. I throbbed, pulsated against my harness-cup, trembling. We both tensed against each other cuming again as she held onto me calling out in pleasure. When we had finished, I fell onto her pressing into her whole body; electrified.

She clung to me ravenous with her inner most dark desire. She was sweaty, and her hair a mess, lipstick and mascara running, a single tear fell from the corner of her right eye, as she breathed heavily, passionately, keeping me deep inside of her.

I breathed deeply, mentally exhausted.

"Oh… God, yes! Oh, that was fucking awesome!" she blurted out. "Fuck, oh yeah, yes!" she concluded letting her hands and legs fall from me lying open on the bed.

I tried not to laugh at her, the frankness, the openness, the way in which she said it. I could only nod my hair tangled head in agreement. I was winded, still coming down from my sexual euphoria.

We lay together, her body next to mine, sweating; panting. She held one of my breast as she snuggled into me. The air and our bodies saturated in the scents of exotic sex, sweat, Hibiscus, and perfume as we lay wallowing in our wet sheets.

Charlotte looked out at the ocean view through our glass bedroom doors lost in thought, embarrassed a little maybe by that onslaught of her lustful hedonistic need.

I held her tenderly. My touch reassuring her that everything was OK.

"Well…," Charlotte said suddenly and assertively. "Is there any of that Porterhouse left? I'm fucking starving."

I busted out laughing at her; she began to laugh out too.

Laughing together, we rolled around kissing with great passion for a while longer then fixed ourselves a bit to eat.

That sex toy was our little secret between her and me, reserved for special times, or especially bad work weeks when escape was desperately needed. It made me love her even more than I already did, not the act but the surrender of her vulnerability to me; her absolute trust in me.

CHAPTER 17

It had been a year and six months, and we both felt it was time that we completed our union. We were going to Capri where I had bought a home on the South-Eastern part of the island facing into the Tyrrhenian Sea near the upper most part of the island close to the Punta di Tragara overlook many years ago, around 1930. I was timing our trip for a full moon. It was there where I was going to ask her to marry me; above the Faraglioni rocks and ebbing cobalt blue sea below in the warm midnight's sweet honeysuckle and bougainvillea scented air.

My home was the last home before reaching the lookout, set high above it upon the cliffs actually, embedded partially into the hillside rock. It was mostly hidden from the view of passing visitors by a wild expanse of growing rose bushes and other flowering vined plants which formed an organic canopy-wall. Only a small plainly ornate wrought iron gate suggested there was anything to be seen beyond.

The house was old, quaint, and typical of the early 1900s Caprisian lifestyle. Made of traditional Roman style stucco and cut stone, it had a secret access path from the backyard near the pool to the Punta di Tragara lookout and its view of the Faraglioni rocks and the Scoglio del Monacone below, the Mediterranean Sea to the South, and mainland Italy to the North. It was a place of absolute romance and would serve as our honeymoon getaway as well.

Inside, the hand troweled walls gently undulated over the foot-thick hand-cut sandstone. I had goat's milk blended into the stucco mix, an old but traditional technique, which reflected a cool, soft off-white almost honey like glow at most times of the day. Other walls were painted in antiqued whites then burnished or accented with analogous colors of light lemon yellows and light blues. Clean, crisp, invigoratingly romantic, it was a balance of both modern and antique. I knew Charlotte would go nuts, reveling in her "Shabby Chic" sense of style there.

The furniture was mostly Italian in design consisting of hard woods, forged steel, and cast-iron furnishings. Italian glass table tops and soft textured canvas materials completed the seaside look.

The flooring, a soft seashell-white colored marble flowed from end-to-end. It felt luxurious on bare feet, like silky sand. It kept the house cool in the summer. In the winter, large beige, thick, hand-corded woven throw rugs from Northern Italian weavers were brought out to warm the floors.

The beds were covered in comfy, thick, white cotton, fluffy, duvets awaiting owner and guest alike, for a quiet restful nap or a full night's sleep.

Plush cream and light beige couches and chairs sat waiting throughout my home, placed to optimize either the view of the sea below or clustered for small gatherings and intimate conversation. One could lounge all day, engulfed within their soft, textured fabrics and powder blue and light-yellow accent pillows and throws.

Large retracting windows let in ample ocean breezes during the height of summer, and a large fireplace in the main living room stood ready to ward off the chill in the often-stormy winters.

A vast collection of rare books, consisting mostly of art and photography, filled the library. But there were also rare literature and assorted poetry books.

A small collection of movies; classics such as *Casablanca*, *Ben Hur*, or *Some Like It Hot* on old school film reels were available for viewing using a vintage 1950s-era German-made projector and a pull-down movie screen in the main living room.

For music, records awaited to be played upon an antique Philco console radio and record player. European music mostly, to complement this Caprisian life. I favored classic Italian singers like Laura Pausini, Anna Oxa, and Antonello Venditti among others.

This home was an ode to Italy, to Capri and its history; an honor to its global contribution to elegance and luxury, money, fame, and power. Capri is where the rich come to gather most summers; to visit and relax, to mingle with fans or patrons as equals.

There, also, was one of my most prized earthly possessions, my collection of most rare concept drawings and wax renderings by Pietro Capuano and Salvatore Aprea, creators of the now world renowned Chantecler bells and jewelry. Vintage drawings, color renderings, finalized gouch paintings of these jewelry-bells are placed throughout my home, framed in elegant dark gold leafed frames.

There were original wax modelings of much of their classic designs which I kept under glass upon eloquent pedestals, many of which were from the nearby Villa Jovis, Emperor Tiberius's summer retreat. I hosted unvielling parties often on behalf of the Chantecler family, for their most special patrons. A time for clients to make one of a kind purchases and see some of the original works first produced, that I keep in my private collection.

Outside, my home revels in the classic; encased in soft white sandstone and stucco molded in the typical Italian-Moorish construct. Its massive glass windows and sliding doors take full advantage of the natural light and changing weather. Cobalt blue awnings and cypress wood pergolas provide shade and cover for outdoor seating and garden dining.

My garden grows tirelessly in an almost never-ending percussion of flowers of every hue. Lemon, lime, and orange trees grow strong, along with red and white grape vines and all manner of vegetable and herb plants. It is, I think my one true home on this world. The place most sacred to me on earth.

CHAPTER 18

Capri is a secret, sacred, timeless place; a place to rest the heart and soul. To allow the mind to dream, remember and recover what it is to be in this life.

Life is easy on Capri. One can be indifferent to time, allow the world and all its worries to fall away from you as you slip into the dream of love and lost romance. It's where you go to eat, to drink, and to immerse yourself in the finer things; to find friends and lovers, even if for but a single day or night.

I take late lunches in my garden, mostly, and then wander into Capri proper, down the Funicular and to the Marina Grande to sit and catch up on life's happenings with local friends and acquaintances, or with friends aboard one of the many yachts always docked there.

Then, after a few hours, I make my way back up to the Piazzetta Umberto; the main plaza. There, I would sit in one of the balconies of the Ristorante Pulalli wine bar; the mini one designed to seat just two, to the left of the piazzetta's central clock tower. From there I had the best view to observe life, and most importantly love, and romance in motion. Ristorante Pulalli is considered one of the top five restaurants in Capri. I know the owners well; I was a lover once of a now long dead family member and an original proprietor of Pulalli.

I had history on that island reaching back to Roman times, when Emperor Tiberius first constructed Villa Jovis in 27 AD. I was one of many advisors there, a personal manager of his private accounts and estate. And secret lover to his wife Vipsania Agrippina for a short while.

I have stayed connected to Capri because it has a great secret. There, at Tragara, when the full moon is at its zenith, all the romance the world could ever hope to offer for any who were truly in love revealed itself in full. There, in that place, on that lookout, any who proposed or committed to one another was assured eternal love.

It had been this way long before I had ever known of it, and I think, will stand vigil for such love even as the world falls down into the sea below and is swallowed up by space and time. There in that place, I am quite sure, is one of God's greatest works.

At midnight, I would purpose to Charlotte. It would be just the two of us standing under that full moon, before the world, before God, the universe, and the ghosts of all long-dead lovers, immortalized by one simple phrase; "I do!"

In the quiet of that night I would make my promise to Charlotte, to say the words "to have and to hold", and "to love and cherish until death do we part". It would only be us to hear them, but the ghosts of lovers past would witness our binding matrimony; my eternal commitment.

And there I would tell her of whom and of what I am, to bare my soul to her, to let her decide our final fate. And, I think, I hoped, that she would understand and take the gift of which only I could give her, a lifetime of complete and absolute devotion, comfort and happiness for as long as God would grant us.

I felt my excitement growing as I envisioned that coming night, our night, when the phone rang. It was Charlotte, and she told me that she was going to die.

CHAPTER 19

Tears ran down my face at the sound of Charlotte's trembling voice on the other end of the line. I think I knew what was coming; I had been in denial for a while.

"I…I…need to see you. Come to the hospital…I…I, I have cancer, it's…it's…terminal, I.., I.., I don't have much time," she stammered, unable to get the words out.

She sobbed quietly in disbelief at her own sudden mortality. There was so much she, we, wanted to do in this life.

I was powerless in that moment. Unable to say or do anything but cry, be weak, and utterly crushed. I hated that part of your existence; death.

She had gone to her doctor's that morning. The pain, the unrelenting exhaustion finely convinced her that she had better take action. She had been called back that afternoon.

I was helpless to do anything.

"I…I…," I stammered, unable to tell her that I had suspected for a while now that there was something seriously wrong.

"There admitting me right now!"

I heard her voice tremble in fear; lost.

"Daddy is on his way, I need you!" she whimpered. "I need you…"

"Y…Ye...Yes, I am on the way!"

"Please hurry, I, I'm freighted…," she trailed off.

"I…I know sweetie, just, just hold on…I am coming!"

We listened to the sounds of each other over the phone for the longest time, neither of us wanting to hang up, to let go, for just in case.

I listened to her crying softly as I remained silent, afraid to say anymore.

"You are going to get better Charlotte." I breathed in, trying to calm myself; to calm her.

My nerves were firing on all cylinders as I trembled uncontrollably.

"We are going to get through this, we are going to get married, and live a long and happy life…," I said quietly, trying to convince her again; to not give up hope.

"O…OK…," she whimpered, trying to be strong for me.

"I've got the money for the best hospitals, the best doctors, sweetie…," I paused.

"You know, I've…I've never told you fully, but, I am rich sweetie, very, very rich!" I said finding strength and power in that fact.

"I mean richer than Bill Gates rich, sweetie," I paused. "I…we can fight this, money is not an object."

I could hear her cry, barely whispering. "Th…thank...thank you. I love you…." I listened to her as she began to completely break down.

I cursed myself. I should have gone with her, but she insisted that it was going to be nothing. Just some stomach problems, perhaps new complications from her car accident several years ago.

"I, I've got to hang up now sweetie-pie, I'm coming, just hold on," I confirmed, suddenly finding myself unable to find my purse or keys, or anything to get myself moving toward her, to be with her.

"OK, please…hurry!" she said as she hung up the phone.

I wavered; standing in the middle of my living room. I was numb; unable to move. I felt the sands of time descend upon me, move through me; swirling. Then the world went black.

I suddenly found myself upon my floor broken and curling up in absolute terror at the thought of losing her. I felt alone and afraid in that moment. Both things I seldom felt.

I thought of her now, my precious Charlotte, her image, her smile in the Coach Store window. Her almost whisper, the night of our first date. And I saw her at the Punta di Tragara overlook in Capri, under the full moon. She was glorious as I knew that place would have her be. I cried at it, the vision of her there in the full moon light, her face, her eyes; that almost whisper that finally spoke their secret; "I know, and I do!"

And then, I watched, as the image of her in that moment, slowly began to fade from me. Her life, her being, her memory. I gasped at the horror of it, of her fading from the annals of time. I saw myself alone again on some other world, standing in some other place of God's grand making, remembering. I knew the memory would be faint by then, a million years or more had passed. The only thing to remain of her, the almost whisper upon her lips that I could never fully hear.

I choked for air, unable to breathe suddenly. I closed my eyes and held myself in an even tighter ball, a protective reaction of the creature I had once been before. It was a defense reaction, a self-refuge from further attack; a defense from the cruelty that is life.

And I cried like I had never cried before over anyone since the loss of my quiet whisper upon the ice that time had washed away.

CHAPTER 20

Charlotte had been diagnosed with an aggressive form of metastatic cancer. No one could really guess how or why it evolved within her exactly. It possibly started in her pancreas or liver. She had been mostly healthy all her life, but it didn't matter now. Cancer by its very nature is spontaneous, mysterious, secretive; destructive. It is universal, and I have come to believe, God's contempt against all Its own creations.

It was spreading fast and beginning to form in her nervous system and brain. Time was short, a few weeks at best, maybe a little longer.

I found myself still unable to accept this fate as I sat at Charlotte's bedside; having in all probability now to plan for a funeral; for death; when I had planned so long for love and life.

I found myself caught up in a whirlwind of agony and anger. Normally clam and calculating, I began to unravel, lose control of my inner desires. The thing that is what I truly am. I quickly fell into contempt against life, against mankind, against God and this universe. I seethed over It, God, Its uncaring, unknowing, indifference. I felt that I had been cheated; again.

I was also continually haunted by the image of the girl upon the ice from so long ago. It seemed to continually replay in my head. The vision, the dream; the ghostly ballerina.

And, too, I found that I needed to feed to console my anguish. To help erase the images. I was angry. My natural instinctual blood-lust was clawing its way up inside of me. I wanted power over life; as our kind always did and had. I found relief in the violence, the consumption of the flesh, my power over human kind.

I would take many in those first days after Charlotte's admittance to the hospital. My prey, mostly, evil men or women, common criminals and thugs. But I took innocents too; anyone that I found obtrusive or annoying. I snuffed them out, consumed them and felt my power grow.

I was ashamed of myself. I hungered to satisfy my hatred, to try to ease my pain in some way. I starved for power, the power to erase my feeling of powerlessness.

And, I was beginning to believe, to convince myself, that Charlotte had betrayed me in some way. She was weak after all, human in all of its fragility; a being of God's lesser creation. A soul with no memory, no real destination.

Stoya had only reiterated this fact, confirmed what was a truth. She had little pity when it came to such things. Her indifference only seemed to support what I was allowing myself to believe.

"I told you…Ianthe, that this world, its life, it is here for us. Use it, take of it, do not fall in love with them, or it," she spoke coldly.

But I knew too, she was not entirely convinced by her own words.

Still, I was invincible, timeless, free of disease, and the frailties of the body. I cried constantly over the feelings that came to me, at the fact that I began to resent Charlotte, her life, our passion, my love for her; for us. I even came to resent having ever fallen to this weak and pathetic world in the first place.

I thought of Stoya more and more. Of the connection that we had. Of the timeless love that she could give me. Of how we could rule in this world together, rise up and become gods to your kind. I could endure her brutal smothering; at least we could be together forever.

And I thought of the others; of E'ban and Tyr. Maybe I could bring them together, I was of royal lineage only second to Tyr, and together the four of us could rule in glory over human kind.

I had many unflattering thoughts in those unending days. I felt my heart withering and dying.

CHAPTER
21

“Haven’t I told you, time and time again?” Stoya replied smugly, rudely, at the latest news of Charlotte’s condition, indignant of my pain as I sat utterly defeated before her in my executive suite at the Ramada overlooking Sibiu, Romania.

She had come down from her mountain home in Arefu for the day, hoping to take me back with her.

I looked out across Sibiu and its rooftops covered with traditional red and gray tiles. It was peaceful, enticing. Ancient memories of Stoya and I in the court of Bran came flooding back.

“They are inferior, playthings, food; nothing more,” she let a long stream of smoke exit her lungs through her mouth while clenching her teeth. “Leave her, there is nothing one can do, they are weak!” she went on.

I wept softly thinking of how I should be with Charlotte. I hated myself. I was the one who was weak now.

“Come, my sweet, don’t fret. It is God’s will after all,” she mocked.

“God’s will…,” she seemed to snarl, more at God than at Charlotte’s plight.

I have no idea why I went to her, confided in her. It just seemed the thing to do. I needed to be with my sister, my lover; a woman my equal.

E'ban had been more comforting, even by phone from thirteen hundred miles away. I should have gone to him instead.

"I'm going home to Arefu, Poenari!" Stoya exclaimed. "Come with me to my home, your home as it once was," she spoke enthusiastically.

"I will take care of you there, love you. And, if you want, I will end it for her, because I love you so."

I shuddered at that thought, my eyes welled again.

"Mercy! I will do that for you, for Charlotte, this thing you love, I will make it pleasurable, complete," she paused reassuring me.

"In time, the memory of her will fade…like the other before…"

She seemed to snarl at something, a memory within me.

I looked to her suddenly, what did she know of that? My dreams, the woman upon the ice? And it was then that I fully remembered something, of who Charlotte really was.

I began to cry again, but Stoya made no effort to hold or even touch me. I felt her gaze penetrate deep into me. I felt her condemnation for me; her thoughts burned their way into my heart.

"It is not for you to have this time either Ianthe, we all must lose in this game. It is as it is and forever will be. Loss…"

She exhaled slowly sneering again with contempt. "Souls have their own journeys, it is not your place to question why it is as it is made. God is contempt, be lucky we may live to survive Its will. Forget her and come with me. We are forever, I will care for you as she could never do…I have offered…let it be remembered."

Stoya sat back convinced of her own resolution.

But Stoya was more bark than bite. She had been in love, too; bitter sweet love. All with horrible men, but it was love to her pure and true. Her heart had been broken many more times than mine. She was the hopeless romantic, even if she couldn't admit it to herself.

She sat back in her chair, her left leg kicking back and forth frantically, annoyed by the burden I had laid upon her.

I knew she loved me more than she would ever admit. But she smothered her lovers, trapped them and bound them to her will. She was poison to the soul. She saw Charlotte's death as an advantage, a tactical move to draw me in again.

We sat for a long time in silence. I could feel her energy come down upon me, coaxing me, pulling at me. Dark, seductive, an end unto itself.

"Fine!" she said as readied herself to leave. "Call me if you need…"

She stood up, lit another cigarette, her eyes blazed angrily at me. "I will give you time…but not too long," she paused; about to say something else, then stopped herself.

"I will be waiting…"

She bent down and kissed me on the cheek, pausing for a moment, hoping maybe I would concede to her desire and leave with her in that moment.

I remained seated as she left my room closing the door behind her.

I sat for the longest time contemplating what she had said. Maybe it was all true. *"They were food, playthings, and nothing more…"* I thought of God, the cruelty.

I did not want to go back to see Charlotte slowly die. And I could not leave with Stoya, to be with her in the way she would demand.

E'ban would have forced me to face this end with Charlotte, to fulfill my promises to her, and if I didn't do that, he would have abandoned me also.

I sat, sunken down, defeated; lost in thought over all this. Staring mindlessly out at the landscape beyond my room, out into time itself. I sought a solution to an impossible problem. Charlotte was, after all, only human. Her soul, its course, already predestined. I wondered over it, her soul; its purpose in this life. Its inevitable end whatever that could be.

But was this impossible? I worked my mind searching for options and carefully began systematically building possible mathematical constructs and probable solutions that would dictate my next move.

I picked up a still smoldering Insignia brand cigarette from the ashtray Stoya had been using and took a long drag, letting the smoke fill me like I had filled this body so long ago. I exhaled, and as the smoke slowly exited, I thought of all of my past loves and lovers in a slow motion, black and white reel of *Casablanca* movie-like highlights. But always there was that one face, that one image, Charlotte, the many incarnations of her. The eyes, the mouth, the spirited dancer. And I understood then, that the game wasn't fixed, that there are other possible ends whether God accounted for them or not.

I am not going to give up this time. I am not going to lose again. I had found my love, my purpose; the one I had been subconsciously searching for all these years. Charlotte the body, the soul within, was going to live. I began to contemplate my situation, my next move.

Then, suddenly, a thought came into my head. I began to consider something I had not considered in a very, very long time. I thought of a child born of our kind that both Tyr and E'ban could give me. Of how it would save Charlotte, inhabit her and make her one of us, the Nosferatu, immortal. She would be saved from this fate of hers, to live forever until the end of time. Together, with me. There would be no more desperate searching, no more passing but for a lifetimes short flickering moment.

"No, we could be together then...," I said aloud to myself. "She will be as us."

I took another drag and drifted deep into thought, hunching forward.

I thought of Tyr again. I thought of his miserable existence and began to boil within.

“It is time!” I thought for some reason. An image of his death came suddenly. My hands drenched in his blood.

There was going to be a new soul born, one that will love and cherish her existence, and in time do something wonderful I was sure.

Yes, I reassured myself, I would take what I needed and finish off the old and weak. It’s what we did wasn’t it? Our kind, the culler of the herd. Shapers of God’s evolution.

I sat back and let the smoke exit me, a release of sorts, the punctuation to my new-found conviction.

“I am going to save Charlotte,” I said aloud. “I am going to save love from God.”

CHAPTER 22

The flight back to the states was restful despite my worries. The first-class flight attendant was a sexy Neapolitan woman with big boobs and a beautiful smile. Her name was Ciosa. She was maybe fifty, but she had a timeless beauty about her, so it was hard to tell. We hit it off the minute I stepped onto the plane. It was almost as if she had been waiting for me.

"Welcome aboard, Ms. Gold. I hope that I will provide you with an experience you will remember," she greeted me, smiling broadly.

But it was in the way she said it that drew me to her, made me wonder over her.

I have flown through Italy a thousand times or more, I had never seen her in my travels until now. Yet it was as if she had always been there. She was a welcomed relief to my current pain, and seemed to perceive of my troubles instantly. Perhaps expectantly.

Business men of all sorts walked past my seat, disappointed they were not to be my flight partner.

No one would be. I bought out the first two rows in my aisle; left hand side, bulkhead seats and directly behind. I wanted to be alone and unhindered by wanton advances.

Ciosa took care of me. She seemed to know that I was in great need without even asking. She was busy, but found moments to sit with me throughout the flight, holding my hand, soothing it like how my kind can, but it was different somehow. In what way, I could not fully tell.

A strange energy filled me, rejuvenating me. As if shaving away the ages upon me. I puzzled over it. Of who or what Ciosa might be.

I felt compelled for some reason, to spill my guts, to tell her everything of what I was going to do. She sat silent staring off into some unseen space, some place of which only existed in her mind.

"Love…," she spoke after listening. "Will always win out," she said quietly, gently, smiling, when I was done with my story. "It is God's will, Its intent...for us; love. For that is what life is really, what our soul is meant to do. But love is fleeting, God's creation, life, is struggle," she said quietly, patiently, ensuring I understood her.

"Life is as it was made to be, and will always be. It is what is done with it, this life, your one chance at it. But it is elusive, uncertain…filled with infinite variables of which we can only guess at…," she finished softly, evasively as if speaking to herself another thought entirely.

The look of deep thought and concern seemed to set upon her frowning lips. Her eyes, like mine, endless in their depth drifting back again to the space in time of which only she knew and could see.

We both sat in silence for a while, both contemplating those words. It was strange, I thought. How she seemed to know me, of what I really am inside this human body.

"Well, I wonder sometimes about that…about God," I responded carefully.

"Yes, it is difficult to understand now," she replied comforting me. "But there are things at play in this universe and beyond, that even God Itself cannot understand…," she trailed off cryptically, almost as if she had revealed something she should not have. "Nor ever come to understand fully..." She seemed distant again, thinking. "We...," she stopped suddenly.

"Well," she changed direction, smiling. "Anyways, I see a future with you two again, it is time for that union to be completed...," she spoke confirming that idea to herself I think, more than to me.

"It's been a long time, souls are eternal, and eternity passes quickly," she spoke as confirmation to me, to herself I was sure.

I saw her smile at something as if remembering a vision. "Ice...," she said fondly whispering. "Love is timeless...," her voice trailed off.

"Yes, Charlotte must be reborn before the end...she...must...," Ciosa seemed to cut herself off again, looking back to me with a slight smile, a spark in her eye.

I wondered over it.

Ciosa quickly slipped back into her in-flight attendant bearing, and smiled as if any of what we had spoken somehow never been said. As if it somehow no longer mattered.

"Well, the old will be new again, that is for sure!"

I felt my mind penetrated, like Stoya did to me, but at a much higher level.

"Yes!" she concluded. "Yes. I believe that is the design for this..." she said as she looked straight at me.

I felt her mind within mine. "Yes, Ianthe, it is time!" she said playfully, her Neapolitan accent thickening, her eyes seeming to lose their infinity as if to conceal a true identity, as our kind so often does.

I thought of my self-confirmation in Sibiu; *"It is time."*

I asked why she chose those specific words. *"It is time."*

She just shook her head, saying furtively, avoiding any further questioning. "Because, it just feels like it is so."

She smiled, laughing and kissed me on the cheek playfully. "Because you believe it to be so..."

She smiled broadly then got up to set about her in-flight duties.

When we arrived in LaGuardia, New York, I gave her a one-thousand-dollar tip, a hug, and a kiss.

She handed my money back and gave me her card.

"Money means little to me Ianthe Gold…," she spoke with a playful, but disapproving tone.

"But, take this, call me, when you really need of me...but not until then." She softly smiled again. "When Jonathan Nelson Davis will need of me," her dark, penetrating, chocolate brown eyes seemed to implore me caringly.

I was thrown off by this out of the blue comment. What did my best friend have to do with any of this, I wondered?

"I will think about you and Charlotte. You must do this….," she paused again. "It will work out, it is as planned, or, so as it is meant to be. Have faith in that Ianthe Gold; that it will be as you believe it to be."

She took my hand for a moment, then backed away, lingering to look deep into my eyes as if she was trying to see something within me; read my very soul.

She paused then spoke again, as if a thing she almost forgot. "Do not be afraid, Ianthe, in this thing you are about to do. It is in this thing, that there will be salvation for many. In your betrayal, there will be a defining moment, and a love so strong will flourish. Have faith, Ianthe Gold…that in you forever has its chance, that through this, we will all live again, this thing forever."

I went to speak.

Ciosa, quickly backed away and playfully waved saying, "ciao!" as she turned and walked back down the ramp and onto the plane.

I stood for the longest time staring down the ramp. I felt life move by me, people on their way, each to some destination, each into their own lives, their personal forevers.

I looked at her card.

Love is Timeless, souls are eternal. Eternity passes quickly within forever.

010 – *Ciosa*

I stepped out through the gateway and out into the awaiting world, strangely uplifted; empowered. I seemed to have a courage I had not had had before. I breathed out letting all my worries exit me.

"It is time!" I thought and turned to my sole endeavor, saving Charlotte; saving love.

CHAPTER 23

Charlotte lay upon her hospital bed awake, but exhausted from yet another round of chemotherapy. Her treatments were aggressive, but it was going to be a losing battle. Her father, seeing me through the room's partition window got up as I walked into the seating area.

I had arranged for her admittance to America's finest hospital and research center the Johnson Memorial Cancer Center, New York City. I simply wrote a check for five million dollars and told them to bill me when that ran out.

I sighed as her father came to greet me outside of her room.

"How is she?" I asked. It had been a few days since I had last seen her.

"Ah, good, good," he said trying to reassure himself more than me.

But I could tell that he was angry deep inside; at the situation, at the world, and at me for leaving.

"Good!" I said as I squeezed his shoulder.

"Father…," I spoke, looking into his eyes.

"Things are going to get better, but you have got to trust in me," I said softly and with conviction hoping he was one who could read between the lines.

"I know this is hard to understand, but I can fix this! I just need you to know that everything that I am doing, and that I am going to do, is for Charlotte."

He began to break down and cry, leaving before I could say anymore. Leaving to hide his weakness.

"Ianthe, is that you?" the weakened voice of Charlotte asked from beyond the glass wall.

"Yes, honey. It is!" I said rushing into the clean white room.

Her room was decorated in all white, accentuated by colored reprints of Galen Rowell and Philip Hyde landscape photos.

I had arranged for fresh flower bouquets, which were changed daily. I bought a fern and other tropical plants to make her surroundings as pleasant as possible; Bird of Paradise, Bougainvillea, and Orchids. A small plug in water feature completed the tranquility I sought to give her.

A game of checkers stood ready to be played at her desire. She had everything and anything; the best.

I had brought in one of Switzerland's best up and coming cancer specialists, Dr. Yash Mehra.

He was from a moderately wealthy family in Northern India and had a specialization in advanced cancer research. He had graduated from Harvard Medical School with distinction and was summa cum laude in DNA-cancer stasis research utilizing a very rare radioactive isotope.

After he completed his studies, he was immediately offered a job at the Genolier Clinic in Switzerland, a privately-run hospital that is at the cutting edge of cancer treatment. The clinic is known for its highly advanced, experimental and bold approaches to treating cancer.

He was brilliant, and Charlotte's one and only chance.

I had purchased for Dr. Mehra and his family, a large apartment, with full in-home maid service, staff, and an on-call driver, just three blocks away from her hospital.

I got his children accepted into a private school close by and even arraigned for an interview for their eldest son at

Vassar College in upstate New York. I knew the dean well. We were old friends from long ago.

I would spare no expense; the world had shit enough gold to last its lifetime.

I purchased a long-term residence agreement in two of the superior room suites at the nearby Bentley Hotel overlooking the East waterway and Franklin Roosevelt Island for Charlotte's family so they could have a place to stay when they visited.

A business agreement with a certain airline guaranteed a perpetual first-class ticket system for her family. It allowed for immediate, first priority boarding and full transport services to and from the airport with unrestricted access through security and full club room access. I wanted any family member from anywhere in the country to be able to see her at a moment's notice.

Don't ask about the price tag and the red tape issues I had to deal with; money is power. I probably funded the TSA and its operations for at least two years. Not to mention the airlines CEO's month-long vacation to Bora Bora.

"I'm glad your back," she mumbled, tired, broken, and high on pain medication.

I kissed her on the forehead and sat down next to her; taking her hand in mine. Her hand was cold, clammy, and weak. I felt her pulse and began to work her blood, warming it, and moving it throughout her.

"Oh, that's so nice, I'm cold always," she spoke meekly.

I watched as her skin regained its coloring for a while.

"I'm so tired! she exclaimed. "Stay with me while I sleep, please."

"Yes sweetie, as long as you want."

I sat holding her hand and warming her blood while I softly cried.

I thought of Capri and our night of union, it was nearing the full moon. We wouldn't be making that night now.

I thought of the girl upon the ice again. The coldness of Charlotte's skin brought about a flood of memories.

I saw the death of the girl on the ice. The day I held her in my arms as the storms came, blotting out the sun for nearly a year. Black and cold. I saw the driving snow piling up, erasing the vision of my Chantecler anklet, like in my dreams, from the memory of time.

When I was certain Charlotte was fast asleep, I leaned forward to whisper carefully into her delicate ear. I told her of my plan. I told her of whom and what I was. I whispered to her the memories that I had of her in another life, the girl upon the ice; a fairy tale of such grand imagination; a love story for the ages.

I told her I was going to fix her and make her whole again. I told her that we would live forever, lovers she and I, to the end of time.

I held her hand tightly as I wept.

I placed a diamond ring on her finger, nothing gaudy. I had it designed specifically for her by Tiffany's of New York. It's what she had dreamed of since she was just a little girl. I looked at her angelic face, as she slept in silence.

"I'm going to do this," I exclaimed to myself aloud. "Even if it means my death."

CHAPTER 24

I found that Charlotte was feeling a little better when I went to see her on Sunday afternoon. She was having an up day, which meant the chemo was finally working. It bought me time.

I brought Chinese, Kung Pao Chicken, her favorite, and hot coco as well. It was rainy outside and I knew that both would cheer her up.

Her family was there when I arrived, along with the family's minister and close personal friend, Father Boughan.

I shrank from them, from their family's spiritual guide especially. The way they looked at me. I took his presence as a bad omen and a sign that the believers were choosing to give up in the hope that miracles can and do happen. I also knew that he was there to absolve her of her sinful lifestyle; our lesbian relationship.

I gritted my teeth and seethed. I saw Charlotte smile at me and weakly wave, beckoning me to join them.

"So, you are Ms. Gold!" Father Boughan announced as he approached me coming out of Charlotte's room and into the adjacent sitting area, seemingly pleased to finally meet with me.

His voice carried a slight New York Irish-English accent. His greeting was an attempt, I believed, to defend his flock, his benefactors, his friends from further outside influences and intrusions.

I stood frozen, unable to act at this sudden betrayal. I flushed with anger.

"Yes…I am," I pronounced, catching myself before letting my anger show.

"It's so good to finally meet you Ms. Gold!" Father Boughan extended his hand to shake mine.

"Same," I said sharply as I curtsied slightly and took up his hand firmly in mine. This was business now.

"You know, I keep missing you, the wedding, and other family events…," he said laughing.

"Yeah…I'm busy often, global travel and all…," I responded.

In truth, I had avoided meeting him, one of the few things Charlotte and I did actually fight over.

"But, please, Ianthe will be fine."

"Well, OK then…Ms. Gold."

He resisted more friendly familiarity, wanting to ensure formal barriers were not crossed; a form of control.

We stood looking at each other for a long while.

I thought of Stoya in that moment. How would she deal with this encounter? I chuckled to myself, and then smiled; relaxing while thinking of her words

"They are nothing to us…"

"A little early to be begin last rites, isn't it?" I spoke confidently, sarcastically in regard to Charlotte.

Father Boughan stood silent for a moment then opined. "Oh, no, just here for moral support, and to say a good word for Charlotte. That's all. You know…I christened her when she was born."

I smiled at the thought of his memory, musing. "Yeah, I'll bet she was adorable."

"Oh yes! The sweetest thing I've ever seen and it was my pleasure to watch grow up," he paused.

"You know I say that to everyone about their children, but for Charlotte, well, I am not lying at all about that. She is a child of God that one."

I stepped back laughing. "Well, a lie, Father? Are not all children beautiful; of God?"

"Well…yes…yes…," he stammered. "But you know, a little fudging of the truth every now and again doesn't hurt anyone."

He recovered trying to play it off as a little inside joke between us.

"Well, good, then, perhaps I still have got a chance," I said easing myself and laughing as I thought of my truth and the lies I tell to keep them.

"I think God will understand then...," I winked at him.

Father Boughan began to chuckle to himself at that comment as he looked me over; the uniqueness of me. I could tell he saw something in me. But what, he was unsure.

I knew he did not approve of Charlotte and me. We were sinners in his eyes, and he was there to save her soul upon her passing, if he could, and to improve her family's "standing" in heaven.

"Well," I spoke standing up tall and powerful again, exercising my peculiar feminine prowess. "The Chinese food is getting cold," I said as I jiggled the bag a bit. "And we shouldn't keep Charlotte waiting," I softly directed.

He stood staring at me wanting of something, a relinquishment maybe, of my hold on Charlotte, of our love I am sure. A confession by me perhaps.

I smiled, trying not to smirk at the thought of that meaningless gesture as I stepped past him.

"Uh, oh?" he stammered again. "I…I wanted to ask you about something. If…"

I turned and faced him. He seemed to have lost his conviction with me. I thought of how lucky he was that Stoya was not here.

"Yes; anything."

"Well…well, we are a little concerned about something…"

He looked back at me nervously wiping his forehead with a white handkerchief.

"It's OK, sweetie, what's on your mind?" I softened, trying to ease his fears.

"Well, its Charlotte, she, she, keeps mentioning vampires in her sleep. We… we just wondered if you knew anything about that?"

I almost cracked up, but refrained from doing so. I smiled back at him grinning.

"Well," I paused. "I suspect she's talking about the nurses and such. You know all the blood draws going on each day…," I trailed off trying to keep my composure.

I was dying inside from laughter.

He seemed to like that idea; my convincing lie.

"Well! You know I hadn't thought of that." He seemed pleased with himself, of his new-found answer.

"Yeah, I'm sure that's all it is," I smiled devilishly back at him. "She's so silly you know!"

We both laughed, looking at Charlotte through the glass partition.

"Yes!" we said almost in unison.

"You know I'm glad I met you, Ms. Gold, thank you!" Father Boughan said genuinely.

I had given him something to give to her family, an explanation to further deem his worth to them. It didn't matter to me; I was there to do anything I could for Charlotte, and Charlotte alone.

"Visit me sometime Ms. Gold, we are always open to any and all!" He said kindly, imploringly.

"Even vampires?" I asked, grinning.

"Sure…we help all kinds of lost souls," he replied back to me slightly laughing at what he thought was a joke.

"Good! It's a date then, and I'll bring my sister Stoya. I think she could use a little spiritual uplift; a word or two maybe from the good book; from God," I laughed trying to keep my sarcasm buried.

"Yes, well then, see you soon, the three of us!" I concluded and then turned my attentions to Charlotte wondering if he could catch that hint, my little tease of what I was now about to do.

CHAPTER 25

Our reproduction cycle is complicated and at times dangerous. And it is nothing as you would fantasize of us. In truth, reproduction of our kind, the "Birth-Rebirth" process, is quite unglamorous, despite the seduction and chaos that can be involved. There is no "eternal kiss", no "gift", no exchange of blood or a passing of a venom, nor any other magical transaction as the traditions and mythoi so attributed to the earthly vampire might have you believing. There is no grand illusion. No magical transpiration, save one, inhabitation. Those are the ideals of fictitious minds, an all too easy explanation, an all too easy dismissal of God's one true miracle; conception.

In that lies the real miracle of us, this universe, of all our making, a thing greater than any other thing of which God has designed. Birth and rebirth is everything we are, you and I. A perfect union of atoms, of indifferent cells, a formula forever unknown, a thought in the mind of God alone. A mathematical construct which concludes in a single moment, with only one outcome; life. That is the real magic, the joining of those cells, the chromosomes, and the inhabitation of one into another, a blending to make a new thing.

Yes, we are as you in so many ways, and vice versa. The result of an inhabitation of one body into another. A grafting at the cellular level. Of chromosomic cellular joining; sperm and egg and the cellular division and unification which occurs thereafter.

We create and bear our children both within our natural forms and through the bodies of which we have inhabited; create them through sex. A grand and yet so simple and pleasurable thing, a magical thing unto its own. Such is the devilish side of God; Its grand trick essential to the propagation of life. The desire for it, the need for it, the fact that life can die in the face of it. Yet another way in which all life is challenged, to ensure only the fittest survive.

I had a chance at that now, to mate, to breed, and to give birth. To make a new thing, another of our kind, to unify it with Charlotte, to fulfill its life as sentient being, make it into what we are, to ensure our kind continued to exist.

On our world, in our culture, reproduction is as much a status position as it is a natural selection process. Often violent, wars have ensued over the rights to breed, for sex partners, and at times, over the resulting offspring. So much like as on your world over the centuries between rival clans and kingdoms and for eons in the animal world.

Usually only the strongest of us get to reproduce. Traditionally, rights to breed are granted only to those of elevated social status, or those who were born during certain powerful celestial events, or within specific lunar and solar cycles. Though many were conceived outside our normal standards.

I am of the house of N'I-Nari'd, our center sun, the God-Sun, and was born during the thousand-year eclipse when our moon, Namri'd, passes N'I-Nari'd, blotting it out for three of your earth days.

I am of high nobility. Only those born under the four-month phase when Etonar, our farthest and largest moon, N'I-Nari'd, and Namri'd align every one hundred thousand years, are higher.

Tyr is of this house; the house of "the Great Aligning", or the Massar'id as we know it.

Our reproduction process resembles most other male to female sex processes in this universe but with a slight twist. Normally, the process requires just one of each sex, a male and a female, to join and complete the transaction. In our case it requires the union of two males and one female to achieve that conception; two sperm, one egg. But that too, is complicated.

Conception is selective, violent at the cellular level. For us even more so. There can be no single contributor. There must be one succeeding sperm from each male and they must be of equal strength. They must fight, spermo a spermo so to speak, until the one remaining spermatozoa reach a "mutual" submission, both joining chemically, an inhabitation of one into the other to form one super-sperm. Together, as one, they will attempt to fertilize the egg. But that can, and often did, fail.

The egg in our species is the final gatekeeper. It seeks to remain pure and un-inseminated. It alone determines the final outcome; whether there will be life. It determines if the incoming genetic coding, the DNA, was of acceptable elevation and quality to ensure that only strength and perfection existed; that our species remained strong.

If the super sperm failed to gain penetration, the egg would turn on it, attack and devour it thus negating the conception entirely. It was just how our kind did things, how we were made; products of near impossible conceptions. And I think another firewall on behalf of God to keep my species in check.

But biology can be overcome, and most often is. It is the social aspects that often stands in the way of any possible interaction. On this world, the social structure between Tyr, Stoya and E'ban, and I was virtually non-existent in that sense. Especially concerning Tyr and E'ban. My two male contributors. To move forward in this process, I would need approval for mating by all; a serious obstacle.

Tyr considered E'ban a lesser in our social structure. A person of no house and no stature. Tyr would not allow his seed to be tainted, not allow the possibility of imperfection.

Stoya was at odds with E'ban as well. She too considered him a lesser, considered him a threat to Tyr's elevation, his rule on this world. She sought Tyr for herself, and thus, was jealous of me in that regard. For Tyr had always favored me over her as the potential carrier of his spawn.

E'ban, on the other hand, would fully support me in this endeavor. Not out of malice towards Stoya or Tyr, or for any another thing, but for his love for me. Our long and lasting friendship. It was going to be an adventure to say the least, and quite possibly result in my death. All of our deaths.

I would need to gain consent from Stoya, Tyr, and E'ban to breed. An approval which helps to set into motion, my body's chemistry, activate my one and only egg, to set the course for conception.

Consent to breed and initiate it requires approval, the "mark"; known as the Narun'an in our language. The "mark" mainly a series of deep bites upon the chest or neck, usually placed upon each other, was our way of "approving" others for breeding. A thing from where some of the vampire myth was born.

Other visual "marks" also occurred, scratches, tears, and bruises. Brutal but effective, a display of power and endurance among our kind indicating strength and virility. A thing similar to many other species on this world, and others, like my last one, where visual physical acceptance is needed to demonstrate possession and keep social order.

But the "mark" is not just about "approvals". It is the only way in which our reproductive systems activated chemically. Without which, neither the sperm nor my egg would act and simply lay dormant, producing nothing. This is why I cannot conceive with humans who lack both that ability to give me the right "chemical" initiating approval, and the complementing DNA ignitors that comprises our species. Conception is simply impossible without this and the sperm of two males from my kind, that specific cooperative chemical union, and is why new children of our kind are so rarely made.

CHAPTER 26

There would be no ritual gathering for us. No formal congregation of all involved. No mass sexual interludes as are so normally the custom in the process. This union would be complicated and messy. Dangerous for all involved.

Tyr could not be awakened to accomplish this. It would mean death, of me, of us on this world, and quite possibly your whole world if he could build within himself enough power to truly rise again. A thing I was prepared to try to prevent if it all went horribly wrong.

E'ban would grant me his seed. He had always wanted to have a child; he had always wanted me to be a part of that dream.

But Stoya, I believed, would most likely attempt to thwart my chances if she discovered my plan, and would never knowingly accept the "mark" given to me by E'ban.

I knew I could seduce Tyr. Steal his seed. I had a plan for that, to keep him docile; sedated actually.

I had a plan; a shaky one, but a plan. I knew I could "fake" Tyr's consent, steal a kiss if you will, and use it to induce Stoya's consent. Fool her, and the creature's lust within, in the last minutes of passion to get her mark. Instinct would take over, if I was lucky, and she would be unable to control herself. And I would leave before she could realize what I had done.

Once I had Stoya's "mark", I would go to E'ban for his "approval" and the first of the impregnation process; receive his sperm. Then dash back to Tyr and seduce him under sedation, and complete the process.

If all was successful, if conception occurred, I would have about 40 hours before the child would be born.

When the child was ready to be birthed, I would have to deposit it into Charlotte immediately in order for it to flourish on this world. I would have to cut her open for the best chance for an easy inhabitation, a messy ordeal to say the least and unfortunately painful. If that failed, there would be little choice but to find any host available, and I would lose Charlotte to the mortal coil forever.

Once the transaction was accomplished and the child began its union with Charlotte, I would need to attend to her, to nurture her while she rested. Protect her and ensure everything went accordingly. The child would need to connect to her to repair and absorb her being, her soul, and make her into what we are. It was process that could take weeks, months, or even years.

I wasn't fooled into thinking this would be an easy ordeal. There was going to be problems along the way starting with the geographical location of where Tyr now rested, Mt. Everest.

I had work to do now, careful planning and a precise unforgiving schedule to adhere to once it was initiated. I had to give E'ban's sperm the best chance against Tyr's for them both to be able to bond. I was going to have transportation and logistics issues. And, at the very end, I would have to steal Charlotte away from the hospital, from her family, her life, the world as she knew it; forever.

Luckily, I had powerful friends and the contacts with which to do it.

CHAPTER 27

Navigations Air and Emerald Inc. are little side projects of mine. A gift really to a lover and her husband, a retired three-star general and now multi-millionaire, who run a firm providing high-end private jets, personal security, and protective services for the world's global elite and governments.

It is a long story of which I will not tell out of respect for their privacy. But we are friends and they remain trusted entities and strong business partners to this day.

I made a call to them now, Navigations Air Division, this was the kind of work they did; secretive, high risk, no questions asked. I would have six operatives, as they liked to be called, at my disposal along with two pilots. There would be four "expedition experts", one advanced life support medic, Mike, a field-doctor really, and one international security travel expert, a former CIA officer, John, who knew how to expedite things fast and diplomatically across any boarder. There would also be a host of back up aircraft, pilots, and other assorted crew as we made our way around the globe. We would take cash, lots of it, a few business contracts, if those were needed, and some of my gold holdings in case things turned nasty.

My team had little knowledge of who I was. And no idea of what I was, or what I was up to. To them, I was just some rich bitch with an endless bank account that had this crazy notion to see Mt. Everest, first class all the way. My crew only cared about two things, seeing that their client got what she wanted safely and the million-dollar cash bonus they each would receive at the end of this adventure.

But it's what they did, "Anyone, Anywhere, Anytime", was the company motto. They were all former shadow operators of some form or fashion and knew the drill well.

I placed them on standby now, fifty thousand dollars a day to hold their services for me alone. I would need to do a few things first and, most importantly, see Charlotte as her human self one last time.

I wondered how she was going to react to all of this, when I made her into one of us. Would she have wanted this? Would she grow to hate me for doing such a thing to her?

I was going to condemn her to a life of eternity. A life in which all will pass before her to the hands of fate and time; her father, mother, siblings, the rest of her family, her life-long friends old and new, would all pass in time along with entire worlds and their histories. All things she knows now will fade, change, and become lost to time, a faint memory.

But there would be new worlds to see and explore. Some will be very alien to her, and at times downright frightening. She would become a part of life in its fullest; apart of the great cosmic feast that is the universe at play. See the great "savage garden" play out as only God knows of the next scene.

She would partake of the blood and flesh, become a predator. She would come face-to-face with others of us who are not so kind to the living or the dead. Like Tyr and Stoya. She would be of no house, no order, no standing but for what I say she is to me, my mate.

I wondered, also, if our romance could endure that test of time. The end of forever is a long, long ways away. Would she become bored and wish to leave me? I knew I could endure that. I myself have left the side of those of my kind that I've loved.

Change is inevitable. Sometimes love isn't always literally forever. But I could accept that, if it came to it, as I always have.

But despite my reservations, something told me deep, deep inside that it was time, for what I did not know. But I just knew that for some unimaginable reason Charlotte was here on this world for me, for this the great change. It was her time to evolve, or so I had convinced myself.

I thought of Ciosa, her simple confirmation, "it is time…" and wondered over it. Of what she could possibly know or be in all of this.

CHAPTER 28

I held Charlotte's hand. It was almost impossible to keep from totally breaking down before her. She was going to lose this fight if I couldn't finish what I was about to start. She had taken a turn for the worst again. Her pulse was weak, and she seemed sunken, her eyes lackluster. Her beautiful blonde hair was flat and getting sparse from the chemo therapy.

"I've missed you, Ianthe…," she meekly pleaded.

"Daddy…I…you…"

"I don't…would you stay? Don't…don't go away anymore. Please."

I almost broke. "No sweetie, I won't but…,"

She tried to sit up more to talk. "I'm sorry I, I'm not looking well for you…I'm so tired. I…I think, I'm going to go away soon…"

I broke down and began to cry shriveling up into a ball beside her.

"No, no, oh God no, sweetie, no it doesn't matter to me, please hang in there a little bit longer, just a little bit longer."

"I need more time, more time…," I pleaded with her, with God.

I composed myself again. Looking at her and moving closer to her face, I lay next to her, soothing her hair back over her delicate little ears. I sobbed some more then took her face in my hands forcing her to look back at me, to acknowledge me; then spoke.

"Would you want me to if I could make you live forever?" I asked imploringly.

"If it meant a life so very different from this one that you have, would you let me take you away from all of this pain even though it would mean an eternity of loss?"

She smiled at me. "You're so silly, Ianthe, but yes I think I would. I just wish that you could."

I smiled at her again. "I am going to hold you to that Charlotte Bell Aberdeen. I can, and will, make you live forever…," I trailed off.

"Do you remember Stoya, how you always tease us about being vampires?"

"Yes."

She smiled weakly, but somehow still managed to be her adorable self.

"Well…Charlotte, we are vampires. Charlotte, I am immortal, I am forever!"

It was the easiest way to explain something so complex. To use earth's most famous known immortal ideal.

She seemed confused, in disbelief. I was wishing I had fangs or could perform some strange magic trick to show her my truth. I wished that I could turn her right there and then with just one simple bite or kiss.

"Yes, sweetie," I spoke clearly and perhaps too loudly. "I am a vampire!" I paused. "Look at me now, into my eyes, listen to my voice, see me. Please…see me for who I really am," I pleaded gently, coaxing her to look more closely at me.

"See the thing behind this human body, see me for what I really am…," I pleaded softly again, forcing her to look into my eyes.

"I see you…silly," she said meekly, not understanding my plea.

"Silly Ianthe, you look so perfectly human to me…oh, such a beautiful human…," she said forcing another pained smile, sinking back into her bed, into the pillow; she was already exhausted after just five minutes.

I wept again.

"Oh…but how I wish you were Ianthe. Oh, how I wish you were…," she sighed sinking deeper into her bed then drifting off to sleep barely whispering one word. "Vampire."

"And you will, God willing, be of us!" I whispered. "Together with me; forever."

I watched the IV fluids, its sugar hydration and chemicals drip down along the clear plastic tube and into her veins. I could hear her little heart pumping away quietly. She breathed shallow; slow.

Oh God, how I missed my clumsy, goofy, caring Charlotte; her spunky personality and her ever wondrous demeanor. I was lost in her, even now, in her worst condition imaginable. I was still totally and utterly in love.

"Just hold on as long as you can, sweetie. I am going to save you!"

"I will make you mine forever."

Just then, my cell phone chimed, it relayed a text message.

Phone Number: 010
IT IS TIME.

I jumped up at this knowing, in that instant, that I had to begin what I had planned to do. I tucked Charlotte in and kissed her forehead.

"I love you; see you soon, just hold on!"

As I rushed out of Charlotte's room I found her father. He looked at me suspiciously.

"What, I thought you…?"

"I'm sorry…I can't," I put my hands up in protest. And in that moment, I realized what I would have to do; betrayal.

"I just can't right now, I've got to go!" I told him. "I just can't anymore, not today, not for a while."

It was the ultimate betrayal. I had promised him to care for her to the end. I saw him brew to anger, but there was nothing to say. I went to leave, then stopped. I was crying again, it seemed to never stop now; the tears.

"I, I, I asked you to trust me once…," I pleaded, shouting. "Please, just…," I cut it off and turned to leave then stopped not turning to face him. Looking instead at the doors beyond, the escape from this house of the desperately dying. My escape. Charlotte's escape.

I took a deep breath and realized that this was our break, Charlotte and I, the first step into an eternity of steps. It was time for this now.

"It's what you wanted, and always have. Charlotte and I, our love; well, then, there! You win!" I paused, crying. "It's over!"

"I'll stay away, I do this for you, for her, for all I ever wanted was for her to be loved. For her to be happy. Your family to be happy."

I stood looking to the doorway trembling. "When the time comes, I ask only that you call to let me know. I will do as you desire and will uphold my financial promises. No expense too great, you know where to send the bill," I spoke coldly now, trying to find strength in this cruelty. I felt numb and so ashamed.

I looked at Ciosa's text again, it gave me strength.

I turned one last time gathering up as much courage as I possibly could and faced Charlotte's father.

I smiled slightly then spoke with a cruelty I did not know I had.

"Goodbye!"

I turned and left.

I called Navigations Air. “I’m coming to the airport; we leave now!”

The voice on the other end of the phone spoke clearly and concisely. “Copy that Ms. Gold. Don’t be late or we’ll leave without you.”

I had to smile at that, at least I knew I could count on someone and something.

CHAPTER 29

Everything was set into motion as the Bombardier 6000 lifted off and into the air. Our first objective was Mt. Everest base camp.

The chief pilot ordered me to me to relax, have a few drinks, and not to worry. Everything was running smooth and taken care of; out of my hands.

I sank back into the plush, hand-stitched leather seat finding myself utterly exhausted and it was only the beginning.

It would take almost 20 hours to get there. We would have to stop in Guangzhou, China, to refuel. Then fly into Kathmandu Airport and exchange planes for the two-hour flight up to Tenzig-Hillary Airport, also known as Lukla, in a remote Nepalese village at the base of Everest.

But I could breathe easy enough. Emerald Inc., Navigation Air's security and support services division would take care of everything for me now. They were the personal staffing service I used for most of my domestic and foreign business and housekeeping affairs, among other things. They supplied me with a host of professionals to manage my every day work and life-details; maid services, home maintenance, and business services mostly. It's why I had invested in them in the first place, to maintain a level of secrecy about my life and that of other friends and associates who needed such level of services.

A full time professional house sitter-manager was deployed to oversee my LA condo. They would not only provide the necessary maintenance and upkeep of my home while I was gone, but also the little daily life details; collect mail, pay bills, and so on.

But their most important task was to begin the process of selling my condo. They would ensure that my antiques and other treasures were packed up properly and put into storage. All the rest would stay with the house as part of the sale.

It was time to take a short break from the world, to slip into hiding for a while as Charlotte made the coming transformation. But we would return to California, the San Diego area. From there we could still venture into LA. I knew Charlotte could have some difficulties coping with her new reality when she awoke. She would need an adjustment period, familiar surroundings. I wanted to keep her close to the city she loved. The places she loved. Those thoughts brought me courage again; our lives together. A new setting, with familiar destinations. It was going to be grand. We were going to live life to its fullest.

My most pressing business-related issues would also be temporarily transferred into the hands of Emerald Inc.'s business staff of which I also used to some extent over the years.

A small team of lawyers and a top-tier free-lance personal investor was hired for just that purpose. But most of my business dealing were set on auto-pilot, there was little to attend to daily, much of my money being managed by the major global investment firms such as Berkshire & Hathaway, UBS, and Reach, among others. Emerald Inc. would be my face now for a while, manage my brand name, and manage what little interaction I did have within the greater business world.

I also had Emerald Inc. outsource a professional caregiver to sit with Charlotte in my stead and to handle any medical intricacies that might arise. Having both a nursing and psychology degree, she would be able to deal with Charlotte's father, family, and other related issues in my abrupt absence. Be my inside eyes and ears, fulfill that part of my obligations to Charlotte's father and her family.

The hospital was more than willing to sign the necessary legal documents which ensured her ability to interact as a private entity on my behalf, for another contribution of one million dollars, of course.

Charlotte's father's protest went little heeded by the hospital and its staff. He simply didn't understand the power I had, the depth of my checkbook, and the loyalty it could buy.

Besides, the never-ending flood of fresh baked goods, deluxe coffees, and other little perks sent on behalf of Ianthe Gold to the nursing stations on all floors daily, ensured even the most sympathetic of staff to Mr. Aberdeen's plight remained muted.

I chuckled over the thought of the nurses and other staff fighting over the random gift cards with values of no less than $500.00 to Victoria Secrets, Michal Kors, Total Wine and More, among other stores I also had sent.

I smiled at my med-tech, Mike, a former Special Forces operator, now pressing me to conduct his medical examination of me not even ten minutes after take-off.

It was his job on this assignment to know my baselines, my medical issues, if there were any, and to monitor me and keep me well. He would also rescue me and save me from my injuries if the need should arise.

If he only knew what he would up against by the end of the week.

I smiled holding my arm out for him to take his readings.

He silently checked off the boxes on his medical chart.

He was strong, confident, and manly in every way. His well-muscled, tattooed arms, scruffy long hair, and beard made me a little aroused. He wasn't pretty, but ruggedly handsome with a boyish smile, his green eyes were intense in both color and experience.

I cooed, pleased at his gentle touch.

"Hmm…so, Mike, what is your background? If I can ask that?" I spoke coyly.

Mike looked up at me, I had read his profile, knew it well, but I wanted to hear it from him.

He smiled, there was some hesitancy then he spoke. "Special Forces, First Special Forces, Delta...ma'am. Ranger, for the first five, then fast tracked to SF Medic, and somehow managed to pass into Delta where I served for fourteen years," he paused to take some more notes and to reflect I think, on his life.

"I spent nearly ten years bouncing between Iraq and Afghanistan before Emerald conned me into working for them…," he chuckled.

"They paid for even more medical training, all kinds of certifications for stuff I doubt I'll ever use, and now I am here, with you Ms. Gold!"

He spoke reassuringly, looking back directly into my eyes. He seemed to look me over, and I think, saw something in me that he was not sure about.

I smiled back and winked at him.

"Well, Mike, you might be surprised at what you will need on this little trip, I am glad I have you on my side."

He seemed puzzled by what I said.

I watched him finish off his medical chart on me and prepare another document which he might need in case of an injury or sickness. When he was done he breathed out seeming relieved.

"Well, you look fine Ms. Gold, very healthy, better than healthy actually, everything is in order. Is there anything else I should know?" he asked professionally again.

I smiled back at him. “Thank you, and yes, there is one thing…how are you at delivering babies?”

The look on his face was priceless as I leaned forward and kissed him softly; laughing.

He straightened up trying to regain his composure; his military bearing and professionalism. He looked long at me, then cracked a smile.

“Mine or yours?” he asked as we both broke out laughing in full.

It was to be the beginning of a new, long, and most trusted friendship.

CHAPTER 30

The helicopter flight up to Everest base camp was a bit turbulent. I watched the trail below and wondered if walking might not have been a better option. My ground "adventure guides" for Everest were already in place along with their Sherpa attendant. They had been sent forward to prepare for our arrival and had been in place and waiting for nearly a week. There was no time to waste now. The stopwatch had been started for the conception to come.

I watched as the consortium of international climbers and their associated support teams wondered over who I was and how it was that I came by private helicopter. The intrusion of such aircraft normally reserved for military or emergency medical extraction only was an interruption of the peaceful atmosphere.

First class service and amenities here were limited. Yet, I swooped down in a glossy, black Navigations Air helicopter. I am sure many were disgusted.

Once on ground, we would move immediately to the Khumbu icefall and began the six plus hour trek across it; something that never happens here either.

I had an extremely experienced team, my "adventure guides" had climbed both Everest, successfully summiting it three times, and K-2, twice. They were experts in mountaineering, in many things actually. War and killing was just a basic skill for them.

The entrance to Tyr's lair lay just beyond the ice flow, hidden within the great boulder field. From there, I would go alone.

On May 29, 1953, Sir Edmund Hillary and legendary Sherpa Tenzig Norgay successfully summited Mt. Everest, surpassing George Mallory and his 1921 expedition. It was a triumph of human stamina, dedication, and will.

In addition to summiting Mt. Everest, the expedition was also able to obtain many photos of the ever-elusive snow leopard, indigenous to that mountain range, along with some interesting human looking foot prints in the snow.

Deemed a hoax, or some snow-melt anomaly, the photos of the footprints remain subject of stipulation to this day.

The Sherpas who have lived there for centuries begged to differ. To them it was proof that the Yeti was not a myth. I suspected it was Tyr.

It was the photo of a section of rock freed from its normal icy cloak that had caught my eye.

The rock contained an elegant hand carved writing, our ancient filigree-stylized runes, that proclaimed "Tyr, God of Gods".

I knew in an instant that that mountain is where he had made his lair.

Those photos were also discredited as nothing more than some odd anomaly of light and shadow.

But I knew better. I had personally interviewed Sir Hillary, Mr. Norgay, and the rest of their team. They knew what they saw and were mystified.

The truth, along with the photos were buried in the basement of the Smithsonian, lost to the history of man and time. Perhaps it was a good thing.

Many months later I would launch my own secret expedition with a small team of four Sherpas lead by Mr. Norgay. There on the far side of the Khumbu ice flow, hidden within a small field of ancient, massive boulders, I found the entrance to Tyr's eternal lair.

Tyr had made his lair near the top of the summit, inside of the mountain, within the solid rock. He had fashioned a stairway intricately carved from within the heart of the mountain, which lead to his chamber there. It's where he rested, in the great sleep, emerging at times, as a god to early man and throughout millennia. He waged wars and brought strife and misery, killing and devouring hundreds of thousands. Then, as his stamina faded he would return to this place to sleep, to wait, to dream.

His last earthly visit was during the Viking age when he came to the ancient Norsemen as a god. Many gods actually, but always favoring the god of war.

I would go before him now to begin the process of securing his seed for Charlotte's sake so that life could spring forth from this place, his wretched existence, and eternal damning dreams.

CHAPTER 31

The hand-hewn granite stairway wound itself up and up without mercy toward Tyr's chamber within the top of the mountain.

I did not need the extra oxygen intake as others do at such high altitudes, my re-engineered human lungs would compensate for that. The stairs, though strenuous, bothered me little.

It had been a long time since I had entered his frozen, isolated realm. And though my body had a high tolerance to both extreme cold and heat, I shivered slightly despite the warmth of my most rare, down-filled Snow Leopard coat; the fur of an animal once populace here but now was nearly extinct.

My coat, a relic, was a souvenir from my first journey to this place nearly 65 years ago. I had hunted him, ate him, and wear him now.

I moved ever forward, spurned by Ciosa's text.

What did she know? Who was she in all of this? I pondered as I navigated the great stone stairs, perfectly cut and perfectly spaced, spiraling ever upwards in a near precise mathematical ascent.

I marveled over Tyr's work, the intellect, the skill. All of this was done by hand, hammer, and chisel.

I could feel the ages wash away from me as I climbed ever higher. I could trace the history of life upon this world from its creation and evolution from a swirl of cosmic particles and rock-trash garnered from other long dead worlds into a new planet, a new solar system, just as my home world was so very long ago.

Though not the oldest mountain range on earth, the Himalayan Mountains still spans over 65 million years of earth's roughly 4.5 billion years of existence. This mountain once laid at the bottom of an endless sea. Slowly rising over time, it was the by-product of the separation the Indian subcontinent from the Tibetan Plateau.

The rock, the God-made molecular materials it is comprised of, had seen the beginning of life on earth, and was in fact comprised of much of the beginnings of life.

This mountain had given birth to the first algae and the first slithering things that crawled out of the still infant seas. It had seen the age of dinosaurs pass and witnessed the rise of the mammalian age; man, and your human evolution into what you are today. It has stood sentinel through the ages, a testament to God's true power, and had become home to something not of this earth, the resting place of a being that quite literally shaped the mythologies of modern man and perhaps much of your evolution.

I tried to remember of where I was in the cosmos when this place, this mountain was born. It was cloudy, that memory, a thought stored away long, long ago. I felt old in that moment. Realizing that I was born before this mountain was even a ridge, a fault line at the bottom of earth's ancient Neotethys Sea.

"How long have I traveled?" I pondered, trying to connect the dots from my inception to this very moment; my eternal lifetime.

And then, I questioned it all again. What I was doing now? Should I give this fate to Charlotte? Consign her to this eternity of ours. She would soon, too, know herself as I did that day, feel the ages bare down upon her. Understand just how long forever really is.

CHAPTER 32

I climbed on.

I felt weary suddenly. Tired, weathered, and aged. I doubted my conviction and thought of turning back.

I heard Stoya's words in my head, maybe she was right.

"They are human, mortal, food and nothing more..."

And then I thought of my promise to Charlotte and to the time-lost memory of the woman I once knew upon a world so far from here. The woman I once loved so completely. The woman upon the ice that I could not help but to know and see in in Charlotte now.

I had promised her that I would look for her when she died; her soul, her reincarnation in mortal flesh, for her race believed in such things. That I would be with her forever, wherever it was that she would be born again; if she was reborn again.

No, I not going to lose this time, I confirmed to myself.

I had the power and the means to make this happen. It was going to happen.

As I climbed on, I began to remember more of her world of so long ago, of my time there. It was a place of great wonder; a world of floating ice-rock above a great frozen sea, Phét-mthilliu'm it was called, if memory served me right.

I smiled at the memory of it, its tranquil frozen beauty, and at the first time that I saw her. Her pale blue eyes and her delicate smile. What was it, that she was always about to say, but never did or could?

I thought of Charlotte, her almost whisper also.

I could see clearly in my mind how she danced and played upon the endless fields of ice, upon a sea which once was warm and raged as the winds and driving snows did when I arrived. She danced barefooted and naked to feel the sun, to feel what little warmth it offered upon the endless clear blue horizons.

I saw her ice-white hair blow long and flowing, like spun silver. So long that it trailed behind her as if she was forever being chased by a rumbling avalanche. Her body was pale white, long and thin; she towered. But she was so silly. Although her body was adapted to such extreme temperatures, she had always complained of the cold.

"I want it to return...," she said. "To the days long ago when our world was warm, how the historians say it used to be, when we could swim in the sea below us...," she'd lament always. "Be as the fish, forever swimming...forever dancing within the sea you and me."

She'd spend hours, at times, peering through the ice to see the giant ice-fish below lumbering along through the thick, half frozen water.

And I remembered that she was a princess; a healer, a savior of sorts. Her way was gentle, uniting. Her birth had brought peace after a long war. It was her purpose, her birth, to unite two houses. That was the prophecy. They would have a girl, a beautiful woman who could heal deep seeded wounds with soft words and quiet whispers; a touch that vanished all pains. If a male had been born, it would have been cause for utter destruction.

I stopped dead in my tracks and saw so clearly in that moment that the girl upon the ice, the woman in my dreams, my memory, had died of age and a cancer also. That she had found her way back to me, or, I to her. That she was indeed Charlotte, the soul within, that fate had chanced us to be together again.

I had been powerless to save her then, for I was the only one of my kind on that world. I could only hold her as her body faded from my arms like the melting snow, as was her kind's way in death and dying.

I began to tear at the memory of her body as it dissipated into the winds of a great storm and the sound of the ice tinkling in the wind. The sound of tiny bells.

It was in that moment, too, that I remembered something not to be forgotten; what God had designed. Of what Ciosa's card had said; Love is eternal, souls are forever. *Eternity passes quickly within forever.* I understood then in that moment that time is no barrier to love, and that love will make its way in this, God's grand design. I looked up into the heavens beyond the ancient stone to God. I smiled and laughed at the mind that creates such torturous details. at the mind that has somehow managed to ensure that I would be where I am in that exact moment, at the mind that has allowed for chance.

Having faith again and feeling uplifted, I climbed on moving ever faster. I realized I had the chance now to make her as me, immortal. To keep that promise, the promise of a past, present, and future. I thought of Charlotte and the girl upon the ice and her ability to heal. And in that moment, I understood what Charlotte, her soul within, was born to do.

CHAPTER 33

I entered through the archway and into the chamber, the lair of Tyr. It was ironically disappointing after such an ardent climb. Tyr cared little of this world, its artifacts, its beauty, or anything. His chamber merely served as a place to sleep the great sleep, to wait for an opportunity to leave this world, or to possibly die at the end of time.

It was not grand save for the skill and precision of which it was carved. But, there was a comfort in it, the perfectly measured mathematical height and width of his simple granite tomb. Stark and cold, the only light came from his body and his armor, a space suit actually, the uniform of a star traveler from some far away world.

It was intricate, a strange combination of some unknown metal and plastic-like plates and an artificial fibrous skin material. It shone pale blue-gray and bright silver in places. Upon the cuffs, a sort of gauntlet like computer system was attached. The small screen, now black, the system long dead, was unable to be powered by anything upon this world. It looked worn, evidence of damage upon it from earthly weapons and was stained from the blood of humankind; Tyr's enemies.

The armored space suit hung suspended upon a crude stone armature. In its gloved hands it clasped Tyr's favorite earthly weapon, a massive war hammer of alien metal forged from a support beam of his long-lost space craft, gone now to earth's evolutional memory at the deepest depths of the Mariana

Trench. It shone radiantly like burning gold. And, when it struck other objects it sparked as if lightening. The simple plate and ring mail armor and flesh of man was little match for this weapon. It was the metal's property. Light, strong, fast to wield, spectacular to behold, it struck fear in the enemy and was deadly; a god's weapon against man.

I knew not of its origin, that metal, or the peculiar technologies of Tyr's space suit. I suspect its creators have long since vanished from known universal history.

Other weapons lay stacked in the corners of his room, human weapons made of earth-born, blended metal alloys of which only Tyr knew how to make. A great two-sided war ax, a multitude of swords, and a great bow of springy steel. And, as if somehow forgotten, a weapon of unusual size and proportion. It was a gun of some kind that I had never seen before in my travels. It appears it may have lost its power long ago. Its odd, spike-tentacle-like prongs were petrified, frozen; unable to act. Its energy cylinder seemingly burnt out, devoid of power. I suspected it was capable of great destruction, like of what the bible speaks of at the beginning of man, and perhaps still prophesied in The Book of Revelation.

Tyr lay upon a black granite slab bed. His human body glowed softly, a pale violet light, a thing our kind does when in the great sleep. It was an aura of our dreams, or so it is said.

His bed was massive in size and perfectly cut. Its edges sharp even after many millennia. Of how or where it came and how it arrived here was also a mystery.

There was no such colored granite found here except deep within this mountain range. Granite is of a lower substrate mostly found at or well below the heart of a mountain. Softer stone such as sandstone and shale come from the summits.

Yet there it lay, so great that even Tyr would have been challenged by it. It was beautiful, almost translucent, black and rich. It seemed like some solidified oil-like fluid. Like the obsidian colored seas upon Ckathñu; a dark world upon which I dwelled upon long ago. There the seas were thick, viscus, seldom ebbing, and poisonous to all save the creatures that lived in it.

Tyr remained silent, lost in the great sleep, trapped in an eternally slow-motion dream. He was naked to the world in majestic glory. Immersed in secret dreams that awaits our kind during the great sleep; a dream of unfathomable timelessness and forever falling.

There in that dream we become time, the sand, the strands, the fiber of it; falling forever, into and through it. We see the ages of the universe pass us by, unable to neither move nor act.

Time has substance. It is molecular like all else that God created. But time is not of God's making. It is something much deeper, a living thing unto its own.

You would not understand fully my explanation of it, the great sleep. For each of us it is always different. For you, only to be experienced in death. Death of the body upon the parting of the soul.

Tyr was aware of my presence, but unable to move, to act, or to speak; to even really comprehend the moment.

My presence would be like a dream to him, a fragmented memory; some apparition of which he could not fully tell of when or where. He would be unable to place my presence in any real context, to place it in a specific time. I might have appeared to him as a kind of super slow motion animated ghost figure; something similar to a reverse déjà vu moment possibly based from my own experiences when I am in my deep sleep to heal or pass through time.

I smiled down upon him, he was truly magnificent, a god in so many ways; as God. He was beautiful, terrible, and without mercy.

I felt the being within me waver at him, my egg trembled at the prospect of joining with his seed. This instinctual desire to breed with him welled deep inside, almost hurting.

My egg was wanting of him, his supreme genetic DNA, his power. It had awakened from its hibernation, a built-in instinct that I could not control. It sensed him, his scent, his aura, his social elevation of our being.

I felt myself becoming wet to prepare for him, my body self-activating in that and other ways; at the thoughts of the penetration, the semen, the life forming carrier of God's secret code. A fire grew within.

I began to connect with his mind and saw the visions of him, his long life when he traveled the universe. I saw his ever-changing bodies and his great beastly being devouring all in his way. I saw the blood and the bodies of both his victims and of his worshipers. The flesh discarded upon long worn ramparts of the earliest temples.

I saw his life before earth. His great rise to power on our world and the death and destruction he wrought. I saw his travels to other worlds, how often he was as a god to them and how he destroyed their worlds without mercy.

Here on earth, Tyr was a giant; the Nephilim of old. Another word taken by mankind to describe the union-inhabitation that is our existence. He, the creature within, had the power to manipulate the body, to exercise the physical flesh. He stood just over eight feet and was massive in all proportions, muscular, lean, and arrogant in his physical adornment, his manhood.

He had fashioned himself a penis of large proportions, at fourteen inches fully erect and well over three inches at its largest circumference. It was a symbol of his projection of power over man, over the primal and social order of both early and modern society.

It was circumcised and pierced with a single platinum ring just below the tip, underneath where the frenulum concludes. The ring was made of an ounce of pure platinum. His massive testicles hung waiting to release his dominant spermatozoa. He was a breeder of the highest order.

Tyr was prideful, superior, and abusive. He took little heed of women on this world, save for the boldest, strongest, most dangerous; the women of the Viking and Celtic ages mostly.

He had preferred young men, boys really, and delighted in their suffering of his penetration. He kept many, imprisoned often and tortured daily. He was cruel and unfeeling. To him you are mere animals, unintelligent, physically impure and useless, food and little more.

He had ruled empires where great and powerful beings waged wars for glory and consumption of power. That was his only real goal in life, power and the blood and flesh. To one day be god of all things.

Tyr was magnificent. At his best, he was all commanding, soft, sensual, and sexually powerful. He was what much of our kind aspired to; the ideal.

Here in this moment, I felt myself faltering, sexually aroused and desirous of waking him, such was his power upon the women of our world. It was embedded in me to breed with, and to die for him.

He was god-like beautiful, handsome like in the description of the ancient gods of man. His red-blond violet undertone hair streamed down from his head and out upon his stone-alter-bed. He wore a great braided beard, tightly woven, it hung to just above his solar plexus. His face had sharp, stern features. His skin tough and leathery; scared from many battles. He chose not to heal his scars like I did, but to proudly bare them as proof to the non-believers of his power over immortality. Upon his massive chest was branded in our filigree like writing:

"N'summarŭ-l I'illithia LǸae'D'I'ah-thårus N'I"

"Succumb, for I am the death of God."

A simple translation in your language that is much more complex in ours.

For us the word God, or It, N'I in our language, means "Life" or "Birth." Our view of God is that of a life-giver, the birther, or womb, of our universe. Tyr was openly declaring his intentions for this world and any other.

"Succumb for I am the death of Life."

I looked him over for a great while, entranced by his being again, his history; then remembered why I had come. I removed my clothes and slid up onto him, to feel him, to collect his scent upon me. His body was intoxicating, strong, hard, and mighty. I took in the vision of him, then slowly touched his body, his manhood. I sighed at the thought of him, what power for good he could have chosen. I could be his, and we would rule entire galaxies together. Justly, fairly, free of war and strife. But it would never be his way.

I straddled him just below his chest. I ran my fingers through his chest hair up and over his pectoral muscles. I traced the branded, scarified lines gently musing over his power to do as he proclaimed. I melted in that, the manliness, the power. I fantasized over him, the sex we could have. My tiny frame upon him, under him; being ravaged by him. But I also was abhorred by him, his wanton destruction and absolute disregard for any life.

Stirring myself out of my thoughts, I quickly pricked my neck with a small surgical scalpel and bent down so that I could let my blood drip upon his mouth, then fully rested my neck upon his lips. I could feel them move, instinct taking over even in sleep. I felt his mouth began to open, to suck at my blood. I felt my blood being drawn to him, move into him. My being, the creature within began to move to him also. It had no choice but to obey his calling. I had no choice and fought now to slow the inevitable.

I pushed my neck into his mouth grinding on his teeth, letting them cut into me hoping to achieve a convincing “mark”. My heart skipped; he was starting to stir. He knew me, I felt his manhood stiffen.

I quickly injected him with 40 milligrams of Propofol. He seemed to move a bit then let out a long sigh and fell back into the great sleep. His human element, the body, would succumb to such a dose.

I caught my breath. “Fucking shit,” I let out, relieved, then quickly donned my clothes and left back to the ice flow and my awaiting Navigations Air/Emerald Inc. team.

CHAPTER 34

Mike had a full glass of Stoli Elit Himalayan Edition Vodka with a single large, crystal-clear ice cube ready for me as I boarded the Bombardier 6000. The ice clinked against the Baccarat glass and for a moment I was mesmerized by the sound. The tinkling of the ice. I was exhausted and desperately needed a drink. We were off to Sibiu now and then Arefu where Stoya resided.

I playfully stuck my arm out for Mike to play doctor with.

He looked at Tyr's bite-mark on my neck, it was still bleeding slightly.

"Band-Aid?" he asked me as I laughed at the look on his face.

"Possibly, after this next round…," I said thinking of Stoya and the coming sex or fight we were going to have, perhaps both.

Mike looked at me quietly for a while then pronounced me "fit and healthy" as he silently checked of his boxes on my client medical chart.

My vitals were good, though slightly elevated from my ascent and descent of Mt. Everest and my encounter with Tyr. I am sure he noticed other things, the flustered vibe I had about me for one.

"Trust me, Mike, you don't want to know!" I spoke handing him my empty glass. "Please, just keep them coming!"

He smiled and waved to the flight attendant for a refill.

"And bring back whatever steak you have back there, extra, extra rare, bloody please," I paused. "Make that two, if you can."

"Yes ma'am, right away!" the flight attendant said as I watched her well-shaped but generous ass bounce as she made for the galley.

I sighed as thoughts of Charlotte began to creep back into my mind. I made a call to the caregiver and found that Charlotte was still hanging in there. I was relieved. I then made a call to Stoya, she answered right away.

"Fine, it's about time," she said seemingly annoyed. "I will care for you now; it will be just you and me."

"Yes…just you and me now…," I trailed off, knowing my lie.

I began to weep, then cry as I hung up the phone.

Mike hesitantly took me into his arms and let me bawl. He knew I was in some deep personal pain. Of what he could only guess.

I was missing Charlotte, afraid suddenly that I might not make this thing happen. Afraid I might not save her. I thought of Stoya and her love for me. I was going to betray that now. Destroy our connection, our love for one another. It would not be the first time. I prayed for some form of redemption; for her to understand. I was going to kill her in so many ways.

CHAPTER
35

An hour out from Sibiu International Airport I got an unexpected call. It was from someone whom I considered to be one of my closest friends and confidants, Jonathan Nelson Davis, an old-school international photo journalist of the highest order. I immediately thought of Ciosa, her message concerning him and wondered over it.

Jonathan had just returned from Bolivia where he had been covering the never-ending drug war and was "just checking in" as he called it. He was a breath of fresh air, another much needed uplift.

I told him about Charlotte's condition. He was depressed by the news but as always, did his best to remain positive for me. Though they had only met once over dinner, they hit it off right away. I knew that in time they would become the best of friends.

Jonathan was back in LA for a few days, then leaving for Afghanistan again on a six-month embedded assignment with some joint DEA and Special Forces unit tasked with trying to stem the tide of opium leaving the country. Before he would leave for Afghanistan he would go to visit Charlotte in New York.

Always ready to come to my aid, he had offered to not take the assignment, to stay and wait to be with me for when the time came for Charlotte's passing. But I told him no.

“Jonathan, I appreciate your offer. But you and I both know that these types of assignments are getting fewer and fewer with the Iraq-Afghan wars winding down. I want you to take the assignment,” I told him.

“You need to keep yourself in that game!” I spoke knowing how hard it was getting for him, for anyone in that line of work, to stay active, do what they love.”

He understood.

He had no idea of me and of what I truly was, of what was coming if my plan went through. It was best I thought, the less he knew.

“OK, Ianthe, just let me know,” he spoke softly. “Just give me the word, I’ll jump on the next transport. It’ll be a bit, but I will be there!” he reassured me.

“Yes, Jonathan, I know you will, I love you, be safe now, I can’t lose you too!”

We remained silent on the phone together for a moment then both hung up at the same time. I began to cry again as I looked out to the Carpathian Mountains beyond as we descended into Sibiu. I took a deep breath and finished my drink.

I thought of him now, my Jonathan. He had always been a consideration for a deeper relationship, but somehow, someway, it just wasn’t in the cards.

I love women too much and have learned through the years that sometimes people are just meant to be as best friends and little more.

And, I think, the feeling was mutual. We were both content with that, best friends, best buds. And I believed that deep down, he was searching for something else, someone else.

“It’s time!” I thought out loud. “It is time!”

CHAPTER 36

At Sibiu, Stoya was waiting on the tarmac with a bouquet of white lilies, two blood red roses embedded within them, bound by a black silk ribbon. It was her declaration, her intent, of us, together, forever.

I smiled and fell into her arms crying and sobbing, an utter wreck.

She held me and soothed me, her unique energy enwrapping me, protecting me. She snarled at my poor Navigations Air team and at Mike, threatened for no other reason than that to her they were beneath her, beneath us, an invasion to our love.

I winked at Mike and mouthed, "just be ready."

He smiled back at me nodding as Stoya rushed me into her Jaguar XKX.

I had to smile, she was going to try to fix everything, my world, my life, our love, us; everything.

We rode in silence from Sibiu to her hidden mountain refuge and lair near Arefu, a high mountain pass cliff top dwelling within sight of Vlad Tepes III's ancient war castle and refuge, Poenari.

It was there in that backdrop, its deep and mysterious blood-soaked history, that Stoya had chosen to make her earth-bound stand against this world and her time upon it. Sibiu, Arefu, and in fact all of Romania was her land, her country, her first and only love.

I pressed back into the luxurious, skin soft black leather seat of her exotic custom crafted Jaguar and watched the ancient trees and cliffs drift by us like a dream. I thought of Bram Stoker's *Dracula*, the opening scene with the intrepid Jonathan Harker in the black carriage being whisked away into a world he had little way to prepare for. I also thought of the real-life dramas played out here, the vicious war that Stoya and Vlad Tepes III waged against the Turks and in so many ways, against the world, life, and God's hypocrisy.

This was Romania, dark, mysterious, romantically sad, and eternally unforgiving, like Stoya.

She was anxious, puzzled, and aroused over the scent of me, of Tyr. She knew we had been together I was sure. Stoya, for all her faults was no one's fool.

I could see her mind at work over this discovery as she gently, thoughtfully, inhaled the smoke from her long, thin Insignia brand cigarette and the scent of Tyr upon my body.

I had concealed his mark, a few tricks learned from a famous Hollywood make-up artist long ago. You would know his work if you're a fan of the greats; Frankenstein, the Werewolf, and Dracula, among others. But I doubted she was fooled about that either.

Once at her home, Stoya set about her seduction of me, releasing her full lurid sexual prowess. She would wine and dine me, and as the saying goes "sixty-nine me".

I hate to admit it, but she was entirely impossible to resist. Stoya was a master seductress. She could be soft and sensual, meek and innocent. But she preferred to be bold, aggressive, and domineering. She could and always did win out with either approach; that was her peculiar charm. She chose the loving caring approach now, with just enough cold indifference to keep my heart wanting, needing.

After a grand and eloquent dinner of which she had masterfully prepared, we sat out upon her massive ancient stone patio to watch the quarter moon rise gently over the castle Poenari; her most passionate pastime.

I watched as she seemed to dream over it, the beauty of it, the cool mountain night; the quarter moon, as it softly illuminated her sanctuous obsession, the thing there that held her in such sway, a memory. A great love.

I watched her quietly from the far end of her massive outdoor couch and admired her statuesque body. She looked as if she was made of some fine marble or porcelain, some opaque venetian glass, the recipe of which was long ago lost. Her figure and her face shone in the cool blue light of night, the reflection of the moon upon it. It was hard to not tear slightly at the vision of her, her beauty, the stoic moviesque image. Her romance. The sadness within of which she could never fully hide.

My eyes drifted over her body, her shoulders, her breasts, her legs, and her long slender bare feet. She was heroically elegant, like some grand romantic fantasy animation figure from some strange Gothic dystopian movie. A dark hero. A blatantly horrible monster.

Stoya may have been the youngest of us by birth, but she had an ancient mind and a very, very, ancient soul. Stoya was a masterpiece of intellect, physical beauty, and artistic aptitude. God, or perhaps something even greater, had reached deep when making her. She was perfection in both our kind's ideal and in human being.

Stoya was complicated, misunderstood, and dangerous. She was often taken for being an absolute psychopath, a sociopath, a rapist of the body and soul. She was all of this, and more. It's what made her so special, the emotional roller coaster vice-grip ride that was her mind, will, and being.

She bore abilities that our kind do not, or so as I have yet to meet. Her unique powers are where much of mythical attributes of the vampire emerged in human lore. How she had come to have these powers none of us knew.

To keep or transfer those things of which she had learned through the centuries across the stars, into her mind, her being, the creature within, was not within our talents. Maybe it was just how well she was made. God's little darling; an epoch of celestial being.

Stoya could vanish into thin air. Not literally mind you, but she could in some strange way manipulate light and shadow, becoming the thing in-between the two, a void, rendering her all but invisible, a ghost of the mind's imagination.

Time also, or the reasoning of time, the passage of time, she seemed able to manipulate. To make you forget, or to remember, often against your deepest will. To shift it in some way, making one trip up on the logic of it, to wonder if you had indeed taken part in what had just happened. In effect, she had the power to inflict a sort of déjà vu moment, a glitch in one's own personal time continuum.

Stoya's great mental powers allowed her to amplify her physical strength by many times. She could destroy things, solid steel or stone; a combination of mind over matter, an absolute focusing of mental energy, laser like, deadly in execution.

Mentally, emotionally, she could bend you, manipulate you to her will. Make you do things that you would never even consider doing. And, she could, at times, move things with her mind, a form of telekinesis; another very dangerous ability.

She could read thoughts, fragments of thoughts anyways. Enough to form a picture of you and your intentions, to aid her in her manipulations. She could at times even put her thoughts into your mind. Another dangerous ability.

She was cunning, a tactician. A warrior with unsurpassed skills in the art of war, weapons, and killing. She, in a past life, and past being, conquered many galaxies, commanding millions upon millions of warriors in battles where billions died.

But her most dangerous ability was her power to conjure up a horrible alien-like darkness which created a void, a vacuum of sorts, an energy cloud of absolute dark, stifling, encompassing, defeating; so powerful it can devour you, and for the weakest of heart and mind, kill.

Stoya was all intellect. Highly focused and ever watchful. She had a complete understanding of things, of how it all worked, the universe, the grand design, and God. She knew the how and why of the narrative of life, how it all fell into the order of time. She used this insight to manipulate destiny, her influences lay behind many things upon this world.

She had an advantage. She had seen God, the great burning light upon the endless horizon, confronted It, questioned It. Came to understand It's mind. She has never told anyone of what had been revealed. Nor I think she ever will. It is their little secret, and, I think, her inside joke on us all.

I quietly watched her, my perfect mistress of the night, my eternal vampire. I saw her eyes blaze in search of something she could not seem to find, a thing only known to her. This was her one weakness I had always thought, this thing she seemed to ever search for. But what it was fully, I did not know, nor I think, ever will. But I was in love with her; I always had been since the day we first met. A turbulent love full of mistrust, chaos, violence, and misunderstanding. I just hoped that one day she would learn to forgive me. Forgive me for the past, and forgive me for what I was about to do. That one day she and I could just simply love again.

CHAPTER 37

I moved closer to Stoya, to touch her. To love and feel her. But I found her guarded, distracted. I took her hand into mine kissing it.

I whispered the words, "I love you."

Which she seemed to ignore.

I felt her wall, the impenetrable fortress that was her being, stand strong before me. Unwavering. I could feel her mind work at something, but it was shielded from me completely. I paused, then attempted to move in on her, to submit to her.

I had become desirous of her. The egg within me seeking yet more approval, further confirmation. To know chemically, its place within the social order.

I felt the archaic beauty of Arefu and the sadness of Poenari creep over me, penetrate me; seduce me and elevate the dark hedonistic fantasy of her I had in me. I thought of our time on this world, of the dark sex we had had, and found myself wanting it, now, again.

I felt Stoya's mind begin to pry at me. I felt her probe me with her senses. What did she see in me, my body and mind? Did she already know?

Stoya stood up abruptly, shrugging me off, and walked to the edge of her massive stone patio. Its primitive hand-cut granite blocks jutted slightly out and over a one-thousand-foot sheer cliff face into the river Argeş below.

She seemed sad, disappointed in me I was sure. I watched as she looked to Poenari and then seemingly to force herself back into reality, into the now. I waited as she gathered herself up and turned to speak.

"Come, it is time that you feed," she paused, thinking. "Yes, you must feed for what's to come...," she trailed off penetrating me with her ice-cold stare.

I saw a slight smile form upon her lips.

"There is a Gypsy camp not far from here, five men and three women," she spoke quietly. "The patriarch, Florica, my servant, has been disobedient. She has allowed outsiders here on my land without permission. They will be punished. There flesh will serve me better than the mouths I will have to keep fed."

I felt the cold indifference of her voice, the matter-of-factness of it. Death and the consummation. It was how she viewed this world, the universe, a simple math equation, survival by numbers only. Each to a purpose, each to live or die when that purpose was fulfilled, there was little else.

"You will need strength now, in the light of all that is to come."

She smiled softly, if not forcefully, the hurt on her face buried within her lips and the paleness of her complexion.

I watched as she took one last drag from her half-finished cigarette. She breathed deep and slow, then as she turned back to watch Poenari, she exhaled; then let the cigarette fall from her hand.

I saw it descend and collide upon the granite stone of her patio. The burning end crashed and flicked outwards like some small explosion. I saw her elegant bare foot descend upon it and crush out its life.

She turned grinning wickedly. "We can't have a fire, now can we?" she said with an air of challenge and disregard.

"Come, I hunger...and I thirst."

CHAPTER 38

The Gypsy camp was not far from Stoya's home. I had seen the campfire in the distance. We had chosen to walk hand-in-hand to them through the ancient, damp, Medieval forest. I thought of centuries past, back to when men had feared wilderness like this. In these forests there were still monsters. From these forests, we used to take our prey.

I trembled at what was to come, at the hunger pains growing in my stomach, my being, at Stoya's absolute resolve in the coming feast.

They were a small regional family of five members, Gypsy foragers, drifters, sheep herders, common to this area, and a visiting group of men. The core family consisted of the grandfather and matriarch-grandmother Florica, a long-time servant of Stoya's. Their daughter and her husband both of about forty-five years of age and their sole offspring, a daughter of perhaps sixteen. They belonged here and were, in essence, still trapped to servitude to their immortal master.

Their ancestors of at least eighteen or more generations ago had sworn an allegiance, a contract to serve their lord, Vlad Tepes II, his son Vlad Tepes III, and many other Wallachian lords, the paternal Order of the Drăculeşti, or, Dragon. Loyalists to their landlords, defenders of the faith, and long-dead ideals from some 650 years ago.

This family's ancestors had fought against the Turks from the shadows, as conscripts, mercenaries, spies, and assassins. They killed without mercy and enforced the Order's rule and reputation upon these parts and much of greater Romania.

This allegiance to the Order was a sacred pact, an eternal pact. I doubt they could have ever known just how long they would have been bound to it, this family and many others like them.

In return for that servitude, these families had been granted certain protections, ensured that they would earn a good living, have land to roam, and be forever exempt from normal social and governmental standards. Stoya cared for her Gypsy clans, her social outcasts, but there were rules governing this care, this servitude. Rules that now had been broken.

Stoya would remind them that night, of that sacred oath, the rules governing the blood-penned signatures of so long ago. Enforce her will and power and set an example in an effort to carry on a tradition, a relic of serfdom from a long lurid past. It was her way.

This was Romania after all, the heartland, Arefu, Poenari, its great and powerful mystique which still captures the attentions of modern society to this day. Here, in this land, long forgotten things still dwell, ancient orders and vampiric manifestations. Here in this land, the ghosts of the languishing dead still call out one sacred, eternal name; Dracula.

CHAPTER 39

The egg within me ached, churned, wanted. Aroused by Tyr's mark and now seeking approval from Stoya, it wanted to revel in the flesh, the nourishment for a coming conception. I felt ashamed. Instinct was taking over me as I began to salivate over the coming feast slipping back into my true nature, the hunter-beast, the monster within.

We watched the camp from inside the tree line as they drank and prattled on around the fire. The men ordered two of the women around, Florica's daughter and granddaughter, as they passed a bottle of cheap vodka. Having them fetch this or that as they ate and drank; telling tall tales and other lies.

Three of the men, who were of Polish Gypsy origin, were not from these parts. They had come down from Poland in search of work. They had brought a small herd of sheep with them, their main occupation and source of income. They sat with the two other men, the grandfather and mid-aged son of Florica's family, sharing drink and laughter. Forgetful of what the night still brings in this part of the world.

The eldest woman, Florica the familial matriarch, was at least seventy-five, and seemed indifferent to the rudeness of the men. This was a way of life for her, the Gypsy's life. Women in most clans were second best to the men. The daughter of Florica, hovered about waiting upon the men's every want.

The youngest, the teenage daughter, sat bored, texting away on her cheap cell phone, indifferent to the leering eyes of the three visiting men.

I watched as they lusted over her, her sweet, young body.

I knew at least one would make a move tonight, late when the fire was long dead, and all the others had passed out from their drink. Force himself upon her most likely.

A hind section of lamb roasted on a spit near the bonfire.

We listened as one of the younger men attempted to play at an old guitar, to serenade the young girl. He sang Extreme's "More Than Words". It was dreadful. Both his version and the song as a whole.

I watched Stoya's lips curl into a sneer at the sight and sound of that song, the rendition, at him, the others. Classless twits, I knew she thought. Gypsy. That very word offended her, their sight so common throughout Europe, offended her. And, I am sure, if she could, she would rid the world of them.

I never really understood her hatred for Gypsies. And she never said much of it, nor explained why exactly.

She spoke of it only once. "They left me to die," (her human self). "One less mouth to feed. I was a burden, an expense. My only sister, a child of twelve, was worth more as a whore than I."

One thing I did know; however, to her they were dirt.

She had Gypsies in her direct employment and other dealings, but they were servants to her and nothing more. A contract. The rest were an inconvenience, a soiled mark upon her lands. Demanding children that needed constant attention and punishing.

"Come, it is time to feast," Stoya snarled, cracking into a devilishly wry grin.

Her eyes seemed to increase with intensity, glowing in the dark a wild violet light, like a demon, the devil, or some unfathomable ancient evil.

"Look, they have flavored themselves with herbed meats, tobacco, and vodka," she said, snickering as she walked out from the shadows and into the fire light.

"They will be a tasty delight!" she smirked again and began to laugh wickedly as we walked blatantly into their camp.

Florica, her servant, shrieked at the sight of us and our naked bodies. At Stoya, her master.

Stoya's marble white skin reflected the firelight's red-orange glow, making her appear in body as if some demon had risen up from hell.

I, her minion, looked like some ancient Egyptian djinn-queen cast from the sandy ruins of ancient Egypt.

We had removed our clothes, precautions for the modern day where science can detect the slightest things in murder investigations.

"Oh, my sweet children, why was I not invited," Stoya's voice seared with disdain. "To this, the feasts of feasts…?" she hissed.

"Why have you not heeded my warnings, my sweetest Florica?" Stoya directed her question to the old lady and her husband.

"The rules of your servitude are clear," she confirmed. "Outsiders are not welcome here."

Florica groveled, pleaded for mercy in a rare, more ancient Romanian dialect, an inflection I had not heard for a long time.

"Did I not take you in when you were but a girl?" Stoya asked almost imploringly. "Gave you a trade and matched you with this man?" Stoya glared at the elder man as he hunched over his wife Florica, submissive, protectively.

"Have I not been fair and let you to your own free will? To live here and keep my secrets, and now...?"

I heard Florica uttering prayers in Latin, the old language of the Orthodox Church.

"I grow weary of you," Stoya condemned them. "I tire of your insolence…"

Stoya held up a long sword before them holding it upside down so that the hilt looked like a cross. The gold pommel shone in the firelight to expose the dragon symbol of the Drăculeşti, the blade of Vlad Tepes, a weapon which had directly sent hundreds if not thousands of Turks and others, who were disobedient, to their death.

Here in this part of the world, to this day, the symbol of the Drăculeşti, is held sacred. Worshiped by some, and bound by an honor long forgotten to many.

"I am your master Florica, and I am displeased!" Stoya scowled condemningly.

The old lady went prostate praying and begging for mercy. She knew the symbol of power. The eternal damning death. She knew she had wronged, and that she would pay.

"Come now, sweet Florica, you were warned and yet chose to disobey…," she addressed the old lady again.

"How do we settle this, my faithful Florica?"

The old woman shrieked again and began praying to God with even more fervor, unable to fully answer Stoya or fight against her oppressive power. Florica cursed her husband, this trespass, this invite of strangers not of this land into their camp, professing that it was his idea alone.

"It was not me!" Florica lamented. "It was him, I promise, please let us go!" she began to sob. "Mercy!"

"I told you!" Florica condemned her husband. "I told you, but you never listen!" she lamented in Romanian.

"Oh, Ms. Dracŭ, oh! My lord and master please…!" Florica pleaded. "Spare us! Mercy!" she gasped.

The second eldest woman, Florica's daughter, panicked not quite understanding that the old stories her mother had still spoken of, were true.

The young girl seemed to almost smile as if thinking this was some kind of joke. She fumbled with her cell phone to snap a picture, probably hoping for a selfie with us.

The old man went to speak, to defend his wife and I was sure, to confess to his trespass.

"Silence!" Stoya seethed. "You are but a husband to provide for my Florica, and nothing more to me. I never cared for you then, and I care not for you now. You serve one purpose and even that you have now failed…" Stoya spoke bitterly.

"So much for your family name, Ústie, your ancestors would be ashamed and would willingly die now, again, as they once did, to make amends for displeasing their lord and master, and yet…here you grovel, such is the disgrace of modern men, of family who once died nobly and with honor" Stoya scolded.

"What man allows his family such shame I wonder? Allows it to stray so far and into its ruin?" she hissed with disdain.

Stoya turned her attention back to the group as a whole. "Oh, my children, he is always watching. I am always watching! Betrayal, defiance, disobedience does not bode kindly here in my land."

Stoya scolded them, Florica. "As if it ever did!"

The old man tried to shield his aged wife as he too began to pray to God.

Stoya scoffed at them and circled them, seeming to herd them all tighter together, like lions or wolves do to a heard of antelope.

"What have you to say Florica Elsi Gabalean?" Stoya mocked. "So much for that name also. The loss of honor upon it…"

The youngest of the visiting Polish men stood up and withdrew a sheering knife and yelled back at Stoya trying to defend his host as honor would dictate amongst these peoples.

"Fuck you!" he bellowed in Polish.

Stoya laughed out, mocking him, her voice seeming to echo across the great farmland valley and beyond onto the winds of the world.

"Fuck...you?" she hissed. "Well, such a brash little mouth," Stoya countered, turning her attention to the young man, her head cocked slightly to the side to consider this new display of insolence.

"Well yes, I am fucked!" she laughed out heartily.

"Yes, I have been fucked! By God and the devil...by time immortal, forever. And by things you could only guess at," she laughed again, a sinister laugh. "By time itself!" she hissed.

"I am the great fucking of the fuckers and the fucked!" Stoya moved toward the young man, prowling. Her alien-darkness, her power descending upon the whole scene.

I felt stifled in it. It was thick and unmoving, unforgiving. A spider web, a barely invisible mass of which escape is impossible. I saw her seem to grow in strength and stature. Her shoulders squared and ready. I knew that time had stopped in this part of the world. Reversed itself possibly, back to the time when Stoya Tepes Dracŭ was the real monster behind the monster.

"I am the great fuck, the end to all things as I see fit! You can pray and swear and sacrifice to old gods and new gods, and gods that humans shall never know exist. It matters not for I am a god, of God, and I will take as I please. I will fuck you and all upon this world at my desire..." she paused.

"Would you like to fuck...me?" she asked of him displaying a sudden act of flirtation, turning in a complete circle to show off her body.

"Little old me?" she asked playfully cocking her head to the other side now, and licking her lips.

"A fuck for the fucked?" she stood tall again, towering.

I saw her muscles coil, wind up for the final pounce.

"Well, pity…you are just a boy after all!"

"F…fu…Fuck you!" the young man stammered back uncertain now about himself, about Stoya, and what it was before him.

"Hmmm…yes, then, let us fuck! You and I, shall we?" She grinned moving in on him. "But careful, I bite!" she mused, laughing.

"I like the taste of virgin flesh, the flesh of whores also. Which are you?" she smiled. "Both I suspect…maybe?"

I saw him cower suddenly as prey does when it knows it has lost the right to survive.

She lunged, striking him instantly with her ancient blade with such skill one had to wonder at it. It was a perfect penetrating blow, a heart shot, an instant kill. So fast, so accurate, that the quiet sucking sound of the blade going in and out of his body still seemed to resonate upon the air long after the act.

I, too, became terrified of her, her mastership of that ancient weapon of war and death. To know that she was that much a killer, the eraser of men, of worlds. A stark reminder of God and the unforgiving things in this universe It has put into play.

I saw absolute terror wash over the rest of this Gypsy clan. The instinct to flee took over them as they darted about seeking escape.

She lunged at another young Polish man as he tried to run, striking him down quickly, effortlessly. Her blade dripped with blood.

The third man drew a small switch blade and readied to defend himself. He trembled uncontrollably, uncertain of his ability. I could smell his urine and the coming defecation.

He quickly looked toward the young girl to find some renewed courage. He would save her if he could, I am sure he had thought.

"Well, courage now child I am sure heaven awaits you, too!" Stoya snarled at him.

"God will welcome you, maybe, but I highly doubt it such as Its disregard for us…" She smiled circling him, keeping him off guard.

"She will be hers tonight…" Stoya smiled at him as she gestured towards me, glancing furtively to the young girl caught in panic.

"She will be of us soon, our consummation, a small apart of the cosmic feast, the sacrament of flesh to your God!" she sneered.

"Have courage my sweet, die with honor, hold your ground!"

She circled the boy, taunting, encouraging. "I would remember you for that, I am a sucker for all things honorable and noble, fearless deaths."

I saw Stoya move in on him, smiling, the blood from the others splashed across her body; it glistened like unpolished rubies in the firelight.

"Take them now, these women!" Stoya commanded me, while intently closing in on the last of the young Polish men; her bloodlust on full display. Flexing her might in the art of death, destruction, and war.

"Take them now, and be quick before the meat spoils!" she snarled.

Spurned by the sudden surge of my own instinctual blood-lust, and the absoluteness of Stoya's commands, I lunged, leaping over the fire taking up both women who cowered at my feat of biomechanical mastery. I took them both, gathering them up into my arms one on each side and squeezed them into me. I held them to me, each arm over their chest griping at them into their arm pit pressing against the long thoracic artery and nerve bundle there. I pressed it, sending a pulse like energy wave into them immediately causing them to seize and then fall limp. A trick we had found that worked on human bodies.

Quickly, I reached up and took them by their throats. Holding them, I twisted my hands in such a way that shut of their air supply and circulation instantly.

I breathed heavily, the heat of their bodies against me. I salivated, longed, wetted. I thought of their blood, the flesh, so sweet, so young. Their bodies against me. The flesh of like I had had here so long ago when the Turks had fled this land and Stoya laid her love to rest.

I squeezed the life from them. I moved the blood in them, drowning their hearts, overwhelming that organ, a pleasure that they themselves did not know could be felt by such an act. Strangulation, erotic-asphyxiation, drowning of the blood, they had no concept of this, a thing left only for the decadent of society; the rich, the emotionally bored of this world.

Their bodies began to weep and struggle reflexively. Their mouths gasped, but they soon found the arousal in it. This death. Unwittingly, their bodies would build into climax from the sensation. Their thoughts a jumble of confusion, death, or pleasure and pain. What was this new thing they would wonder as they passed.

I was the master of it.

I watched as Stoya took up Florica's husband by the back of his neck, scowling down at him, as she snapped it like it was nothing. The crack seeming to echo amidst the other sounds of death. She cared nothing for him. He was but another pawn in Stoya's circle of servitude. He did not plea for forgiveness. Instead he remained defiant. A sin as far as Stoya and her relationship with these people went. Death for insubordination.

She then turned her attention to the last young man again. He held his small knife tightly, trembling as fear continued to paralyze him.

Stoya smiled at this, like a wolf that has cornered the baby lamb. Her mouth opened a bit barring her teeth as if to compliment him, his willingness to fight.

She lunged at him, her sword thrusting into vacant space as he dodged her and the blade, swinging back at her, missing also. Fear can make humans quick.

"Well, my sweet! You, I shall savor last, you are a brave little one, worthy to be called dessert," she mocked. "My favorite meal is dessert!"

She seemed to admire him in that moment as she circled him. Her eyes transfixed on his.

She licked at her lips delicately. "Yes, a sweet, sweet dessert!"

Then in a sudden, barely detectable flash she lunged at the young man. The war sword thrusting into him with such great force, that it lifted him up high and off of his feet. She held him there suspended for a moment, like the impaled Turks in Dracula's forest of the dead.

Stoya grabbed at him as he gasped from his mortal wound. She took him by the throat as she withdrew the sword from his chest while still holding him up to admire him. She stared at him for the longest time wondering over him. Her head cocked to one side then the other.

"Did he remind her of someone from her past?" I wondered.

"Brave…," she spoke quietly to him. "Brave."

I heard the snap of his neck and he knew no more.

I went to stand and take pursuit of Florica, who had by now managed to make her way into the dark forest.

"Leave her!" Stoya ordered me. "She is no bother. I will deal with her myself at another time."

I watched Stoya drop the young man as if in sudden disappointment, then turn to the other dead to begin her feast. She kept her promises. She would save him for last, he her sweet dessert.

Kneeling, holding my prey, the two women, I breathed in their scent, thick musky, human; sensual in every animalistic way. They had not bathed for a while, normal for their way of life, this outdoor camp living. But there was cheap perfume on them, an attempt to feel feminine, to belong to the finer world.

I was intoxicated by them, their look, their smell, their sex. I wanted their blood, their being, their flesh inside of me. I wanted to know them on an intimate cellular level, to absorb their DNA, their power.

I watched as Stoya began her feast. For such a monstrous thing, she had made it a ritual of grace and beauty. I had always wondered over that contrast in her. She was so brutal, violent, when taking life. But she had somehow found a way to make the final consumption something elegant, sensual, slow, delicate, and above all, thoughtful. She was as always, a deep dark study in contrast.

I held my two women close to me as I watched Stoya's consume her prey. My stomach, my being, panged at the sight of it, the raw flesh being stripped from the bone.

This was death. This was the universe at play. The vision of red and orange flickering firelight upon the black and moon-blue colored forest backdrop, the *Night of the Living Dead* reality that was God's final end of all things living. This was the grand design in motion. What God has intended of us; for you, to die and be reborn.

I had consumed the mother first, saving her daughter for last. In truth, I felt sexual toward the daughter. She wasn't beautiful, nor was she ugly. Her thick, black, curling locks of semi-oily hair and sun-weathered face already had signs aging.

Life as a Gypsy was often harsh and cruel. They were hated, despised even in some places. Their existence, their deaths meant little to a modern world.

She was firm to the touch, thicker than most girls, but hard boned and thick-skinned from long days of servitude to her elders, her family-clan. This young girl knew how to split firewood, to cook and sew; worst and knit wool into clothing and blankets. To milk goats and make cheese, and how to do many things that other girls her age in the world had no idea existed. She cared for her family, was loyal to it, defended it with honor, and aided it to prosper.

I smiled down upon her; she was motionless, asleep in death, cool, soft, supple, enduring to look at.

I gently touched her clothes, some of which she had probably made herself. Her sweater so finely crafted. I touched her arms and unshaven legs. I could tell she always went barefoot. Her hands were callused from her labors. She kept her nails short, clean, polished with an off-putting purple color. She had little in the way of makeup, but her eyeliner and pink lipstick was applied near perfectly.

I suspected there was a boy somewhere, waiting to see her again, to run off into the night together, and make love, to consummate a union that most likely was not sanctioned by either family.

Yes, she was perfect to me; a liar, a thief, a seductress, and at times, for the right price, a whore. All these things her family would make her do so that they could survive. She was of the noblest of women in my mind.

I held her tenderly, as I kissed her gently, softly upon her brow, her cheeks, then upon her lips as my hand gently outlined the curves of her face, her mouth. I began to undress her, and thought of how even now some things in life stand still while others speed by. This Gypsy girl, like so many before, was a relic of a way of life that still seems to linger on behind the veil of the modern world.

I sighed fondly at such memories, the reality, touching her hair and gently pulling it back up and over her ears. I whispered to her in that moment a secret, the thing she must know.

"Do not fear this my sweet, this thing called death. It is your evolution. You will see a great burning light upon an endless horizon. Do not fear it. Walk into it, and never stop walking. Never!" I paused. "There is where rebirth awaits, there you can be timeless, forever." I paused again. "And in me also, you will reside eternal, forever of my blood and bones, my memories; a part of me, this body for as long as I keep it. It is as God intends of your flesh. For the journey or your soul within."

I kissed her gently then slowly began to open my mouth. I thought in that moment of how she will be remembered by me, my body, my mind. Of that joining of she and I through God's mystical programming, her DNA. I began to take her in, to feel her slip down part-by-part, sweet, delicate, and life-giving.

I thought about how I will speak of her, about her, throughout time when I fall upon the next world in my great journey. How I would tell them, the beings there on my new world, all about human kind. I would tell them of her, this Gypsy girl from Romania, and of many others. This life, humankind, this world. And they, then, would understand of this place, earth, the human story, of you, the human race.

"What were they? Who were they? Where have they gone?" they will ask of me.

And weeping, I will reply to them; gone to the will of God and time. Dead at their own hands. Dead from a dying sun.

I wept at that thought now; of your kind's inevitable demise. At least she, I thought, will be remembered and live on as a part of me, when so many of you will not.

CHAPTER 40

Stoya was forever ravenous and had delighted in our feasting. Sated, we retired to her lair, exhausted and needing to rest. We had bathed and drank more wine. I, being careful not to disturb the scent of Tyr, something that did not go unnoticed by Stoya.

Then stood out again upon on her massive stone patio to take in the coming morning hour. We listened to Romania's elusive black wolves howl in the distance, as they rallied to the remains of our kill; the blood, the bones, the leftovers that Stoya left for them. Owls, too, and other predatory creatures of the night called out to each other, a secret language that only they and Stoya understood. It was a communion of sorts, the feast of the flesh, a gift from their human master. She smiled at the prospect of such things so dark and unforgiving.

Stoya stood dreaming again at the edge of the abyss below. A silent statue cloaked in a blood-red colored dress, its train flowing out upon the ground behind her as if a trail of blood in the dark.

Her dress was very old, a velvet of some Medieval weave indicative to this region. Her long, jet-black hair was let loose to gently flow in the light, cool mountain breeze.

She lit a cigarette and thoughtfully inhaled the fine rich tobacco.

I watched her dream over the distant Poenari again.

Her eyes, blazing in the dark, seemed to glisten with sadness. She thought of our feast, of their feasts, so long ago. She was forever a sad soul, I truly felt sorry for her.

I approached her as she spoke quietly to me still looking toward her sacred temple illuminated under the waning crescent moon. A silent testimonial to obscene death and terror like this night had been.

"I loved him…," she quibbled, sneering at the memory of Vlad Tepes III and their torrid love affair.

"I know…," I answered quietly.

How anyone could have loved such a man was beyond me I thought to myself. He was cruel, to her and to the world.

"He was a great man, a hero. He saved a country," she exhaled. "Saved God for them…saved me."

"He tried to kill you!" I exclaimed, saddened, angered at her stubbornness to let his memory go.

She stood silent for a long time. "It's what all great men do, kill love. Shatter the romance of it. Who can live in such shadows?" she lamented.

"Not all men kill love!" I pleaded angrily.

I thought of Jesus and his last moments. Of my OSS lover, the acts of great courage and love he shared while alive. Of others, men and women, who had risen to defend what was right, love and life, over the centuries here on this world and others.

"No, but the quest for power does, the quest for power that lies in all men's hearts. It is the way of things, of great men; warrior-men. Love, it cannot exist against that. There is no place for love to flourish under that exaltation," she paused.

"The resolve for absolute power. To be as if a god," she concluded.

I knew she was referring to Tyr.

I marveled at how clearly she saw things, the world; the universe at play. How the truth was like bones to her, stripped away of the complications of the rest of the body and soul to reveal the standing structure. It is in the bones that one's inner truth lies immortal. For they stand the test of time, the last thing that is ever known of a man or woman or anything upon their death. That and what history has written of them, their mortal deeds.

She was right in that conclusion, of course. It is difficult for love to flourish in the raging seas of the pursuit of power and the death and chaos that comes with its obtainment. It evolves all lives, here on this world and the universe.

Power, the desire to have it, and the want to keep it, is yet another of God's hideous designs. Power, no matter what form it takes, means survival. It is what drives evolution forward; it's what corrupts the mind, the body, the soul, and the essence of what created us; love.

It is an irony of ironies. I thought of myself, my quest for power over love, over what God had already intended.

Or did God intend for love to exist? I wavered at my own ambitions.

And then in my head, I heard her thoughts. "Yes…women kill love also…"

I stepped to the edge and took her hand, to face the oblivion. To jump if she so desired, together forever, to our deaths; if we could die from that.

She stirred, exhaling. "But, there will be an absolution soon," she whispered toward Poenari.

More to it, the stone sentinel in the distance, than to me.

"There will be a revelation," she confirmed again. "And then we will see, you and I, this cruel thing of your making."

She then turned and looked into my eyes. I felt her mind penetrate me again, searching for something, the truth. Her thoughts were cold and precise. It prodded at me, chipping away bit by bit. Driving like a knife. She wasn't fooled by me, my motive, she knew me better than I knew myself.

"Yes, a resurrection in the betrayal."

Her face reflected a wave of emotions. Did she see my truth of what I was here to do, or simply my memories of all my failures? I felt her mind bare down into me, my soul, tearing its way down, ever down into the very essence, the chemical reaction that is thought and memory.

This was supposed to be so simple, this heroic love story of mine, to find my one true love again and live blissfully forever.

Now there was only pain, death and great sorrow, a failing love. I was so naive really, for all my millions of years of existence.

Stoya, frowning, looked back to Poenari mournfully, but seemed to shrink from it, suddenly. What did she see in that dark tower?

"Well...," she lightly huffed, annoyed, catching herself.

"In the end he was weak. They are all weak! Mortal, useless, human…," she trailed off.

"Undeserving of my love; our love…," she seemed to be addressing me, possibly, looking hesitantly back to Poenari, seemingly to lose her iron-willed convictions. Seemingly to lose the thing she so wanted most to say.

I touched her gently, her shoulders and arms. She was cold to the touch in the cool night air, but a warmth welled deep within her, a burning, raging fire was rising; a super nova waiting to happen. I shuddered at the touch her skin, the luxury of it. The contrast between the cold and the inferno just below it.

She moved toward me suddenly, forcing me right out upon the edge, my heels barely touching, waiting for one fatal mistake. I thought now of our interludes over the centuries.

I trembled; finding myself wanting of her, the intensity, the dangerous truth of her, and her sex.

I took her scent in deeply. It was as mine, that of the rose at full bloom an hour before it turns to die, but fuller, stronger, completely intoxicating, and of the Bvlgari eau de parfum Noorah. Its scents akin to some dark hidden bar. An opium den possibly, found at the end of the world's worst alleyway; the place where all sin meets and breeds yet more sin in an unending unforgiving whoredom. I withered into her, submitting to her as she took me in.

Her nails were long and painted blood red. Her lips were still stained and tasted of blood. I could smell that, too, on her, the blood; the sweet sugary metallic nectar.

She inhaled again the smoke from her cigarette. Her eyes and her slightly parted lips challenging me to darker pleasures.

I felt time begin to slip away again, to stop and freeze in that moment. I heard the wolves snarl and bay as they tore at the bones of the dead. The owls and other beastly night things rattle at their mortal cages, yearning to run and rage across the world, to tear at it, to devour it. To throttle the bars of their nature-cages which held them at bay; the eternal damning night for which they are consigned.

Our lips met, partly open, interlocking, poised. I felt her gently blow the smoke of her cigarette back into me and onto my wet, wanting tongue, her death whisper; an apparition of thing's best left unspoken.

I felt the smoke gently roll over and between our tongues and then down into our lungs. The noxious sweet tobacco was of a most cultivated and refined process. I could taste the blood of those of which we had consumed upon her lips. The combination of which was sensual, an aphrodisiac. Like the flesh and juice of raw oyster is to human lovers.

I felt her power envelope me. Her alien darkness gathered me in, binding me to her; holding me tightly. Choking. I found the thoughts of Charlotte begin to slip away from my mind, torn away by Stoya, made to become some long-ago dream, her vision of us, together, replacing sweeter memories.

Stoya towered over me as I teetered upon the ledge and the oblivion below. Then I felt her gently push against me to touch me, my shoulders; my breasts. There was nothing to stop me. I felt gravity pull at me, drawing me down. She seemed to smirk as her hand traced its way across my body then down and up under my dress line to touch me, my wanting sex.

I trembled, balancing upon the edge of her oblivion.

She took another long, sultry drag from her cigarette, as her eyes tore down through me and into my soul. She was bold and unforgiving. Stoya took what she wanted from her lovers. I had always found pleasure in that. She would be cruel. Sex was pain. Sex was control. She would want me to know of it, to remember it, to know the warning of it; the warning of her.

I leaned back, to open myself to her. To fall from her down onto the rocks below if she had so desired.

"God will not forgive us…," she whispered with a defined certainty. "We will sin against Its designs, betray the covenant by which we are consigned…" She seemed to revel in that thought; to relish that betrayal.

"And you, my sister, will be the nail that seals Charlotte's fate, my fate, the fate that is forever."

CHAPTER
41

In her dark, candle lit bed chamber, Stoya came upon me in an avalanche of perversion and forced subjugation as she pushed me down onto my knees and into her waiting sex.

I was prepared to submit to that act, willing, in fact, to indulge. But even here in this most intimate of acts, she had managed to pervert it, to inflict her will upon others. To make it a point that she was queen.

I recoiled at the small, gold-plated nail-ring pierced through her clitoris. It was a gift, a sacred thing from man's antiquity; meant to be a bond of our love, our sisterhood. It was fashioned to be a ring for her finger; it shone gleaming now before me in the low, orange-yellow light.

Stoya had perverted it, the thought, the sentiment, like so many things in her life. It hung boldly, a symbol of her power over love and God's only spoken words to man and as a testament to betrayal.

It was the small nail I had taken when Jesus was brought down from the cross, a memento of a great sacrifice. The nail that had held in place the sign above his head, INRI, Iesvs Nazarenvs Rex Ivdaeorvm, "Jesus of Nazareth; the King of the Jews", the final insult to a dying man. It was a cherished relic of mine from one of earth's darkest days.

I had it gold plated and fashioned to be a ring, a symbol of our connection, our bond and our love; Stoya and I. It hung now, a testament to destruction, perverted as only Stoya could pervert love and sacrifice.

I wavered, holding back before she forced me into her.

She had bound up my hair into her fist for control.

I began to lick and suck at her clitoris, to suck at the ring, as she sneered down at me, holding me there.

"It's how I keep you close to me my love…," she scorned as she looked down upon me with disdain.

"How I will remember this night and the coming betrayal."

Her lips partly open, sneering in anticipation, open to breath out, to speak yet more cruel words. Her eyes ablaze with delight at my submission.

I was going to pay for this defiance, this little secret of mine. If I wanted love eternal for Charlotte and me, there would be a price to pay.

She held me there suffocating me within her, taking sex by force.

I tasted her sex, her juices, sweet like a thick rose-honey.

She moaned and grunted with anger squeezing the back of my neck forcing me to perform harder.

I found myself falling into the role, submissive to her violence, aroused at the forcefulness of it. I felt disgusted inside, in my heart, my soul, that I took pleasure from this explicit degrading way she had of me, took of me. Defiled me.

Satisfied, Stoya pulled me up by my hair then threw me onto her bed and lunged upon me, pinning me down with great strength. A singular focus.

"You are my whore and you now need of me, again!" she moaned. "A weak needful whore to suck at my breasts, the milk of which only I can give…approval."

"Yes…," I let out inexplicably, reaching up to hold her breasts, weeping.

She clutched at my neck, choking me with force as she positioned herself over me.

"Yes," I said again assuring her I was going to submit to her will.

"My whore of many whores!" she gasped longingly. "My little deceitful whore!"

She hoisted my left leg up onto her shoulder as she slid herself up onto my pussy in a scissor like fashion, preparing to fuck me. The nail, the symbol of her wanton perversions, dug at me, making me bleed.

"How you will take of me…," she languished angrily.

"Of how you will use me again…this thing, this love we had…," she paused. "Funny, it's always me that seems to pay for you Ianthe, your will, these things, this forever wanting…."

She grabbed at my breasts squeezing them, pinching my nipples, the pain eliciting pleasure.

I felt our cum mingle, wet and dripping. I could smell my blood in it, it oozed down my buttocks, onto our inner thighs onto her sheets as I breathed hard and sweated. My body reacted willingly, if not entirely wantonly.

"I have waited a long time for you, Ianthe…," she gasped. "For your weakness to reveal itself again and to admit…that you are just as selfish, just as horrid as I."

She clawed at me with her long, sharp nails breaking the skin in places.

"Can you admit this, Ianthe?" she gloated. "That you are weak now in this moment of need?"

I saw the walls of her bedroom chamber covered with "mementos" of past loves. Their skulls prominently displayed upon alters, Vlad Tepes III the center of it all on a pedestal with his sword and his armor. Even now, he seemed to grin down upon me as if still able to watch the world, me, suffer.

"Come begging, like some junkie whore to her street pimp…," she condemned as she bent forward and kissed me hard on the mouth, biting me on my lower lip, tearing at it to make it bleed. "Such a beautiful, perfect whore…"

I saw her almost tear. I kissed her as she lapped at my blood, her soft talented tongue upon mine dominating even that sensual thing.

"Like God has done, in Its moments of delusion." She looked down wickedly.

I was nearing orgasm. I felt her sex press down into me. I couldn't resist her, the cruel love, and the eons old instincts kicking in.

This sex, the way of our species from the dawn of time when we were young and had to fight the other of God's children for our place in this universe. This sex, her sex, assured only the strong survived, that it could endure. And it was a way in which Stoya loved her lovers, tested their fortitude and conviction to be with her. Violence.

"That you are Its delusion, God …," she continued, aroused and obsessed. "Deceived by Its own mind into thinking It is greater than all else…," she laughed out.

"Your delusion that you are greater and deserving in this…"

I felt her kiss at my neck; lick it where I had concealed Tyr's mark. I felt her darkness envelope me like a womb.

She snarled, breathed deeply, lustfully, grunting louder as she ground herself into me, her sex into mine.

She licked at the inside of my left foot at the arch then bit into it, breaking the skin.

My back stiffened automatically at the sensual feel of it. I shuddered, arching and thrashing.

"Well, we are as God, aren't we? Liars and thieves, deceivers…murderers…left lost, desperate for a lasting love in an ageless life. Afraid to be alone in our forever as God is..."

She seemed to laugh condemningly, taunting me, at our weakness in that.

"Weak!" she seethed.

"We are alone my love, that is our fate, our fucking over by the thing beyond the veil of God…forever. We are all alone…these drifting souls of ours," she spoke coldly. "Why we took of the bodies…," she seemed to scorn our own kind.

"At least some know death, get to be reborn," she spoke sarcastically of man. "At least they get a blank slate, get to forget the unpleasantries of the past, live alone briefly…"

My head fell back, my eyes closed tightly as I strained to gather in all of her unforgiving pleasure. I felt my egg ignite as if on fire. I felt Stoya suck at my toes, putting them into her mouth.

With her left hand, she reached up to my face and inserted her three middle fingers into my mouth, forcing me to suck at them like a cock, to gag me; the cup of her hand gripping at my chin, pushing my head back into the pillows as if to snuff me out.

"I am alone like God, Ianthe. Do you hear me whine about it?"

Gathering up my legs, she bent them forward to more fully expose my pussy and anus.

I felt her slide her right hand down over my buttocks, caressing them firmly, claw at them, grabbing at them. She massaged me, moaning at the feel of them. Then, unhesitant in her desires, inserted her fingers into me, two into each hole.

I gasped out at the suddenness, the deliberateness, the roughness of it.

Leaning into me as she moved her hips into me, violently fucking me with her fingers as she rubbed upon her own hand, pushing her fingers deeper inside me.

"Cry, be weak!" Her mouth grinned devilishly. "Long ago, when I crawled from the sea…," she laughed. "Even as I stood under It…I understood that God did not see me, think of me, nor even, I think, remember making me…"

My back arched as I choked, gasping for air. I felt her nails inside of me; digging. I came again, unable to control it. I felt the weight of her press down onto me, her right hand and arm pushing down onto my chin, her fingers pushing deeper into my mouth.

She breathed deeply, elated at my suffering.

"Yet, I did not whine, search for Its love. I accepted in that moment, Its truth, that we are and will be alone, forever…," she laughed again, mocking.

"Yes, the immortal life-thing…Ianthe…God has fucked you. Us. You and I, our race, the universe and all its lost and aimless souls…in constant rebirth, this immortal, timeless existence never to be with those we love, but for some utterly fleeting random moment…"

"It takes and takes and takes without any end…God, the thing beyond..." she lamented. "Forever!" she paused. "Its cruelty has no bounds…"

"Even in death, It is slow and unremorseful. Uncaring and unselective…random and chaotic…," she seemed to anger. "But you will know this also, soon, again."

Her eyes blazed, her mind penetrating me, sharp and focused.

"What does It know of love, of being alone anyways?" she paused. "What does It know of anything, of suffering? Nothing. Because God Itself is suffering...the thing within…time. The cancer even It cannot escape."

She seemed to relish this fact.

"Even God will die alone in Its end, and cannot do anything to stop it. It cannot save Itself against the endless thing that lies beyond…"

She invaded me like our kind did to all that we encountered. The taking of the body, the soul. Her fingers fully into me, searching, prodding, as if inseminating me. My blood was drawn to these places, streaming, pulsing.

She rode me, smothering me, not caring, not giving; only taking her pleasure. A deliberate uncaring taking, a raping of which you cannot keep yourself from wanting. A thing so decadent, so dark, a thing deep within the mind of all things, the most primal of thoughts; to be taken, to submit, or be devoured.

"We are, all of us, a fate set into motion that cannot be undone, unmade, or reborn without consequences…it is the math of it…forever to be alone…all that is made and lives, this unending death march of the body and soul…," she seemed to languish. "To forever be alone. It is as intended, and it cannot be undone…"

She pulled her fingers out of me, roughly, and yanked my legs back down, positioning them so she could mount me, pussy-to-pussy.

I felt the nail-ring again as she ground herself against me. Her smooth sex, seemingly violent in and of its own self, against me.

Opening my eyes, I looked back up at her as I felt surrender wash over my body. Shuddering in that moment, I lost myself to the violence. To be humiliated, oppressed, beaten down; the coming abandonment. To feel the stark contrast of her soft, sweet sex and the violent way in which she used it. And found that I loved her all over again.

"I was here for you, eternal. I could have been that love…," she spoke quietly, sneering.

"It is as all are to me, it is the one truth so painfully revealed. We could have faced it together, but in the end, you, too, are weak," she laughed again.

"Well…," she seemed to grin as she rode me slowly deeply pushing herself down into me. "What is love anyways…but God's failing of the heart."

She snarled looking down upon me with great hate and came upon me in tremendous violence. I felt her sex pump into me, a long, deep thrust downwards. Her body trembled as she came, her hands gripping my breasts. Her sweat poured from her, the beads glistening in the candlelight.

I melted back into her bed, my head falling back. I felt time descend upon me, my body release itself, all inhibitions.

Stoya reached down and ripped away the prosthetic wax-flesh-cover from my neck which had concealed Tyr's mark. She grinned wickedly, knowing that I was all that she had discovered me to be. The betrayer. But I saw in her face, a tear, a glimmer of a truth that lay behind her wicked smile. Self-sacrifice.

Stoya, enrapt in her orgasm, lost to the feeling of my utter submission, lunged instinctually, purposefully upon Tyr's mark and bit down, nearly severing my carotid artery. She sucked hard, grinding her teeth into it. Into me. Taking in my blood, my being within that blood.

I felt her body give as she completely lost herself and came with great force. I felt her lunge into me, her juices, her cum seem to flush into me. The world would hear it, I thought, the beast's conception.

Her hips plunged into me as I yelled out, grasping at her.

I felt her shudder and tremble over and over. I felt her cum seep its way into me, a feeling so sensual. A rare and unique joining of a woman to another woman. She had mated with me, inseminated me in so many ways. And as she fell on me dripping wet with sweat and sex and blood, I took her into my arms, gently holding her. To love her. Keeping her locked within my legs against me tightly, encouraging her to completely drain herself within me.

I wept openly. I felt her breathing, as I lay saturated within her body, soul, and being. The alien cloud tightening around us. Smothering me, crushing me.

"There is nothing sacred left between us now my love…," she whispered gently, scornfully. "My ideal of you lays broken upon my bed!"

"You will be my Judas…her Judas...," she quietly whispered. "You will be the thing that reminds me of how cruel and ugly this all is…God, love, forever. And I will be there laughing at the end of it!"

"You will soon come to understand of what you really are…," she hissed.

"A monster just as I; maybe even more so. You need, and want and take of it all, your personal selfish desires. And yet you think yourself noble in it, deny your real being. You don't understand, or want to understand, that love and the innocent die in the face of us…that you cannot force anything upon forever."

"That Charlotte will lose all that you have come to love in her, her innocence, her fragile human being; the thing that draws you to her so. That she, too, will come to kill as we. She will know of the blood and of the flesh. She will become as me, as you. As you have become this night…"

"The great deceiver. The betrayer. The eternal damnation despite what she is meant to be, what she is meant to do…," she paused, thinking on those things.

"But, I assure you, Charlotte, your love, this thing that you will do, will not go unpunished," Stoya looked at me, her eyes blazing, her face an inch from mine.

"You cannot play God…tamper with the master design. And you cannot trick forever…" she cut herself off, smiling wickedly.

I felt her hand gently caress the side of my face, I saw in her eyes a thing I had not seen before. I shrank from it. And then in my mind, I saw an image. An endless expanse of utter nothingness before me, black and frozen. I was alone, and longed inexplicably.

And I began to weep at the thing in my mind, a whisper, words that had been spoken from out of the darkness, from Stoya's mind and from Charlotte's lips. I cried out, tried to understand them, and then they were gone. Gone before I could even fully grasp them, speak them upon my lips. Only the tinkling of ice remained as the image, the whisper, the words faded from my mind, falling into a great silence.

I felt Stoya's dark alien power, the oppressive aura that had encompassed me, lift from me, pulling upwards into the universe above from whence it came.

I gasped out, suddenly able to breathe again.

Stoya lifted up off of me, standing, then turned to leave smiling wickedly, and all knowing.

"Go now…"

Her words cut.

"It is time!" she smirked looking dead into my eyes with an unrelenting absolution.

"Charlotte awaits the betrayal of her mortal innocence, to know the cruelty of God and the thing beyond all this, the monster that is forever," she whispered, then vanished from me as it had all been nothing more than a distant fading dream.

CHAPTER 42

I was bruised, battered, and bitten. The smell of Stoya and her sex upon me hung in the air uncomfortably. I was exhausted. It took all my strength to board my plane which stood ready, waiting to whisk me to safety, to Paris, France, where E'ban was waiting. I had betrayed Stoya; there was no coming back from that anytime soon.

Mike kneeled before me.

I looked like a whore at church on Sunday morning, having just crawled out from my bed of sin.

He remained silent and did not bother to take my vitals. Sitting down next to me, I lay with my head in his lap as he gently held my upper arm. It's what I needed right then, no judgments, just silent understanding. I am sure he wondered over the mystery of which he now was finding himself in.

"Judas…," I whispered to myself, crying, as I drifted off into a deep sleep. My mind still searching for that word of which Stoya had spoken in my mind.

We arrived in Paris without any problems. My team needed some rest and to switch out planes. Another Bombardier 6000 had been prepped and was ready to go.

Most of my wounds were already healing, only slight scratches and bruises remained. I had to focus on keeping them in that state; visual cues for E'ban and Tyr, the approval from Stoya that put me in high regard for insemination.

Mike seemed to shrug this off, my miraculous healing ability, keeping his silence.

The rest of the team did their best to ignore this strange anomaly also, instead choosing to focus on their one-million-dollar cash bonuses.

Outside on the tarmac, E'ban picked me up gently in his muscular arms holding me, caressing me, loving me.

I was emotionally wrecked by Stoya, by my ugly truth.

He just held onto me telling me that everything was going to be OK. We had little time to be together now, but when this was over, I was coming back with Charlotte, here, to where E'ban would tend to us and only us.

CHAPTER 43

I found myself in E'ban's massive, top floor apartment in the heart of Paris looking out of one of the guest rooms' massive floor-to-ceiling windows, taking in the sight of La Seine River and the Eiffel tower. I smiled at the memories of this place now flooding back to me, and breathed a sigh of relief. Ah Paris!

E'ban's Paris home was located directly on the river just across from the iconic Eiffel tower and the Pont d'Iéna bridge and the surrounding parkways, Paris's foremost meeting grounds for both tourists and Parisians alike, a place where history and romance were born.

I sighed, weeping again at the voice of Stoya, her warnings still echoing in my head.

E'ban had purchased this place in 1910 and held occupancy of the entire top two floors at the north-east corner of the late 1800s apartment complex situated at the vibrant corner of Rue le Nôtre and Avenue de New-York.

Outside, the building's facade held to its quaint elder Parisian charm. But once inside, once in E'ban's quarters, one found a clean, sleek, crisp, modern abode.

Clearly meant to imitate the classic image of the black and white photograph so indicative of Paris's great photographers, his apartment presented a color palette of stark and yet soft analogous gradations of whites, grays, and subtly defying blacks.

Steel, iron, leather, and French quarried marbles formed the grounding upon which a plethora of Parisian furniture and antiques were presented, often boldly and starkly.

As if awaiting some secret French partisan-agent phone call to his handler, an old wrought iron phone booth sat in a far corner. Set alone and illuminated by a soft white light from above, it was wired and still worked.

In the opposite corner, an 1800s aluminum cast, ornate street lamp stood ready to illuminate a large well-worn black leather chair and ottoman with its well-used cushions and rabbit skinned blanket, which sat ready for an easy quiet night of reading and intellectual ponder.

Books of all sorts and sizes, both fictional and fact, lay stacked, piled up along the walls, in the corners, and next to the chair. Newspapers and all manner of editorial magazines accompanied the books.

This was E'ban's reading corner. His chief pastime was education of the mind. It was a fact, that there was little in the way of earthly writing that E'ban had not read. He had a library kept in his lair that would astound modern intellects, or any collector of rare, one-of-a-kind books.

At the center of his main living room, before a large black leather couch, an etched, glass-topped coffee table held stacks of French and Italian photography books and rare signed portfolios. Its legs and supporting body was without a doubt designed in pure Art Nouveau of the highest and most decadent order.

In other parts of his home, more black leather chairs, couches, and love seats sat ready to comfort the weary visitor.

Bathrooms bore classic French-styled tiles and antique wrought iron faucets, towel bars, hooks, and mirrors.

Guest room closets held elegant designer clothes of varying types, sizes, and styles. Their inner drawers held all that is needed to spend a day, a night, a week for any who may find themselves the center of E'ban's exceptional hospitality.

The kitchen, a chef's kitchen, was simple in design and function. Formed of stainless steel, copper, and brass, it always stood ready for the preparation of most any desired meal. Cold decanters containing orange-minted water waited on the counter to quench one's thirst. And of course, champagne remained on ice, always.

Here in this home the romance of Paris, its simple essence, was elevated to the highest order. It celebrated everything so very typical of France, Paris specifically, its rich artistic and culinary history.

Paris was E'ban's city as much as LA and New York were mine. He had fought hard over the centuries to keep it safe from outsiders, to liberate it during World War II, and still works diligently, politically, and socially to keep its vibrancy, the quaintness of it all, its traditions alive today.

As I made my way out into his large living room and kitchen area, I paused to examine the black and white photos that adorned his walls. Many were of Paris by morning, noon, and night, the lights at night in particular, most were by very famous artists.

There were also photos and paintings of Paris's women, E'ban's past wives and girlfriends specifically. Loves both great and small from over the years starting from when the camera was first invented in 1839. Many of the photos had turned to sepia.

These women were smiling contentedly back at me, the look of love upon their faces. They were cared for, catered to, and enjoyed all that love had to offer when in E'ban's life.

I knew the feeling. E'ban was a wonderful soul, a fantastic lover and being in all ways. Like me, he had no cares of what or who, of fat or thin, or of color or not. He cared little of one's elevation, a whore from the street, a princess, or some other woman of high esteem, to him it made no difference. Women were special, on this world in particular, and he prized their company above all else.

But there were portraits of men as well. A few here and there, from over the years, young beautiful handsome men; mostly princes, lords, or other prominent men of political position and power.

But there were also commoners. Soldiers with whom he fought alongside. A Huron warrior from the New World, was one. Together they had fought a silent war against the British during the war for America's Independence. Often alone and deep behind enemy lines, a bond had formed, not out of sexual attraction, that came ultimately later, but out of absolute trust and kindred spirit. He was handsome, a warrior's warrior.

But women, always, remained E'ban's sole passion. We were kindred in that regard.

CHAPTER 44

I felt used and dirty, but could not shower or bathe. I had to keep Tyr and Stoya's scents upon me. The bites, the scratches, the bruises, Stoya's mark, the approval, must remain visible. And that of E'ban's when the time came.

E'ban had taken care to ensure that the tub in my guest bath was filled with hot water so as to provide a bit of revitalizing steam to help me freshened up. He had scented it with rose buds, orange rind, and clove.

It was refreshing, and I felt revived and ready to finally accomplish something E'ban and I had considered for a very long time, making a child that would be of us. A child to love, nurture, and see grow through the eons, to be together as time and our journey allowed.

Charlotte would be our contribution to the universe. And, I was coming to believe, something very special.

E'ban had lunch waiting for me out on his balcony. It had been a while since we had visited with each other, something not unusual for our kind.

We are solitary by nature, prefer to be alone and anonymous save for our lovers, and are content with small circles of trusted friends. And, it was not like anyone of us was going anywhere anytime soon. We were imprisoned on this world due to a lack of materials to construct and power the technology needed to get anywhere else, in any length of time. Such is the vastness of this universe, the distances, the technology needed to surpass it. You have no idea of this, the great unending distances, and I doubt you will ever come to know of it.

Unfortunately, on this re-acquaintance, there would be no going out, no partying as we always had done. This trip was all business. He was going to shelter me from the world for a few short hours and then when I was ready, plant his seed so that Charlotte could have a chance at life.

I had changed into a light summer robe, an antique 1940s Coco Chanel design. E'ban had bought it just for me, for this occasion. A remnant of a rare collection series pulled from the design vaults of her most esteemed family empire for this special night. It was a light silk with a kind of modern Art Nouveau-ish design that swirled across the fabric. It was elegant and ladylike, reminiscent of Paris between the two world wars.

I padded around barefoot looking at his other art collections, paintings, mostly by Monet. But he had a few Nicolas Poussin's, Henry Matisse, Paul Cezanne, and others. Gifts from over the years rather than purposefully collected. E'ban was a patron of the arts and supported some of France's greats.

These paintings were special, most were sketchings of now famous works, of which E'ban had garnered from close personal friends and lovers. These sketches, in truth, were more valuable than the final renderings for these were the raw ideas of the mind, rather than the polished story for public consumption.

I marveled over the rough watercolor and quick oil sketched possibilities of Monet's mind; powerful, sad, and moving. One could trace the oncoming blindness invading his mortal body.

Stoya was in love with Monet. Not so much the body, but the mind, the talent, the ability to see the world as she saw it. I had seen her weep as she watched him paint where the water lilies grew upon the pond. There under the shade trees, through his eyes, she knew she was powerless.

Stoya had always hated the fact that Monet seemed to favor E'ban's company over hers, yet another point of conflict between the two. Just before his death was the last time Stoya and E'ban had seen each other.

But it was E'ban's photographs and paintings of his many loves over the centuries that were his real treasure, his life-long collection; for E'ban had many relationships and many marriages. He took great pleasure in these loves, his sole earthly devotion really.

I teased him always, his penchant for husband-hood. I have watched him for centuries, ever the perfect boyfriend, lover, and husband in life and at time of death. A hopeless romantic, like Stoya.

Funny how they were at such odds, being so bound by that one thing; love.

E'ban ever loyal, ever devoted, did something very special, as each love faded away or passed. He would write a short book about them, a memoir really of their lives, their history, and of their time together. He kept these books and modern-day flash drives, hidden away in his lair deep within the French Alps for safe keeping. For someone to know and read about at some time in the future when he was ready, a time capsule of love and romance of sorts. It was, I think, such a beautiful way to remember the ones you loved. It was a way to keep them alive eternal. A way to keep your human kind eternal.

We sat upon his balcony in the cool, early fall Paris afternoon. I wore a light knitted shawl about my shoulders. Not so much to ward off the cold, but to embrace the memories of Paris, its fashion and way of life even more.

We sat side-by-side taking in all that was Paris. He had prepared a delightful lunch of French ham and pea quiche, light and flaky, buttery, perfect. Only Stoya could have done better. A small spinach and fresh baby green salad accompanied it along with E'ban's famous baguettes and homemade butter. And as always, just for me, a perfect herbed butter Porterhouse just barely seared, thick, red, rare.

For dessert, he had made an orange, vanilla, and cinnamon custard. Light, creamy, delightful. Stoya was jealous of it, E'ban's secret recipe. Another source of great contention. He was a master cook, a master homemaker, a master host, and a master lover and husband.

We sipped at a Bollinger Special Cuvee, light and bubbly, a hint of roasted apple compote and pear fruit tempered with a hint of walnut. It was velvety in texture, but smooth on the teeth and tongue like a soft, white Tahitian pearl. It pared perfectly with both the meal he had prepared and the cool fall Paris day.

I looked at E'ban as he sat daydreaming over the place that he had called home, this apartment that held such great memories. He was, as always, magnificently handsome. I saw the sun reflecting upon his dark, black, ebony body revealing the slight blue that is the color of his deep pure African heritage. He had the perfect smile, warm, smooth, friendly, confident, open to any and all.

He stood tall and proud at 6'3" and walked with great power and poise. Muscular of body, he was clean, slick, devoid of all bodily hair. He, too, had chosen to disconnect that hair follicle gene code. His muscles were large and well formed, tight and rippling, they demonstrated the ability for both great brutality and gentle, protective caring.

I was aroused by him as I looked him over, talked with him, enjoyed the memories of him and our time together as we traveled through time and space, and of our time upon this world thus far.

I pinched playfully at him. His silk Armani T-shirt stretched tightly over his huge iron-like chest and arms. He was so easy, so casual.

E'ban pinched and poked me back. Laughing, poking me in the ticklish spot just under my ribs to the right side of my stomach.

I saw the bulge that was his manhood. It had been a long time since we had connected sexually. I thought of that last encounter, when the century turned to the year 2000, as I looked out over the to the bridge over the Seine not one hundred feet from his balcony. We were so drunk and aroused that night, we couldn't even wait to traverse the last few meters to his apartment and his bed.

We both laughed at ourselves now, at the memory of looking up at his bedroom window as we took each other on the bridge.

My egg began to pain again, begging for sex. It longed for the fight, to be dominated, to make life. I moved in closer to him, submissively pawing at him, he smiled and placed his massive arm around me, collecting me in so that I could nuzzle at him, his neck, his face.

"Let's take this slow," he reassured me.

"We need to wait, Ianthe, it's all about timing; we have until midnight," he spoke gently to me. His slight African accent was such a turn on.

"I want this to succeed. I want this to be special, the start of a new beginning," he trailed off quietly looking away now suddenly verklempt.

I thought of his sentiment, "a new beginning." I knew he was thinking about all of us, about Charlotte whom would be re-born if all went well, of me and Stoya. Of Tyr even, though he did not know of that part of my plan, the execution.

E'ban wanted a family, an eternal family. Something we had never been able to fully cultivate here on this world. The divisions were just too great. He would, I think, even have been willing to completely submit to Tyr for the sake of family, if it could have ever been possible.

I sighed and moved ever closer, deeper into him, tearing. I wanted that so desperately, too; family.

"It's going to happen this time, Ianthe, just take this easy, I want it to be slow, memorable. It's going to happen I am sure of it," he said reassuringly.

He moved in to kiss me, gently, lovingly, as I shrank against him, finding myself in utter love with this man again.

CHAPTER 44

The man before me, E'ban Jabari Magoro and the creature within had a most unusual start on this world. A union born from mortal combat; a fight for the ages, the ultimate contest between two apex predators from two very different worlds.

E'ban, the human, was a warrior and a hunter. His people were of the first Nilotic groups which had begun to inhabit the region of Africa that is now called the Serengeti; southern Kenya and Tanzania. They had called themselves the Masai, or "God's work", in their language. They were proud, fierce, and strong, surviving by hunting, gathering, and herding.

E'ban had found the reptilian-anthropoid beast that had fallen from the stars while on a hunt for a great black lion; one which had taken to eating human flesh and had become a scourge of his land. E'ban had seen the streaking meteorites falling from the stars and crashing down upon the great plain. Curious, he went to investigate to see what his gods had offered, or what calamity might be coming to his tribe and his family.

It took nearly two days of travel to find the place upon where the star rocks of iron-ore and granite obsidian glass fell. It was there, within the nearby scrub, that he had found the strange space-beast laying in ambush, waiting to kill. It was alive and healthy, and ready to fight for its life, its right to survive upon this alien world, to make it its new home.

E'ban was delighted in that meeting, unafraid of the creature before him. To E'ban, it was a beast, a demon to be mastered, destroyed, and displayed. Such was his resoluteness as a warrior. The creature's death would elevate him politically, a kingship possibly, over all his clan, his people.

Without hesitation, E'ban lunged at it laughing and barring his razor-sharp, shark-like teeth; the self-sharpened, hand filed teeth, a self-inflicted rite of passage for the Masai warrior class.

The creature was fast and strong, honed by millions of years of vicious and unforgiving evolution, advantaged by the knowledge of the thing within it also, our species. It was ferocious, out sizing and out weighing E'ban, it towered over him. It reveled in this defiance, the coming fight, and easily absorbed the first blow of E'ban's mighty sand-cast iron spear.

The creature returned the favor reaching out with one of its six arms and swung, easily knocking E'ban down to the ground tearing him open with razor sharp claws.

But E'ban was smart, wise in the ways of the hunt and combat, and recognized many earthly living things in this new beast. Quickly, he scanned the beast's body. It looked as if a lizard to him, and of the dung beetle, and the armored mud dwelling catfish. He knew the weak parts, the chinks in that armor, the neck, and underneath the arms, the soft supple membrane-skin that must exist to affect movement. And he saw, too, of how it moved hyena-like, hunched over with the cunning quickness of the Meerkat or Mongoose. Accounting for all these things, E'ban made ready to strike again.

But the beast from the stars also had knowledge. It knew anatomy by instinct and had vision similar to a thermal imager. It saw the heart, the primary veins and arteries of the body, the weakness of the spine, the ribs, the place up underneath them; a likely place for an instant death blow.

It was the clash of clashes, man against alien super predator. It was fast, brutal, and short. Another victory for our kind really, it would be chance to experience life a s a human.

E'ban's triumph over the beast, its death, was the chance for an evolution of our kind. It would be a chance to become all that is now E'ban Jabari Magoro on this world.

The sun struck its high-noon zenith as the dusts of the Serengeti settled. Flies and other creatures of opportunity descended upon the dying bodies of both man and beast.

But evolution was not going to let death stand in its way. From within the dying space-beast, another creature emerged, that of our kind. Spurned by the mortal blow of which this new, human creature delivered, it fled from its ages old host body and sought a more resilient being, the body of the still barely living E'ban.

It rushed upon him, entering him through the hideous gaping wounds. It flooded this new body, filing it quickly, and sealing the wounds behind it.

By dusk of the following day, E'ban's fellow warriors had found him. They had begun searching for him when he had not returned from his hunt. Barely alive, he was carried back to his village along with the great beast's head, a trophy of battle, an assurance of political elevation.

It took E'ban many weeks to recover from his wounds and for the creature within to assimilate, to awaken from his death-like sleep.

At first E'ban was exalted as a hero. A kingship was in short order. But his strange, new, more powerful body and mind, the voice and the violet eyes, troubled his clan.

Soon, E'ban began to thirst for blood and would often drink fresh, raw blood that he would siphon from his herd of goats. Not an unusual practice in times of starvation and ceremony, but unusual as an everyday occurrence. Then, an even more powerful need consumed him, the desire for fresh, raw, living flesh. Within weeks of his healing, E'ban had begun to consume great quantities of raw, uncooked animal meat, often, devouring entire goats in one sitting.

He began to hunt for larger and larger animals to sate his thirst, his hunger. But this hunger would ultimately demand the flesh of man. We needed to consume the same flesh as our host bodies in order to survive and flourish. A thing E'ban found hard to hide within such a close and tightly knit social structure.

Soon members of other clans began disappearing. Sometimes their bones were found striped clean and piled neatly miles from their village. Other times, there was nothing at all but blood-stained sands.

In time, E'ban became shunned, suspected of these monstrous acts. Cannibalism amongst the Masai rarely occurred, reserved for only the most sacred of ceremonies and was frowned upon by all, even by the witch doctors that partook of it.

He was soon disavowed from his clan, his tribe; his people. He was labeled the Impundulu; the African name for vampire, the death bringer and consumer of living flesh. He became an outcast doomed to wander, always keeping to the shadows of night, to feed upon the African landscape alone and alienated until I found him again.

It was the strange stories of that Impundulu, the flesh-eating man that drew me into middle Africa from my Egyptian home.

I knew of what I had sought. I knew I was not alone. E'ban and I were united after our 100,000-year sleep-voyage through space. A love and friendship from another world renewed again for the ages.

From Africa, we would set out upon this world together to travel and take up residence in fast growing cities of Egypt along the great Nile River in the year 2600 BC. In the beginning of what history knows as the Middle Kingdom.

There, in what soon would become Cairo, I presented myself as a princess from the faraway lands of Aram, what is now Syria. E'ban was introduced as my warrior protector from the lands of Cush, now Ethiopia, Sudan, and Somalia. We would live there in that city, to rise within the political and royal class as esteemed investors, purveyors of water and gold and other precious commodities. Builders of empires that lay at the core of your global order to this day.

We would travel through the centuries of this world, ever moving forward with mankind and its quest for elevation of life and purpose. We were quiet in our existence, going little noticed, save for when Tyr emerged to wage war and when Stoya, our sister, fell here and set about her manipulations and the building of the greatest empire, The Church of Rome.

Europe; France, Italy, and Spain had become our home for many years, well into the early 19th century. Much of our money was made then as we began to trade and invest within the new empires.

When the Dutch and British successfully invaded Africa and began the slaughter and enslavement of the African peoples, E'ban would return periodically to fight them from the shadows of the night, a lone warrior, known only as the Azali Kivuli, or, Eternal Ghost, a name given to him because of his apparent ability to never die despite being wounded on several occasions.

With the European discovery and subsequent colonization of the New World and the ultimate birth of America, slavery found its stride there as well. Torn between the ideals of the new democratic republic and the horrors of human captivity, E'ban and I worked the system.

I would help influence the agenda that was to be a new way of life, freedom and equality for all, while E'ban quietly, secretly constructed the way to freedom for thousands, and ultimately a civil war which would determine a nation's modern history.

By the turn of the 20th century, E'ban had returned to France, traditionally a country which had always exulted freedom and equality for all, here he was at home. He found acceptance and a place within its society. Here he would stay, make his home, and defend it through political upheaval, two world wars, and many other modern day political issues.

Sighing, I stood up and went to the balcony railing to see the streets below, the river Seine, the Eiffel tower and the city of Paris beyond. The sun was beginning to set and cast a light pinkish red hue over everything.

The colors of love, I thought to myself.

"I am coming back with Charlotte, when this is done," I declared to E'ban. "We are going to need you."

E'ban stood and came in behind me to encompass me. I fell back into him, to feel his strength, his love and warmth.

"I await that hour…," he spoke softly. "I am going to love her as my daughter," he said, fully kissing me for the first time, as I turned to look up at him.

I felt his tongue, large and firm, commanding in the art of the kiss, upon mine. It filled my mouth, luxurious, dominating. My knees buckled; weak from the intoxication of this pleasure. He was a master at this.

"We are going to be a family again," he said, lost in the sentimental moment.

"Stoya, too…it is time!"

I looked at him puzzled, thinking of Stoya and Ciosa's words, my own decree; *"It is time."*

"Yes, it is, isn't it?" I whispered back longingly at that thought. "But it will take much time for her…I think. I have crushed her soul."

He smiled gently, sadly at that fact. "That is all we are, Ianthe, time!" E'ban whispered back to me reassuringly. "Time...," he paused.

"Stoya is strong and will rise up again, it is her nature, it is why I love her so."

Tyr had kept us from this, uniting as one as we might be on our own home world.

E'ban smiled knowing we were in agreement; this was going to happen now. It was time.

"Come!" he quietly spoke again, gently pulling back his body suggesting that it was time for our consummation.

It was 9PM when I called my guys at Navigations Air, Mike and the crew, to confirm we were still on schedule.

It was all going to happen fast now. A helicopter was to be dispatched to the open parkway beneath the Eiffel Tower at midnight for my transport to the airport and the Bombardier 6000 and then back to Nepal and Mt. Everest for the final insemination and the death of Tyr.

It was hard to keep control of myself. Hours of talking, the reminiscing of old journeys, and the casual foreplay had me wanting E'ban so much I could hardly breathe. I sweated, burned to have him, to conceive. I cramped, the egg was more than ready now as E'ban lay me down upon his thick quilted, white satin sheeted bed.

This was not the way either of us wanted it, but time was of the essence. And in a flash, I would be off in the last fervid rush to save Charlotte. It would be a marvel of timing, of flying, of everything now, to complete my goal.

The Emerald Inc. hired professional caregiver somberly informed me that Charlotte had at best three to four days.

I was over whelmed. E'ban and I wept at the news.

I trembled, weeping and emotional over all this as E'ban gently kissed me, weeping also in consolation. The air was charged, raw, unyielding, consuming our feelings in the pyre of uncertainty. This was the sum of all things for us, for our kind, this little coven on this little world. I found myself enamored and confused over his seduction, over the underlying feeling that I was somehow betraying Charlotte as she lay dying so far away. I felt guilty as I tried to take comfort in the fact that this was for the better of all things, that this was the only way to save Charlotte.

I laid back to surrender myself to E'ban so that we could surrender ourselves to each other, to love this man, my cosmic best friend. I felt him close in upon me, to make love to me, us together, alone in time, alone in this one sacred thing like we all are in the act of making love.

CHAPTER
46

I lay back fully onto the bed, luxuriating in the cool sheets and the sounds of nighttime Paris as the city began to come alive on the streets below. I saw the reflection of the city lights dance upon the ceiling of E'ban's bedroom. The soft white antique stucco with its Art Nouveau neo-classic soffit molding and Rococo design centerpiece reliefs caught as if dancing in the flickering shadows of the candle-lit antique sconces set to either side of his headboard above the night stands.

I thought of La Bohème, my first date with Charlotte, remembering how she looked that night under the faux candle chandeliers, the red velvet and rich walnut black browns.

I heard voices of lovers, of friends meeting again down on the streets of Paris below through the open window, of life and laughter, and wondered over them, those voices, of what and where they shall go and do tonight? Of who they shall meet and of what romance could be about to bloom.

It brought back memories of long ago, good memories of times when I loved and lusted here in the streets of Paris, of friends and lovers long dead to the ages when Paris was the ideal of an elder Europe.

I took another sip of my Cuvee and let myself slip into the scene of it, of Paris at night, and old-fashioned romance.

Laying side-by-side, naked, I turned and kissed E'ban running my fingers up and over his chest and back down and over onto his back, feeling the muscles of him; tight, defined and massive. E'ban worked out religiously, weights, running, soccer, and a little rugby from time-to-time.

I felt his ass, firm, hard, sexy as hell. I giggled at it, at myself touching it.

He caressed me also. His large hands and strong fingers gently touch me stroking my hair, my face, my shoulders, my breasts, and my stomach. E'ban gently kissed my neck, the spot where Tyr and Stoya had made their marks.

I did not hide the wounds or the marks from him. I bore myself to him in my fullest.

He became erect at that; the scents, the tastes, the visual approvals left from the others. I felt his heart rate increase; his veins swell and pulse across his body. His eyes, the dark violet irises, his pupils dilating, transfixed upon my body. His breathing became heavier, more rapid. He was everything a woman could want, everything I wanted in that moment.

We began to press harder into each other, our passion, our desire, the creature within us both began to need, to consume this sex. I slid my left leg up along his, hooking it over his ass. I felt his stomach, his abs, hard and tight; I touched them, the creases in between, tracing my fingers along the lines circling his belly button, an outie.

I giggled as his stomach flexed inward responding to that sensation. I played with him, poking him, tickling him, teasing him in that way. He responded in kind. We kissed again as I reached down to touch him, his sex, to remember the length and the girth, the firmness of his cock. I cooed, delighted, it seemed to vibrate slightly, to twitch, to jump at my delicate touch.

E'ban was uncircumcised. I teased that now, the foreskin, tugging at it gently, running my finger around it, between the tip and skin eliciting excitement within him. A slight moan of pleasure emanated from within him. I felt a drop of semen emerge and I rubbed it around gently in small circles upon the hole.

We moved even closer into each other, beginning to touch, caress, to grope harder, more ravenously. He slid up partly upon me, his cock just barely touching me upon my clitoris. It teased at me, a suggestion of what was to come.

I moved my right leg up and over his ass fully to lock him in onto me; my foot resting in the small of his back. I felt his weight upon me. My back arching slightly as he began to kiss and suck at my breasts and nipples.

I held him tightly as I ran my hands up and down his back and along his sides to feel the "V" shape of his body. My legs caressed him as I squirmed slightly under him, hooking my legs over his and moving them up and down slowly.

I could remember now; see and feel the first time we made love under the stars upon the bank of the great river Nile, there in the new sand-stone city. I caught the memories from his mind, as he had mine, together to share in that moment, to arouse our lust further.

It had been warm and balmy that night, long ago in the still infant city of Cairo; the heat was saturating, humid, wet, silencing, save for the slight murmurs of family life that went on behind mud-brick walls and thatched doors. It hung on us as we sweated under the endless stars upon the river bank.

I breathed deeply, taking in the scent of E'ban and chuckled lightly, fondly, at our memories. The smell of Old Spice cologne; such a simple inexpensive thing, one of his favorites. He wore it now, his signature scent. It reminded him of the Nile, that night, the spices traded upon the banks, the date-nut and palm trees, and the incense to keep the beastly insects away. Of that night when we first had sex on this world, in our human forms, under the stars on the ancient earthly sands of oldest river in the world; the river that had birthed man.

Back then he used to create his own colognes. A blend of cinnamon, cardamom, vanilla, and other peppery spices mixed into juniper oil, sometimes adding orange or another sweet citrus. I inhaled his natural musk too, just beneath the spice, his human scent, and that of the creature within. The smell of the rose an hour before it begins to die, only, it was lighter in him, as with all males are of our kind. That smell, more-subtle, perhaps more of the stem than actual flower, green, leafy, faded to the nose.

I wiggled around playfully under the pleasure of him, smiling, awakening to the fact that this was going to happen. I tilted my head back so that he could kiss at my neck some more, the mark. I held onto him tighter as he kissed me working his way down to my wet, wanting pussy. I laughed playfully, letting myself forget Charlotte, time, and death, giving way to the sounds of Paris rising into the murmured crescendo of people living life. Of individuals coming together united under the one thing we all have in common, the need to be with others, to live and laugh and love.

I saw, remembered images of a younger Paris, when the streets were still cobbled and narrow, and life, as now, ever in motion. I thought of our old haunts, the bars and adjoining hostels, the numerous brothels. Memories flooded in my mind of those long-past lamp flame and candle lite nights.

Oh, how I missed it sometimes, the elegant, young, hopeful city; the revolutionary spirit, with its aspiring politician-idealists; the princes and princesses, drunk and without care. And, the commoners, the soldiers and sailors; the drunks, the thieves, and the whores. I missed the late-night orgies of endless wine, gambling, and sex. I missed the mad ranting of the poets and the piano-songs of which now great historical musicians had sang and played; the soundtrack to the political and social intrigues of turbulent changing times. I smiled, deeply content at such thoughts, such adventure. The world was finding modernism. And that modernism is now, today, slowly killing it.

I was lost in this moment, in E'ban, as he so expertly began to work my clitoris, his huge tongue lapped and tickled at me. I giggled out at first playfully, then laughed out heartily, and moaned and groaned, and spoke out loud words of sex; commands, instructions, unashamed like in the old days with our favorite mistresses and whore-men, high above in the most expensive boudoirs money could buy.

"Oh, fuck yes! More, harder! Oh! Yes, my love, right there, that's it!" I told him, encouraging him and the memories.

And I began to sense, to see in short, slow sepia and vintage color washed film-like flashes of us; the eternal travelers of time, friends, lovers, partners. I could see us together through the ages, the good times and the bad, the love and the adventures. These shared visions of the mind that were enabled during the heat of things, violence, love, sex, intimacy, exchange of memories and thoughts psychically, emotionally.

Together in one joined thought of our time in the dens of debauchery as we traveled this world, oh, how we loved to party! How the champagne flowed, and the wine drank by the hundreds of bottles. The uninhibited sex and wanton desires we satisfied so very explicitly with ourselves and others. Life was and always had been for us, a grand experiment; an adventure.

I began to pull at him playfully, I wanted him inside me. My egg seemed to swell and toss and turn, aching, wanting, it's needing ever more powerful. I was more than wet. I was flowing, ready to join with him to seize that moment, and take the journey once again.

Letting myself completely go, like back in the boudoirs of old, I shouted out laughing, bucking; rocking as I drug him up upon me with all of my might. Grasping him at the waist with my legs, I reached down and pulled him into me. He was large, wide, it felt wonderful, full, invigorating.

He gasped with great pleasure as he slid all the way into me. Down fully into the bottom of my sex. I was fresh and tight, a virgin from infrequent penetration of that magnitude or any other really.

I laughed playfully, coaxing him verbally. "Oh, fuck...yeah baby, all the way now my love, let me feel it, the pain and that pleasure!"

He looked at me for a moment staring into my eyes. We smiled at each other, and kissed and laughed, for it was a reunion really, a celebration, a confirmation.

I teased at him verbally; "Don't just lay there, love…" I commanded gently. "I want it good, long, and hard!" I gasped laughing again.

"Do you remember Bethany? And Lilly? And Annette? And our young poet, Samuel?" I laughed again, the memory of a summer long ago in the 17th century brothel of Versailles, France. Of our six-way summer days and nights.

"Oh, yes! I do my sweetest Ianthe, oh, yes, the love we shared the six of us!"

E'ban smiled at such fond things, biting and kissing me playfully on the lips and my neck as he began to move in and out of me as I bucked back at him; rocking my hips we soon found our old unison again.

"I want to go back to them…"

His eyes tearing slightly.

"I want to go back and freeze that time, stay there and never leave," he lamented. "It was good days, then, the world was calm enough and optimism out shadowed uncertainty…."

"I know my love, as do I. Come, let us remember them now, that time…!" I trailed off recalling those memories of a better more innocent time.

"Let's pretend we are them and of them, and taking of them!" I moaned. "Know that they are and forever will be of us in memory and spirit!" I gushed with emotion.

"Now fuck me E'ban, like we did then, love me to the fullest, as I love you in the fullest, this thing between you and I, eternal..."

It had been a while since I had been with a man, a man like E'ban. And E'ban was every bit a man, skilled, artful, well versed in the art of sex, in the art fucking.

We could feel ourselves winding up into a rhythm, we looked at the clock upon his night stand, "1115 PM" it read, and thought of the memories of old lover-friends.

Then, looking back to each other, smiling, knowing this was it, the race to the finish. Who would win?

I held onto him tighter as we became more furious. He had saved himself for this night, to make his mark, to prepare for the battle, "the fight" that was going to happen in just a few short desperate hours between his seed, his semen against that of the mighty Tyr's.

As we rocked back and forth together, our hips circular in movement at times, I felt him move in and out of me, filling me to my maximum volume as I clung to him. We were becoming one, our spirit, our souls, our minds. We could see the ages now, a high-speed movie reel of our lives, together and apart from when we were born to this very moment. We understood everything about the other, experiences, feelings, emotions, memories.

We called out, loudly, the sounds of the most passionate and intense sex. Lost in ourselves, the memories of other partners, of long ago loves that we shared. I could feel the waves of lust slowly rise in him as he made his way to cuming.

He could feel me also, bucking, rolling, undulating, my sex gripping upon him. We both could feel the pull of my egg, the imminent release of what we are into each other, his sperm, my egg, both now preparing for the moment when there would be a union. The one moment where upon God would do his most amazing work.

And in that moment as we began to fall into ourselves and the coming orgasm, we saw a vision of Charlotte. She was beautiful, godlike; exquisite. She wore all white, and smiled out upon the universe.

We saw her mouth, the almost whisper of things that only she must know. We longed for it, her mouth; her whispers. Her secrets. To know what was still unknown. I shuddered and came in waves. I tilted my head back to fully reveal my neck, the marks laid bare for E'ban to approve and further activate the process within me. I felt his mouth clamp down upon it, to bite carefully but firmly into my neck.

I was choked, the air unable to pass in or out from his massive mouth. I felt and smelt my blood, the raw flesh. I felt him suck at me, bite me as he came into me. I felt myself clamp down upon him, tighten and hold him there.

He tried his best to keep still and in the right biological position deep inside me. He grunted as I gasped out loudly. I felt him spasm and twitch inside me, releasing everything he had. His seed would have a journey ahead of it. It had to be placed perfectly. He released me from his bite, my blood upon his lips, as he came and came.

I reached down and tugged at him to help him continue. He sweated and grunted, his eyes closed. His teeth gritting as he worked himself to absolute emptiness. The smell of our sex filed the air, musky, sweet, salty, Old Spice cologne, of human man and woman, of the thing deep within. Insemination and conception.

I so wanted him to collapse on me, to be smothered by his magnificent body, to feel him breath heavily, to take in his air, to lay with him for hours, days, weeks. To repeat and repeat what we had just done. I longed for that so intimate of connections; that final thing, the feel of where two are so utterly spent; the melting into one.

I sighed as E'ban ever so carefully removed himself from me. I immediately lifted my hips up as he slid a large down filed pillow under me. He seemed almost ashamed now at the clinical aspects of what was taking place. It was not how it usually happened. Our sex, our kind's sex, would go on and on until all were utterly depleted and conception was identified; the woman and her two male lovers, the others that may have been invited. It was all somehow emotionally distant now, a disappointing, cold reality.

He left the room as I carefully removed the 3M Tegaderm transparent wound dressing from its wrapper. A special bandage meant for burns really, but would perfectly cover my vagina and seal in E'ban's sperm, to keep it in place until the time of Tyr's insemination.

The clock said "1145". E'ban was already ready. He had thrown on a pair of slacks and a soft Armani T-shirt. I quickly slipped into some panties, to help keep the bandage in place, and my dress and shoes. I felt like a cheap bar fling. I knew E'ban felt the same.

I laughed at him, smiling. "Sorry, babe, but ah.... I don't do sleepovers."

"That's OK," he replied pretending to look at his watch then taping it like I should hurry up and go. "I've got another date anyways she'll be here any minute."

Then he rolled his eyes toward the doorway as if saying "Get out!"

We both laughed.

"We're quite the little whores, aren't we?" I said flirtatiously.

We laughed together pronouncing "Ah, Paris!"

It broke the tension.

CHAPTER 47

E'ban's F80 Ferrari limited model concept car came to sudden but graceful stop as my Navigations Air helicopter swooped down and landed upon the open walk of the Pont d'Iéna. Though it was only a ten-minute walk at best from E'ban's apartment, he wanted me to rest and to relax. To avoid too much movement so his seed could set.

As always, Navigations Air was on time and ready to roll.

Mike, my med-tech super hero, opened the door for me and helped me out of E'ban's car.

"Hey you!" I smiled and hugged him tightly finding myself slightly verklempt.

"Hey!" he quietly, coolly greeted back.

"Everything's ready Ms. Gold. Next stop Everest!" he informed me.

Taking my hand, we headed for the awaiting chopper.

E'ban grabbed Mike by the arm, pulled him aside and seemed to hurriedly discuss something.

I saw Mike smile, nodding often, standing tall and bold, like a warrior. When the conversation had concluded Mike gave E'ban the thumbs up. I wondered over what they had said to each other.

Once on the helicopter, Mike would only say that he was ordered to "take good care of you!"

I smiled and leaned against him, happy but exhausted.

"When this is all over Mike," I spoke into the headset. "We're going meet here and have a nice, long lunch and a good, long chat," I said pointing to the Eiffel tower and the world-famous Jules Vern restaurant.

He smiled and replied. "It's a date!"

I thought for a moment then spoke cryptically. "Funny you should say that, Mike."

I already had a good idea of whom I was bringing along with me to meet him. I thought of my good friend Gretchen Brandt as I looked down upon the Paris lights below. Yes, it is time for that also.

Mike couldn't help but look at me, my still bleeding neck, and the fact that it was obvious I had just had sex. The smell, the tussled hair made it obvious.

I smiled back at him coyly, shyly, playfully musing. "What…?"

He looked away quickly, embarrassed.

I took his hand and held it tightly looking back out the helicopter's window as I rocked our clasped hands gently upon his knee.

"I'm so glad you are here with me, Mike, I am not sure I could do this without you."

"Thank you, Ma'am."

"No, really Mike, I promise, I'm going to make it up to you."

He remained silent.

I thought of Gretchen, she was a single mom with a young boy of nine. She had gone through a bitter divorce. Her son was bi-racial; white and African-American. Mike was twice married with two children. His daughter, ten, was also bi-racial. His son, nine, was half white and Asian mix. The first marriage had ended in divorce, the second in a tragic death.

Gretchen and Mike were both alone in this world. It was time to fix that. I knew it would be an instant match.

Gretchen had worked for the German Police as an anti-terrorism specialist, and then worked as a security contractor overseas for two years with GK Sierra and a year with Control Risk group. She had been wounded in the line of duty several times. Tall powerful, thick boned and thick bodied, she was the best of all that a good German woman had to offer.

She was one of the few women to participate in the European Society for Creative Anachronism, full armored combat circuit. She won against men often. Her weapon of choice was the Grosse Messer, the German hand and a half sword, weapon of choice for its world class mercenaries of the Medieval period of which she was from a long, long line. She had always been very, very proud of that fact, embracing that lifestyle. They were going to have much in common. I knew lasting love would bloom.

"Yeah, when this is done, Mike…" I trailed off, thinking of Charlotte, of our coming new life together. Of E'ban, and Stoya, our coming resurrected family, and of friends that we are going to take care of when we are strong again.

"And oh, I almost forgot, you had better brush up on prenatal care right quick!"

I turned suddenly to him.

"I'm going to be pregnant soon," I announced, smiling.

I busted out laughing at the look on his face. And could not resist what I said next.

"And by the way, it's going to be a girl, a full-grown woman actually!"

I watched Mike's head sink. "Fuck!"

I'm sure what he was thinking. "I knew I should have opted for a tour in Afghanistan flying US Army generals through the Hindu Kush."

CHAPTER 48

The flight into Lukla Tenzig-Hillary airport just 23 miles NE from the international base camp of Mt. Everest was horrific. There was a storm moving in fast. This type of weather was normal for any time of the year, especially in September when weather systems are fighting over the transition from summer to winter.

The plane bumped and rocked and went up and down, ascending and descending by fifty feet or more. Our landing was harrowing, death defying, to say the least. My short nails clawed into the seat arm rests as we slid almost fully sideways upon the sleet and ice down the length of the 460 Meter uphill runway.

My species does not have bowl movements like what humans do; we tend to burn off all of what we eat. But I will say this, I almost had one by the time we came to a complete stop.

We all laughed apprehensively, when Mike shouted out to our aircraft captain. "Fuck dude, why stop now, I can see the bar, it's just three more feet that way!" he said as he pointed to the building's window of which the nose of the plane had actually tapped and fractured.

But it wasn't over yet. It was going to get worse. God was just getting started. We were behind schedule by several hours. Time was running out fast for this leg of my journey.

We readied for our helicopter flight up to base camp. It was beginning to fully blizzard now. I saw my pilots cross-themselves and make some last-minute phone calls to their wives.

Mike, and our former CIA cross-border facilitator extraordinaire John, had come up with a somewhat horrifying solution. We were going to fly up into base camp, and then beyond to the far side of the Khumbu ice flow, where we were going to set down near the entrance to Tyr's lair only a few hundred feet beyond. It was the only way to save time now, to avoid an impossible trek by foot.

"You're fucking kidding me, right?" I gasped out.

Mike laughed. "Welcome to this side of crazy, ma'am."

"But…"

"We've got a tiny window Ms. Gold, if you want this it's now or never…," John spoke, hoping I would change my mind on this.

"But you have just one catch, I'm going with you!" Mike chimed in.

I went to speak, to tell him no way but I was met with sudden insubordination.

"Shush! My way or no way!" Mike scolded me firmly.

I leaned back, shocked at this sudden retaliation of sorts against my wishes. I squirmed, I knew the consequences.

"Just need to know one thing ma'am. Are you up to this?" Mike grinned thinking, no doubt, about my apparent pregnancy joke.

I thought of time now, and suddenly found there was none. It had taken over twenty hours to get back here. There was no timelessness in that moment, no putting it off, anything. Time was short, moments are fleeting. I felt Mike firmly grasp my knee.

"It's time to shit or get of the pot, ma'am," he paused. "I say its time take that leap of faith."

He smiled reassuringly.

"I am here, ain't nothing gonna' happen to you, I made that promise…," he trailed off looking away suddenly.

I thought of the words exchanged between E'ban and Mike at the Pont d'Iéna parkway.

"Besides," he paused looking at me long and hard. "Charlotte is counting on you, you made a promise to her, and I'm not going to let you fuck that up!"

I gasped, surprised again. How did he know? I broke out almost crying at his words.

Mike reached out and took my hand as I balked. He was tall and powerful, and ready to face the gates of hell, death, anything to see this mission through.

"Let's go!" he commanded.

"It's time to make that jump!" he said as I moved forward and gathered myself together.

"Besides Ms. Gold, it would be an epic day to die!" he spoke with confidence waving out at the blistering white ice storm about us.

"An epic day!"

I saw John's head sink down. This was not in his realm of things. He had been a CIA analyst, a station chief, not an "operator" like Mike. He did not have that particular attitude towards life or dangerous situations as Mike did.

Mike had seen the worst the world could offer. Picked up the pieces of fallen friends, literally, and carried on "into the breach" as it is known in his world. He had almost died several times, the "Unclassified" portion of his military record showing no less than eight Purple Hearts and two Bronze Stars.

Though I am not afraid of death per se, I have never enjoyed the part of it as it is about to happen, the dying of my host body. It's often painful, not in feeling always, but in the detachment of it. Death of the body is a lonely thing, cold and unforgiving no matter how gentle it may be. There in that time is the realization that one is truly alone and God, often, cannot be found. I shuddered at that prospect, about being trapped on the ice and the cold end of it for my human body.

I clenched the hand rails of my seat as the Navigations Air chopper bumped and swerved its way up to base camp and the Khumbu ice field beyond; a feat of masterful flying. It was white out conditions. The windows frosted over save for a small opening that my pilots had. It was freezing inside. They both had their door windows folded down and open attempting to get better views so as not to crash.

I marveled at the skill and bravery of my pilots. They were Navigations Air's best. The Chief Pilot had actually flown one of the then 'Top-Secret" helicopters that were used in the Osama bin Laden raid in 2011; the one that did not fail and crash.

I listened as Mike and John lambasted our intrepid pilots at every yank and bank. "Damn it "slick" do you fly like this on the raid?" Mike shouted, ridiculing our Chief Pilot.

In return, the pilots shot back dirty remarks about Mike being a dumb-ass "pretty boy Delta-fuck" and "sorry, Delta couldn't make the grade bro!"

In John's case, they referred to him as the "Bourgeois intel-retarded station chief, who read *Time* and *Bloomberg* magazines for his intel."

It was hard not to be strangely comforted over this abusive yet loving post-military camaraderie, these brave men who knew no such thing as "it can't be done".

Navigations Air and Emerald Inc. advertised the best of the best. I knew now I had invested wisely in that business plan.

I looked up at the great mountain of wintery death, to God beyond and thanked It. That It had seen fit to supply me with some pretty awesome company, soon to be new and most trusted friends after this crazy journey of mine.

I tried to hide my womb-pains from Mike that by now were almost searing. It knew of the second mating to come. My egg wanted to fight and submit, to be fulfilled, completed, and to achieve evolution.

Mike held onto my knee tightly as we made our final approach onto the ice flow below us. The helicopter bounced and jumped in the wind driven air.

"When we get off the chopper, get on the ground, go prone just in case," he paused, and then made a whirling gesture with his finger and thumbs down motion, indicating the possibility of a crash occurring during the de-boarding process.

"Once on location and on the ground, you do your thing, but make it fast; I doubt this storm is going to get any better," Mike confirmed. "I will be tracking the storm via my computer and radio."

I smiled and grabbed his knee. "I couldn't have better company." I spoke looking deep into his eyes.

The helicopter hit the deck hard and skidded across the ice for at least fifty feet before stopping.

Mike threw out his pack then exited quickly pulling me behind him forcefully, unflinchingly.

John, with his snow boot on my ass, quite literally, kicked me out as Mike pulled at me and shut the door behind us.

I was coated in ice and snow instantly, both from the storm and the rotor wash. I fell into the icy snow with Mike on top of me to protect me, as the chopper took off yanking back up and sharply to the side then made its way back down into the valley.

Mike pulled me up and slung his pack onto his back as we made our way to the massive snow, ice-covered boulders and the entrance to Tyr's lair.

I tried to hide my super human abilities from Mike as he pulled me along in urgency to get into some cover. I really just wanted to pick him up and carry him while running at full speed.

Once inside the entrance, Mike dusted me off and made sure I was "all secure" and ready to do my thing. He looked up into the black hand-hewn stairwell that wound its way up into oblivion. I watch him shake his head, seeming to already try to find a way to disbelieve what he was seeing.

"OK Ms. Gold…," Mike spoke firmly. "Make it fuckin' quick, we ain't got long before hell freezes completely over," he said firmly.

Ice hung off his frozen face and beard.

I smiled and gave him a big hug and a kiss. Then spoke with a conviction that he was not expecting.

"No matter what, do not go up there, Mike, I am begging you!" I lamented. "There is something very dangerous here. Something I hope soon no one will ever have to know of again...," I paused.

"Here, Mike, there are monsters. Up there is the death of worlds. Please, I am begging you!"

Mike took me seriously; he knew the tone, nodding his head in acknowledgement. Still in disbelief of this fantasy he found himself in now.

"In time, I will tell you of this, but not now; this is our eternal secret, OK?"

Mike smiled again and shook his head. "Yes, Ms. Gold, but I doubt anyone would ever believe me anyways!" he paused to look back up into the staircase hesitantly.

"Now go! Be quick, Charlotte is waiting."

Encouraged, uplifted, and supported, I sprang forth up and into the darkness that was Tyr's icy lair.

I thanked God for humans such as Mike, men who would go willingly into death for the sake of another. This, I thought, is why I fell here, to this world, so that I can cherish him, exalt him, and remember him through the echoes of time.

CHAPTER 49

My watch beeped as I entered the great chamber of Tyr. It was the countdown I had set to keep me moving forward and to mark my steps as I moved through these next series of events, and to track and manage my coming pregnancy and the subsequent birth. It also marked the last few hours of Charlotte's human life.

I shook. I was terrified for I was alone in this now, to suffer and most likely die at the hands of Tyr.

Tyr lay silent upon his great stone bed, unmoved, unchanged. I was relieved. Perhaps he had not fully understood what had happened to him only three short days ago, a dream to him perhaps, one of many in the endless dream.

I produced a syringe and quickly injected Tyr with its clear, cold substance. A concoction Mike had made up for me. A tranquilizer mostly, but with some other things like sodium pentothal and a minuscule dose of Viagra just to ensure an erection.

The look on Mike's face over my request, the chemical cocktail, the Viagra portion, was priceless.

I needed Tyr alert enough to be able to have sex, but docile enough to give me a chance if things turned violent. I had identified the sword I could use if things took a bad turn, an ancient rune-engraved Viking sword of normal human proportions. I thought of Gretchen, she would have killed for it to add to her collection.

Tyr stirred a bit from the injection. Sighing out and moving a bit upon his great bed of oil-black granite.

I removed my clothes. I had little on under my down-filled snow leopard coat. Nothing more than a pair of Kühl fleece-lined leggings, a long-sleeved top, and my rabbit fur lined Sorrel Tofino boots equipped with mini screw-in ice spikes.

I stood naked before Tyr in the icy air. I began to shiver again, to tremble. More from the sudden onset of yearning to mate with this being, a god of our kind, than from the fear of him. I climbed up onto him. I nuzzled at him, submissively, demurely; it was instinct taking over, the wanting of the creature, the so very alien woman within.

I removed the 3M Tegaderm dressing that covered my vagina and stuck it on the inside of my left thigh. I would need it later, to keep the semen in until I knew the sperm and egg had taken. Until I knew conception was complete.

I held him, soothed him, careful to let my clitoris gently rub upon the end of his manhood. I shuddered at the cold of his platinum cock-ring piercing, the thought of it and his enormity inside of me.

I thought of Stoya, too, and her torturous nail-ring, my innocent gift that she bore upon her sex, her womanhood.

I moved closer to his face, biting at him gently as I went along his chest and about his neck. Bites of submission, appeasement, to call into action his desire to breed. I moved up to his face let him smell at my neck; my scent and that of the others, to let his lips feel and taste of the marks, the approvals of E'ban and Stoya.

It was risky, he knew the smell of E'ban, I worried that I could anger him, awaken him.

He murmured something and moved slightly. I felt him becoming erect at Stoya's scent. The smell of another female's approval of me. I slid up to move myself forward and near his face so that he could smell my sex and the scent of Stoya and of E'ban's seed. I was wet and dripped from want.

He moved again and tried to open his eyes, but the dream, the great sleep, and the drugs were hard to emerge from.

"Shhh...," I whispered to him as my heart raced with fear. "I am here now, your great earthly want, ready for you, my love. The child will be great and powerful!" I purred. "Our child will level this world, this solar system."

I hissed assuring Tyr that this would be our legacy, his legacy. "Even if you cannot awaken, your name will be soon known!"

"I tire of this life and want now to be a queen. To ensure our houses, our families are known again as they once were on our world, in our galaxy," I said to him as I caressed him.

"Stoya, also, will rule with us...she will raise an army the world has never seen, kill millions as you feed on their flesh. And she will be my lover, your lover, she will submit for you, for me, for our kind...she has approved of me, this mating..."

He murmured something inaudible in our spoken language, of what I could not tell.

"Shhh...take me now, we will be gods of gods to rule and destroy this world and many others. We'll drain it and eat of its flesh. E'ban will serve also, he will be yours as you please, your lover. He has submitted to me, my will, feel him in me now, the seed, your seed. We will love you so, and will abide by your every wish. We will all rise and kill the elder gods, God Itself...," I said, pausing.

"We are the last of our kind, we must rise and rebuild anew," I spoke confidently, a lie to save myself, the others, human kind.

He murmured something again, moved but did not wake. I slid back down along his chest turning so that I could kiss his massive cock, to tease it with my tongue, to ensure its wetness for me. To taste the cum that even now began to find its way out, looking for my egg. He groaned as I gently stroked him, wetted him, prepared him.

I played with him. I wanted this to be quick. It had been a very long time since he had last had sex. Five centuries at least, I was sure. I felt him begin to twitch, to thicken and well quickly. I saw his testicles ascend slightly upward; his pelvic muscles undulate as the semen mixed within him.

When I was certain he was close to orgasm, I slowly lowered myself onto him as much as I could bear. I felt his massiveness fill me, stretching me as I winced and gritted my teeth. I felt the platinum ring inside of me. I could not help but to shudder at this sensation, the pain, the searing coldness of it, the grating metal within seem to claw at me. I could feel his cum begin to seep as I started to ride him slowly at first then faster in a long, slow rhythm.

I clawed at his mighty chest, the message to a world; "*Succumb, for I am the death of Life.*"

"Fill me…," I spoke quietly. "Let me know that you are my god, our god, the child will be great, and we will rule this universe and beyond." I assured him again.

I continued to ride him, to push down upon him. I began to lose myself to his sex as I pushed myself ever more at each decent upon him. I felt myself delighted despite the pain. A new-found hedonistic pleasure of which I had not experienced before in this body.

My hips began to undulate, to savor the intensity. I wished his hands upon me, my breasts, my ass. Wanting him to touch me back, pull at my hair, to ravage me. I found myself falling to another place; the power of Tyr's sex over the human body, over our kind.

I wanted to take all of him, to please him in entirety. To be utterly filled by him. I felt his piercing begin to heat within me. Its wet metal upon the place that elicits the highest arousal. It moved, rubbing, grating there. I thrust ever harder upon him, driving myself mercilessly down upon him. The sensation quickly eliciting climax.

And in the heat of sex, I began to pull from his mind, the great dream of which he was within. I saw, then began to feel the sands of time descend upon me. It was black, fine, soft, and velvety, an endless void. It began to envelope me, move through me as if I was no longer there in physical body.

It was as if I was falling through it, or rising up through it, of which I did not know. There is no true up or down or left or right there, nor any other orientation when in the clutches of time. Just a void of moving particles, a sand of sorts, if it was a sand at all. A molecule of some unidentified thing which seemed to move ever faster toward something, a black hole, a void of eternal emptiness, the end of time itself perhaps. This was the great sleep, the place where all is as death. Time the only living thing left in motion, if time is a living thing.

Then, there was beyond this great emptiness, in the distance a light, a great white burning light, pure and blinding, isolated in the black upon an endless horizon of absolute desolation. It radiated, scorching just above. It drew all things to it. And from it I saw the things that it had made even before our kind ever existed. Elder things, most of which I cannot explain. Things living yet so long dead in an eternal nothing, floating there waiting, forever waiting.

And then It made a solar system, a world, a new form of eco system, a new way of being. I saw my world, dark, exotic, alien. I saw the things upon it, the writhing amoebas; the sketch-like experimental models of things yet to come. So, great where they; beautiful, perfect, it was God's first attempt at things of the flesh.

And there, in the water, I saw the rise of us, our kind; the great consumers. And then of other great beasts and beings, and found that I knew what they knew, saw what they saw, and realized suddenly that this was Tyr's memories, his rise from the sea, his journey of evolution and his inhabitation of other beings.

And then I saw them, the Angels of which they called themselves, those who were perfect. They were radiant, the highest order of flesh-spirit from upon our world. So very human in form, like you are. Majestic they were, as we fell about them in awe and love. For they were of God's eyes, the favored ones, or so we believed. But they were not immortal, not forever as we are until we made them so.

It was the love of them, to be as them, in the same form as them, that drove us to inhabit them, to turn them into us, our kind.

I saw that first ascension, the first inhabitation. Tyr had taken one, the first of our kind to do so, drained it and filled it and became as one of them. It was a magnificent evolution, the joining of two most perfect beings, the Nephilim, as it is known to us.

I began to feel Tyr move under me, to feel him twitch inside of me. He was going to cum as I writhed upon him, lost in his memory. I closed my eyes again to search for other visions of his memory.

I saw a great space craft, intricate, glimmering like a pale star, it bended space to move the great distances of which man will never understand exists, or ever experience. And I saw the worlds of which he visited before he had fallen here, strange violent exotic worlds with beings so inconceivable, even to me.

I saw his lovers, great and beautiful in every way. I saw myself, the way he saw me, I was splendid, godlike; a dream in the great burning light. And then, I knew these things were what Tyr wanted me to see. I looked down and found that he was fully awake and knowing, an evil smirk upon his face.

I watched as he reached up to me as if in slow motion and then felt his mighty hand crush around my neck. In a feat of unearthly agility, I found myself flipped onto my back upon his cold, granite stone bed. Tyr was on top of me grinning down upon me, intently silent save for his steady meditated breathing.

I felt him push deep into me with his cock without any mercy, pushing, tearing, and release his sperm. The sensation made my body shuddered and climax as I felt my life being crushed. He squeezed at my neck shutting off the air. I felt faint, frightened.

I thought of the irony. At how I tried so hard to make my kills pleasurable, the use of strangulation often, but in truth, for my victims, it was horrifying and humiliating. An event filled with fear, uncertainty, and emotional, if not physical pain.

I was remorseful for my victims in my own moment of imminent death as the velvety black sands of time and Tyr's life-images slipped away from me. I found myself falling, sinking through space. I had the sensation of falling ever falling through the sands of time. Into the black endless hole at the end of life.

I felt Tyr and E'ban's sperm begin their war within me, swirling, fighting, and preparing for the final union. A conception already consigned to end as quickly as it began.

I thought of Charlotte, my promise that would go unfulfilled, fated like my love upon the ice before.

I felt Tyr push down into me with all his might, his hand close around my neck, his sex pushing ever deeper into me, impaling me. I was helpless. I felt the sands of time begin to fall through me faster and faster. A strange rush of electricity maybe, a negative charge through my body, my soul being drawn out of it. Then, my vision went black.

As I slipped down into my death, I became aware of a sound; a cataclysm that rang out, echoing. The thunder of what I was certain to be the end. A calling, perhaps, the summoning of God. The summoning of the soul perhaps back to It, to be reabsorbed by It into the forever.

Again, and again it rang out. I was aware of something wet. Blood, I think, splattered across my face and upon the walls of Tyr's frozen lair. Another volley rang out, the summoning of an apocalypse. It echoed, deafening me.

CHAPTER 50

I saw Tyr rise up, clutching at his chest. The blood poured out as he yelled out in a great fury. I saw the thing that is us, its blood mixed with the human blood, becoming as one. The other receding back already regrouping beginning the healing process of its host body. Collecting itself to form anew.

I felt my chance to live again return as Tyr turned his attention to this thing now calling out in defiance to him. Gasping, returning from the brink, I gathered up all of my strength. I moved, stumbling off of the great stone bed in one last effort to survive, that which is within working fast to heal my human body, to recover from near death.

I moved to the Viking sword I knew I could wield. I had rehearsed this in my mind, over and over. I sputtered and wheezed, struggling to breath.

Taking up the sword, finding my courage, I lashed out blindly with what little skill in the arts of war I had, and slit Tyr's neck open as he was turning to stand and face this new violator of his realm.

It was then that I saw Mike. He trembled at Tyr's might, his god-like wrath, for what thing on earth can absorb such wounds as he had inflicted? But Mike was strong also, honed by decades at war and a never-ending cycle of training. He did not know how to lose, to fail, to give up, to retreat. He would stand his ground despite the insurmountable odds before him.

I watched as he gripped his weapon tighter, bore down upon it, sighting it. Aligning, re-readying his modern assault rifle, leveling it fast and true, and made ready for another round of attack.

He moved, hunched over slightly, stealthy, like a great cat, moving rapidly, diagonally to align himself for the best shots, and to avoid any counter attack.

I had never seen a human so determined in the face of such overwhelming consequence. It was the face of certainty in the sea of chaos of war. Like the knights of the Middle Ages upon their steeds into the charge, as the soldiers at Verdun and Normandy running into certain death, he moved, determined that I would survive.

Mike seemed to stagger; however, and move with difficulty, utterly exhausted, winded; depleted of all oxygen from the harrowing climb of the stairs below us. He fired again, three more rounds of .50 caliber Beowulf hollow points, the bullets ripping through Tyr's stomach and chest.

Tyr called out in an ancient Nosferatuin war cry. An old language that was seldom spoken even on my home world. I saw him move forward and reach for his most powerful earthly weapon, his great war hammer. Taking it up he seemed to almost grow. His pride, his honor, his very earthly being entwined with his horrible weapon. With it on this world, he had never been defeated. And he was certain of victory now.

I knew that if I did not act Mike would die. For all his courage, he was no match for Tyr. I breathed deep and lunged forth into Tyr again plunging the blade into his back where his human heart was. I pulled the blade out again, and thrust for the spine. I heard it crack, grate, and pop. The tip of my sword broke off in him.

Tyr turned on me and swung with his hammer.

I ducked and struck at him again piercing his right side in-between the fifth and sixth rib, into the lung.

He scowled, howling out like a mad, wounded beast. But he was fast in recovery, a master of war-craft. Swinging his hammer again he caught me, smashing into my chest, sending me hurling through the air into the far side of his lair and against the wall.

Instinctively, I curled up to protect my womb and the child within. The conception, I instinctively knew, was being completed.

I saw Mike move to fire on Tyr again. Angling, vectoring, hunched over, and moving, his training taking over completely. He was hardwired to protect me, his charge. To die with his weapon in his hands if need be.

But his weapon malfunctioned suddenly, and fear caught hold of him. There was little option as he struggled to get it working again. Attempting to clear a jammed shell casing from the breech, I heard him mumble something to himself. To scorn himself over this mishap.

He moved, trying to guard himself with his jammed rifle as Tyr swung at him with his mighty fist which caught him, sending Mike crashing backwards onto the hard granite floor.

Mike's weapon skittered across the hard stone, the magazine dropped out and slammed down upon the floor; its baseplate popping open as the remaining three rounds sprung out of it bouncing and separating in three completely different directions, rolling away from any hope of ever being used to end this fight.

I heard Mike grunt from the pain as he tried to scramble for safety, reaching for his secondary weapon, a pistol, from inside of his jacket.

But Tyr was upon him, caught him and lifted him up by the throat as Mikes pistol fell out of his hand.

Mike instinctively attempted to deny the full closing about his neck by Tyr's hand, producing a small combat type folding knife and slicing at Tyr's wrist.

I cried out and tried to stand up feeling again for the Viking sword that I had dropped.

I saw Tyr smile wickedly and begin to open his mouth.

"Fight!" was all I could utter to Mike. "Fight!"

I saw Mike struggle as he was losing consciousness, dropping his knife. He had tried to apply some sort of martial art pressure point technique upon Tyr's wrist as a last-ditch effort, but to no avail.

Tyr was just too powerful.

I lunged at Tyr only to be stuck down again, crumpling upon the ice-cold floor.

Tyr turned his attention back to Mike and began to laugh at him.

"Insignificant!" Tyr hissed. "Worthless evolution!" he laughed wickedly.

"I am your God…," he spoke again, his voice echoing throughout the chamber and down into the stairwell below.

"This is my world!" Tyr scorned again. "Monkey!" he laughed.

I heard Mike rasp back. "Fuck, fuck you...asshole!" he said as he squirmed trying to kick at Tyr and then passed out from the crushing upon his neck from Tyr's hand.

"This is what I do to worlds!" Tyr proclaimed, turning to me as he opened his mouth again to devour my friend and companion on this journey.

"This is what I will do to you, to E'ban, to Stoya…and the child within you!" he condemned me.

"Betrayers!" he spoke of us.

His very voice made me weak, fearful, submissive as it thundered.

I coward before him. Unable to act further.

"I have been betrayed by my own kind. You will all suffer the consequences. This world will suffer your treachery."

"No!"

I rose up determined.

"NO!" I screamed.

I found the strength, despite my injuries, to move forward to raise my sword and strike again.

But God, fate, or something even greater, it seemed, had other plans that day.

CHAPTER 51

"Today old gods die!"

I heard a familiar voice echo forth from the doorway.

"Today, I will claim your place!" it said again. "As I have said that I would of you, so long ago…"

From out of the dark stairwell emerged E'ban in all his glory.

He snarled, saliva spitted out from him. His sharp Masai warrior, shark-like teeth now revealed and gleamed open and ready for an attack. He was almost naked save for the pair of tight, tan adventure shorts he always wore when on a hunt. And he carried with him his great sand-cast iron spear of which he had hunted with for centuries, the spear that killed the beast from the stars so very long ago; the spear that sealed his own human destiny.

Tyr threw Mike down and quickly moved, striking at E'ban with his war hammer howling in anger at this intrusion of intrusions. Tyr's eyes blazed as he screamed out to E'ban.

"Know my power over you. Know that you will be the one who dies this day!" Tyr commanded of E'ban as they faced off with each other.

"That of which is of no house, no rights." Tyr ridiculed E'ban. "That which has mated and defiled our God seed, this slut of which you so hold dear…"

"You who should not have been born…," Tyr insulted again.

"I will kill your love, Ianthe, and your child, devour them for their power," Tyr hissed again. "You will watch as you lay broken!"

E'ban remained silent, focused, and lunged upon Tyr driving his great spear into him with such speed and force that it lifted Tyr off the floor for a brief moment.

E'ban twisted his spear-blade then pushed upwards and pulling out in a cutting fashion splitting open Tyr's stomach and chest.

I heard the shuck-shuck sound of his spear, the ripping of flesh and bone, the sound of air being released from inside the body.

Blood poured out of Tyr. His human insides bulged and began to drop out upon the ground, and so too the creature within, mingled, swirling as it attempted to swim against the current of blood and gore, to stay reunited with its own self.

Tyr looked astonished for a moment, wavered, then lunged at E'ban, screaming with anger.

But E'ban was quick and skilled, honed by centuries of hunting the most wild and dangerous of beasts. Swinging his great spear as if a sword, I heard a loud ripping slicing sound as Tyr's severed head went flying across his lair and into the far corner.

I rose to my feet; I could feel the process of the embryonic chemical construction rapidly excel within me. I staggered, holding my stomach, smiled down at it knowing in that second that Charlotte was going to have a chance to live.

I saw Tyr's eyes still watching us, the absolute hate and malice burned through my soul even in his death. His giant mouth seemed to scowl, to condemn us even then, our insignificance to him. But it was a temporary win.

As E'ban and I tried to recover ourselves, the creature within Tyr sought to rejoin its body in an effort to heal and resume the fight.

"Quick!" E'ban commanded me as he took up Tyr's massive human body, holding it up for me.

"Take him, consume him, his power!" his voice echoed, rumbling within the stone walls.

I saw Mike hunched against the wall, terrified at all that he had witnessed.

He saw the blood and insides of Tyr swirl like a mass of writhing worms, tentacles perhaps, so alien, wriggling, seething, seeking their way back into Tyr's human flesh. Blood-red-violet, they streamed, slithered back crawling up into him, even now the corpse seeming to reanimate, to twitch and move.

"Take of him! Now!" E'ban commanded of me again, desperate, holding onto a long creeping violet tentacle, trying to make its way to Tyr's head.

"For Charlotte!"

I saw the glowing violet amoeba that was Tyr's real self begin to gather itself up inside, to grow and become its true form again, to rise up against us. It would be almost unstoppable if it could do that, a force and thing so terrifying.

And when it was done with us, it would take Mike, inhabit him and return to its human splendor. It's inhuman power. It would become Tyr again, and want to finish its task, to live and to destroy this world.

I thought of Stoya, she would welcome this thing, destruction, and revel in the wars to come, and the never-ending blood. I shuddered at the power they would have over this world's fate.

E'ban stood tall, powerful; sweating as he held up Tyr's corpse.

"Take him, Charlotte must be strong!" he commanded again with urgency.

I moved to him, to Tyr. Standing before the headless corpse I saw the amoeba within swirl and gather itself. I saw the memories of us in it again and felt the black falling sand of time.

I opened my mouth and began to suck at the great corpse of Tyr. To take in and consume the creature within, the thing which had become of the blood and flesh. All that was the being that is and was the earthly being, Tyr.

I felt it pull back from me as I swallowed it down into myself. It was sweet like some form of condensed rose water, a milk possibly, sticky like some strange and alien honey. I reached for it and gathered it up as it desperately clung to the body it had known for 200,000 years. It shrieked and cursed in our language, the alien word-songs that are our natural voice.

I saw Mike cower in absolute terror at this so unearthly sight. His eyes wide and lost in absolute disbelief, a horror he could never have guessed at.

It was then he knew my words; "here there are monsters..."

It was in that moment that he fully came to understand that he, his insignificant human race, was far from being alone in this universe and beyond.

E'ban held Tyr up higher, his mouth opening also. He was going to consume the flesh, the blood. There was residual power left, the physical remnants of the connections our kind creates to inhabit bodies not of our own.

I heard the ripping and cracking sound of skin, muscle, and bone. The smell of torn raw flesh filled the air as the last of Tyr's inner being slipped down my throat and into my stomach where its power would be reborn.

Stepping back, I watched for a moment as E'ban began to devour Tyr's earthly body.

I saw Mike turn white and to gag at the sight before him. This thing, cannibalism, the eaters and the eaten.

I felt the warmth grow within me then a burning heat. It was Tyr's essence, his being. I was absorbing it, him into me. My injuries began to heal, and I felt the child within me grow.

E'ban smiled, instinctively knowing that the conception was complete and going to take form.

"Go now!" E'ban spoke quietly. "Take Mike and go!" he commanded.

"I must complete this and I will erase all memory of Tyr and this place," he spoke almost mournfully, respectfully.

"Go now! Hurry!"

I nodded and turned my attention to Mike. I began to weep at the sight of him; my broken human hero.

He looked up at me, unable to speak from the horror he had witnessed, astounded by my presence.

I was naked. I shone upon him, radiating a soft healthy violet light. I was warm to the touch, heating his body slightly.

He saw the bump that was already beginning to show upon my stomach, the coming miracle.

I smiled down at him as I knelt down and took his hand. I warmed it, his blood within, soothed him and pulled him up to his feet.

"Come, Mike…we must go!" I spoke gently.

"Do not watch...this…," I spoke again, persuading Mike to look away from the feast that was now occurring before him.

"Come!"

I pulled at him, down and into the stairwell.

"Hurry, Charlotte is waiting!"

"Your future, our friendship, is waiting!"

CHAPTER 52

Once in the entranceway at the bottom of Tyr's lair, we found the wrath of God and Mother Nature raging outside. An absolute torrent of pure white hell.

Mike slumped over and fell down against the wall, injured and utterly spent.

I suspected he was suffering from hypobaropathy, edema, from his rapid ascent and descent within the mountain.

I radioed John for our helicopter.

Static competed with his simple devastating message. "We can't, there's no way, the mountain is gone!"

I knew what he meant, a total whiteout. There was no way they could get to us even if they wanted to. I listened to the winds howl like some rabid yeti-beast or worse. It reminded me of the deathly ice storms that occurred, often suddenly, upon Phét-mthilliu'm, especially the year-long one that had arrived on the day my love upon the ice had died.

The wind howled at us, daring us to venture into its oblivion.

I wavered, Mike was going to die here. Charlotte was going to die as well if I could not find a way past this new obstacle.

I couldn't help but to break out laughing to myself as I contemplated my situation and then at the fact that I was still stark naked.

I looked up to God. "Always fun and games with you, isn't it?" I spoke vindictively.

I looked down at Mike. I knew I had to try to save him.

"Well Mike, have you ever been carried through a high mountain blizzard on Mt. Everest by a naked, pregnant vampire?"

He looked back up at me and smiled trying to laugh with his fractured ribs and gasping lungs, his body succumbing rapidly to the edema.

"No, but I did wake up drunk in bed with two transvestites in Thailand once!" he proclaimed.

I could tell by his eyes, this was a great secret of which he had told no one.

"Ahhh…Kathoeys…"

I mused, laughing over some long, past memories. "Who hasn't!" I said back gleefully.

We chuckled together for a bit.

"Well, then, Mike, this will be your second-best story, won't it?"

I radioed John again and told him that he had better be ready. We were coming to him and we were leaving Lukla airport hell or high water.

He was silent for the longest time probably wondering how on earth I was going to accomplish such a feat; then reluctantly confirmed my plan.

I am sure he was wishing he had chosen another assignment, a contract analyst desk job. Some place sane like Iraq or Syria.

"Well, Mike…it's time to shit or get off the pot…" I smiled down at him, reaching for his hand.

He smirked and took my hand in his.

"Please, Ms. Gold…Ianthe…don't tell anyone about this," he pleaded somewhat jokingly.

We laughed again.

"Sure sweetie, mum's the word!" I said laughing, eluding to the fact I might just tell everyone.

I got Mike up and onto my back. I was feeling strong and powerful from the consumption of Tyr. But desperate also to complete my plan and get back to Charlotte. I couldn't help but laugh at thought of the sight of us, me carrying Mike through the blinding mountain snow and at life and all of its fucked-up situations.

I sighed, took in a deep breath and stepped out into the pitch white icy void that was God's testament that the universe It had made was indeed cruel and unforgiving.

I laughed out defiantly. I wasn't going to let It win.

CHAPTER 53

I would leave Mike at Everest base camp with the resident expedition doctor and a handful of medically trained Sherpas. I couldn't help but laugh at their faces when I showed up carrying Mike on my back from out of the blinding snow storm.

The Sherpas had immediately believed I was a mountain spirit. Some fair and beautiful snow goddess sent to test their reverence for the mountain. Seeing that I was unclothed and with child, they eagerly presented clothes for me and rained great blessings upon me.

The camp's doctor was mystified, but heeded little the prattling of the Sherpa's conviction that I was there to test their will and veneration for this place.

"Well, Mike…"

Tears welled in my eyes.

"I, I've got to…"

"Go! Ianthe. Go and finish the mission, save Charlotte!" he spoke with difficulty as he coughed up some blood. He was half frozen, frostbitten, and fading in and out of consciousness.

I held his hand for a moment longer trying not to cry. I warmed his blood one last time, to energize it so as to give him more time.

"He not going to die, we promise!" The lead medical Sherpa lamented, pleaded with me.

"We take him down the mountain to hospital. We take him soon!" he proclaimed again pointing to the sky, indicating that the storm would clear.

Fighting broke out between the lead Sherpa, his men, the doctor, and the western med-tech staff.

"No! He goes soon, soon, in one hour!" the head Sherpa yelled at the Western guide-doctor defiantly.

"We go! No listen now, the mountain has spoken, this thing must be done! Fire me, I no care!"

I smiled and kissed him gently, taking his hand in mine.

"Do this and you will be greatly rewarded," I confirmed to the lead Sherpa, crying.

I removed my small hooped earrings and gave them to him.

"I will bring a mountain of gold and wealth if you do this one thing for me," I exclaimed.

I saw his eyes widen as he shook his head. "Yes! We leave in one hour!"

I shook his hand and bowed before him in great respect. Then turned and left the medical tent, back out into the blinding tormenting snows.

CHAPTER 54

John shook his head when I appeared from out of the blizzard on foot at the edge of the runway at Lukla Airport. He muttered something about how fucked up the situation was getting as we entered the small De Havilland Canada DHC-6 Twin Otter aircraft specifically rented by Navigations Air to fly from Kathmandu Tribhuvan International Airport.

The blizzard was showing no signs of subsiding. John and I argued for a while about our situation.

I felt the child growing within me.

A message on my phone told me that Charlotte was going to die; soon. She was entering the organ failure stage, it wouldn't be long.

"Get this fucking plane in the air now!" I demanded. "Do what you're getting paid for," I yelled like a spoiled rotten bitch.

"We will all die if we take off in this, you won't be saving anybody!" John snapped back puzzling over my ranting about saving Charlotte.

I was wishing Mike was here. I knew he'd be on my side.

I saw the half inch-thick ice continuing to build upon the wings of our plane. Like a cancer I thought, this universe, absorbing everything, anything to make life a fucking hell.

How does anyone or anything survive and flourish? I wondered. Move forward and get anything done, like simple evolution. I angered.

"There's no way we'll make it!" he confirmed. "This thing you're doing, it's over!"

I felt myself anger inside. Thoughts began to enter me. I felt betrayed. I wanted to hurt him. I thought of consuming him.

Images of Tyr's past, his wars and power entered my mind.

I listened to our two pilots who argued amongst themselves. The captain was siding with John. The co-pilot, a former F-22 raptor pilot who had logged thousands of hours of combat flight time, was up for it. He wanted to test himself, and with a new wife and baby on the way, he needed his bonus.

Seeing an opportunity, I spoke loudly and clearly. "Fine, fuck it!" I turned to the pilots ignoring John's command seniority. "Get me off this mountain now and I'll double your bonus, cash in a bag!" I confirmed.

I almost laughed at the sudden absolute silence; then smirked as my pilots set about readying for take-off.

Money was the one great motivator after fear of death.

I sat back and buckled in looking at John. I smiled at him. "Sorry guy, you're fired, I'm taking over now," I spoke sarcastically.

"If you want, you can get off here," I spoke harshly. "Or sit down and shut the fuck up!"

John moved to the back of the plane and looked out the window grasping his armrest with white knuckles as the plane began its short slip and slide take-off into the ice-white horizon.

Navigations Air soon found itself in big trouble for this act of dangerous and reckless behavior. Our Bombardier Global 6000 ground crew at Kathmandu Tribhuvan International

Airport had reported contact with Nepalese government officials who intended to ground us from further flight.

I held up my satellite phone, and ordered John to fix it. We had the cash.

The first thirty minutes of the forty-minute flight to Kathmandu was truly a nightmare. Ascending and descending by hundreds of feet to avoid being driven into the mountains by air-storm pockets and associated turbulence. Often, it seemed as if we were flying sideways and at all sorts of other odd angles.

I laughed as the co-pilot tried to throw up into a giant coffee mug. The captain didn't bother to be polite and just leaned over and puked on the floor from time-to-time.

John had chosen to just pretend it all wasn't happening and leaned back into his chair and whispered prayers to God, his eyes closed tightly.

I sat back and let myself drift into a sort of meditative or semi-hibernated state, something we can do even under stressful conditions. But it was hard to concentrate on it.

I felt sick, also, and I worried over my growing child. It needed nourishment, I needed to consume flesh. I hungered over the thought of dining upon a few lightly seared porterhouse steaks and a bottle of red Burgundy.

I looked back at John, still annoyed at his disobedience and found myself licking at my lips.

As the plane bounced and swerved around, I couldn't help but think of it all, the chaos of this coming birth and of all the death and destruction becoming associated with it. Of how Charlotte was dying, being disconnected piece-by-piece, cell-by-cell. Of how her only hope was this thing from another world growing within me, forming molecule-by-molecule, part-by-part. And how the baby was already learning, becoming sentient through the chemical information transference occurring within. I thought of the violence of it all, this life, and life in general and of how death begets life which in turn begets death.

God was truly cruel in Its math, Its science, Its meticulous arithmetical plan, the grand design. I wondered over It, what kind of mind conceives of such things, gives birth to such things, allows such horrible things to be.

CHAPTER 55

It took fifty-thousand dollars in bribe money to get us out of Kathmandu and moving forward again back to the good old US of A. I would have paid a hundred times that; we got off easy I guess.

My apparent pregnancy helped us also. I told them the baby was sick and we needed to get to more advanced care. The Nepalese are respectful in that regard. They even said a prayer for me as I boarded the plane.

Our next stop was London then New York. I was showing now. I appeared to be somewhere around six months maybe a little less, my baby-bump did not go unnoticed.

Our flight attendant was a wreck over it. Such things are simply not possible in normal human understanding. She trembled while serving me three six-ounce lightly seared filet mignons and a nice, dark earthy, Burgundy.

I was famished.

She seemed to turn white when I ordered three more.

I had to eat, the child was demanding it.

I found myself watching her. Disturbed at the ideas, the images that came to my head. I starved for her, her blood, her flesh.

She was healthy, thick, and full in body. She dropped a crystal wine glass when I touched her arm, then held it for a moment. An attempt to seduce her, to make her succumb to me as I drew her blood to me. The sound of the glass breaking, and her terrified gasp stirred me out of my lust.

By the time we arrived in London, we were in need of repairs. A wing hydraulic had partially failed to deploy an aileron correctly.

I stormed up and down the plane, constantly checking my watch, as I watched the private airplane repair crew outside working frantically. I was furious, another charter plane would have taken hours to secure.

I video called Dr. Yashi Mehra and pleaded with him and the other doctors to do anything to keep her going. I threatened to withdraw future funding from the institute. I threatened them with malpractice law suits. I had power, and they knew it.

I didn't just scream at them, I cried, too, as I pleaded with them. It was the worst situation possible.

"There is one thing...," Dr. Mehra finally injected, nervously, after long pause over the conference phone.

Amidst the moans and groans of the other doctors working on Charlotte's care, I could hear the hospital's owner, director, and CEO attempting to thwart the idea that was about to be introduced.

"What? Anything?" I pleaded.

"Well, Ms. Gold...," Dr. Mehra spoke clearly thoughtfully, calculatingly. "There is a drug, it's called Noradismol. It's new, raw; not even fully ready for final laboratory live tissue testing...," he paused. "Something I've been working with...," he paused again.

I heard the moans, muffled coughs, and words of condemnation from the others over such a preposterous idea.

"Well?" I demanded.

"Well...well, it might...might delay shut down, maybe, for a few hours, at best," he said with great reservation.

"It, well, has promise, future use for this kind of thing…," his voice was clear concise. "It stops cellular regeneration, degeneration specifically. Halts it actually, putting the body in a state of suspension, a stasis, like hibernation…" he paused again. "The cancer, the cells, will stop their aggressive behaviors for a time being…also, hopefully."

"Then do it!" I demanded. "At whatever costs."

I assured him that money was no object; that I would pay him privately as well.

"Well, that's just it, there…," he paused long and hard.

I could hear him think. I could hear his mind turning, considering the ramifications of the drug's use, some reason to not use it that I could only guess at.

"What?" I gasped, pleading sobbing.

"Ah, well…we don't know exactly, but initial research suggests…"

"I don't care, just do it, just fucking do it!"

"We need permission from…"

"Fuck them, fuck you," I said, pointing at the rest of the staff on the video teleconference as I heard them quibbling, balking.

"Just go in there and do it!" Turning my gaze toward Dr. Mehra, "I'll have your back, I will make you rich. You can have your own hospital," I paused.

"Go talk to Charlotte's private care nurse, she will put you into contact with my lawyers, the papers are ready signed! The money will be in the bank in minutes!" I pleaded.

"It's already done!" I said as I clicked enter on my bank app.

"I don't want your money Ms. Gold," he posited rationally, calmly, almost insulted.

"I just want…you…to…know…"

"Please!" I broke down. "Just do it!"

I sobbed now caught up in a swirl of desperation, confusion, and fear of the unknown. What was going to happen if she received this drug, I wondered. In fact, in truth, I doubt I even cared in that moment.

"Please, please, anything…just do it! NOW!"

I fell to the floor of the plane utterly broken. I was alone in this, against God's desire for death over life, against evolution taking place.

I longed for Stoya, for E'ban, even Tyr in this moment, for some sort of power to defeat my powerlessness.

"OK, Ms. Gold, I, I, I will get it to her now…I've got to…"

"Please!" I pleaded with all the fear and dread and earth-shattering desperation of which I had never felt before in a million years, if ever.

"And you all…don't even think about stopping him, I will end you, all of you if you do! You have no idea of my power!" I screamed at the monitor. "I will end you all!" I cut myself short.

I wanted to tell them I would do more than that; end their careers, their personal hopes and dreams. I wanted to tell them, that I would end their lives.

"Please…"

I redirected my attention to Dr. Mehra. "Just do it now!"

I went numb as the teleconference suddenly went dead. The phone's long, death-like tone, the white grainy screen grated on me.

Cut off from the final resolution, I desperately needed to know whether Charlotte was going to get the drug or not. I lay crumpled, withered, looking up at the airplane's ceiling. My eyes transfixed to some point in space and time, the center of it all; God.

"Please!" was all I could mutter, sobbing. "God, please…"

CHAPTER 56

I didn't think compassion from John was possible. He was aloof from the start; disinterested in anything, overly professional and impatient. But he came to me now, picked me up from the floor and gently deposited me in my seat as the Bombardier Global 6000 made its way down the runway and eventually out over the great Atlantic Ocean.

He sat next to me and handed me a clear, short whisky glass.

I sobbed as he poured the sweet, amber Macallan Lalique 50-year single malt Scotch into my glass. My hand trembled. I smiled back at him, my eyes and face red with sorrow, fear, and panic.

Our glasses clinked as we made a silent toast to Charlotte, Mike, me, us, our team.

He didn't bother asking any further questions. In his mind, I think, he just wanted it to be over with. This adventure. And I am sure he would purposefully forget all that he had now seen and experienced, especially my apparent miraculous pregnancy.

We downed our shots quickly, then he poured us off one more.

"I am going to have another kid myself...," he trailed off.

He seemed reluctant at the thought of it, his continuing to be a father and husband.

I took his hand.

"Boy or girl?" I asked, distracted from my avalanche of thoughts.

"Boy…," he sighed out.

"Well good, maybe…," I cut myself off, knowing somehow, he did not care anymore.

His marriage, I'm sure, was already long over.

"Your Ducati is waiting at the Nav-Air hanger," he said, changing the subject.

I wasn't much for motorcycles, but I would need one now for the coming plan.

I had Emerald Inc. purchase for me, a Ducati 595 Panigale, European-spec, for my entrance into, and escape, from New York City. Some slight modifications were made, enabling it to endure a little extra road abuse and accommodate two riders instead of one.

"We're making good headway. The captain is pushing full-throttle," John reported.

"Once you get to the hospital, call on the burner phone that will be provided. The event will take place on your confirmation," he paused hesitatingly.

He didn't know fully of the plan, but enough I am sure so as to be able to help keep the entire mission in play. He only knew his own personal time tables and objectives to be completed as we made our way in all of this. But he was used to this "compartmentalization" so often involved in mission planning that it was second nature to him. And, I am sure, he would not want to have known anyways, such was the magnitude of what was to go down.

"Once you finish what you're doing, a contact will be waiting for you at Lebanon Valley State park. You'll find a closed-up gas station and defunct diner. We'll have your Bugatti waiting there."

He paused, then poured himself another drink.

"Once that transaction is completed, you're on your own. Let me be the first to wish you the best of luck in all this…," he trailed off again.

"Thank you," I said quietly.

I took another sip from my glass and contemplated life and of how fragile love is; the relationship between two souls. Of how I was willing to do anything for it, while John had already given up long ago.

I reclined my seat and held his hand tightly and began to weep again. I looked at John who was distant already as he stared off into the unknown memories and thoughts that is his life.

"I am sorry for your marriage…," I offered up to John.

I watched as he sat back and reclined; closing his eyes.

"Nothing lasts forever…," he muttered to himself more than to me. "Nothing is forever…"

I began to weep again, to feel that God, the grand design, was and always would be about sacrifice and loss. About thwarting love at every turn. About being alone.

"Please, save them!" I whispered to God a little prayer for John and his family as I looked out over into the endless cloud-dotted horizon of the ocean below.

"Please, save them…"

CHAPTER
57

Our plane set down at precisely 5PM at LaGuardia Airport, in New York**.** I thought of the traffic that I was about to encounter. It was quitting time for at least half the city. The fight to get home was on for millions.

I looked out of my window and up to God again. I thought of the struggle of life. It wasn't going to make this easy.

Navigations Air was in trouble with yet another control tower.

We had been told to move into a holding pattern to wait for another inbound plane that was still five minutes away, some form of emergency.

My pilots ignored the warnings, bent on their million-dollar bonuses.

We listened to the radio squelch of airport security over the plane's speaker.

"Don't worry John, what's another million or two in legal fees anyways?" I offered up. "I'm good for it!"

He broke a smile, then we both began to break out laughing.

The folding stairs of the plane barely hit the tarmac when I was off and running.

Emerald Inc's hanger security team was waiting to intercept airport security.

John raged across the tarmac, shouting and waving his security credentials at the now bewildered airport security guards who were being held by gun point at Navigation's compound perimeter fence. John was going to make an "incident" of all this, I was sure, call in favors from his old friends at the CIA.

Navigations Air and Emerald Inc. was a CIA asset, actually, not to be fucked with by civilians.

I was ushered by two Emerald Inc. security personnel to my awaiting Ducati which was fully fueled and ready to go.

"Our security teams are expecting you at the back gates as you exit. God speed and good luck Ms. Gold!" was all they said as I suited up and made ready for the race ahead of me.

The experimental drug, Noradismol, had bought me a little more time. But it had been reported that Charlotte had only had an hour or two left at best.

I thought only about the ticking clock now as I recklessly tore my way through New York City.

I connected myself to my new machine, my soon to be mechanical lover. I knew it, it knew me. We were one, together in that moment. We were going to accomplish something even the best racers wouldn't dare to achieve. I heard it roar, purr with delight as I shifted gears, ready to race the race of races.

We moved, this machine and I, like a great angry beast through the traffic-jammed highways and onto the surface streets with unrelenting agility. An intensity that only we could accomplish, it was not going to let me down. Together, we were not going to let Charlotte down.

I did not stop for anything as I weaved intricately through every possible opening.

By now there was a police helicopter in the air and a few squad cars winding through the streets trying to intercept me. But traffic was bad, and I, we, were too cunning, too quick; too elusive, too fast.

Like some modern-day aluminum-carbon-fiber and flesh raptor, we moved through the herds of lumbering steel beasts, planning, plotting; hunting.

The child was coming. I had little time.

Nearing the hospital, I made my call to start the last evolution of this venture into motion. I couldn't help but gloat a bit at my power right then. The money I had, its influence of which could get this impossible, horrible thing done. Even Stoya would have been impressed.

Within one minute of my call, electrical power across Southeast New York, to include Long Island was cut. An explosion at a major electrical grid sub-station sent other hubs cascading into failure, ending the hope for many of ever getting home in time for dinner.

Made to look like an accident of some kind, it's what money, power, and a willing partner with highly capable employees with dangerous skill sets can achieve.

Leaving the Ducati in the alleyway adjacent to the hospital, I quickly crossed the street and into the chaos of a mass power outage in a major city.

The hospital, full of dying patients, would soon find itself without reserve power.

I breathed in, the final push to save my love was now at hand.

Charlotte, I hoped, would be waiting alone for me in the darkness.

I passed many of her family members as they sought to find an exit as directed by the hospital staff. I was a ghost, moving forward against the stream of confusion, adorned in a tight black and red leather motorcycle racing suite, gloves, and boots. The mirrored visor of my helmet, down to shield my face. I had cut my hair short also, an attempt to hid my full sex.

In her room, I found Charlotte and her father. I smiled and wept as he held her hand as he cried. Her life support machines were off from the power failure; the end was imminent.

Hospital maintenance had found their back-up generators sabotaged. The automatic ignition switches removed and left on a work bench. They would be working furiously to get them reinstalled. Time was of the essence for many patients there.

Charlotte's father's back was to me. It made what had to be done so much easier.

I swiftly slid my arm around his neck and put him into a sleeper hold. He knew little as I let his body slowly sink back deep into his chair.

I watched a moment as Charlotte gasped faintly. I knew the signs of death. I smelt it come now, drifting in, an invisible but palpable cloud.

Death is real. It is a thing, a presence, an existence in and of its own. It is, like God, an unknown thing, a consumer like me. A great and ever hungry devourer of life, of energy, of God's very will.

"Hey, you! You need to exit, hurry please!" a young male nurse told me, excitedly. "You can't stay here!" he paused looking at me funny, my motorcycle helmet still on.

But he was panicked and turned his attention back to Charlotte's father. "And wake him up! Let's go!" he exclaimed again. "Let's go!"

"Yes! Coming!" I said as I moved to him.

I was going to remove him from my way, kill him if I needed to. But he continued on his way down the hallway forcefully urging visitors to leave.

I felt a sharp pain suddenly and doubled over. I was going into labor.

The child was coming. It knew there was a potential host-body before it. It knew my thoughts. It knew of what I had intended to happen; its joining with her.

I felt for the first time, the small, delicate tendril emerge from me, sliding around between my skin and the leather suit, its first attempt to discover the world it would soon become of.

I stood up, desperate, catching myself, instinctively cupping myself, trying to slow the coming birth.

"Fuck!" I uttered. "I need more time!" I said out loud, pleading to myself, to anyone or anything listening.

I moved to Charlotte and gathered her up. She was limp, a dead weight. Her heart beat so weak and sporadic even I could barely feel it. I felt her blood becoming still, moving little, pooling at the ends of her limbs, thickening.

I turned and carried her to the door. I knew of a back stairwell that led to an alley way and loading docks that only the staff used. My bike parked across from it for escape.

"Hey, what the hell are you doing?!" The young male nurse's voice yelled at me from behind.

"You can't…"

I turned to him angry, desperate. "I, I just…"

I stopped myself then turned and ran into the chaos of nurses and other hospital staff trying to save lives and calm the living, and families trying to find their way out or their way to loved ones that they had sought to visit. I knew he was following me, there was little else to do but run.

I could see the other patients clearly in the dim light as they struggled to hang on. I saw the weak and the dying; children, mothers, fathers in their last breaths. I saw their families cry and pray to a God that they had no idea did not care. I heard the pleas for help, the desperation as I ran on.

And in that moment, I also heard the words of Stoya.

"You are a monster just as I. Maybe even more so…you need, and want and take of it all, your personal, selfish desires. And yet you think yourself noble in it, deny your real being. You don't understand, or want to understand that love and the innocent die in the face of us…"

I knew in that moment that she was right, I was a monster. I was the great lie, the great deceiver. I lived in a world of created falsities. While I gave of my time and money freely with one hand, helping many, I took away with the other hand, other people's loved ones, possibly even, a family member of someone I that had just helped. And then in that act, I so arrogantly attributed it to natural selection and to God's will.

Here in that moment, I realized that with all of my power and wealth I chose to focus on this one life. To make it immortal when others here were not even going to fulfill a normal span of life, to reach their dreams and intended life-purpose.

Was this life of Charlotte more important than any other? That question nagged at me now. Who was to say that Charlotte was worth saving over any other? But for out of my own personal wants and desire.

I moved on through my living deception. I saw the faces of the hopeless dying before their time and heard the pointless prayers of those who were powerless to do anything but cry and become utterly weak like I was not so long ago.

"They are nothing; food, playthings, and nothing more..."

I repeated Stoya's scathing words in my head. It was the only way I could justify my so uncaring selfish actions.

"Security! Security!"

I heard the young male nurse scream after me on his radio as I entered the stairwell. I turned on him quickly and lashed out now with all of my inhuman power, punching him in the throat. I heard a crack and a choking sound as he fell down onto the cold concrete stair well landing.

I stood over him, holding my precious Charlotte, glairing down upon him as he sought to call again on his radio, gasping.

"Nothing more…" echoed in my head as I raised my steel reinforced racing boot and crushed his skull, killing him instantly.

I thought of Stoya and her blood lust, her ease at taking life and her indignancy to it all, to these human beings.

And in that moment, I knew of it too. That we are superior in every way and that we will exist beyond human's known universal memory. That this life, this person under me, was already forgotten to time, save for its bones that might whisper my truth to whoever might care.

And even they, his bones would soon be long gone to time, and we, Charlotte and I would be on another world far away laughing and playing and living and loving. It was our right and what God had intended, was it not? Or so I had convinced myself in that desperate moment. Of what I realized perhaps, I had always believed all along.

CHAPTER 58

I turned and continued my descent to the ground floor racing down, leaping several steps at a time. I could feel the last of Charlotte's life ebb. The smell of death coming down upon us more quickly, chasing after us. I cursed it, defied it openly. I felt the child sliding down through me seeking to be free.

Outside in the alley way near the loading docks, I laid Charlotte on a pile of old carpets and cardboard boxes. Pigeons pecked away at the ground seemingly oblivious to my intrusion. The light was dim and the air chill as the sun began the last seconds to finality and into another horizon.

It was not how I wanted it, but it was too late. Time had come to an end in that moment.

Charlotte's eyes fluttered open. She seemed to look up at me, frightened, already so close to death, what could she know?

"I am so sorry Charlotte…," I spoke softly, crying, tears streaming down my face, the birth wasn't going to wait anymore.

I presented the surgical knife Mike had given me. Its long, curved blade gleamed as I withdrew it from my boot.

I had to make sure the transformation succeeded and there was only one way. Her normal orifices may not suffice, the child within me might be in-experience, confused as to how to make its first inhabitation.

"Stop! Freeze!" a voice screamed at me, commanding me.

I stood up and turned to see an overweight security guard coming at me, his gun drawn.

"Stop, put the knife down. Do it now!" the fat, unshaven, sweaty face screamed at me.

I looked down at Charlotte. I saw her life leaving.

"I said stop! Back away from her and get on the ground, now! Do it now!" the guard yelled again.

I turned to fully face him. "I am so sorry…," I spoke clearly through the face shield of my helmet, trying to have empathy as I moved my head from side-to-side pleading for him in silence to leave.

"Please, I am so sorry…"

Then moving with great speed, I seized him, breaking his arm. I heard the gun drop and skitter across the rough asphalt. I heard my surgical blade make a swoosh sound as it sliced through his neck, windpipe, vocal cords, and carotid arteries.

I felt his warm blood upon me, enticing me instantly to feed.

He fell back from me in pain and horror at this sudden life changing event. His death, so fast so simple, a way I am sure he never envisioned to be.

I saw him fall back onto the ground as blood spurted and oozed.

I turned my attention back to Charlotte again. I felt the child begin to leave me.

"I'm so, so sorry Charlotte…," I said as I cut open her hospital gown exposing her naked, withered body.

"If there was another way," I whispered.

She looked at me in horror, or so it seemed, too weak to act in any way. She could only watch as I lowered the knife.

"I am so sorry, Charlotte. Just know that I love you, and without this you will die, pass forever. Your memory, your legacy, lost to the annals of time."

The child within me began its final painful decent, the violet mucus amoeba creeping past my labia searching for its first host.

I reached down and cut deeply into Charlotte from just above her lower pelvic area up into her chest, exposing her insides. They steamed in the cold, bulging out slightly.

I almost lost it as Charlotte seemed to miraculously awaken. She cried out for a brief moment from the pain before passing into oblivion.

Unzipping my leather racing suit all the way to expose myself, I lowered myself above her, over the gaping wound, allowing the child to reach out with its feelers then begin to reach into Charlotte, grabbing hold of her spine. The connection between me and it told me there was but a second left. But that life would return in time, thrive again.

It crawled out of me as I choked back the pain and sobbed softly.

I could only look at her, crying, trying to think of our future life together.

Just as I felt the last of my child slip down into Charlotte, I heard a new voice, as it gasped, afraid of what it had found. Of what it was seeing.

It was another hospital guard. He saw his partner lying dead nearly decapitated, the gaping wound in Charlotte, and the thing, the strange violet-purple thing that had slipped out of me and was moving within her. He saw it seem to pull the wound closed behind it, Charlotte's body reanimate for a second.

He saw me standing over her, my lower body exposed, my vagina still dripping with violet-red mucus afterbirth, and, holding a weapon of torture and murder.

I stood tall and defiant, an alien mother-beast. I postured, by which he knew instinctively that he was next.

But he found he could not draw his weapon, nor speak, or do anything but turn pale and begin to vomit.

I was exhausted, weak from the birth. But I couldn't allow any more impediments to the task that lay at hand.

I turned to him holding the long, curved surgical knife, dripping with blood, in my ungloved hand.

He reached, shaking uncontrollably, for his radio, then to his gun, unable to decide of which option was best for this situation.

I moved on him. I made it quick, painless.

He would know no more.

Desperate, I gathered up Charlotte and quickly duck taped her wound together with some strips I had kept on my arm.

The child had taken hold and even now had begun the process of closing the wound behind it. To begin the healing and the process of assimilation. To reignite her body at every level.

Charlotte had passed from near death into a comma like state, the dream-sleep of one who is in transition. She would remain this way for a great while. I turned and ran with her in my arms. I was weak, stumbling, only the thoughts of her and our lives together spurned me on.

I made my way across the street to the awaiting Ducati. It was our only passage now from this gridlocked city. I held Charlotte tightly in front of me as we moved through the streets of gray in the power disrupted dark and chaos upon my willing machine. I was lost in a dream of past life memories, oblivious to the fact that I was endangering many and heeding little to our own safety.

Outside on the open road we found our freedom. I could smell Charlotte; feel even now her life coming back, a newly blooming rose.

I smiled and nuzzled into her, holding her tightly. I felt my promise to her regain its reality. I felt her begin to heal and radiate.

At Lebanon, near Valley State park, New Jersey, I would pick up my trusty Bugatti Chiron from the Emerald Inc. contact there. We would make for Sedona, Arizona, to my lair, deep in an isolated part of the mountains. It was there that Charlotte and I would start the rest of our lives together. To live as our kind does.

I thought of it now, and of the time when I could finally propose to her under the Caprisian full moon at midnight when long dead lovers unite in that one moment to remind the world, the universe and God, that love is real, wanting, and eternal.

CHAPTER
59

My home near Casper Mountain, Sedona Arizona, was a welcome reprieve. It was my primary lair. A place built long ago by a small team of master masons and stone cutters from Italy whose relatives still do work for me to this day.

It was isolated, hidden, and centering, a part of the Sedonan energy vortex. Time and energy did not move here, nor gain or lose momentum, but it remained a steadfast constant. Here, in this mountain, deep beneath the earth was a point within space where no time trajectories intersected, creating the chaos-friction that is so often felt most everywhere else.

It was a lost place, a quiet place in the universe, the grand design, where nothing occurred, and God had long forgotten about. There are many places like this where my kind go to rest, heal, and renew on this world and others.

These places, akin to the coffin of the movie-vampire, a tomb deep within the earth, mathematically and geographically positioned within an astral geometric plane, is where I came to sleep and prepare for the next cycle, physical participation of my interaction on this world.

I was utterly exhausted and starved.

When the opportunity readily presented itself near Winslow, I had gorged upon a hitchhiker, a rapist and murderer of young unsuspecting girls. We were too tempting of a target, two beautiful women and a two and a half million-dollar car.

I took comfort in knowing he will never hurt or kill innocents again. But I was still ravenous. It took many porterhouse steaks and bottles of rare red burgundy wine to get me settled and fully centered again after all that had happened.

I had wrapped up my business dealings with Navigations Air and Emerald Inc., all cash paid in full to everyone involved. A verbal contract with little paperwork other than the ordinary costs of day-to-day aviation operations and miscellaneous security services was all that could be discovered to any further investigation into its recent activities regarding me.

There would be some lawsuits and other litigatory issues leveled at Navigations Air for its renegade activity in Nepal and LaGuardia International of which I knew would eventually be swept away. That is the power of money within the private security contracting world, with its rich and famous and government clientele. An industry that finds itself exempt often when there are deep secrets to be revealed.

My investments would remain on autopilot for a while longer; in care of Emerald Inc. and my other associates. My condo had been sold and the word put out that I was on a business sabbatical in Northern Europe. Charlotte was to be my sole interest now; my sole dedication would be to her well-being and that of the new life that she was about to have.

Mike had returned stateside safely and was expected to make a full recovery. We spoke at length on the phone.

It was time for him to retire, to "fade off into the sunset" as he said. He still had trouble with what had happened on Everest, what he had seen. Nightmares made sleeping difficult.

I could only apologize repeatedly, assure him that in time, I would explain it all, and that these things will fade from his memory.

CHAPTER 60

I awoke three days later still holding Charlotte's hand as she lay resting, hibernating beside me. I could already see the changes in her, she was simply radiating. I watched as her eyes moved back and forth rapidly from behind her closed eyelids which made them flutter slightly.

I saw her body twitch in places here and there at times. Other times her body would twitch, almost in its entirety, like a full body seizure almost, reflexes from the healing and the changes the child, the creature within, was orchestrating.

It would take a little over six months for her to reawaken.

I watched over her constantly.

The change that was taking place, an event I had never witnessed before, was comical at times. She muttered things in English, Spanish, and in our language, disjointed thoughts of memories both human and alien. Other times she called out for her father and for me which made me weep.

I would also laugh listening to her stomach groan. She would fart or belch at times. Sometimes sneeze or cough. She even had an orgasm. All these things were products of the creature connecting itself to its host, understanding how its new body worked.

Her body became lean and slender. Her hair thickened and grew; turning an even purer blonde with slight violet undertones.

I chuckled over the fact that the child within, inexperienced in habitation, did not disconnect the genes that affected bodily hair growth. I saw her armpit and leg hairs grow out. Her pubic area, too, flourished, thick and full, I was sure that Charlotte would change that inconvenience later in her next hibernation-sleep cycle.

I found myself ever more infatuated over her eyebrows. Already perfect, beautiful, they had somehow managed to become even more so.

Her lips became fuller, firmer; sexier. They glistened, still keeping that almost whisper of which I am forever still so enamored with. Charlotte had secrets to tell now, of her being, and of things that are beyond human comprehension.

On an early Sunday morning in the fifth month, I was startled when her eyes opened big and wide. They were a bright, rich violet. And most unusual, they glowed like Stoya's did. Radiating cool and clear in the low-light of my cave-like bedroom. I wondered over it, and thought of Stoya, of what this secret thing was that they both now shared.

In the last week before her first awakening, Charlotte became restless in her sleep. Tossing and turning, sometimes sitting straight up then sinking back down into another position. It was a strange thing to watch at times, eerie like some undead reanimation science fiction horror film.

Then, on a Wednesday in the late evening, she awoke stretching and yawning squeaking out a long, sleepy sigh. Sitting up, she was startled at first of the unfamiliar surroundings. She was supposed to be dead I am sure she thought, suddenly realizing that she was not. She recoiled; curling up under the blankets of the bed and peering out at me innocently.

"Ianthe?" she whispered.

"Yes dearest, it is me!"

"Wh…wha…what's going on?" she squeaked still frightened.

"It's OK sweetie!"

I tried to comfort her. "You are all better now…," I said moving quickly to her, pulling the sheets up and tucking them tighter about her.

"You have been healed Charlotte. You are all better now!" I whispered earnestly. "You need to rest more, but you'll be up and about soon!"

"I'm, I'm very hungry and thirsty," she squeaked out meekly.

"Oh, yes dear!" I spoke joyfully, hardly able to contain myself. "Give me a moment, I'll be right back!"

I fetched what would be her first experience as her new being. Her first real experience as our kind, a vampire, the Nosferatu.

I returned with clear, cold mountain spring water lightly flavored with orange and mint, along with a small plate of fresh assorted fruits and berries, dried dates, and a few slices of hard goat cheese with honey dripped over it. They were Charlotte's favorite snacks.

She drank a full glass of water, then a second one as she nibbled at the berries and fruit that I hand fed her. She was confused and groggy, weak from her ordeal and from the inhabitation process.

I thought about my awakening in the desert under the stars all alone. The awakening can be difficult, especially the first few. It gets easier with time, but you are almost always alone and often thrust immediately into survival mode. It's very frightening for the uninitiated.

At least she was not alone on her first. Would not be thrust into an often, unforgiving situation as I have been.

When she was done, she continued to complain of hunger.

I returned yet again, this time with a plate of thinly sliced filet minion, which had been quickly seared in a light sweet French style pan sauce.

She hesitated at first, but the creature was desirous of the flesh, the protein that she so desperately needed. She ate it all and asked for more.

I laughed at her as she nibbled away at the rare beef making slight grunting noises in approval of the taste and the satisfaction it had in her.

Three helpings later and fully sated she lay back down to access this new reality for a moment, then quickly fell back into a deep peaceful sleep.

When she had awoken again at 2AM she was more alert, but still unable to get out of bed, her mind still paralyzed by the reality that she was still, indeed quite alive. Frightened, she remained there as I soothed her fears.

"You made it sweetie, survived just as I had promised you would."

I soothed her, smoothing her thick, vibrant blonde hair up over her delicate little ears. I held her hands, drawing her blood to me then back into her. But it was different now; the act between us was much deeper. It was our kind's connection.

Her blood, the creature within it, rushed now, to and from me on its own accord, slow, steady, concentrated.

We passed our energy to each other, our thoughts; our power, like two waves meeting in the riptide of the sea.

"Where's daddy?"

"He's out my love," I smiled gently. "He needs to conduct business for a while."

Charlotte pouted in disappointment.

"But, he knows you're safe, and well," I posited.

"My family?" she sat upright hopeful. "My sister, my brother, mother?"

"They are at your California home in Modesto...," I calmed her.

She slowly slid the blankets back exposing her naked body, her faintly showing stomach muscles rippled as she stretched, breathing in and out. She had become a vision that even Michelangelo would have had difficulty portraying.

She looked about her and took in the sights of my cavernous bedroom with its soft red, pink, and orange walls made of Sedonan slate and stone. She marveled at the arcing steel and concrete supports designed to complement the naturally occurring stone cavern of what is my deep, earthly home.

"Wh...where are we?" Charlotte asked cautiously as she moved to sit up.

Her eyes moved about slowly, taking in this strange earthly environment, the rough-hewn stone and wood furniture, the large traditional Navajo rugs upon the floor, many of which were well over two hundred years old.

"My home...," I paused. "Our home."

I spoke cautiously. "Near Sedona, I had mentioned it before..."

"Ye..yes, I remember something about that," she said meekly, confused still.

I smiled down upon her, then stood to help her up onto her feet.

It would take a few minutes for her to rediscover her balance, to reignite her human perceptive senses. The creature-child needed to learn how to use the faculties of its new host, its first host. To adjust itself to the way its host experiences the world.

"Our, our, home?" she trembled slightly not understanding fully of what was taking place, that this was not heaven or some other mystical after-life abode.

"Yes, my home, your new home; our place to be away from the world. A place for you to heal and become whole again...," I trailed off, speaking gently, reassuringly.

"Wha...what day is it?" she asked quietly.

I remained silent for a while as we slowly walked across the floor of our bedroom chamber hoping to let the question, and the answer to it, slip away for the time being.

She was not ready for such precise information. I wanted her to enter this new life slowly. She would have a lot of catching up to do. A lot to wrap her head around.

As she slowly moved, she caught her reflection in a large dressing mirror and startled. Recoiling, her face turning white. It was then that she fully understood the truth of things. That she was not dead, and she was not in heaven. She turned as if to flee from her own vision. Then turned back again, frightened, to face herself.

"I, I, I...." she stammered. "I am not...."

I saw fear come to her face, panic begin to set in.

"I, I'm not dead?"

I almost laughed in the way that she had said it.

"I am not...I am supposed to be...dead!" she proclaimed again astonished over the fact.

"No sweetie, my love, you are not!"

I held her gently from behind, encouraging her to look at herself fully, her absolute splendor.

"It is as I promised you; you have won the battle over cancer," I confirmed.

"But, I, I died, I, I...," she trailed off.

"No sweetie, you did not, but maybe for a second, but you are back now, and that is all that matters."

She saw her eyes, the bright glowing violet, blazing back at her, her pure blonde hair with its violet undertones, her perfect body.

"But…I, I am not me…!" she squeaked, startled from the way she now looked and the changes that had been made. What she suddenly knew to be of herself in that moment.

"I am, not me!" she began to weep at the thought of this implausible proposition.

"Yes, yes, my love, it is you, but…better now," I reassured her.

"But how? How can this….?"

I smiled at her, soothing her, pulling her hair back slightly as I turned her into the mirror again and gently moved her closer to it. She had to face this, understand of who she now is.

"My eyes, they…I…" She stepped forward to look into them, into herself, her soul, at the thing, the creature within that she had now become.

I saw her look at me through the mirror's reflection, realizing suddenly that my eyes were of the same color as hers. Her hair and my hair were of the same violet undertones, our bodies; the perfection that humans seldom obtain.

"This isn't…how?"

I smiled warmly and soothed her again. "Well, …. sweetie…"

I squirmed. I was afraid of this moment, the revelation of a so very alien truth.

"Do…do you remember what I told you…," I paused. "A…about me?" I spoke hesitantly.

She looked at me, my reflection in the mirror again.

I saw confusion in her eyes. I saw her brow furrow and a look of disbelief wash over her face like a cascade of ice cold water. Then I saw it in her face, the realization, the memory coming back, of the thing, the secret thing that I had confided to her. The implausible reality that I was not of this world; that I was as I had said I was, an alien, a vampire.

"No! You? No! It's not…not possible!" she confirmed to herself, to me in the mirror her body gesturing in disbelief.

She looked faint, and doubted herself, her own thoughts; the realization.

Then she heard the voice within her, a new voice, the other voice that quietly echoed within her human brain. "Yes, Charlotte Bell Aberdeen, you are!"

"A…a…v…va…vampire?" she uttered as I saw her go weak and begin to fall back into me.

I caught Charlotte as she fell backwards into my arms and fainted. I put her back into bed and tucked her in to sleep again for what would be another week.

I lay down next to her and watched her.

I saw her eyebrows furl as if in deep thought. Her lips slightly parted, breathing, murmuring thoughts known only to herself. This was the moment in time for her mind, her body, and soul to come to terms with this new truth, to make amends with itself and accept this new reality.

I wept again for her in that moment as I heard the words of Stoya so clearly again.

"Charlotte will lose all that you have come to love in her. Her innocence, her fragile human being. The thing that draws you to her…she will be as us…"

I thought now of that one thing that I had taken away from Charlotte, her unique human body, her spirit, her soul, its personal journey as God had planned it to be, all that was that I had fallen in love with. Charlotte Bell Aberdeen the mortal human being.

I lay back into our bed next to her and pleaded with God, lobbied with It, that my decision was indeed a good one. It was the indifferent deafening silence that made me break down and cry again.

CHAPTER 61

Charlotte sat at the far end of the living room's grand leather couch clutching at a large Southwestern style throw pillow. Her knees were up as she pushed herself back into the deep corner of the couch as if to defend herself from me, from the coming truth.

She was clothed in her favorite set of old worn out pajamas which depicted little Snoopy and Woodstock characters dancing joyfully across its fabric. It was her down and out "life sucks!" go-to comfort ensemble, a relic from her college years. She had worn them often in her last weeks as a human being before her admission into intensive care. They brought her comfort, an armor of sorts against an unfair world. It was the first thing I packed for this new and unusual start to her new, most unusual life.

It was hard not to fawn at her, her child-like vulnerability in that moment, the way she looked down at the floor to avoid direct eye contact with me.

I had microwaved some frozen Chinese food and made a tall cup of hot chocolate with extra marshmallows. They were set before her on the large, carved Juniper wood and glass-topped coffee table.

She sat listening to me, guarded, still expectant that this was all some kind of elaborate prank.

When she had re-awakened, she had realized that none of this was a dream and that, in fact, she was indeed very alive and well. And she knew, intuitively, that she was now somehow different. She saw and heard things that she didn't before. She found she knew things she could not possibly know. Memories of past lives not of this world flooded her.

Her body felt perfect, inside and out, unhindered by any pains or muscular restrictions. Her heart beat strong, her breath deep and fully oxygenating. She felt alive in a way that she had never had.

It took a long time for me to get the words out right despite my having rehearsed "the talk" that I was going to have with her. But how do you explain such a thing as this? That she was now inhabited by an alien life-form and would be for the most part, as herself forever, or, at least, until she found a new, more appropriate body.

I thought of my parents, the explanation they had to give to that alien being for which I had been birthed to inhabit so long ago.

Charlotte was frightened, and unsure; in total disbelief.

I sat next to her, gently massaging the arch of her left foot, drawing her blood to me and then back into her, warming, calming, centering; charging.

She cooed at my touch, that memory of my most unusual thing I could do. But now, it was even more exhilarating.

I smiled at her, and began to speak, to tell her the story of how it was that she had come to be what she was now in this moment. A story so vast in scope and deep in details, so very fantastic, that even great fiction writers would have a hard time conceiving of such a thing. I saw her beautiful, rich, violet eyes blaze and widened with each and every sentence. I saw the questions in her mind build and pile upon each other.

I told her about what and who we were, about our creation and how we had evolved into what we are today, of whom I have once been, the lives that I have lived.

I told her our species' story and of the long journeys we have made from other planets beyond this galaxy, planets that mankind will most likely never see or experience. I told her of my travels through space and time, of my coming here, and the little girl upon the desert sands whose body I had claimed for my own. The body now before her.

I looked into her innocent eyes and could see that deep inside she knew this was not a hoax, that it was not some kind of grand prank. For the creature-child within her told her otherwise, its instinct, its memories of mine that I had passed to her; those of my experiences, and that of my parents and their parents and all those that have come before and still live. These things in her mind confirmed to her all that I had said to be the truth.

Charlotte sat in silence for hours looking out through the massive inch-thick sliding glass windows to the snow-dusted mountain ranges beyond and the red and brown-pink Arizonian desert, still trying to take in all that I had told her.

The human part of her mind worked to process the information. To put into place the chronological order of things as I had told it. To ultimately conclude that she was now what I had told her that she was, an alien being on the inside with a human on the outside, the perfect immortal symbiont. That she was of us now, the Nosferatu, the cosmic space drifting vampire. That she would take her place amongst our race, begin her part in our greater history; her new-found story.

Then, in silence, she garnered the strength to walk into the enormous stone and marble bathroom with its warm, spring fed soaking pool and trickling water fall under which a shower could be had. She approached a massive floor to ceiling mirror and in it saw herself again.

Removing her clothes, she marveled at the exquisiteness of her newly reformed body, now shaped and molded into perfect strength and beauty. She was petite, slight, gingerly feminine. Her body glowed, slightly ebbing with her inner emotions. She smiled, seemingly pleased at what she saw. But, also, still horrified by what it all meant now.

I watched as she turned and twisted slowly to view herself.

"So…so…then…I am a vampire…now?" she asked of me cocking her head looking at herself, trying to make that final confirmation in her mind.

"Yes, that is the easiest way to think of yourself." I offered.

"But we…we are much, much greater than that!" I confirmed.

"But I can see myself, you!" she wondered as she starred at the mirror before her.

I chuckled lightly.

She was going to have a hard time with the idea that we are not the creature of myth as humans would have of us, that we are of a far grander idea.

"Yes, we cast reflections, dear, we cast shadows; we are quite real, corporeal, of flesh and blood." I trailed of in thought.

"Entirely human in so many ways," I concluded.

"We are the Nosferatu, "one of the flesh" is what it means in our language," I paused.

"We are of the flesh, inhabitators of the body...," I encouraged her. "Of the flesh, both in our natural forms and as human kind save for our unique life span and some other abilities. We are warm and soft to the touch. We feel emotions, we feel pleasure and pain. Hurt, both physically and emotionally. We love and make love as humans can, eat as humans eat, sleep as human's sleep, we are as human as any human can be, perhaps even more so."

I spoke quietly, thinking upon the fact of how I feel more human at times than of my other self.

I saw her muse over that concept, of being so different yet so very humbly human.

"So…I am…alien, immortal?" she asked seemingly afraid of that answer, the ramifications of which she could only begin to fathom.

"Yes! You are forever now," I told her lovingly. "But that too is far grander than what you could imagine. You will live to see this world go through its changes. Watch the human race grow; to reach its intended evolutional peak and then most likely pass from cosmic memory."

I watched her turn sad at that sentiment. Consider that concept.

"But you and I will live beyond this place, in this form or another, a new being, visitors on some new and alien world. We are eternal; there is no end for us, save the great sleep," I reassured her again. She looked back at me in wonder.

"The…the great sleep?" she inquired, turning to view herself in the mirror again.

"Yes, the sleep that will take you to an eternal place beyond time, but it is a long way off for you my love, a billion years or more maybe...if ever."

She smiled back into the mirror, moving closer now, peering into her own eyes, noticing the larger pupils, the violet hue. She saw them glowing, different from mine. I could only shrug back at her as to why this was so for her and not me.

"Like Stoya…?" she whispered to herself again, wondering.

"Yes," I mused shrugging, for I did not know why Charlotte had this strange anomaly.

"Yes, like Stoya's, but I could not tell you why."

I wondered about this myself, Stoya's eyes. What did it mean?

She stood starring into herself, her reflection, slowly understanding that all that I said was true. She could feel it, instinctively begin to understand the math of it.

"For…ever?" her voice cracked slightly again.

I approached her gently touching her presenting her to the mirror further.

"Forever!" I pronounced to her again.

She smiled back into the mirror still not fully wanting to believe that this had become her truth.

I breathed in at the sight of her, the vision of her. She was a goddess of purity and light, the earth I knew was going to be lifted because of her.

She looked long and hard at my reflection in the mirror; then mouthed the words "thank you!" trembling slightly, at what they meant, what I had done for her.

"No, my greatest love, thank you!" I broke slightly.

She smiled back at me seeming to whisper something else but of what I did not hear and did not ask.

She moved closer to the mirror, her face a few short inches from it.

I saw her lips pull back to reveal her teeth.

I busted out laughing at her suddenly, as she bared them, straining her face attempting to make her canines grow as she turned her head from side-to-side.

"Oh silly, silly Charlotte, we don't have fangs!"

"No fangs?" she seemed to whimper, disappointed; stepping back slightly. Her face frowning as she tried once again to grow them.

"No, my sweet; no fangs!"

"But how then…?"

I chomped my teeth. "Well…it's just like eating big, thick, juicy steak," I said. "Like a porterhouse…"

"But without utensils…," I paused over that grizzly fact.

She recoiled, realizing the truth of what I had said. She turned pale, the romance of the fantasy of the sexy vampire kiss quickly slipping away.

"Do I…do…?" she paused looking back at herself in the mirror and stepping away from it afraid again.

"Drink…drink, blood?"

"Well…," I said playfully moving to her. "Yeah…it's sort of a package deal."

I stopped behind her, smoothing her hair back feeling the airiness of it, longing to feel it upon my body.

"But for right now…" I stirred wanting to keep her thoughts positive and moving forward in this coming new life of hers. "I think you'd better shave those hairy legs of yours!"

She held herself tightly, looking at herself for a long time. I saw her lick at her lips like in the way Stoya did. Her eyes seemed to ebb in and out, the intensity of their light.

"Well… yeah, I guess I can't go around looking like this, can I?" she said as she looked herself over. "It's pretty grody!"

Chuckling at her, I touched her lightly on the shoulders again.

"Yeah, it's hard to seduce your lover-prey, little vampire, when you look like you just stepped out of the jungle…ape-girl!"

I paused a moment then saw her crack a smile, giggle at herself then laugh, her silly goofy fun-loving laugh that I had not heard for such a long time.

She continued to look herself over for a bit, turning, moving.

"Well, shit!" she spoke happy with what she saw moving closer to the mirror again. "I am a sexy little bitch, aren't I?" she concluded resting her hands on her hips standing tall, her feet spaced widely apart boldly looking over herself again.

"Even with armpit and leg hair!" she declared out loud.

"Yeah, you are! You certainly are!" I exclaimed as my sexual desire for her began to flood over me from the sight of her heavenly body.

"A sexy little bitch!" I repeated.

We both began to laugh and for the first time in so long of a time, we hugged each other long, hard, out of love and passion.

I wept again. I had missed this, my goofy little Charlotte, her silliness and joy for life. I felt my fears beginning to slip away again, to have hope for the future, for us.

CHAPTER
62

As usual, Charlotte recovered quickly from the shock of it all. She was strong in that way. She had always been able to move on quickly, brush herself off, and carry onward. It was just one of many things I had been intrigued with by her from the first few weeks of dating her. A trait that, I felt, had assured me she would be up to this new life. Still, it was going take time for her to fully catch up to the reality of this new existence.

I lay outside on our patio taking in the mid-morning sun. It was warm and serene in the growing desert heat. A light, warm wind blew gently as birds of many kinds sang and flittered about upon the surrounding boulder landscape. I lay back naked, exposed to the world; the universe, to absorb this gift of warmth and solitude, to watch the dusted snows upon the mountains beyond slowly melt away, the scene turning back into the sage-rose-gray and browns that was the Arizonan desert.

"So…let me get this straight," Charlotte interrupted my thoughts as she sat down in the reclining teak lawn chair next to me. "I am not…dead, undead?" Charlotte said seemingly hesitant to be outside with me in the sunlight.

The thoughts of bursting into flames, stubbornly stuck in her head from reading too many fictitious books on what society wanted us to be.

I laughed at her. She had been thumbing through many of her more favorite vampire novels, among her other most treasured things, of which I had packed for her to help ease her transition.

"No!" I tried to keep from laughing at her silliness. "You are, quite alive my dear!"

"Alive?"

"Oh yes! Very, very alive!" I chuckled. "Living, breathing, thinking, moving, all so very human. Can't you feel that?"

"But…I…I have a creature inside of me?"

I paused, thinking about that idea for a moment.

"Well, yes, our kind, a sentient being, but you are it now, together in body and soul as one," I paused. "A symbiotic relationship. But of the highest order."

"But how?"

"Well, it's complicated…we connect to our host at every level. Become one with it, as it. Two systems joining as one, the mind and body all things united into one cohesive, near seamless entity, a new form of being really."

I saw Charlotte squirm; I had not answered her question.

"No. I mean…how?" she paused. "How is it inside of me?"

I choked for a moment. "Well…as I've said, I put you in there!"

I saw her look at me oddly.

"H, ho, how?" she questioned, her head cocking slightly wondering, fidgeting at my rather vague answer.

I suddenly understood of how a human mother or father felt when their child became aware that babies are not delivered by a white magical stork. I took a long sip from my ice-cold lime margarita.

"Well…I birthed you Charlotte, like a woman does a child…" I stopped myself.

I saw her look at me funny, her face contorted in disbelief.

It was an ugly truth. There was no glamour in our kind's birth, no magical blood-kiss or some other mystical process. Just plain old conception, fucking, like just about everything else in this universe.

"You…you, birthed…me?"

"Yes, Charlotte, I birthed you. I, we, made you. I carried you and put you into your human body. It is the only way we can procreate, to make more of us. Sex. Make you as you, you in that human body."

I stopped, finding myself confused over the explanation of it myself, as I laughed.

"Wha, buuu…t."

I watched Charlotte sit back somewhat bewildered looking up to the sun, then tensed at it.

I laughed. "Don't worry Charlotte, the sun will not hurt you, in fact, it will only make you stronger."

She seemed to ignore that fact, still finding the strange truth of her existence, her "birth" somewhat incomprehensible.

"So...no… biting?" she paused long. "No blood transfers, venoms, spiritual inhabitations?"

I chuckled again as she seemed to grip at her vampire book.

"No, sweetie, as I explained before, no blood or biting…," I paused. "Just normal human intercourse and a somewhat normal birth."

"No spirit-demon?"

She seemed to whimper over that romantic ideal also.

I laughed out snorting, spilling some of my drink.

"Oh! How you crack me up sweetie-pie! No…no spirits, demons for you my love, just simple plain old sex and out you popped!" I laughed again. "But that in and of itself is a complicated matter also…"

I settled in my chair looking back at her trying to be serious again.

"But…but… how? Wh…who?" she looked at me oddly.

"Well, Charlotte, I know you've always been strictly lesbian but…"

"Oh, poop on you! You know what I mean!" she huffed at me.

"You are born of two fathers, Nosferatu, like me. E'ban, of whom you will meet soon and Tyr, who is now dead and is another story in and of itself. Like most any other creatures, you, the creature within you is the byproduct of that union. What you are now, before me, is the product of that child's inhabitation of your human self…the symbiont."

"Ssss, sooo, I am not Charlotte, my human self?"

"Oh, funny!" I laughed. "Yes, yes, you are, but enhanced now. Better than you could be naturally in human form; gifted with an alien knowledge and increased senses and physical powers; quite boring, actually, when compared to human myths."

I reached over and tapped on Anne Rice's *Interview with a Vampire*.

"But an amazing feat of evolution and biomechanical engineering none the less!"

She paused long then spoke. "But…how, is it inside of me?

She seemed still confused.

"Well…" I straightened sighing. "I cut you open…"

I saw her squirm, did she remember? Her face contorted as if in pain, her hand instinctively moving to her stomach.

"It was the only way, I assure you, for you to survive. That you and the child that I bore, and put inside of you, would survive as Charlotte…," I trailed off.

"It is as we are, inhabitators. Under normal conditions, you would have had to find your own way in, through…," I laughed out. "Well, I think you get that picture."

Charlotte looked incredulous, wanting to speak but could not.

"Unfortunately, inhabitation is well…sometimes messy, painful. But open wounds are the best way, in your case, the easiest quickest way. But we can enter through the skin, a process much more difficult and time consuming, painful also for most."

"Through the skin…?"

She looked at me then at her arm touching it.

"Yes, but most normally a mouth or…," I chuckled. "Well, you know…"

I glanced down at myself, my vagina, motioning towards it, then my butt, laughing.

"It is as it is Charlotte, such as God sees fit for whomever we meet. Some are easy, some are quite difficult to inhabit, but all bodies have a way in, or so far that I have found, be it micro orifices upon the skin, or large openings of some kind, all things must take in, and all things must expel. It is as designed, in this universe anyways, the body always like any other machine, a process of consumption and a resulting expulsion of unused materials…," I broke off, laughing.

"Anyways, you get the picture. Everything has an in, everything has an out."

I sighed, I hadn't thought this out fully, I forgotten the part where there would be questions. I laughed to myself, the fuzzy memory of the time when I was born. I suspected I, too, drove my parents nuts.

CHAPTER 63

"But what of my old self?" Charlotte asked again.

I laughed. "Old self? It's quite fine really, can you tell the difference?"

She paused for a long time to wonder over, herself, her body and mind, finding ultimately how much it was all still the same.

"I suppose not, I feel the same as I always did, before I got sick. Just…just…well smarter, stronger, faster as you said. Almost like the *Six Million Dollar Man*," she said, laughing. "Well…woman!" she blushed feeling dumb over her comment.

"Well, that is our gift to you, any host being actually, empowerment of the mind and body!"

She seemed uneasy looking at the sun again.

"Don't worry dear, the sun is our friend, it is life. You won't burn up I assure you!"

I reached over again and tickled her making a sizzling sound.

She giggled and slapped my hand away.

"You poop!" she said turning serious again.

"But wait? You said birthed me?" she paused trying to figure it all out. "Then are you?"

"No, sweetie…well yes…," I paused, feeling rattled at this interrogation.

"Yes! But we don't look at it in that way. Our children, you of me, is sentient, born an individual and of a collective gene pool, less than the blending of male and female parental genes. I am apart of you as is E'ban and Tyr, but you are also a part of a much more complex chemical reaction. You are of millions, a direct linage in physical make-up," I paused to finish my drink.

"You are independent and have no need of me or any other to make it in this world. We consider our children free of us once they have left the womb. Like an earthly vampire and its chosen mate, the blood-birth does not hold one to the differentiation between father or mother and that of the lover. You, Charlotte, are as the same to me, my lover and not my child in that conventional way. You are of your own body now, I think that is the separation. In time, you will feel and understand this to be true, as hard as it is to understand now."

I emptied the contents of the margarita pitcher into my glass. Closed my eyes and knew Charlotte's questions were just beginning. I had to chuckle to myself. I may not have been her mother in the conventional sense, but I was to be her parent, the one person in charge of her growth process until she could find her resolve and sentient independence as all children come to do.

CHAPTER 64

"And what about fire, holy water, silver bullets, stakes and such?" she asked after a while, worried again. "Can we be harmed from that?"

She contemplated herself, her books, still hopeful there could still be some romance in this new life, I think.

"No! Sorry dear, those things hurt, yes, maybe kill your host body, but you, that of which is now inside; will survive."

She seemed incredulous over that, but also disappointed that there was so little element of danger.

"We are…well, pretty damn hard to kill. Our make-up, our chemical-cellular composition is too fluid, too difficult to inflict damage upon. We are flexible you could say, able to separate ourselves and reform…like water on a hot pan, or mercury on a mirror, always able to bead or separate, but always reconnecting at every chance it gets."

She paused, thinking on that.

"But, if I did have to leave this body, what happens to it, my human body? Do I become me again; my old self, remember what I had known to this day?"

"No! The host body becomes vacant, empty, understanding little, like a zombie perhaps…or close to it, if you chose to leave it. But, I am not fully sure. I have never left a body that hasn't suffered a mortal injury except to change into something more adapted to the environment I am in, I find it uncaring and distasteful to do so."

"You two are joined now. When the creature within, what has now become you, leaves its host body, your human body, it will take your memories with it, your collective knowledge, your soul, that which makes Charlotte Bell Aberdeen, Charlotte Bell Aberdeen, leaving it to function at only the most basic levels," I paused.

"The few bodies I have left intentionally, I showed mercy, and ended that life…"

Charlotte seemed to recoil from that statement, that unnerving fact.

"But I choose to work with it, the body I am given, improve it. I think that is really living then. To make do with what you've inherited, and work to improve it, oneself. I think anything else is cheating perhaps," I paused, thinking over long past lives.

"But it means survival to inhabit the highest order of being on whatever world you are on. I think there is an exception for that. To arrive in one form, and change to another for the sole purpose of survival."

I paused long, stretching out and remembering something of great importance. Something that was of second nature to me from since I could remember.

"Remember my love, that we must assimilate, adapt to the demands of the environment, the order, the hierarchy of what exists. Become whatever the apex predator or the apex being is, to be as them; to blend and conceal our true identities within a society, an ecosystem, and to become as one with it. Live within it, and love it. Love them as I do here on earth," I paused.

"Just make sure that the body you choose is one that you will want and see yourself falling in love with it, as I have with this body now."

I saw her smile at that so thoughtful idea. To love one's own self for all its faults and fragilities.

I spoke again. "I love this body, this woman I have become. We have become a grand thing, beautiful; vivacious…I love humankind Charlotte, I am so glad to experience it, you, this world."

"Oh, do…do you love us…I mean earth, the human race?" she asked afraid of the answer.

I wavered for a moment at the thought of you, this human race.

"Yes Charlotte, I do. More than you could understand right now."

"I have lived on many worlds, lived many different lives…and I can honestly say that when this life of mine is at an end here on this world…when this world's time is at an end, I am going to cry for many, many years over it. That is how much I have come to love this place, this earth, the human race."

"I pray each night, thankful that I have fallen here, thankful for each and every day. It may be hard for you to understand this right now, but in time you will. This place is very special. Your kind is very special."

Charlotte thought on that for a great while relaxing to take in the sun with me.

"Yes, you have always been happy, haven't you? You care for others, help when and where you can."

She looked at me.

"Yes, I do what I can, try to love and nurture them."

"But we must remain in the shadows, do our part from afar. Let them believe of you, the vampire, even though they themselves do not believe that you are truly possible," I spoke quietly.

"This world, I assure you, would turn on us if it ever knew we actually existed. I fear this fact, for there is still Stoya and she is perhaps as dangerous, or even more so than Tyr. We are dangerous Charlotte, we could destroy worlds if we so desired. Stoya has destroyed galaxies."

We sat in silence for a while again.

I turned away for a moment, when thoughts of what I had to do to save Charlotte came flooding suddenly back. The lives I destroyed.

It was for the higher good, I thought to myself. It was her time to evolve.

I looked back to smile at Charlotte.

"What of my soul?" she asked me. "You said our kind absorbs the soul upon habitation?"

"Yes, it is what happens to those we inhabit, the loss of that one individuality. But it, the soul, their soul, becomes as us, of us. Lost maybe to its individual journey, but it gets to live, bound to our soul to live forever, if not of its own decision."

"Our soul?" Charlotte asked curiously looking at me again turning onto her side to face me.

"Yes, our soul. We all have souls, Charlotte. All creatures great and small in this universe; it is as God has intended it to be. In truth, the soul really is all we are. It is the life force that is each of us. You, the being within, has a soul, just as much as Charlotte Bell Aberdeen the human did. But, you are together now. Bound eternally, complete. Can't you feel that within yourself, that contentment?"

"I think so…"

She seemed to think on that. Then spoke hesitantly. "So, so my human soul is…"

"Yes, absorbed by you, that is what makes you…you as now."

"But…so, so…"

I laughed again at her, the look on her face.

"Yes, sweetie, here is where life gives itself over to the supernatural. Here, is where perhaps your books can dream up better answers than I, or even God. From here on in, you and the once human-souled Charlotte are as you are and will forever be, save for the future bodies you will inhabit. The first soul, your "human" soul and that of the being within, are as one now, a new soul, a joint soul; not a twin, but utterly one. From here on, in all future bodies, the resident soul, if you will, will become of you also, your soul, in some way. But always joining to be as one. Never to delete or alter much of you the being within and that of what Charlotte Bell Aberdeen is now," I paused again.

"Like Legos my dear. You start with one piece, and add another, then another, then another. Each piece, still a Lego in and of itself, but in time has grown piece-by-piece to become a collective of individual "Legos" which forms a whole, newer thing as each new piece is added. In short, we are like "Legos", an ever-growing thing. But so much more complicated in construction," I paused, impressing myself with that analogy.

"Frankly, my love, I could not tell you of how it all works precisely. There are some things in this universe that God does not allow any to know. This is one such thing. It is what it is and shall always be. Take comfort in this; however, you are Charlotte Bell Aberdeen. What you feel now is forever, just as I am of the soul, the thing which makes me, my being. Makes all that is Ianthe Gold. But I am now in this moment, also, a collection of souls. A collection of memories, as faded as they are. Life experiences unbelievable in their diversity, immense in their span of life within time."

I stood for a while. I needed to stretch my legs. I poured myself another drink.

"Your soul is old Charlotte Bell Aberdeen, despite the youth of this current human reincarnation. But your human bound soul had an inability to remember that, until now. An effect of the mind and body; age. It is the flesh that is forgetful. The chemical deterioration of cells with the natural ageing process. The deterioration of the mind. The soul within unable to rebuild its lifelong memories amidst its failing machine. Like a reappearing hole in a bucket, ever letting out water faster than it can get back in."

I continued.

"In time, the memories of these lives you have lived will return to you. Be reconstructed within our new alien mind. You have been traveling long and far my dearest one, in spirit, your soul, to change often the body with each new birth. Lives are short for most, that is the journey as God intended. That is the miracle, a secret truth, we are all immortal, just not all are immortal of the flesh as we are. That is the one thing I have given you Charlotte, "the gift" as Anne Rice might say, that you are one now of both soul and body, the body within the body. To forever know a continual life, one which suffers no breaks in its pathway, whatever that pathway is."

I paused and reflected upon that thought. Then spoke again.

"I was born the feminine, a girl, a woman of the body and soul within, my natural being on a planet not of our kind. I was placed into a being who was a young female, a teen perhaps. I am of her, my first joining. My personality, my mind, my talents, my essence is as it is before you, as it has been for ages. But I am also of many others, to some extent, the best of what that soul had offered. I was given a body that was dying and gave it life, as I did you. A being all alone, lost, crashed upon the world of which my parents lived. I have been as her, all this time inside. Her thoughts, her dreams, her abilities. Funny isn't it how we are so very much alike in this universe. Could you have ever guessed that my traits and habits are that of another being from so very far from here, of another time, Charlotte? That I am of many other beings also, their knowledge, their memories, and peculiar habits? Think on that Charlotte Bell Aberdeen, of how really the same we all are in this universe and our lives within it. So much so, that as odd as you have found me, I was never so much different than that of any other on your planet. Understand Charlotte Bell Aberdeen, that many times, those who exhibit forms of "mental illness" or other behavioral abnormalities, could very well be humans with memories, habits of things, beings, not of this world, and not of this time. That to them, it is we that are the "crazies". A view through the lens of a memory from another being acting out on this world in human body. This is the nature of what you will come to understand. That all things are not as they seem. That memory, the soul, its experiences are universal if not entirely synchronous to human social understanding."

I paused thinking of some of my friends from the streets of LA and New York, the homeless, the displaced with memories from worlds of which I had lived. I chuckled to myself in that moment.

"There is a Jesus on every bus, in every city, careful now, it may be his memory, his soul, you are talking to in that body sitting next to you. Something to think about."

I continued.

"In time Charlotte, you will see that, how so similar we all are of mind and spirit. To varying degrees, all of us, or so that I have found thus far of intelligent beings. We all love and laugh, hurt and feel pain, and want only to survive and thrive. We all have ambitions, desires, wants. We want to have children, to see them grow, to be better than we, the parents, to move the gene pool forward into time. To make a mark, to accomplish something and to be remembered for as long as time gives us," I paused again.

"I am of the same spirit now as I have been since my first host, imagine that Charlotte. You have been, and are in love with something even deeper than what you could ever imagine. This human body with an alien's soul, the personalities of beings from other worlds, other cultures, and other beliefs. I am alien am I not? But then, so were you to me once long ago, your human race. The only difference now, is that you will come to remember who you once were also. Come to inherit those ages old peculiarities also. Develop habits perhaps, of someone long ago."

I stopped a moment smiling blissfully at her, the memories of the woman upon the ice replaying in my mind.

"That is our miracle my love, to remember and be always."

I smiled at her and winked. Would she soon remember her time upon the ice so long ago? Will she remember me, the soul within, and understand then, that we are all each of us destine to meet, that only time and distance stands between us, in that forever reuniting?

"Well, some lives…," I paused, speaking more to myself than Charlotte, looking back up and past the sun into the darkening blue of space, "however, are quite dull," I paused again.

"Like my last one. But then, what would they have become in time and evolution if their world had not died, perhaps, one day, as we are now."

I thought about that, and others like us, and of the things not yet evolved to a higher level of understanding. That in this moment, somewhere, they scratch and crawl, and creep slowly forward into it, life, existence, as we once did, as my human body once did, unknowing now, perhaps, but they will soon. Of what things will they do, when man has passed so far into memory that even the footnote no longer exists. I sighed out stretching, and attempting to melt farther down into my chair, to bask under a sun, which may not exist a billion years from now.

I thought of Charlotte. Envious that her adventure had just begun.

CHAPTER
65

By the end of the month Charlotte was beginning to drive me batty. She was always talkative, gossipy, and it seemed worse now than when she was entirely human. The questions seemed to never end, and my liquor cabinet and wine cellar were beginning to thin. I had no one to blame but myself after all.

"If nothing bad happens, would I have to leave this body at the end of the world, for example?" she posited one day over lunch on the patio.

"No, not necessarily, it, you, can live forever in it. Even travel the stars within it, most times. But only as long as your human body is able to adapt. There are always issues when it comes to surviving on other worlds. Not all worlds are as earth."

"But how is it that my body stays forever, exactly?"

"Well…"

I took another sip from my glass, a nice crisp white 2013 Rhys's Chardonnay.

"It's a bit complicated, the science, the chemical construct of it, but we can keep this body because we, what is within, is capable of continual regeneration and DNA chromosome augmentation assimilation. We have no stem cell replication limits because we have no Telomere limits for cell reproduction. Our kind, and by default, the body of which we inhabit and inter-mesh with will self-heal, self-repair constantly, never ending. When we take of the blood and flesh, we absorb new DNA components from it, sequence cells that are useful to us. Re-engineer them into our own, to continue our bodies functions. To further improve upon it. That is why we must eat of the blood and flesh, of the human body. To absorb the same components of which is as our host body in order to continue on."

I thought about that now, in that moment, that Charlotte was going to need to feed soon, on human blood and flesh. She had taken quite nicely to rare red meat and understood now my obsession with Porterhouse cuts. But Charlotte being Charlotte had begun to prefer Wagyu beef. The taste of which she saw as refined and lady like.

I laughed at her, sitting before me in a light cotton Tommy Bahama sun dress, her mirrored Prada sunglasses, and fancy sun hat, delicately, if not veraciously dining on bloody, barely seared beef.

"But anything other than meat will suffice?" she said gently chewing.

"No and yes, we can eat most earthly foods, but we must eat of the flesh, it is what we are made to do. We cannot thrive long without it. Any flesh will do to satisfy our hunger, our basic chemical needs. We consume animal proteins, but to truly thrive, we must eat of the same flesh as of the body we currently exist in. Human bodies, human flesh. If we were apes, we must consume other apes, a fish for a fish, a lion for a lion, and so on."

"So…I must kill then, sometime soon…"

I saw her frown, sadden, and sink in her chair, the ugly reality of the vampire coming home to roost.

"Yes, this isn't Hollywood, but there is time still."

I thought carefully over my next words. I stopped eating, took another sip of my wine, and leaned forward toward her, speaking quietly.

"The act of killing for us is not out of malice, Charlotte. Not out of barbarity. Not out of some desire to harm or to do evil. It is the way of things, of what we are designed to do. Like the lion on the Serengeti, we take of the sick and the dying, the weak and unfit to survive. We weed out those that will pass on unfit genes; genes that may hinder growth of the species, whatever that may be. We cultivate worlds. Ensure it succeeds in its evolution. We are mercy; we are the propagators of life."

"I choose to take of the man-on-man predators here on this world, those that prey on the helpless and the meek for no other reason but self-gratification and greed; murderers, rapists, criminals of all kinds; those whose actions inhibit growth and unbalance evolution. But I also take of the sick and the dying, the infirm. This is my mercy. To mindfully eliminate needless suffering and help propagate the strong and healthy, the fit of mind and body in order to produce the next generation; perhaps a better generation. If this world ever achieves some of what other worlds have achieved, it will be in part of my doing, our kind's doing."

I saw sadness flood over her. And I began to fear again, of what I have done. I reached over and took her hand, holding it gently.

"You are here now, Charlotte Bell Aberdeen, to do good in this world. More good than you could have ever thought possible. You are rich beyond all comparison both in physical wealth and in body and spirit. You have only time now. Time to do good, to keep the balance. There are many who will need of you, your kindness, you're very being. To believe that there is hope. That God does exist. To know that there are otherworldly things at play in the final moments of their life. You are the reckoning for the evil of others and the light for the those that are good, those worthy to succeed. I assure you Charlotte, you can make more of a difference now than your humble human existence ever could. It is what you have always wanted, and have always tried to do. To make a difference."

I paused remembering her, my mighty lawyer on this world, my girl upon the ice; the princess with the gift to heal great divides; the body, the soul, and the mind.

"Yes Charlotte, you may not understand it right now, but life for you, your dreams to make a difference in this world, this universe perhaps, have just begun."

I saw her smile at that fact. She stood up and removed her sun dress to reveal her naked body. Moving to the lawn chairs, she sat laying back to stretch fully under the noon day sun. There was romance in this I believed she thought; to be, possibly, a hero in a world with few heroes. Money and time, her ultimate super powers.

I watched as she sat looking out over the desert valley beyond. In that moment, I saw also, the girl upon the ice, the way she also looked out into the horizon, ever searching. And I knew then that they were truly one and the same of soul.

CHAPTER 66

Charlotte was quickly coming to terms with her new life, its alien reality. She found that she was strong and healthy. Her body worked now. Free of normal human aches and pains. Free of limitations, both self-imposed and real. I'd watch her stretch into yoga poses that even those who had practiced for many years could seldom achieve in entirety.

She moved gracefully, quietly, tip-toeing around as she always did in our apartment back in LA but with even more poise. My clumsy Charlotte of old was forever gone to such awkward human conventions.

Mentally, her mind, her thoughts, her collective human knowledge had all become clear to her now. Re-focused and articulately organized.

Memory for humans, is often cloudy, disjointed, not out of any deficiency, but because the mind is always trapped in the dying process chemically, as time moves on and the body ages. A tragedy really, that even that thing, a thing so cherished, also fades with time. Left in the end, as it was in the beginning, a blank slate, yearning for information.

But Charlotte's memory had been resurrected, re-built and catalogued in a clear concise way now. It is our ability with knowledge, a thing built out of evolution in order to survive. She could instantly recall, in entirety, almost anything she had ever experienced or learned. Things even that were not there before; memories from other lives.

"There not dreams!" she concluded one day. "They are memories. I see that now, how my human mind interpreted them, using images of this world to explain something it could not fully understand from another!" she puzzled.

I laughed. "Yes, that's what I believed to be of your kind, your dreams are memories really, disjointed, and masked by things familiar. Pity, what things could humans do if they could ever remember of themselves more fully, a past life where technologies or some other thing could be made to ease this suffering."

She found, too, that she could recite nearly verbatim, line-by-line, section-by-section, the multitudes of Case Law books of which she struggled to remember all through college.

She discovered a near complete understanding of advanced science and math formula and theory, understood much higher levels of philosophical discourse. Charlotte was not dumb in any sense, but the average human mind is incapable of verbatim memory recall, with rare exceptions. The inhabitation of our kind changes all that. It was all beginning to make sense now. Her memory had recovered itself and had added our ability for advanced understanding.

"Shit!" she said one day. "Wish I had these brains in college, it might have taken me maybe three years to finish instead of seven"

I laughed at her; she was so damn funny.

Other things became intuitive to her as well. The principles of advanced engineering for example. Something she neither had the aptitude, nor desire to learn. She found that she understood and even enjoyed it now. She would look at images of mechanical diagrams on-line and found enjoyment.

I found her outside with the engine hood up on my Bugatti one day.

"You know, daddy tried to teach me basic mechanics for just in case...," she laughed fondly at the memory. "It all makes sense now."

I went to her and gently lowered the hood.

"Sweetie-pie I will tell you once and only once. Don't ever touch my baby boy again, or so help me!"

We both laughed out as she darted around pretending to be "working" on my Bugatti.

"I can give him an oil change!" she laughed. "And oh! How about the spark plugs? Those need changing too!"

She taunted, touching his hood, pretending to turn a wrench.

"Shit! I'll just take him all apart and rebuild him into something better!" she teased.

I stood tall and firm shaking my finger at her gritting my teeth.

"Touch him and I'll file for divorce, miss missy!" I threatened.

Charlotte also found her artistic side. Always languishing to be able to draw and paint, she understood for the first time how to apply light and dark marks to form shadow and light, the foundation of all image. She could create an image in her mind and turn it into the physical, something that even I still struggled with.

I found delight in that ability of hers. Contented as I watched her draw or paint or sculpt images in wet clay.

"I will leave you to live with Stoya for a while...," I told her one day. "She is a master artist in her own right," I thought fondly. "She will teach you many things."

I was never good at the arts, creating something of the mind in that way. My mastery was of business; numbers, math and science, of gold, investments, and how to profit from them.

Charlotte also reveled in her new-found physical strength and senses, and soon began to run and jump between the giant red and pink boulders upon the nearby mountains.

However, Charlotte was extremely disappointed in our lack of magical vampire abilities. Having read the earthly myths of what a vampire should be, she had expected to be able to fly, maybe turn into a cloud of bats. She wanted to be able to climb walls and walk across ceilings, to be able to vanish into thin air.

"This sucks!" she blurted out one day annoyed over the inability to achieve her fantasy.

"What good is being a vampire if you can't do vampire stuff?!" she huffed.

I laughed at her. She was such a dork.

"We don't even sparkle!"

She pouted again.

"What good is sparkle?" I quipped; becoming a little annoyed at her constant petulance of late.

"In what way, ever, could that be of any purpose?" I demanded.

Charlotte pouted.

"Well, at least Lestat can fly and read minds!" she quibbled. referring to Anne Rice's now very famous character. "That would be useful!" she posited.

I thought of Stoya and shuddered at her abilities, the words and images she had put into my mind still nagging at me even now, the one word that I could not seem find.

"We don't even sleep in coffins!" she said continuing the argument.

"Well, you can if you want too...," I shot back. "But I prefer my comfy, cushy bed to any of that."

Charlotte huffed at me again.

"But we have no super powers!" she demanded as if God was listening.

"Well, Charlotte, you can see clearly as if day in absolute dark. Smell, hear and sense things very far away. And, you can eat a human whole!" I scolded. "Maybe two or three!" I laughed.

Then added. "You can endure the cold vacuum of space and see other worlds," I paused. "Change bodies at will and live until time itself ends." I countered sarcastically. "Let's see Lestat do any of that!" I joked.

"Well…but, Lestat is sexy…dark and romantic!" Charlotte naively countered.

"You have met Stoya, right?" I condemned her. "Lestat doesn't hold a candle-wick-flame to that piece of work!" I posited. "It doesn't get any darker, more dangerously sexy than Stoya, I assure you."

I thought of her now, Stoya's absolute power over me and anyone she chooses. Even Lestat would have found her absolutely irresistible. Dead by her hand if she had wanted it. I thought of that scene now, and smiled, the look on Lestat's face when he came face-to-face with a real monster.

She pouted. "But, well…he's 'Lestat!" she posited coyly implying of his sex appeal. "You know, fucking hot and…" she paused, ashamed to admit some young girl fantasy.

I thought of Stoya again. Oh, how she would be insulted!

"And limp as a wet rag," I offered up. "What good is that?" I laughed.

"To live forever and not enjoy sex, the feeling of one's skin upon yours, to be within your lover, to be so beautiful and never get to use your functions. Perhaps even, to make another of one's kind…to have a child one day. That would be truly sad, Charlotte, if you think about it. To have so much but, but yet in the end, achieve so little, even Lestat would die in the face of us. He is immortal, but not forever."

Charlotte frustrated, huffed again, annoyed at my sarcasm of her grand illusions; my practicality. Our so very human attributes.

"Well...," she protested at last. "At least Lestat doesn't eat his lover-prey. It's disgusting!"

She pouted angrily.

I mused over her assumptions then spoke sarcastically.

"Well, I've eaten you and don't have any complaints about that, do you now?"

I watched her lips form into a grimace of disapproval as she turned away and stormed off taking her copy of *The Vampire Lestat* with her.

"Poop on you!" she exclaimed back at me. "Fucking poop!"

I couldn't help but laugh at her. Perhaps she would have been happier being reborn in the 17th century, I thought.

At least then she would have had all the illusions of the fantasy, the elegant frilly dresses and the corsets and capes and all the grandeur of the courts of Europe.

I chuckled quietly at the memories. I saw the dusty bottle of Grand Marnier 1880 given to me as a gift from Stoya many years ago sitting on my liquor cabinet. It was the original 1880 blend.

Yes..., I thought about Charlotte's fantasies. I do miss the grandeur of elder times.

I sighed out missing suddenly that elegance also, then thought of our modern times, the global complications and efficient corporate like coldness so often occurring in this day and age.

"Poop!" I said loudly to myself. "Fucking poop!"

CHAPTER 67

But Charlotte would remain Charlotte, cute, innocent, idealistic, and kind. The person I fell in love with that day so long ago at the Coach Store, that day I first saw her upon the ice.

She had ideas in her head, of how things should be. She wanted the romance of it, the fantasy of being a vampire. And was finding it wasn't there. We, our being, were the opposite of that. We were God's ugly fucking truth.

Killing is a horrible, ugly, painful thing. Charlotte would need to commit to it if she was to survive. I had explained that a few drops here and there would suffice most of the time. That she could take of friends and lovers in order to sustain herself. And that most of us only needed to feast, to consume flesh infrequently, often waiting months or even in some cases, years. It was what it was. It was God's grand design.

"And what of God?" Charlotte saddened at that thought. "Will he turn against me?"

She became afraid of that thought due to her Christian view of things.

"No sweetie, you are of God!" I paused, smiling gently at her. "You are the love that is God; you are Its greatest gift."

"It?" she puzzled, shocked at that word used to describe her heavenly master.

"Yes, the N'I, It, what describes life in our language; the Great Burning Light that is what God is to us and many other beings in this cosmos," I paused.

"God is not what you have thought he or she is. It is real. It does exist in form and matter…It is not a thought nor an idea, It is so very real," I thought for a moment then spoke again.

"It is neither a he nor a she, nor anything but the birther of life. Its own entity. It simply is, makes and takes and does as Its mind has thought fit to do. No one could tell you of why or how, or any other motive, It simply is and does and will do until It is done, such is Its makeup, Its purpose of which none, save but some other elder gods understand. And It is elder, a thing from beyond our time, from beyond time itself quite possibly," I spoke ceremoniously, introspectively and smiled again at this thing so grand.

"But, am I evil, my being…vampire? Am I of the devil?" Charlotte paused to reflect on that thought slumping down slightly, waiting for an answer.

"No! You are the Nosferatu, the feaster of the cosmic blood and flesh, nothing more and nothing less. And…," I chuckled. "There is no devil…," I stopped to think of Stoya and Tyr, and others like them.

"No, no devil, unless you wish to be," I chuckled slightly. "You are as God intended you to be, of us, our kind, predators and little more," I reassured her.

"In time, you will understand this, and what your place is in this infinite universe. That true evil is what you do, or do not do with your time. Your life and the purpose you give it, that is the gift of which God has given us all," I broke off for a moment.

"Time…the only real evil is if you do not choose to make good use of it, your time in this life."

"But doing bad things, is that not evil?" she asked puzzled over my so alien philosophy.

"Yes…and no," I thought for a moment. "In human terms, doing harm is an act of evil. For us evil is an act that misuses time. Time is the gift, the commodity of which we are all given. But the catch is; you may never know how much time you have been given to use...," I paused, thinking.

"Time, Charlotte, the proper use of it, that is the defining moment of what is evil or not, for us."

I saw her puzzle over that so alien of concepts. Our kind's belief that evil is not evil in the human sense. It is in the nature of things, to kill, and destroy, and consume. That to us evil is not making good use of your time in the universe.

"But, to be clear, some of us are bad, evil if you will, like Tyr. Tyr only sought destruction, to master everyone and everything. To consume it all for no other reason than out of spite and hatred for all things lower than himself, than our kind. He sought to be as God, to become God. And though he used his time to such ends earnestly, what good can come of it when you find that you are the only one left to speak of it."

"To kill without mercy or discretion, to take advantage of the meek and innocent who cannot defend themselves, I consider this to be an act of evil, yes. To manipulate things, mislead others in an unethical way, yes. But, we are killers, monsters, and predators like any other. The lion of the Serengeti must eat. It is there to cull the weak and the overly strong, to keep the balance. It neither purposely or wantonly kills, nor is absent of it. It takes what is necessary to survive and nothing more."

I watched Charlotte think hard on that, seeming to be somehow comforted by the logic.

"Boy, are we complicated!" she laughed. "Us vampires!"

"Yes, my love, very, very complicated."

I saw my opportunity in that moment to help her understand.

"Even more so than Lestat and the others in your books could ever hope to be except for their sometimes so very human inner desires and complexities. We are, save for the more glamorous aspect of an author's imagination, them of which they write."

I saw her smile at that thought, complicated, exotic, and unearthly in our being, our deep and ancient way of things. The romance for her was finding its way back.

"Think on this Charlotte, we are the great secret. We are the thing that humans desire to be, but can't be. The thing that has made millions of dollars, a fantasy. We are an ideal, open and in plain sight, so very human. Our guise, living breathing flesh. No different than any other one around you, except for what lays deep within. That my love is the real magic of us. The most fantastic thing; the fact that we could be anyone, that anyone could be as we!"

She perked up at that idea, standing.

"Well, then, I had better not disappoint the human audience shall I. I will be what so many long to be, and I will grace them with it, my being, my so very human-vampire being!"

I mused looking at her vision. Her glow, her enthusiastic eyes blazing in the low light. Her smile and the almost whisper upon her mouth. Of what can she speak I wondered.

"Yes, I think you will quite nicely!"

I thought of her, of Stoya, two polar opposites; the dark vampire and the vampire of light. I thought of E'ban and me, how disappointing to the world we must surely be, our so very quiet, boring human lives.

"I just wish I sparkled!" Charlotte huffed stamping her foot playfully, looking into a small living room mirror.

"It would be so awesome!"

I laughed at her. "Don't worry about sparkling my love, you are positively radiant!"

CHAPTER
68

In Phoenix, Charlotte went bonkers over her new-found power of the body and mind. And it didn't hurt that she was obscenely rich now either. A black card and a hot, size 4 body is a dangerous thing.

We needed to get out. It was time to start reemerging into the world again.

Charlotte was determined to make a show of it, release her pent-up energies, and revel in her new being as we ate and drank and shopped our way up and down the Biltmore Fashion Park Mall. We spent hours upon hours trying things on, ordering Champagne and other luxury services.

I was exhausted and felt old.

But she was beautiful to watch in motion. To see the generosity of her as she lavished praise and cash tips upon the store clerks that attended her. They loved her back, but found that they did not want her money, but her, her presence. She had a power over them. Over people, like Stoya has.

But her way was peaceful. Her touch was soothing, her voice reassuring. A soft glow emanated from her, barely visible, but palpable, uplifting. It brought a sense of hope. The exact opposite I noticed of what Stoya always projected. She listened, empathized, and counseled. She loved them, and they fell about her like some Messiah figure.

Managers offered up deep discounts. Clerks sneaked trinkets into her bags calling them "freebees".

I watched as Charlotte compiled quite a list of phone numbers and email addresses, promises for future dates, dinners, and lunches with these new-found friends for when we were back this way, or anytime. I found myself often left out and sitting alone waiting with the other husbands.

It was 2AM. We were on our way home when we had found a baby deer on the side of the road. Its hind legs and pelvic bone had been broken in an attempt, no doubt, to evade some careless driver.

I stood in the cold, crisp late-night desert mountain air as Charlotte cradled the baby deer. She soothed it, talked to it, as it fought against pain and the fear of dying.

I broke down inside at the sight of her, my gentle Charlotte, as she cradled it, whispering to it eloquent words of comfort, pleaded with God to save it.

I knew what had to be done, what had to be said. I heard the words of Stoya's warning again.

"She will be as us..."

I knew then, that the loss of innocence was upon us.

"Release it from its pain...," I spoke cautiously, gently to Charlotte, as she cradled it, caring for it, its wounds.

I knew the time had come for her to feed. It was a sign, this life, this creature, this moment of truth. It is what we did, feed upon the weak and infirm.

She began to weep uncontrollably. But I could also sense the fight within her, the creature within was awakened and starving, seeking living flesh and blood.

"Set it free to evolve in body and spirit," I reaffirmed gently.

She looked at the wounds on its injured back, its neck, the blood slowly trickling.

"Take of it, release it...," I coaxed her.

"I, I, c, ca, can't…I," she sobbed.

"I…I…I…won't…," she barely uttered.

I kneeled down behind her. "It is within your power to set it free…," I encouraged her.

"Free?"

She trembled.

"Do you feel its blood coming to you? Do you feel it calm within you, its blood reach out to feel your touch?"

"Y, y, yes…," she exhaled forcibly.

"That is your power Charlotte, to bring relief to the dying as you once were dying, to take the pain away. Think of yourself on your bed, dying, the pain and loneliness of it. You can keep it from that now, that pain of which you so well know. Love it, by showing it mercy. Take it, for you are mercy…," I paused thoughtfully.

"Free it from this world, this pain, it suffers," I coaxed her. "Free it now!"

I, too, smelt the blood gnaw at me as I saw it gnaw at her. She wanted it. I could feel the being within her stir, its mind searching my mind, the universe's mind for an approval perhaps.

I could hear the deer's heart beating slowly, its breath was calm as it nestled into her arms. I saw her lean forward, balking at the thought of it, the bite, the blood; the consummation. But the instinct of our kind is strong and the pangs for blood and flesh began to flush throughout her, gnawing at her, calling.

"Think of the vampires, Charlotte. Think of Lestat, the romance of it and the immortal kiss. The freeing kiss. Its soul is immortal, set it free, so that it can find the next evolution," I spoke gently.

Sobbing, she slowly licked at the wound gently, hesitantly.

I saw the baby deer seem to stare out into the great abyss that is the endless beyond, the great eternal burning horizon.

What did it see? I wondered of its next lifetime.

Slowly, Charlotte began to lick, then suck on the wound, taking in the life she needed to survive. Her mouth, the creature-child within, felt the blood rushing to her, into the thing that makes us what we are.

I saw the deer close its eyes and allow itself to completely be absorbed by her, to let go knowing that this was not the end.

It saw the great beyond, the sands of time, and felt time fall through it.

I heard it breathe out long and slow. Blissful was its death in Charlotte's arms. It knew it was of the circle of life, knew that it was of the grand design. And I think, possibly, knew that that night was not an end but a beginning.

Charlotte wept a long time while holding the baby deer in her arms.

I sat with her as she made her peace with this new reality. But she couldn't deny the fact that she felt better, more alive.

We lay the deer in an open meadow of white and yellow desert flowers not far from the road.

I was content to stop short of total consumption; she needed time to come to that. But she would need to feast soon; her new bodily alliance needed to absorb human DNA to continue to be healthy and strong.

CHAPTER 69

Charlotte lay beneath our bed sheets attempting to hide from the world. Images of the dying baby deer and the sensation of drinking its blood haunted her human side. It is; however, something that fades with time and the knowledge that this is who one is cannot be denied. And, there was no denying that she felt better, stronger from it. I cradled her in my arms for a long time listening to the desert sounds beyond the retracting bedroom windows.

"I, I, I feel ashamed…," she whimpered. "I, I wanted to…"

"I know sweetie, it is only natural. Do not let it upset you. There is time to come to terms with that later."

"It made me…feel…"

"Yes, I know…"

"I could see it, its life…something before that also…" she puzzled.

"I know my love, it's the gift we have. To see our prey's life at times, its mind-memories, images of its life as lived in the now, and sometimes of their past lives. Take that story, that of its life and make it apart your own Charlotte. Remember it, for it is how we learn of things, of why we are greater in that regard."

I gently stroked her hair.

"It gets easier with time. Honor it and all that you take from this world. It is what should be done. Love and honor the life taken for us to live on."

I thought for a moment of Lestat and understood a connection.

"That is our gift, my love, to absorb the memories of the souls we take and make them eternal in our own memory."

I contemplated it now, our second magical power over immortality; memory.

"Yes, Charlotte, we are magical…"

I winked at her.

"We have a power that Lestat and the others may not even posse, eternal memory."

I chuckled. "Hmm…perhaps, Charlotte, I am wrong about us. Maybe we are special after all...magical in that way. Yes, I think I like that!"

She seemed to be uplifted again at those thoughts as I gathered her up tighter into my arms. I held her as she fell fast asleep to dream no doubt of the deer and its time within the forest, the time when it was free to live as it was meant to live.

I thought of us now, our kind, in contrast to Charlotte's ideal, the human ideal of us. I thought of the vampire, the thing that is its own ideal, and fell fast asleep to the face of a smiling, all knowing Lestat.

CHAPTER 70

Charlotte's chance to make her first real feast of flesh would come a few weeks later. The local news channel had reported that a prisoner somehow escaped while being transported to a corrections facility up North.

She was a murderer; a lifer with three counts of manslaughter; her own children. She was wanted and considered "dangerous".

When I had found the woman in her red prison jump suit on our property, I knew God's grand design was again set into motion, a clear sign that the time had come for Charlotte to make her first human kill.

I caught the woman hiding between the massive red, pink, and tan boulders that surrounded our home. She was watching, I am sure, for an opportunity. We looked easy enough. It would prove to be a fatal mistake.

I held her down clutching her tightly by her frizzy, ratted hair. Keeping her in a kneeling position upon the sand-rose colored slate-stone patio as Charlotte trembled in fear. Her old human feelings rising up, a natural reaction when confronted by those capable of murder and unspeakable evil.

"Do not fear her…," I spoke clearly. "She is nothing to us…food, a plaything, and nothing more…"

The words of Stoya seeming to apply well in that moment.

"You are so much more than her, in strength and spirit," I reaffirmed to Charlotte. "She could do little harm to you, your body, even if she had the means. You are immortal in the face of her…of them."

I was resolute in this. It had been two months since the deer, it was time for Charlotte to make the final embrace.

"These are the ones that deserve our death," I instructed Charlotte.

"Murderers of the innocent, the meek, takers of promising futures, these are the ones whom God has sent us for. To devour and wipe from this world, or any other, the cancer of humanity, of the universe," I spoke, condemning the woman before me.

"Take of her!" I commanded Charlotte, firm but gentle.

"Think of her children. The innocent, unable to experience the lives of which they were given by God to live and come into their full and intended purpose. This is the evil of which I speak, the waster of God's precious gift, time, the thing that should not be wasted. The thing her children no longer have. Take of this monster, consume it, and rid the universe of this evil," I spoke firmly, indifferently, wanting this person before her to mean little.

"It is the way of things…this is how she chose to be. Use her time on this world to better our own existence. It is selfish, end it, for it is nothing to anyone or anything anymore," I spoke coldly, debasing the woman to a thing, a body to be consumed.

The woman squirmed beneath my grasp and began spouting all sorts of profanity, yelling at Charlotte, telling her that she would kill her, us, like her children, hack us up into pieces, throw us away in the trash as she had had done with her own children.

She fought against me, sought freedom, but I was too powerful.

I saw Charlotte turn red with rage, her little hands clenched into fists. She raged upon the woman, screaming at her. I felt her aura change, an old familiar darkness emerged, descending down upon us, like Stoya could project. I puzzled over it, wondered at that ability.

Charlotte could not understand how anyone could do such a horrible thing. It just wasn't in her makeup, her notion of how life is supposed to be. A thing she battled with in her career of law; liars, thieves, cheaters, rapists; killers of the innocent.

"Why? Why? Why?" was all poor Charlotte could get out.

I felt sorry for her in that moment, my precious love. She felt powerless though she had all the power in the world, the universe.

"Take of her, Charlotte. You have the power to right a wrong. She will kill again. Next time it might be your sister, your brother, a family member, or some other innocent. You have the power to alter destiny in this moment, to right many wrongs. God has sent her to us, it is evolution. It is justified!"

I felt my own self rise within. I hungered for the flesh.

She was ugly, sick of body and mind, but intriguing enough for me to want of her, her flesh. A predator like me. I reveled in thoughts of her, the taste of wicked flesh. The satisfaction of consuming the consumer.

Oh, how Stoya and I would make short work of this. How Stoya relished the consumption of evil. Not to right a wrong, no not ever, but because it was just another way in which she could dominate God's will. Have power over power."

"Fuck you whores! You, nasty cunt bitches!" the woman ridiculed us, taunted us to a fight.

"I'll cut you up and make you my bitch!" she screamed at Charlotte.

I slapped her hard in the face, knocking her over and stunning her, and then pulled her by her hair back up to kneel again.

I smiled down at her, grinning, feeling devilish in that moment.

"We are going to eat you!" I spoke, teasing. "You are going to die today…and you will watch it, your death, there, in the reflection of that glass."

I turned her so she could see her own reflection in the mirrored patio door glass, her coming death.

"In there you will see something most will never know."

I grabbed her face in my hands, forcing her to look at us in the reflection.

"Us, what you really found here amidst this desert home. You have no idea of anything in this world or this universe, have you?" I taunted.

"Of the fact that the feast of flesh is about to begin…," I hissed, mocking.

I looked to Charlotte. I could see past the human being and into the thing within, her face reflected it, the deep seeded desires to feast, to be as God now intended for her, to be the vampire.

"Remove your clothes Charlotte!" I instructed again. "Let this thing see you, know you, and understand that vampires exist. That there are monsters in this world. True monsters. And that we are omnipotent and beautiful. This is your moment, revel in this time, the kiss of kisses. The final kiss!"

I gleamed, hoping to evoke her to action. To become the ideal of what she had so long fantasized.

I watched as Charlotte did as I had told her. Shaking, nervous, she pulled her sun dress up and over to reveal her pale, brilliant naked body.

The woman seemed to baulk suddenly. Her mouth open, aghast, both at the beauty of Charlotte and the action, unable to speak suddenly. To feel fear for the first time, to understand possibly what was happening here.

I felt her fear rise and noticed the smell of the chemical reaction as her adrenalin levels accelerated. Her heart raced, her breath became erratic. She wondered of what satanic thing this was. Realized in that moment most likely, that she, her life was about to end.

"Behold the vampire!" I spoke loudly addressing her, our prey.

"Revel in your glory!" I commanded Charlotte, an encouragement really.

"See the vampire, see the universe at play and know you are but of mortal flesh, that you are *"food, a plaything and nothing more!"* I laughed, redirecting my words to our captive.

I felt the woman squirm hard against me, to fight for freedom. I repositioned my hand upon the back of her neck, clamping it with great force. I felt the flesh of it condense upon her spine, she winced from the pain of that feeling.

I addressed Charlotte again.

"Take her as she took her children…end her, now! Set this wretched soul free and hope that it comes back a better being," I lamented.

"Fuck you, cunts. I'll return and kill you," the woman rebutted, not understanding this thing of life, threatening us with afterlife violence that does not exist.

"And we will be here waiting!" I laughed hideously, finding myself reveling in my horrifying immortal glory.

"We will be here waiting still, for you. For we have forever, your very body, the thing that makes you, you, your flesh will ensure that of us. Your very essence, your DNA.

I grinned devilishly.

"Yes, you are our immortality, your flesh the sacrament by which we shall endure to see the end of time."

"Fuck you, you crazy ass bitch!" the woman shouted back up at me.

"I'll fucking cut your fucking throats, hack you up in pieces…," she labored to threaten.

"Enough!" Charlotte suddenly shouted, her voice breaking the silence of the night, as she stormed upon the woman in a fury.

"No more…," she scolded me also, my taunting.

"No more!" Charlotte screamed again enraged at the whole scene.

I was startled as Charlotte rushed upon us. The woman shrieked as Charlotte grabbed her up from under me and hurled her against a nearby boulder.

The yearning for flesh was too great for Charlotte to ignore any longer.

I marveled at Charlotte's strength that had revealed itself now, like Stoya's, sharp, focused, and in this moment, unforgiving.

The woman, now badly injured and broken from the force of impact, tried to rise up, to run, but could not. Her leg was broken, the wind knocked out of her.

I saw Charlotte move to her with great speed, her eyes blazed down upon the wretch below her. I saw her begin to tremble uncontrollably. I saw her hunger and the desire for the flesh rise up into her, to consume and burn within her. I saw her instinctually bare her teeth as she lorded over her prey.

"Why? Why?" Charlotte snarled at the woman who was broken, crawling.

"Fuck you bitch!" the woman yelled back with her cigarette stained ugly mouth, much of her teeth missing from years of smoking meth and other narcotics.

"Fuck you, you whore!" she screamed at Charlotte again.

"I'm not afraid of you, you bitch. I'll kill you too!" the woman screeched as she tried to stand up and face Charlotte.

I watched her fat, withered, tattooed body make its way up from the ground to stand.

"Take her, now!" I commanded.

"This is your prey, evil to consume!" I prodded Charlotte.

"End it, now! Do not listen to her, she is nothing to us!" I commanded again.

"Fuck you, cunt!" the woman turned on me. Her eyes darted around searching for anything to be used as a weapon.

"Why?" Charlotte pleaded looking for an answer, some form of reasoning.

"Why, what?"

The woman looked back up at her defiantly.

"Your children?"

"Because they were a burden, that's why, a burden to my life!"

I saw Charlotte's face turn cold at those words. Her eyes seemed to burn like ice upon steel. Her mouth went hard. I saw her jaw seem to grind in anger. A single tear fell from her left eye. A storm of emotion rage in her; a storm of reasoning, argument, and counter argument.

She had the power to determine who lived and who died. I watched as her face contorted, her eyebrows furled, and reflected outwardly her rage, her sudden contempt for this wretch. I saw any remaining compassion slip from her, for there was none here to have she now understood despite her best efforts to find it. I saw that she had realized then, that here and now, she could find the retribution, the solution to an ongoing problem. Deliver humanity from a monster.

She thought of all the horrible things she had known and seen in court. Of all the times she had failed to be able to do anything. To watch as the cruel world churned onwards grinding down the innocent.

And in that moment too, it came upon me, upon us, the scene, the alien darkness, driving down and out like a sudden storm.

"Come on, you cunts! Come and get it!" the woman screamed.

She was cornered, outnumbered, and desperate to live.

I grinned at her, licking my lips. I could not help it now, these weeks of endless back and forth with Charlotte and the romance of the fictional vampire. I had to play the game, work the myth.

I thought of Stoya and postured myself as she did when about to make a kill, flexing, coiling, and circling; sneering.

I saw Charlotte fight within herself, the final moment coming when the flood gates were about to loose. I grinned.

"Be careful of what you ask of us, my dear. It's never good to invite the vampire to a feast."

I reveled in my truth again.

"If you are not willing to give of thy own blood and the flesh my sweet!"

"Vampires?" she scoffed. "Fuck you both!" she screamed again. "There ain't no such thing!" she concluded firmly.

But I saw her waiver now, as many do, the sixth sense that tells human kind that they have come face-to-face with the supernatural, something alien.

Then in clear cold voice Charlotte finally spoke her truth.

"Yes, we do!" she spoke cruelly. "We do exist! And you will be my first feast…," she trailed off for affect looking back at me seductively.

I saw her seem to flex also, her body grow in power. I saw her grimace down upon the woman, expectantly.

The woman shrank from us, as fear slowly washed across her face. I removed my clothes also in preparation for this thing to come.

"What thing does such a thing?' I am sure she thought. As I grinned at her, my want projecting with the intensity that is death.

"Take her!" I ordered Charlotte. "Think of her children, the innocent. Erase her memory, set their souls free!"

Charlotte seemed to circle slightly, considering the finality of this thing.

"Yes…," she spoke quietly. "My love is right, we are the vampire and it is time for me to feed…," she paused.

"It is time for you to understand that you are powerless in this moment, for you to understand how your children felt that night so long ago…"

In that moment, Charlotte lunged upon the woman taking her up and into her. Holding the woman tightly, she reached up and gripped her throat instinctively to crush it. To paralyze her prey for an easy kill. I saw her mouth open and begin its descent down upon the woman's neck.

I heard the popping, cracking sound that is flesh and sinew, and the artery being severed and removed from other deeper muscle-skin. The sound that is the release of pressure from within the body. It seemed to echo across the landscape below, punctuate the line between life and death. I could see and smell the blood being drawn from within the woman to where Charlotte had bit down. It spurted out from the corner of Charlotte's mouth and upon the ground, down into the earth.

I saw the woman go stiff, her nervous system unable to cope with the sudden trauma. Her mind suddenly unable in that moment to comprehend the thing that had her now. She saw her own reflection in the light of the setting sun upon the mirrored glass. She saw the reflection of the thing which had her now. A being smaller than she by both height and weight had become a giant in presence, monstrous and absolutely definitive.

Her eyes turned from that vision to me as I grinned.

I saw her lips move, what was it that she said? What was the plea? Something about God as always in the end.

I moved in and cupped her face gently.

"I told you, my sweet. We are the vampire, the Nosferatu. We are not of your world, of Satan or any other thing you could possibly know. But take comfort in this; we are of God. God does exist. And It has sent you to nourish us, our immortal life."

I laughed wickedly as I heard the sound that is blood, rushing into Charlotte's mouth and the sounds the body makes as it fights to retain its life.

"It has sent us here for you to know just how insignificant you really are."

I moved to help Charlotte, to hold the woman still. She was strong and refused to leave this world without a fight. I could respect that, so many others simply give up when the end is near.

"Drink of her," I whispered to Charlotte.

"There is no escaping this."

I smiled upon our victim again, addressing her.

"And God will not forgive you…," I chuckled. "I will tell you a secret; of what little comfort that it is. God exists, but It does not know of you in this moment, your life, and what you have done. It knows not even fully of us, Its first creation…," I paused, musing.

"In fact, I am so sorry to inform you, that in this moment, God does not even care. It made us for this, your death, your consumption. It is what your being is really, food for something greater. But take heart, we are the closest thing to God that you will ever know. We are as God, in fact we are of

God. We will eat your sins; release your soul into the great beyond."

I assured her as I moved into her, holding her body between mine and Charlotte's.

"Pray to us, for we are the reckoning. We are, in this moment, your salvation," I paused, laughing. "We alone are the end of all things, the world's last knowing. Your last everything."

I smiled and kissed her ugly lips gently, tenderly as her eyes remained transfixed with absolute terror.

"See us now, and understand that we are life, the beasts within the "savage garden" and you are merely our prey. That is the mind of God, the math of Its conception…," I paused. "I am so sorry…disappointing, isn't it? That redemption for your soul simply does not exist. For there is nothing to redeem, but your soul within. And even that thing, has no certainty that it will go on."

I saw Charlotte's strength grow. I saw her eyes blaze with a fury I had only seen in Stoya when she took of life.

I watched as the woman faded, her eyes became dull and lost. The spark that is life and her soul released into the cosmic abyss. Her body became a full weight as we let it slip down upon the rose-colored slate.

I saw Charlotte standing over her. The blood dripping from her mouth, the almost whisper of things best left unspoken. Another tear fell from her eye, she had empathy even now.

I felt the presence of death sink down upon us in the cool evening air as the last light of the setting sun danced upon the ancient stone to reveal the full color palette of this desert place.

I looked down upon the woman and smiled.

"Pass now into eternity, unknown and utterly forgotten to the annals of time. Know in this moment that you are nothing…and we are everything."

I watched as her eyes went blank, vacant. The pupils reflexively dilate the sign that there is no longer life. Her body withered, shrinking inwards slightly, collapsing, it seemed, into itself.

I smelt death, my ages old friend, come down to join us for the feast. I breathed in deeply taking in its scent; time in decay. I looked to God. What did It even see of us there upon the rose-colored slate-stone, this predatory interlude, the cycle of life maybe, but little more.

"Eat!" I coaxed Charlotte. "Take of her entirely...," I encouraged.

"Take of the blood and the flesh, the sacrament...," I posited.

"It is God's will!"

I watched Charlotte gently kneel before the woman's body. I saw the steam from it, the vapors of dispersing heat and energy. I saw Charlotte look at it, wonder over it. She saw it all so differently now.

"Eat...my love, take of this universe...the gift of life" I whispered to her again. "Feed!"

I watched Charlotte move closer. I saw her mouth open. I saw her for the first time in full as the thing that I had made, that I had given birth to. The alien from another world, the vampire, and fully knew of the words Stoya had spoken that night in her bed not so long ago.

"Charlotte will lose all that you have come to love in her, her innocence, her fragile human being, the thing that draws you to her. She too will come to kill as we. She will know of the blood and of the flesh...become as we..."

I watched Charlotte begin the consummation and shuddered, repulsed suddenly over the sight of her committing the act. The meat, the flesh, the blood, the sounds of it. The tearing of the fibers, the crunching of the bones, the grisly sounds of predation, the sound that was the final loss of her innocence.

I knelt down behind Charlotte, soothing her as she fed, as she took in the body of God's great measure; sentient life-corporeal. I touched her hair, her back, her body, tracing it. I saw the light of her grow. I saw her eyes blaze hot with violence and desire.

I saw her in the coming last red-orange glow of the blackening night. There was an unearthly silence, save but the sounds of the feast and a lonely howl of a coyote far away.

And I knew then, that she was of me, of our kind, the Nosferatu, the vampire. The eater of the celestial flesh, and I wept.

CHAPTER 71

I watched Charlotte bathe in the ancient, natural cave-pool that was fed by thermally heated mineral waters from deep within the earth. It percolated up through a fissure; then gently rained down from a small opening in the rock just above the pool.

She floated quietly, looking up into the one hundred-foot chasm high above and out through a secret opening in the rock that revealed the stars which flickered bright and silent in the night sky.

She had cleansed herself of the blood and of the lust for it deep within.

I watched as she floated, her eyes transfixed to the heavens searching them intently. I closed my eyes and soon caught her thoughts. She was looking for God and Its approval. She wondered over It, Its being and purpose, over her purpose now and over the journey before her, and of me.

I smiled.

She loved me. She thought of us, our coming "rebirth" to the world, our union, our pledge.

I chuckled.

She wondered if she could be everything I wanted of her.

How silly, I thought, of her thinking that.

If she only knew of how I worried over the exact same thing, being everything for her.

I also saw fragmented, short clips of the past incarnations of her eternal soul. The lives that until now she had no recollection of living save for that occasional déjà vu event, the window into the past. Not all of them were of this world.

I smiled fondly of such things of her. I saw myself through her eyes, the way in which she had seen me that day in the Coach store. I was magnificent to her, a mystery to be explored if only I would make the first move. I saw our first date, our first kiss and the sex that followed. I saw our growing life together and the coming tragedy. Even in my absences to save her, she had thought only of me.

I saw our last encounter before all of this on her hospital bed and I saw the moment that I had cut into her to give her the child, to give her life.

And then I saw Tyr and other ancients of our kind, his memory and his horrors. And I also saw the many moons over the massive ice planet Phét-mthilliu'm' and the floating ice-rock worlds over the sea of eternal ice.

I saw the woman whom I had so deeply loved there, her pale blue eyes and the almost whisper. I saw myself through her eyes, too, the being that was the girl upon the ice, and is now Charlotte.

And we, each together, understood fully in that moment that souls are eternal, forever, and will always find each other again in this grand scheme of God's design.

I held onto myself; let myself slip into the moment, of that love. And as I felt Charlotte's memories of our time together so long ago wash over me, I became aware of her also; that Charlotte, too, had connected with me, a shared memory of us through the other's eyes as we danced upon the great ice sea against the frigid winds.

I saw our kisses, our caresses, and the sex in the open upon the ice.

Charlotte had remembered me now, the strange bold and daring male of their kind with the secret past and the strange violet coloring that no other upon that world had possessed.

I had landed there and taken a male of her kind. He had come to see the glowing craft upon the ice. I had to adapt to survive. His body was attuned to the icy environment, the previous host body would not have survived long.

I saw her look into my eyes, searching, knowing that I was not fully of her kind. There was a thing within, of what she could never tell, until now.

I removed my clothes and slowly entered the warm pool to take my place with Charlotte. We met in the middle of the warm waters. She fell into me, her face against mine; our bodies pressing together, breathing in unison. We rocked slowly to the memory of us dancing on that strange, icy alien world.

"My, my name was…Ra-Ithoru….," she whispered.

"Yes…," I whispered softly back trying not to break at the sound of that name again, the way in which it is spoken, memories of her flooding me.

"You were Isaris, stranger from the southern pole…," she whispered fondly.

"Yes, but so much more wasn't I, than of your kind then."

I wept, slightly trembling in gladness.

"And you were a man then…a male of our kind?"

"Yes, I was. Strong and bold, how I chased you for your love, did I not?" I paused. "Loved you like no other…"

"Yes!" she giggled I think I see that now.

"Do you see it? The soul is what loves, not the body," I spoke.

"We are eternal; we are everything, in time…"

"Yes, I understand now," she said soothing me, feeling the pain of me watching her mortal body die in my arms that day.

"I am so sorry; it's been so long...," I wept.

"But you kept your promise, did you not?" she countered. "That one day we would meet again, be as one again..."

"Yes!"

I broke, trembling.

Charlotte kissed me gently.

"Thank you for that...," she trailed off lost in thought, marveling at this thing called life, her existence, God's plan of us, the eternalness of life; the full circle of it.

Pressing against each other, Charlotte began to kiss me softly, sensually, deeply, stroking my hair, pressing upon me passionately.

I breathed heavily, we were as one again. I needed her to take me now, to lead us in this moment, to empower herself.

I let her position me up against the edge of the pool. Wrapping my legs around her hips we gently moved our bodies together in unison.

I came quickly, deep and long as she gently crashed upon me, the warm mineral waters engulfing us in gentle waves.

I heard the sounds of our love echo, finding its way up and out of the chasm into the night above.

I thought of that world so far away from here and wondered if they could hear us now, to know that we had finally found each other again, if they finally understood of our everlasting promise.

"Forever?"

I heard her softly moan.

"Forever!" I whispered back into her awaiting kiss.

I reflected upon that word forever, the notion, the meaning, the feeling, the mathematical construct of its absolute implication.

"Yes, forever…!" I thought as we fell into the dream of our love beneath the stars on this lost and tiny world within the warm waters that is God's blood, that which binds us all to It, to each other in this, that thing which is all-eternal no matter what the form. Love and life.

CHAPTER 72

It was nearing the time for us to re-join the world again. Charlotte was growing restless. She had come to understand her new body, the things it could and could not do, both as the creature within, and the host body it now occupied.

It had been a year since our little disappearing act. We were ready to begin our new lives together, eager to take on the world as a couple; as eternal lovers.

We had agreed to return to California, choosing to relocate to the northern San Diego area. We purchased a home in the Bella Capri Estates, just a short three-hour drive to Santa Monica and LA; the place we loved.

Our new home was an elegant, but simple five-bedroom, four-bath home with a large pool overlooking the bluffs out onto the Pacific Ocean, situated in a pleasant, quiet neighborhood.

We could soak in the sun by the pool and take long walks along the beach in the mornings or evenings. We were free to travel at will now, unshackled by her old human life, her job and family responsibilities. It was all in life we had envisioned, and more.

Charlotte would also purchase her first home, a top floor, three-bedroom apartment at the Carlyle in West Beverly Hills for our quick weekend getaways. She was well vested now.

In time, she would start up her own charity foundation, The Bell Foundation, sometimes known as the Gold-Bell Foundation when I partnered on special projects. It was divided into two divisions. One, a non-profit law firm to handle domestic violence cases for underprivileged women and children. The other, focused on cancer, the continued fight to illuminate its reality and to find a cure along with a myriad of other related medical and social issues plaguing our world today.

I would fulfill my promise to Dr. Yashi Mehra by building a new, state-of-the art, highly specialized cancer center and hospital named The Yashi Mehra Center of which he was its lead researcher and CEO.

Together, he and Charlotte would fight the good fight, bring comfort and hope. Charlotte would become a fearless humanitarian, championing the most difficult issues that many shied away from, personally overseeing her projects.

She had my support. My brand name, Gold, was a persuasive influence among the most elite of the world. If I was backing, they would also.

But before we could fully move on, we had to make the final break, one final recompense.

Charlotte was missing her family terribly, especially her father. There had been no real closure in her mysterious disappearance.

It was believed that Charlotte had been kidnapped during the blackout, to collect a ransom possibly, but no one knew for sure. Conspiracies abound.

There was no video camera footage to confirm that I was ever there, it had been rendered useless by the power outage. The three eye witnesses that had spoken to police about the "person in the motorcycle suit" had little to offer. Only one description came remotely close to describing me. But how many red and black motorcycle racing suits do you think there are in the state of New York, alone?

The city was in chaos that night and everyone left to fend for themselves. Much went unnoticed in those chaotic hours, too many crimes to count.

Most believed the blackout was caused by an act of terrorism that the government was trying to cover up.

Charlotte's kidnapping was a mere coincidence. But in truth that idea made little sense. NYPD stuck to that claim, that it was a crime of opportunity; someone, possibly a hospital worker, thought they could affect a ransom. Her family was modestly wealthy, good for a million or two. But no ransom request was ever made and after three months of investigation and dead-end leads, they assumed the worst.

She had been dying anyway on the day of her disappearance. There was no way she would survive as a captive for long.

The police had labeled it a cold case, all hospital staff had been accounted for; their activities verified.

The FBI fared little better. No terrorist group, foreign or domestic, claimed responsibility. And after many dead-end leads the case in favor of an act of terrorism turned to a less probable scenario. They concluded it was a freak accident, a power grid overload.

The mayor of New York eventually released a statement vaguely outlining that a series of mishaps had "seemed" to happen during routine maintenance checks which resulted in power loss.

No one was buying it.

Speyer Electric and its host of sub-providers rallied around that scenario to save themselves from deeper investigation, they took the blame and carried on.

The Johnson Memorial Cancer Center, desperate to avoid any serious investigation into their back-up generator issues, was quickly rescued by associated big pharmaceutical investors and a plethora of medical equipment manufacturers. These entities simply could not let this mishap hurt their business and the bigger financial picture. Johnson Memorial was spending millions on the most advanced equipment and pharmaceuticals. Profits needed to be protected at all costs.

Everything was buried. I heard the chief maintenance man lives happily in Hawaii now. His assistant, who was on duty that day, resides somewhere in Mexico.

I had become family enemy number one, suspected by her father of something regarding Charlotte and her disappearance. But there simply was no proof of any involvement on my part. We leave no fingerprints, an advantage in the modern era.

I had called him the following day, when I “heard” that Charlotte “went missing”, using my overseas business number. I had been careful to cover my tracks.

His anger prevented me from getting on a plane right away. I was ordered to stay away from the funeral, the family, period!

It was hard not to both cry and laugh as he commanded these things of me. He even threatened legal action if I attempted to make contact with family, or show at the funeral.

“I understand,” was all I could say. “But I will cover the costs, no expense too great…,” I had confirmed. “I will get you a check soon, when I get back from Europe.”

I heard him steam over the phone, but I also felt his greed. He would make me pay alright, to the tune of $700,000 in funeral expenses.

Charlotte had been placed in Hollywood Forever.

Her father had seen fit to purchase plots on either side of her for himself, his wife and her brother and sister.

I had to laugh.

Even in death he sought elevation for himself and his family. I am sure, if he thought he could get away with it, he would have bought an acre of prime real-estate there for the entire Aberdeen family and extended relatives.

There at Hollywood Forever is buried some of America's greats; performers, actors, composers, writers, singers of all genres, and, of course, the obscenely rich.

Charlotte's mausoleum overlooked the central pond, ironically, within sight of Maila Nurmi's grave. Otherwise known as the infamous Vampira, the1950's actress who set the tone for what was to become the modern-day Goth-vampire genre, among other scenes.

I always had a thing for Maila Nurmi; her dark black and white beauty and the graceful way of her voice and its inflection. I had met her once, at the wrap party and private showing of Ed Wood's iconic film *Plan 9 From Outer Space*, a horrible debauchery of film, save for Vampira's casting.

I was unable to seduce her in the face of Stoya's power. I was always jealous over that.

Stoya still visits her grave to this day from time-to-time, usually under a full moon, at midnight on the anniversary of her death.

Charlotte's tomb was expertly crafted in a modernist French, Art Nouveau, Gothic. It would be flowered daily for exactly one year.

It was hard not to laugh frankly, the grandeur of it, the idea of her somehow being immortalized now. An empty tomb, an empty coffin, filled only with a photograph, her image to be remembered by family only.

"Well, Charlotte, you wanted vampire romance? Maybe we can spend a night or two in your coffin," I smirked, thinking of the expense of such a silly, vain, human thing, the rituals of burial.

"We will visit with Vampira, across the way, and the rest. We will see of what she and Stoya speak," I said cryptically, gathering myself up like Bella Lugosi upon the stairs in *Dracula*.

"Those children of the night…," I laughed ghoulishly in fun.

"Of what whispers the dead tell?" Charlotte replied laughing playfully, moving elegantly like some banshee across the silver screen with a throw blanket over her shoulders like a cape.

"I wonder if Bella Lugosi will join us also?" she joked again.

"Let us hope my love," I said gleefully. "And Akash and Lestat, and Louie and Edward Cullen, and Selene, and the Lost Boys if they are about also. We will have a grand party on All Hallows' Eve!" I spoke enthusiastically.

"Yes, it will be us and them, and the world to see that such things exist. That we are of the world's last knowing," she said laying down onto the couch as if in a coffin, pulling the blanket-cape over her as if a lid.

We laughed over it and her monolithic grave. It would continue to be a joke for many, many years to come.

But for Charlotte, there had to be a solid closure. We, she, had to make amends, see her grave, and say one final goodbye.

CHAPTER 73

Charlotte's father knocked vigorously upon the dark, stained oak door to our suite at the Mandarin Oriental in Las Vegas.

I knew he was anxious to confront me, angry that I had abandoned Charlotte in her last days on earth, angry that I had ever entered their lives. But yet, he was slave to one thing, the one thing I held power over him. Money.

He was here, or so he believed to receive his final recompense. A check to cover all the expenses that Charlotte and her family had incurred and a check for the amount of the pre-nuptial inheritance I had promised so long ago when we had first met. He felt he was due that much, possibly more.

I took a deep breath and opened the door. He was alone as I had instructed. I had paid for his travel expenses first class all the way as he would accept nothing else.

We had four hours now before his plane would leave, taking him away forever. He was visibly agitated as he entered. Immaculately dressed in a suit and tie, he was a handsome man despite the demeanor of his distress.

"Hi," I said trying to break the tension, moving to embrace him.

He was unreceptive to that gesture.

I backed away and led him into the master living room where the drapes were wide open to reveal the city sights and the Spring Mountains beyond.

I offered him some water. “Acqua Panna, Voss, or Perrier?”

“Anything,” he replied impatiently.

I poured him a glass of Voss and brought it to him along with the bottle, setting them down before him upon the black lacquered coffee table.

“Why don’t we sit?” I gestured.

He looked about then, unbuttoning his suit jacket, plunked down on the large white cotton sofa, sipping his water, quietly annoyed.

I sat to the right of him in an accompanying red cushioned chair. Waiting until I could detect that he had calmed a bit.

He didn’t look at me and checked his watch frequently, looking mostly out the window.

Clearing my throat, I spoke softly, firmly. “I know…that you are angry with me…,” I paused as he looked at me intently his eyes began to tear, to rage.

“And you have no idea how much it has hurt me, displeasing you, disregarding your loss, my loss...our loss…,” I paused. “Understand that it was the farthest thing from my intent, to hurt Charlotte, to hurt you and your family. Please forgive me.”

I refrained from calling him father as I had done before Charlotte’s “death”.

He looked at me; then away. His temples pulsed as he fought back the tides of emotion, the anger.

I produced a sealed envelope which contained a check for three million dollars. I saw his attention gravitate to it, his greed for money re-ignited.

“I need you to understand…”

I breathed in, letting it out slowly. “That I have kept my promise to you, to Charlotte.”

He glared at me again, his temper coming back to him, about to boil over.

He went to speak, but I cut him off.

"I do not expect you to understand this, any of it…," I stopped to contemplate my words carefully.

"But, you, I, are nothing in the grand scheme of things. God and all his idiosyncratic power does exist," I said, finding myself stumbling again.

He stared at me, looking at me with disgust, agitated.

"What the hell are you going on about?"

"Me!" Charlotte spoke loudly, proudly, as she stepped quietly out from the master bathroom where she had been making her final touches.

She was going to make a show of this, show her father that she was very much alive and well. Show him that God exists.

Her father went pale at the vision of her, sinking back; gasping at the woman, the daughter, the angel before him.

Charlotte's body glowed, radiated, her eyes blazed softly as she smiled ever so kindly upon him. She was perfect in her white, thick knit Chanel knee length dress with embroidered white roses flowing down across it. She stood tall and proud upon five-inch white Versace heels with their little delicate gold buckles that gleamed in the halogen lighting.

A proper little lady, an angel, her hair long and full, cascaded down around her, her deep, violet eyes, staring back at him intently, lovingly.

I knew it was going to happen; his heart would fail due to this revelation. I moved to him now to slow his heart from its inevitable cardiac arrest. He had survived two minor heart attacks previously. I worried that this one could finish him off.

On my knees before him I reached out touching his chest just over the heart pressing firmly, as he began to gasp.

I looked intently at him, softly speaking. "Breathe with me."

He was panicking. He began to sweat, his face red, unable to talk. I saw him stiffen; he was terrified.

I took his left hand in mine and massaged the palm. Drawing his blood to me, slowly, to move it, warm it, then pushing it around and back into him to circulate throughout his body again. I quelled his rapid heartbeat, slowing it to a normal, solid, pumping rhythm, synching it to mine. I undid his tie and collar, opening it enough to let him breath.

He stared at Charlotte, seized by the idea that his daughter, whatever she was now, walked amongst the living. Was she an angel? A ghost? What? He did not know. The shock of it was just too powerful. He began to reach for her and started to cry uncontrollably.

I soothed him, filling his blood with electrons, a feeling of warmth, love, and resolve.

When he regained himself, I had him drink water, glass after glass, slowly. He was light headed, weakened. I continued to move his blood, his electrons and the water circulating bringing him back in full; making his heart even stronger.

Charlotte watched enthralled, she had a lot to learn about herself, the power that she had.

She went to him and he embraced her at the waist.

He buried his face into her stomach as she stood before him. He continued crying, not understanding, only knowing that she was solid, she was alive.

It took a while for him to calm down and to absorb this new reality. A million questions began to fly, it was all we could do to get him to be quiet to listen, to really listen to what we, what I had to say.

"Father…," I renewed this attachment now.

"When you served in the Army, about 1976, I believe, at Livermore Laboratories. You saw things, at times, unexplainable things, in the labs below," I paused.

He looked incredulously at me and my knowledge of his secret history. A part of his life marked "Top Secret" reemerged. He was nothing special, just a captain in the Military Police Detachment there, but being such, had access to areas of which he had to secure, areas of great secrecy.

"Wha…What, well yes, but…"

He was going to renounce those things, he had a practical explanation I am sure.

Charlotte sat back into the couch coaxing her father to do the same. She leaned up next to him, soothing the palm of his left hand as she had seen me do. She caught on quickly, my little Charlotte.

I took a long, slow sip of wine, then leaning back into the comfort of the soft, red cushioned chair, I paused making sure I could relate the series of events, my birth, my travels, Charlotte's new beginning. I smiled softly reminiscing; then spoke

"The human race is not alone in this galaxy, this universe…," I began. "And God is not a fictitious ideal of man."

He listened to me, fully attentive, quizzical, trying to understand. He would go to speak at times, but Charlotte stopped him, gently soothing him.

When I was done, he was still unable to really comprehend the size and scope of it, my truth, his daughter's new truth. We were beyond anything he had ever experienced, even the strange things in the underground labs at Livermore.

He began to sob as Charlotte and I tried to soothe away his fears. It was all too much for him. He had to believe that aliens do exist, that he, the human race was not that special. That now, his daughter, his single greatest pride and joy, was no longer of this world, but a vampire, a puppet-being of some kind from beyond this galaxy.

"It's not important now daddy, what I am," Charlotte pleaded.

"What's important is that I am here, alive, and I am forever."

He began to cry again at those words. "I am here.... forever."

He was going to miss his plane that I had scheduled. I would have to charter a private jet for him to take later.

I laughed at myself, "four hours", what was I thinking.

It took a long time to get him to realize that after today, this moment, Charlotte, for him would be never more. He pleaded, but there was no going back against the events of time. Charlotte Bell Aberdeen, of Los Angeles, California, Lawyer; age 25 was dead to the world.

I began to sadden as Charlotte took control of her father and the situation; it was time to say the last goodbye.

I had made a few phone calls after I realized I would need to charter a plane. The limousine driver was now waiting patiently at the door. The Navigations Air business jet sat idling on the tarmac.

She held him squarely in front of her by his shoulders. She adjusted his suit and tie, dusting him off both physically and metaphorically. She handed him a large 18" X 20" leather bound Monte Blanc Estate Folio, embossed in gold modern Gothic lettering were the words "Holdings of The Aberdeen Estate". Within its thick vellum parchment pages were the gift that Charlotte would bestow upon her family in her eternal passing.

Its first section outlined the holdings of which was now entrusted to her father. It accounted the net values and calculated yearly approximations thereafter of net income for ten years.

The second section outlined the core investment; gold, tracing its excavation from the earth down the processes which lead to the ring, the necklace, a watch, anything involving the use of gold.

The third section outlined to whom and how it shall be distributed, this new-found wealth. Ensuring each family member got a generous portion upon which to live and further invest.

Lastly, Charlotte had set up a small non-profit entity to care for children with cancer. It was in place and was ready to be managed by her father, who was named the CEO.

"Go now father," she told him. "You have all that you have ever wanted for your family. It's time to retire. Go and do good in this world, for me, the memory of me."

She smiled hopefully.

"I have all that you had ever wanted for me," she said, happy now, glowing.

"I have the man of my dreams…"

She caught herself, laughing; her eyes rolled and then she looked to me

"Oh! Well…"

She nudged her head toward me her eyes rolling.

Her father broke into a smile, laughing at her, his silly little Charlotte.

"I am loved, respected, and valued. I have wealth and want for nothing. It is perfect; my life. Go and be happy knowing that."

She was stoic, strong, at peace.

"This is goodbye father. Know that I will love and remember you always!"

She embraced him lovingly then let him go, stepping back moving into me, against me.

He looked at us now a slight smile washed across his face again.

He whispered "thank you" back to me.

"You are welcome," I mouthed back trembling, trying not to totally break down in that moment.

Charlotte spoke again, the last words of parting that her father would ever hear from her.

"Go now father and remember me, my human self always. But know now that I am forever gone to you, this mortal body and soul. In time, you will forget me, not in entirety, but I will fade from you, my image, my being, save for some lost pictures in an attic somewhere. But, do not worry over it; it is as it should be. Remember, that I am still an Aberdeen, the name will be eternal," she paused, then became resolute.

"Do not seek of me either, do not steal a glance or long to see me pass. When you leave here, it is as if the day you left my graveside as the doors of my tomb were sealed."

"Do not cry for I have been dead to you already. Instead, rejoice in the glory that is God, your faith, and know that he exists, that there is more beyond this place and time. I am evidence of that, his divine glory, for I am of God now. Go in peace father and throw down the earthly desires for any more. It is time to go forth and enact my memory, all that you have made of me, and thought of me. Be kind, gentle, and caring. Give freely and often. It is how I want you to remember me though kindness, charity, and love."

"Go, and never look back for I am but a fond memory now."

I saw Charlotte approach and kiss her father gently on his lips. She whispered something of which neither he or I could tell.

He teared.

"Go now father, and love!"

As I was about to shut the door on Charlotte's past forever, her father turned to me extending his hand. I took it.

He shook it firmly like a father does with the man whom has just taken his daughter away from him to begin a new life.

I smiled, then after a brief moment broke contact and slowly shut the door. Locking it, I leaned up against it and began to cry uncontrollably. I wasn't sad, I wasn't happy I wasn't anything right then but pure, tumbling emotion.

Charlotte smiled at me laughing. "The pool Ianthe…," she gleamed, looking at the pool down below our room window.

"Look, it's beautiful, let's go swimming, please!"

I had to laugh at her pleading, her wanting for fun, her new beginning. I thought of how easy it was for her to say goodbye to her old life, then I began to cry uncontrollably again. I had no idea why.

It took me a few days to recover from that goodbye.

Charlotte, it seemed had her closure and focused now on the new life before her. We would soon be traveling the world. She wanted me to take her to the very places I had been in my travels over time and history, to see and experience it as I had through the centuries. She wanted to know and feel my history, see it through my eyes, of which no history book could ever portray in its entirety. And too, she wanted to see E'ban and perhaps Stoya, for they were her new family now.

I was looking forward to it, the memories of which I could share. We would leave for my home in Capri first thing, to finally say "I do!" upon that sacred place under the full Caprisian moon.

CHAPTER 74

"Uahhh! I can't wait for Paris!"

Charlotte wiggled excitedly across from me at our table at Café La Bohème. We were leaving soon on our world-wide tour, but wanted to renew our ties with close friends and the places and things we loved most. We also wanted to celebrate our three-year anniversary and reminisce over our first date and the beginning of our timeless love.

It was April 15. We had reserved the exact same table up in the crystal both section of La Bohème for dinner. We had gone shopping earlier that day at the Coach Store in the Santa Monica Place Mall, the store where we had first meet.

We had lunch with Ihsan at the Sonoma Wine Garden upstairs on the third floor. We had agreed to meet again soon, before we left for our trip. She wanted to see our new home at Bella Capri in San Diego. and I suspected, engage in a little romance.

Ihsan admitted to us, that on the day of Charlotte and I's meeting, that she had been working up the courage to ask Charlotte out on a date before I had shown up.

I smiled and leaned forward taking up her hand.

"Well…I don't see what's stopping you now?" I laughed devilishly. "Seems like you two still could be friends."

I winked, leaning back to take in the vision of both of them sitting so close together. Thoughts of them both in my bed.

I watched Charlotte and Ihsan touch and hold hands through much of our lunch, whispering things to each other only to burst out laughing from time-to-time while looking back at me. It's what I wanted of it, to keep my lovers close and for Charlotte to take of them also, Ihsan, especially.

"Well, Ms. Gold!" Tim pronounced excitedly. "Ms. Aberdeen!"

He came up to us hurriedly.

Tim was the manager now and, I could tell, proud of it.

"Tim!"

I stood taking him in my arms holding him tightly.

Charlotte stood up gushing over him. They would become good friends in time.

"Hey!" she said merrily, taking him in her arms and kissing him gently on his cheek as she tip-toed up to do so.

"But…"

She held out her engagement ring for him to see.

"It's going to be Gold now!" she giggled over it.

"Well…Aberdeen-Gold for me. But please, just Charlotte will do!"

She smiled.

"Congratulations! Then, to you, Charlotte and Ianthe, Mrs. and Mrs. Gold…"

He beamed. "I just knew it!"

"Come, please sit, dinner is on me tonight!"

We took our seats.

I watched Charlotte's breast bubble up slightly over her tight-fitting black on black Chanel jacquard-flower sheath dress.

I sat back to chuckle at her, the memory from our first date. God, did I love her so.

"Well," Tim spoke. "The usual for you Ms. Gold?"

"Yes, and a Burgundy, a red!"

"Certainly!"

Tim rubbed his hands together, delighted.

"And, I will bring champagne to start!"

"And for you? Charlotte?"

"The same! Porterhouse, extra, extra rare! Just sear it, thirty seconds each side!" she squeaked. "Make it two, I'm hungry!"

I saw the look on Tim's face as he hesitantly took her order.

"Two?"

He cocked his head to the side.

"Yes! Two!"

She pouted. "I've…well, I've developed quite an appetite since my recovery…," she posited matter-of-factly licking at her lips. "Just can't seem to get enough…mmm…meat these days!"

She squirmed.

"In fact, most times, anymore, I am simply ravenous!"

She smiled a little wickedly licking at her lips again.

"Well… OK, then…I will bring that bottle of champagne for starters, if there isn't anything else?" Tim paused, smiling at us, happy to see us again; then turned to place our order.

"And Tim…," Charlotte and I both spoke in unison, laughing.

"Remember, no garlic!"

CHAPTER 75

The music pulsed and vibrated as we entered the LA Vampyr Club. It was midnight and time for Charlotte to make her grand entrance. I watched as her old friends screamed in joy and surprise, racing toward her in a fury of black and red Goth attire.

They jumped up and down before her as she loved them, hugging and kissing them unable to contain her own excitement. They didn't care about the fact that they had all mourned her death over a year ago. Many had attended her funeral.

But, here, in this place, things most unusual happened. Here, it was an automatic that Charlotte Bell Aberdeen had indeed returned from the grave. That she was now, the vampire. At least that was the fantasy they had wanted.

As for the rest of our friends; well, human memory is a funny thing.

We had been gone for some time and while the newspapers read one thing, carefully laid social media posts suggested another.

Charlotte had been declared legally dead even without a body.

Controversies abound but hard evidence went unexamined. And now, she had returned in the flesh. A miraculous chemotherapy, so my Facebook posts had chronicled.

She was, to most, a living, breathing example of what radical and experimental science can achieve.

But we are also, an existence obscured by time, memory and individual personal self-absorptions. Humans are silly in that way, such short memories and so easily distracted. It's how we survive here, most worlds.

We slip past you in the open, unnoticed. Your sense of time and place betrays your very mind. I have lived for decades as I am, while neighbors wither and die. Frequent leaves of absence, does much to hide our truths.

Charlotte stood before them radiating, her eyes glowing softly in the dark lighting. Her aura radiated outwards, drawing them in, healing inner wounds before they could even be revealed to her. She smiled and loved them, the perfect little Miss Perfect, bestowing small gifts upon her closest friends, ones that would soon become lovers; her flock of Black Swans.

Charlotte had decided to embrace her "inner self", like Stoya had. She was not going to hide from it, our truth; the vampire. She wanted the world to know the romance of it, to know God's power.

It didn't matter. You humans never truly believe in us anyways. We are a fantasy, right? The product of a grand imagination, an explanation of the strange in a time when knowledge of the world around and the universe was limited. Life, God, our being, so easily explained away by science. That's what I think I love most about you. Your ignorance to the truth even when it resides right before your eyes.

Charlotte, like Stoya, took up the mantle, carried on the myths and the persona, most often, decked out in white, off-whites, and very light soft pinks. Charlotte favored a more modern vintage look, embracing the 1950s French and American fashion. She selected simple, thick knit sheath and slip dresses that fit tightly and elegantly, no higher or lower than one inch above the knee.

She often wore Pillbox hats, sometimes with the veil. She carried small 1950s styled clamshell handbags and wore white heeled pumps or buckled flats, and most often Tahitian white, pink, or gray-green pearls which finished her vintage look.

I gave her the nick-name of "June" in homage to Barbara Billingsley who played the role of Mrs. Cleaver in *Leave it to Beaver*, and whom I had always found enticing.

Charlotte called it "50s Prissy-Goth".

If she was feeling devilish, she wore similar outfits but in all black or occasionally blood red with six-inch spiked high heels or high heeled boots, mainly over the knee styling and long elegant elbow length satin gloves.

Charlotte had also amassed quite a collection of sunglasses, mostly vintage, a hobby of sorts, a signature look.

She had bought a fully restored classic 1960 VW Beetle complete with roof rack and painted it a soft, pale pink.

We got a lot of looks as people passed by our home, my Bugatti Chiron and Mercedes Maybach S600, with a little VW Bug nestled in between.

I chuckled at it every time.

CHAPTER 76

In Paris, Charlotte and E'ban finally got to meet and bond. He loved her instantly, a father and his pride and joy. They spent long days and nights together walking Paris, talking and understanding, bonding, loving. They became intimate, a passion bloomed but not in any sexual way. They were to be as father and daughter always.

Charlotte was and always would be a lover of women. And E'ban found himself more in love with her as his proxy daughter than anything else. They shared and kept many secrets and would be the first to turn to for as long as time and distance and chance allowed.

While in Paris, I had kept my promise of a lunch date with Mike. I had Mike and Gretchen Brandt flown out to meet us. I had presented this trip as an "adults only" weekend; their children to be left in the care of close relatives. I wanted their time here to be free of parental distractions.

Paris is known for its romance and I knew love was going to bloom.

We found Mike and Gretchen sitting side-by-side under the Eiffel Tower on the Sunday we were to meet them for lunch. In fact, we caught them about to have their first kiss.

"Well, I see you two have met!" I laughed. "When should we plan on attending the wedding?" I chuckled, producing my cell phone as if to save the date on my calendar.

Mike's head bowed down and swung slowly side-to-side as he grinned, knowing in that moment that he had been once again thrust into one of "Ms. Gold's crazy plans".

I laughed at him, teasing him as he stood smiling. He took me slowly, tenderly, into his arms, holding me for a very long time.

I soothed him, petted his muscular back. He was still using a cane but was healing quickly from his most dangerous and unexpected ordeal and the wounds suffered at Tyr's hand.

When we let each other go, I saw his eyes swell with tears.

E'ban shook his hand firmly and then hugged him like men who have suffered in war together do. They had a bond now, warriors who fought in mortal combat against an insurmountable odd. A bond that from then on would continue to cement and flourish.

E'ban presented Mike with the combat folder pocket knife that Mike had resorted to using in his fight against Tyr. Upon the five-inch blade, he had engraved:

"Mighty is he who stands against gods."

"I left the blood to dry upon it, Mike."

E'ban beamed.

"You left a good mark upon him, one that any "human" should be proud of!"

Charlotte then gingerly stepped forward. She curtsied, and moved to Mike.

Taking his hands in hers, she spoke eloquently, respectfully.

"I am Charlotte, Mike!" she announced, glowing radiating, healing him. "Your, goddaughter in so many ways...," she squeaked moving to embrace him.

"Thank you!" she whispered into his ear. "For my birth! For this life!"

I saw Mike break. Crying.

Gretchen moved to him and comforted him.

We all stood in silence, each coming to realize the family we were becoming.

I thought of Stoya, of what it will take to bring her back into our fold; if ever.

"Well, shit!" Charlotte finally announced breaking the somewhat somber mood.

"Let's get some champagne and our party on! Its Paris!" she said taking up Mike and Gretchen's arms into hers.

"Enough of this mushy shit!" she posited. "It's time to fucking celebrate!"

We all broke out laughing at our darling Miss Charlotte.

I watched as Gretchen moved in and kissed Mike fully, their first kiss of many. It was a grand weekend.

When we parted ways at Paris International, I handed Mike an envelope with a personal check.

"Take this Mike; you've earned every penny of it and more!" I assured him. "A nest egg for you both."

"You both can start a new life together. Love each other and do not let go, ever!" I spoke softly, reaffirming.

We all hugged, kissed, and remembered, then parted ways.

Mike and Gretchen would be married just six months later. It was a grand wedding.

I watched the broken rise up again, the lonely find their company. The beginning of a beautiful and long, loving life.

I sat back and lit a cigar; Gretchen was going to have a girl.

Her name was going to be Tyrisa. She was going to be bold and strong, and bore a name that would bring fortune and fame. In time, she would become a most trusted friend and confidant, as her parents are today.

I smiled as I sat back, away from the wedding crowds and took it all in. Life! I thought. That is what this whole thing is really about, to live and to love, and for some to die, so as to be renewed.

I watched Charlotte dance and play and love full heartedly. I found myself hardly being able to wait to live our lives forever.

Gretchen held me as I wept over the that thought, that word; “forever.”

CHAPTER 77

2 Years Later
San Diego, California 8AM

I awoke to the vision of Charlotte standing in the sun on the balcony of our bedroom, clothed in a thin, white, Egyptian cotton weaved Nautica cover up that I had bought for her at Fiore in Capri.

I saw her diamond ring, the symbol of our promise to each other, flash brightly in the rising Californian sun like a daylight star

Her pure blonde hair, long, thick, glass-like, blew softly in the ocean breeze. The violet undertones undulating like some alien sea. She was my wife to love and to cherish until the end of time. I could only think of how lucky I was and little else.

We had returned from over a year's worth of travel to see the world and retrace my history as she had wanted. We caught up with old friends and made many new ones.

But, it was time to settle in, to live and love and enjoy our time together to enjoy our new homes and life adventures, our friends and lovers. This was our life now, so very human really when you think about it. For what else is there on this or any other world, but to live the life you have been given to its fullest, to find that one great love, to cherish it for as long as you can.

I went to go to her when my cell phone rang. I knew the number. I answered. I could feel the silence, the sound of Stoya's slow impatient breath on the other end. I knew in that moment instinctively, that the stipulation had finally come with my promise of "forever".

"How is Charlotte?" Stoya asked quietly.

"She is absolutely beautiful…," I spoke pondering her question.

"I have no doubt about that," she confirmed.

"I want you to see her soon," I offered.

"Someday…"

I felt her voice grow cold, her anger rising toward me and my betrayal. There was a long silence.

"I think you should know something…," she spoke quietly again, pausing.

I waited patiently, fearing the thing inside of me, my inner voice; my turning stomach that told me something was horribly wrong.

"Wh…what…?" I could barely mutter.

"She is going to die...," she paused again. "In time, how long she has it cannot be said."

I began to cry at such cruel words.

"It could be soon, it could be in a few thousand years from now or longer. Only God and time will tell, but she will die. And you will live to see it."

"Why…h…how, how?"

My voice trembled, numbed and knowing that Stoya was going to be right about this, as she always was about everything.

"The drug, Noradismol…," she breathed out, exhaling the smoke from her lungs.

I thought of it now, the experimental drug, the final play to gain me time in the final hours. The doctor's words of worry I had blatantly dismissed.

"I told you they were weak, that she, this thing of yours was not to be in the end," she paused, seeming to feel some pity.

"I warned that you would betray her did I not? Her innocence, deceive her, deceive yourself…"

I heard her pause then take another long drag from her cigarette, then exhale.

"Noradismol…it is dangerous to us, our kind, like a cancer of sorts…it affects our inner bodies, our stem cells, our ability to maintain cellular replication…our immortality…," she paused.

"Kills us slowly over time…how exactly, I am not fully sure," she contemplated. "As if…that matters."

I heard her anger again at her own words.

"How did you…?" I stammered.

"Noradismol, is constructed from a dangerous isotope, a form of radiation developed very far from here…used as fuel on the world from of which I came so long ago…the remnants of a depleted power cell onboard my craft."

She remained silent thinking about something.

"I had warned them, when they had discovered it, the peculiar radioactive dust. They did not listen," she spoke coldly. "They thought they could play God with it, save lives…end lives…"

I heard her pause then speak again.

"Well, it doesn't matter now, I have destroyed it, all record of it, it will not be used ever again. It will not harm us on this world. Nor aid in salvation for anyone…," she seemed to scorn.

"But, I promised her…," I broke down, sobbing.

"What, Ianthe…forever? What is forever anyways?"

I heard her gloat. "Forever. What is forever to anyone…"

She listened to me weep over the phone for the longest time. I felt her power flow into me, but it neither sought to protect me nor hurt me.

"But how do you know?"

I finally mustered up the strength to ask her. To challenge her declaration.

"Her eyes, Ianthe, they are as mine are they not?"

She seemed to anger at my ignorance.

"It is not within our being is it now…Ianthe?"

I choked at this one undeniable fact.

"And she is beginning to do things you cannot, can she not? In time, she will be powerful. Ironic isn't it…the games God plays…," she laughed wickedly.

"The gifts given to the weak…"

"But how do you…?" I asked, afraid, though I found suddenly, that I already knew the answer.

"Well Ianthe, I too, am affected, poisoned by it…"

I felt her words cut like ice, this great secret of hers, burned into me like an iron, the brand of a horrible fate. Charlotte's horrible fate now, my promise of forever.

"I was affected a long time ago…but that is another story in and of itself," she spoke quietly.

"Such is God's will…I too, am dying, slowly, surely…," she sighed, granting a single moment of self-pity.

"Like the water drop upon the rock; drip, drip, drip…," she mocked. "Time isn't merciful. But at least she'll have my company in this!"

She chuckled insidiously at that fact.

I began to cry for them; my loves, my Charlotte, Stoya.

"I am so very sorry, Ianthe…," she spoke again, allowing a moment of sorrow, of compassion.

I sat in silence and looked out to watch Charlotte stare out across the Pacific Ocean and beyond. I found myself trembling again, terrified as the day not so long ago, that Charlotte had told me she was going to die.

"It is as I said, Ianthe; it was not your decision to make nor force, her fate, our fate it is but God's alone. Its random mathematics of this life. It is the way of things, of our kind's evolution. All evolution. God gives us the bodies as random chance dictates. What fate allows. Not of our own making…We are of God, but we are not God…" she trailed off.

"We too have limits. We have upset the balance…" she spoke quietly again pondering the outcome of all of this.

"Your decision has created this situation, like so long ago upon the ice...your promise of forever. Remember? It simply isn't meant to be. God has other plans, God has passed Its judgment."

"I am sorry…," I quibbled, trembling. "So very, very sorry!" I pleaded with Stoya.

"There is little that can be done now Ianthe, just love her for time is fleeting, time is precious, time for her, for all of us has an end."

I remained silent for a long time, listening to Stoya breathe in her quiet steadfast way.

"Is there anything…tha…that we can…?" I pleaded.

"She will need to feed constantly now to thrive, Ianthe, your precious Charlotte…," Stoya trailed off, coldly, knowingly.

"She will be as me, the lust for blood and the flesh will be as you have always feared of me…will grow with the years, she will become forever ravenous from this time until the end. She will kill to save herself, to save you from the loss of her. God has given with one hand and taken with the other. Charlotte has sacrificed much for you Ianthe, will sacrifice much for you, love, but it will all be for not."

I could feel her smirk, sneer, pondering that thought in her own head.

We were quiet again. Her will flooding me with contempt.

"What of us...?" I finally spoke hoping for a chance to begin to make amends, only wanting in that moment, for all of us to be one again.

"Us…?" I heard her exhale, smirking. "There has never been an "us" has there now, Ianthe? Never will there be an us, it is as you have made of that also…a death there too, an end."

I listened to the audible digital click as she hung the up her phone.

I sat in silence and thought of my selfishness of which Stoya had spoken. I was a liar and a thief, the great deceiver. I was a monster. More so, I know now, than I had ever wanted to believe of myself. I took of her without mercy and without thought to a bigger picture. I killed innocents to save one dying love, only to set into motion everything over again. And I knew in that moment that I would not be forgiven nor go unpunished. That God, Its insidious plans for us all, was going to see to that.

I moved out onto the balcony, slipping in behind Charlotte as she leaned back into me and stared out at the glimmering cobalt blue ocean through mirrored Prada sunglasses.

I nuzzled her gently as we melted into each other. It was just us now, she and I, the eternal lovers for as long as time would allow us to be.

She breathed out longingly, then breathed in deep again, taking in the sea below and the world beyond.

"How long again?" Charlotte whispered longingly, dreaming.

"Forever!" I assured her, holding back the tears that were coming despite my best efforts.

"Forever?" she asked again as if somehow knowing that I had lied.

"On this planet; until the sun dies," I spoke softly.

"But what if the sun dies tomorrow?" she asked innocently.

I chuckled lovingly at the question and thought in that moment of how I wish it would die right then so that I could fulfill my promise of forever to her. To us.

"There will always be other planets, Charlotte, more worlds to see and experience, we are forever now…for as long as that is to us."

She sighed, snuggling deeper into me, taking in the beauty of this world.

I held onto her and prayed that when the time came for her to die again, that we had had a good, long life together. That we had seen all that there was to see. That she had done all that she was supposed to do. Be all that she was supposed to be. That she would find it within her at the end, to forgive me; again.

CHAPTER 78

I breathed in her scent as I watched the sea below, slowly exhaling the rose scented, sweet salty air. And I could have sworn there was the smell of ice.

The breeze picked up for a brief moment, and within it I heard the tinkling of tiny bells as the sea foam popped upon the sandy shore. And it was then that I saw the end of the universe, the end of time. The light had died, and all was frozen, devoid of life; black. And upon an endless horizon, I held Charlotte in my arms, sheltering her as she lay dying. I watched as she drifted away from me, our rings, my promise, fall from our hands as her memory begin to rapidly fade. I kissed her lips, the almost whisper, taking in her last breath. I felt her soul ascend as a storm began to rage. I cried out alone into the endless void. And I felt then, too, the building of a torrent so deep and defiant, a raging which screamed out into the universe with unrelenting angst, still determined to live, to love.

And, it was in that moment, that I finally heard the almost whisper, the whisper of Charlotte, and of what Stoya had spoken in my mind.

"Our love will be but a single moment left wanting within forever, an eternity lost WITHOUT the other until the end of time."

End

Arefu, Romania
6:00 PM

Stoya Tepes Dracŭ stood alone in the coming darkness upon the massive ancient stone patio of her home in Arefu, Romania, overlooking the castle ruins of ancient Poenari. She had hung up on Ianthe, letting her phone drop off into the thousand-foot abyss below her.

"What of us…?" still echoed in her mind, cutting like a knife as the phone crashed upon the rocks below. She took another drag from her Insignia brand cigarette, inhaling deeply, contemplatively, indignant.

"Weak!" she sneered at the very thought of Ianthe as she looked toward Poenari.

"Forever…"

She thought of the world before her, the universe, of God's power It tries to lord over her.

She felt the thing inside of her gnaw at her, slow, relentless like lazy water drops upon some long-forgotten stalagmite deep under the earth. Drip…drip…Cancer. Dying. Time. Oblivion.

She snarled again at the thought of it, her illness, the cancer within.

She inhaled, then exhaled, letting the smoke exit slowly, deliberately.

"Well…," she spoke quietly, sneering.

"Forever…," she laughed wickedly, confidently.

She paused for a moment longer; then let her cigarette drop watching it as it exploded upon the ground in a thousand tiny stars. She smiled.

“Forever…,” she mocked as her foot came down upon the dying embers of the cigarette with all the hate she could muster, crushing it into oblivion. She thought of love, of sacrifice, and betrayal. She thought of the word forever.

“Weak…,” she whispered into the wind, out to the world, to Ianthe Gold, to God, the universe, to the thing that is forever.

“Forever…,” she spoke clearly again, laughing, mocking its proposition, the summation of all existence.

“What is forever anyways but a failing heart.”

Epilogue

Upon Forever...

Ciosa stood upon the endless black horizon looking out across the universe to the small, blue world so all alone.

She watched Charlotte dance and swim in the tides of the warm, blue Pacific Ocean as she once did upon the ice so long ago.

She saw Stoya stand upon the edge of the precipice in the night, dreaming; exhibiting the defiance, the pride, the absolute power of her being, as she had the day she had spoken to her the truth.

She watched Jonathan Nelson Davis as he sat quietly sipping at his Turkish coffee taking in the city of Brasov, Romania. He was there to find something, a great secret, maybe, to meet that one great love.

"It is done!" Ciosa spoke quietly as the great burning light within her grew with such intensity that she in that moment had become only light. Pure, blinding. All knowing. She smiled reflecting on this thing before her, the children of her own making.

"What could they ever begin to understand of this…?"

She smiled.

"Could they ever know that this is but the smallest part of something so much more?"

And beyond her light lay many other lights, and beyond them even more. And in them each was a universe. Each with many worlds inhabited by many beings, and in turn, each being inhabited by a soul. The only constant, the soul, for we are all only souls.

"Could they ever understand of this?" she wondered.

"That even we, God, are but the smallest part of a greater whole. That even we, too, have been long forgotten to the mind of what is this, an even greater thing, never to be known by any, ever. The one thing that makes all things possible; forever."

The Author

Brian Dennis Hartford is a published author and writer of fiction. He has a Bachelor's degree in Security Management with a focus on Terrorism Studies and has worked in the private security industry. He currently resides in the beautiful state of New Mexico, a land, a people, a culture, of which he draws much inspiration.

Look for the next edition to WITHOUT

WITHIN

Other Books by Brian Dennis Hartford

2198 A Memoir from the Second Revolution
A Novel

WITHIN

Brasov, Romania
Summer, 3 Years Later

I watched as she stormed across the central plaza of this ancient city, like some all-encompassing, all-devouring avalanche, indifferent to all about her, the world, even the universe perhaps.

Tall, eloquent, statuesque, fierce; she seemed to defy everyone and everything. Even God.

Her blood red Prada sheath dress blazed like a fire in the mid-morning sun as her dark, red Versace high heels with their gold and diamond enhanced buckles stomped their way along the aged, worn coble stone streets, beating them with a deliberate rhythm. Grinding them under her absolute power.

I watched as her waist-long, black hair, thick and straight, bounced slightly as she moved through the crowd. Her skin was white like a fine marble. I could see her bright, blood-red painted lips which seemed to curl into a permanent sneer at all about her, upon a face so fine it was like an opaque, white glass perhaps.

I was struck by the way in which all time seemed to stop in that moment, over the way in which life and the universe seemed to bow to her momentarily as she passed. Her presence becoming the only focus, time's only care.

She was alone. I could feel her defiance in that also, like some forbidden, long dead desert which had forgot any hope for a monsoon. A place no longer caring for life-giving waters, for it had already learned that it can survive without it.

She was ugly in so many ways, but I couldn't deny the fact that she was perhaps the most beautiful and powerful woman I had ever seen.

I could never have known in that moment, of what was about to be. Of what we were about to have. Of the secret before me, of which I believed I would never find. Of the love that would burn eternal.

"Trust me; it will be an adventure, Johnathan!"

I heard Ianthe Gold's words echo in my mind in that moment.

"Yes" I thought; *"An adventure!"*

I smiled taking another sip of my coffee. It was in the woman before me that I would come to understand that life, this universe and even God, was beholden to even greater things. Beholden to her and her alone.

Namri'd
Publishing, LLC

68105980R00246

Made in the USA
San Bernardino, CA
31 January 2018